YOUR OWN PEOPLE

Part 1

NICK OCHERE

authorHOUSE®

AuthorHouse™ UK
1663 Liberty Drive
Bloomington, IN 47403 USA
www.authorhouse.co.uk
Phone: 0800.197.4150

Published by AuthorHouse 06/11/2015

ISBN: 978-1-5049-4138-9 (sc)
ISBN: 978-1-5049-4137-2 (hc)
ISBN: 978-1-5049-4139-6 (e)

Print information available on the last page.

I dedicate this book to my wife and children

CONTENTS

ACKNOWLEDGEMENTS

Words cannot adequately convey my immense gratitude to God for what He has been doing in my life. Years ago when I stepped out of His will, He graciously brought me back on track and has sustained me ever since. To Him be the glory.

I want to thank my big brother, Elder Ampomah Sakyi and his wife, Mary, whom God has used as vessels to shape me into who I am today.

I wish also to record my profound gratitude to Apostle Dr Michael Ntumy for his guidance and taking time to write the Foreword, Apostle Newton Ofosuhene Nyarko for his directions and prayer support, Rev Daniel Kwame Noble-Atsu, Pastor Dr Ben Debrah and many other officers and members of The Church of Pentecost, UK, for their support and encouragement.

Stephanie Amponsah, Adwoa Adoma Antwi, Elder Isaac Appleton, Hannah Dwumah, Diana Fosu, Irene Gyan, Kwadwo Konadu (K.K.), Deborah Aya Kormi, Angela Kumah, Mary Machen and many others helped in diverse ways in bringing this book to publication and I wish to express my thanks to them all. I will cherish what they have done for as long as the cord of memory lengthens.

And now to that woman of substance, that good, supportive, encouraging and understanding wife of mine, Mercy, I wish to thank her so much for standing by me through thick and thin.

What can I say about our lovely children, Patience, Felicia, Joseph and

Nick Jnr? Although I adore them all, I neglected them most of the time while working on this book and I thank them for bearing with me.

Nick Ochere
January 2015

FOREWORD

In the normal scheme of things one's own people should be the first to acknowledge, celebrate or even brag over one's achievements or promotions. Similarly, one would expect the support and protection of family, no matter the extent to which one may have messed things up.

However, history is replete with the contrary, giving credence to the time-honoured saying of the Bible, *"A man's enemies are those of his own household."* Let us consider but a few:

- The first murder in the Bible was fratricidal (Cain against Abel).
- The first Hebrew to be sold into slavery suffered at the hands of his own brothers (Joseph, by his own brothers).
- The first coup d'etat in Israel was staged by a son against a father (Absalom against King David).
- Then we have the supra example of betrayal, Jesus Christ, by Judas Iscariot who was one of His own disciples.

It goes without saying that it is not everybody who will celebrate your success; it is not everybody who will hail you as a hero even when you have done heroic deeds. Many discover later to their shock that sometimes friends, colleagues and even more painfully, family members, are among their secret enemies.

How people react to this discovery varies from person to person. Some go from subtle to open retaliation and confrontation to even causing bodily harm to their perceived enemy. Only very few people meet their perceived or real enemy with love and forgiveness.

Can you predict how you were going to react if you knew that someone very close to you was seeking your downfall or even worse, your destruction? How would you counsel someone who has just made such a discovery?

Well, look no further. You hold in your hand a book which addresses that problem.

Your Own People, authored by Nick Ochere is a fascinating story of how a crafty aunt, by name Cornie, used all means to beguile a young man called Joe. She tried tooth and nail to make her nephew to enter into a relationship with Belinda whose parents were very rich. Auntie Cornie hoped that by so doing, she would rake in some financial advantage.

Her nefarious plans did not work, thanks to the protective hand of God upon Joe's life and of his solid Christian upbringing. Joe stood his grounds and eventually married Evelyn, the lady of his love.

Auntie Cornie, however, was of the pedigree that never gives up. She decided to bite deeper and closer. She teamed up with Brago, Joe's own sister, to make life difficult for the young couple. When after six years the couple had not had a child the heat of the persecution became even more intense- because now, the fires were not just set ablaze by an aunt, but in collaboration with a beloved sister. Cornie kept attacking and castigating Joe to the point of using voodoo on him.

How would Joe and Evelyn react? Will they cave in to their animosity or explode when they can no longer bear it? Read on to discover.

You will not be bored as you read this book. The author holds you spellbound to the very end.

YOUR OWN PEOPLE will jostle you out of your naivety of thinking that being a good person will spare you of enemies. Yet, just because some of your own people could be among your worse enemies should not send you witch-hunting. Meet them with love, benevolence and patience as you trust God to help you win them over.

This is a great book. I recommend it to all.

APOSTLE DR MICHAEL NTUMY

. Former Chairman, The Church of Pentecost

.Former President, Ghana Pentecostal Council

.Former Chancellor, Pentecost University College

.Order of The Volta, Companion, Ghana

CHAPTER ONE

CORNIE BEGINS HER PLOT

The mountainous greenery that surrounds the town of Diasempa has tempted many first time visitors to want to go back there. The rays of the rising sun casting shadows through the big, high trees along the road and the setting of the same in the evening is such a marvellous sight. As you walk or drive down the only winding pot-holed road made up of steep, curved hills and valleys leading to the town, you can't stop thinking of the beauty of nature. The songs of the birds in the woods could make you wish you had these little creatures in your garden at home. The almost over-grown green grass at the edge of the road provides a natural habitat for most rodents and reptiles which sometimes venture onto the road for left-over foods which passers-by have dropped on the sidewalk.

The locals' hospitality, their art of conversation laced with proverbs and jokes are further memorable aspects of Diasempa. The sight of little children playing in open spaces, on the way to school or accompanying their parents to the farm suggests that if all that we see were indeed as it appears to be, then the world would be a better and more peaceful place for all.

Diasempa has three waterfalls which attract tourists. It has a Senior Secondary School educating students from all parts of the country. Three of the Big Six prominent politicians, William Ofori Atta, Arko Adjei and J. B. Danquah, who fought for the independence of Ghana, underwent part of their education in this town. There are six primary and middle schools, a police station, a vocational school, a post office, bank, health centre and local council head quarters. Farming is the main occupation of about ninety percent of the population of Diasempa, the capital of the Awkaetnaf District of Ghana. But the scenery of Diasempa now compared to that of the late sixties and early seventies indicates that no condition is permanent.

Untill the age of thirteen, Joseph Kwadwo Boakye knew no other place than his town of birth, Diasempa, and a few of the surrounding towns and villages. His parents were peasant farmers who wanted the best education for their kids but could hardly afford it. When the second of two children, Joseph, popularly called Joe, passed the Common Entrance Examination, he was admitted to his first choice Senior Secondary School in the city of Kumasi, where one of his aunts worked as a clerk in an insurance firm. Arrangements were made for him to go and stay with his aunt instead of going into the boarding house.

The city life for a thirteen-year-old boy, used only to the rural life, was a completely new thing. Cornie, his aunt, wasn't that harsh, but somehow difficult to please because she liked everything in the house to be spotless and in place. Her only child, Kwaku Odame, was too young to carry out most of the household chores at the time, so Joe had to do them all in addition to his school work.

Joe hardly had time for studies at home, yet he always came out with flying colours after exams. Five years later, when Joe had to go to Sixth Form at Miawani, he enrolled as a boarder. At this point his aunt has had a greater influence on the eighteen-year-old; even more than his biological parents. She could tell Joe what to do or not to do and he dared not challenge what she said. If something was green and Auntie Cornie said to Joe it's blue, it must be blue, because Auntie Cornie said so. It was like she has cast a spell on his young mind. Many times when his parents' suggestions contradicted those of his aunt's, Auntie Cornie would do everything possible to convince Joe to accept what she said as right.

For as long as he remained a student, Joe was pulled in two directions, one by his parents and the other by Auntie Cornie and, of course, he had his own opinion about issues too. A particular case was about Belinda Addo, the daughter of one of Auntie Cornie's old-time wealthy friends who happened to be in the same school where Joe was attending his Sixth Form.

His parents had strongly warned him against having a girlfriend; that it was not a good thing to do as a Christian. Besides, they insisted that as soon as he got into such relationships, it would jeopardise his studies and in the end, affect his future, an opinion which Joe abided by since his parents had advised him long before he went to the city. Auntie Cornie, on the other hand, upon hearing from Joe that the girl was in the same school, suggested that he befriend her. Once when Joe was granted leave to visit his aunt for some cash, she insisted on him having an affair with Belinda.

"Look, the parents are rich, very rich, and if you get her as a girlfriend there is nothing you would lack."

As Joe laughed over this idea, his aunt continued to lecture him on the advantages that could come his way if he befriended her.

"You are a bright boy and you know that all these girls like guys with your kind of intelligence. It will be easy for you to have her by starting to help her with her school work. If she gets to know how brilliant you are academically, you would not have to say a word, she will give in to you straight away."

"I know, Auntie," Joe responded, "but it is against my conviction to involve myself in such relationships at this stage of my life. You are aware as to how some of my mates, both boys and girls, used to come to me for help with their work when I was with you, but my conscience would never have judged me right if I had ever capitalised on my intelligence to take advantage of any of them. I can not and won't do that."

"That was because I was providing you with all that you needed. Now that you are alone there, it is very important that you get a bit of help from other avenues. Some essential commodities and pocket money would never be a problem to you if you listen and do as I say."

Things were a bit hard for Joe because he was not yet fully adjusted to the new school and system of things at Miawani. He has come to solicit for some pocket money from his aunt, and this is the dilemma in which he now finds himself. His parents did send him a specific amount on regular basis but it wasn't enough. He wasn't an extravagant boy, but the money from his parents was just not enough to live on. But this time, he thought it wise to disagree with his aunt.

"Auntie, I'm sorry, I can't do that."

"Think about it, Joe, and you will be amazed by the results," said Auntie Cornie.

Joe bowed down his head for a while as he thought of what was said by his aunt. She got up from her chair, went over to him and tilted his head up.

"What are you thinking about?" she asked.

"I'm thinking about what you said," he responded.

"I know her parents very well," Cornie continued with a smile, "they are rich and she is the only daughter so they do not hesitate in giving her cash and whatever she needs."

"I understand what you mean, Auntie, but I have made up my mind that until I start working and am able to fend for myself, I will not take a girlfriend. Apart from that, I have seen and heard of bright students who messed up their education because of their involvement in such relationships."

"So, you don't agree with me?" asked Cornie.

"I know it can happen as you are saying, but for the first time over the years, I want to make it clear to you that I can't buy what you are selling," Joe said and stood up, heading for the door. "When Kwaku comes, please tell him I was here."

"I will tell him, but think about what I said and some day you'll be back to tell me I was right."

She did not give him any money, neither his transport fare back to campus. When Joe was out of the house, he emptied his pockets to see how much he had. He checked the cash, lifted his eyes up to the sky and made some mental calculations. What he had could take him back to Miawani but could not afford him breakfast the next morning and his parents' money was not due for another four days. This set him thinking about whether to go back to beg his aunt for some cash, the purpose of his visit, or go to Belinda to ask for a cup of *gari* to see how it would go. He lingered in the neighbourhood for a while, pondering over his aunt's suggestion.

'You will lack nothing if you have an affair with the only daughter of a rich man,' his aunt had said to him. *'She will shower you with gifts, and her parents, knowing that you are such an intelligent boy who helps their daughter with her school work, will give you more than you can ever think of.'*

These words kept ringing in his ears and the devil seemed to be putting in some more in support of Auntie Cornie as he spoke to Joe's imagination of how life could be like, having all that he would ever need on campus. Being the boyfriend of the only daughter of a wealthy couple could mean being like the son of the couple who need not struggle much when it came to money matters, as he was experiencing at that time. The master planner of all the evil in our world, Satan, was giving him ideas on how to approach Belinda as soon as he returned to campus, but as fate would have it, he bumped into Bob, an old school friend.

"When did you come, Joe?" asked Bob.

"I came to collect something from my aunt and was on my way back to campus."

"I hear people say sometimes living in the boarding house is a lot better than being a day student," Bob said.

"It depends on many factors, Bob," Joe said. "If you have constant supply of all you need, then indeed, the boarding house is a better place to be because you can have a lot of time to yourself to study. But when you are like me, who has to struggle to get your next meal, living in the boarding house is not very easy."

"Don't tell me you are struggling, Joe, or are you?" Bob asked with a smile.

"It's not really so, but not very easy either," replied Joe. "So what are you doing now?" he asked.

"You know I could not go any further after Form Five due to certain circumstances, so I got myself a job at the post office. But I'm still with my parents because they want me to save a little money before I rent my own room."

"That's good," said Joe.

"Let's go and say hello to my mum; she will be delighted to see you. Of all my friends from school, you are the only one she has been enquiring about. She says you are a good boy so she is always happy when she sees the two of us together."

As they headed for home, Bob told Joe all that has been going on in the locality since his departure. There was a very short route to Bob's home, but they chose to go a different way.

"Why don't we go by the place we used to play football?" asked Joe. "I think it's shorter that way."

"You will be surprised to see the big mansion being built on that plot which had been neglected all these years. We shall pass there on our way back so you can have a look," said Bob.

"It's not been that long since I left here but I'm seeing a lot of changes," Joe commented.

"Yes. Even the refuse dump is being converted into a playground and I hear the market too is to be relocated to the back of the lorry station. The new Assembly Man is a man of action."

"Not a man of words," Joe chipped in.

"Both. He promises and delivers," said Bob.

"Not like some of the Assembly Men you know, who are full of words but no action. They talk a lot and do little."

When they entered the house, Bob's mother was in the kitchen and when he called to tell her Joe was around, she asked excitedly,"

"Where is he?"

"I'm here, Maam," Joe answered.

Bob's mother, a very energetic and easy-going woman in her mid-forties, rushed out of the kitchen to embrace Joe and asked him series of questions which he could not answer at once.

"When did you come? How is school? Are you going back today? How are your parents?"

Some of these questions needed detailed answers but Bob's mother would not wait to ask yet another string of questions.

"Are you coming back to stay here or you would like to stay in the boarding house? I hope you are studying hard?"

The only response from Joe was to smile, because he had no chance of answering one question before another one followed.

"Food is ready, so get yourselves settled and I will be with you in a minute," she said and went back to the kitchen.

They continued to talk about the infrastructural developments in the area and life at school. Bob deduced from the conversation that his friend might need some cash so he gave him a substantial amount from his wallet.

"This is not a loan. It's for you to spend while at school."

"This is too much, Bob."

"Don't worry, Joe. It's okay. I don't spend much here and I don't pay any rent so I always have more than enough."

He told Joe not to tell anyone that he has given him some cash. As they talked, Bob's mother came with food on a tray and laid it on the table.

"Go and get some drinking water, Bob," she said.

When Bob was out of sight, his mother also squeezed some money into Joe's palm and said he should use it as his transport fare back to Miawani.

"Don't tell anyone," she whispered into his ear.

"Thank you very much," Joe said.

When Bob returned with the water, his mother went back to the kitchen to tidy up and left the boys to eat.

"This is real home-made. You can't get this type on campus," Joe said.

Bob's mouth was full so he could not talk. He only smiled and nodded. After swallowing, he drank some water to push it down and told Joe he would get him some foodstuff to take with him.

Not long after Joe had left Auntie Cornie's house, she called Mrs Addo, Belinda's mother. She told her straightaway that she had asked Joe to keep an eye on her daughter and do everything he could to protect and help her, especially in her studies, being a senior student. Mrs Addo sounded happy about the idea and said they were about to arrange for someone to help the daughter after school hours with her work, so if Joe could do that, he would not be doing it for free. She promised to look for Joe on her next visit to the school.

Edinpa Secondary School was the best in the entire district and one had to be either very bright or have wealthy parents to gain admission there. Simply put, it was made up of two categories of students, the very rich and the very bright. Only a handful of them fitted into both categories. The rich kids proved by their every action that they came from a better background. The way they talked and the clothes they wore told who they were. And if they happened to be good academically too, then it was inevitable they would make themselves out to be far more superior to the other poor students, making them feel somewhat inferior in their midst.

The only other boy whose IQ was above that of Joe in the Sixth Form was also from a very poor home, in fact, poorer than Joe's, and they were friends. Patrick Kofi Koduah was his name and he talked like a parrot. He was popularly known by the monogram PKK, the initials of his name. He was always arguing, always trying to prove a point.

He had a red T-shirt with the inscription **BRAINS AND MONEY** in the front and **WHICH WILL YOU CHOOSE?** at the back written in black. According to him, both are good things, money and brains, but the letter 'B' comes before 'M' and because he always wanted to be first, he chose 'B' for brains. His slogan was, *'You can acquire money with brains, but you can't buy brains with money.'* He said you might have a lot of money and lose it all if you don't have brains but if you have brains you can make more money. He was more popular than any other student in the entire school. Even some people from outside knew him as the boy with brains, but he was far too arrogant.

Back in the wealthy couple's house, Joe became the subject of discussion. Mr Addo was suspicious that Joe could take advantage of his innocent girl if he assumed the duty of a protector and a teacher.

"I have been a boy myself," said Mr Addo, "and I can't remember doing anything for a girl for free during my school days, even though, I must confess I wasn't as clever as you claim this boy is, so we must be very careful."

"They say the devil you know is better than the angel you don't know," Mrs Addo said. "We both know Cornie to be from a well respected home. What about employing the services of someone none of us know? He could take advantage of her too. All we have to do is to talk to our daughter to be careful and concentrate on her studies."

"Okay, when you visit her over the weekend, do arrange for a meeting so that we can have both of them at home one of these days. We need to see who this boy is," said Mr Addo.

One could understand Mr Addo's feelings toward the issue at stake. He knew his behaviour in the past, not only as a youth but post marriage. He had never spared any female who needed his help. He was scared that what he had done to others would be done to his own daughter. Everyone who slashes others' throats is himself afraid to lie down face up. Do unto others as you want them to do to you played on his conscience but Joe wasn't having any such idea.

Joe's main aim of going to his aunt was to ask for some cash, but he found himself in a dilemma that, for the first time, made him challenge and disagree with her. However, it was a step in the right direction, because now he was going back to campus with more than he had expected to get from her, a bag full of foodstuff and money from Bob's house and another neighbour.

He had been a well behaved boy while living in the area so each time he visited people showed him hospitality. For the few times that he visited, he always returned with presents but this trip was exceptional in the sense that, although he had refused his aunt's suggestion, he did not return empty-handed.

At the back of his mind, Joe was thinking of the implications of his refusal to accept Cornie's suggestion. Before he left her place, she said to him that he was going to have honey dripping on his tongue and that he should not think of spitting it out. This was an opportunity, a really good chance that others would die for. If Auntie Cornie had simply suggested helping Belinda with her studies, Joe would have gladly obliged. But the other things she added made him think she had ulterior motives, and that was what had put him off.

Cornie separated from her husband when Kwaku, their son, was only six years and for the five years that Joe stayed with her, he keenly observed how she handled the men who came her way. Cornie would do anything she could to get the last penny from your pocket with a smile. Joe didn't like the practice, but he could not do anything about it.

Once a man came to the house to question her as to why she did not come to see him at his office as she had promised. The man was angry and it turned out to be a big scandal because this was a married man known to some of the tenants. It was rumoured that she was having an affair with the man. She claimed to have bought something from the man on credit and the payment date was long overdue and that was why he was angry. But the people who knew this man also knew that he was not a trader, so whatever that something was, which she claimed to have bought from him, remained an unsolved puzzle.

On campus PKK's bragging had landed him into trouble and he was undergoing punishment when Joe arrived. He had said to some fellow students that he was brighter than some of the teachers and that he could teach most of them. When this claim leaked he was questioned by the Headmaster. PKK did not deny it. For his punishment he was asked to clear weeds feom two plots of land at the back of the school garden after which he was to go home on suspension for two weeks.

The source of the rumour was that, a few months earlier, a substitute teacher, a student from Kumasi Polytechnic had approached PKK to explain a topic further to him. The said substitute teacher was no longer at the school but had confided in PKK that his explanation gave him deeper understanding of the subject. PKK took this as a weapon to boast in his ability to teach some of the teachers. His punishment was used as an example to instil discipline into other students, in that no matter how intelligent you are as a student, you were not considered equal to your teacher, let alone brag that you were better than them.

PKK's punishment caused a divide in the student front. Some said he went a bit too far, while others supported his claim. The third group chose to remain neutral. They knew he was the brightest boy in Lower Six; however, claiming to be above the teacher was a bit too far, but condemning his claim as false was also false in itself. So they chose to shut their mouth, ears and eyes to what was going on. We have this type of people everywhere, so, it wasn't a big surprise that some either supported, condemned or remained neutral about the comment that landed the brightest boy in the school in this situation. When Joe approached PKK, he was furious and did not show any remorse at all.

"I accept the punishment as being the consequences of my comment, but I won't lick back my spit. I still stick to my guns that I know more than some of them."

"Reserve those words, PK," said Joe. "Sometimes it's good not to talk about your feeling, even though you may be boiling with anger."

"Joe, let's face facts. What do some of these guys know, that you and I don't, tell me? I was there a few days ago when the Maths teacher was fumbling with the Pythagoras theory until you came to his aid. You surprised all of us that day with your explanation. These are facts, so why can't we talk about them?"

"Yes, you can talk about them but be careful whom you talk to, because they may go out there and explain it differently," said Joe.

"You know me too well, Joe, I will always stand for what I believe in, the facts. They can do whatever they want to do to me but I will never beg them for what I believe is the truth," PKK maintained.

"I am not saying you should go and beg them because that's too late now. What I mean is, be careful of what you say and to whom you say it. Everyone in the school knows that you are the brightest boy, so a time will come when those who stand for the truth will fight for you. You have become a target now, so if I were you I would be quiet and let my brains do the talking," Joe advised.

From an open window, the Housemaster spotted Joe and PKK having a chat so he called out to Joe to go to the dormitory in order to give PKK the time to serve his punishment.

"Can't I even have a chat with my mate? Is that part of the punishment? If you want to banish me from this school forever, let me know and I shall be on my way," PKK shouted.

Joe walked away and promised to talk to him later. Although the Housemaster heard PKK's rantings, he did not respond. Just around that time, in a telephone conversation to tell Belinda she would be visiting during the weekend, Mrs Addo asked her if she knew a boy called Joseph Boakye from Diasempa in the school.

"Yes, Mum, he is a very clever boy, second only to an arrogant boy who is always bragging about his intelligence. How did you know him?" asked Belinda.

"His aunt is a good friend of mine and she mentioned him to me when I told her I would visit you this weekend," said Mrs Addo.

"I will introduce him to you when you come, Mum. I have actually not spoken to him before, just hello and hi when we meet each other, but now that I know you know his aunt, I will let you see him when you come. Please don't forget the pink trainers," she reminded her mother.

"It is among the things that I have packed to bring to you," said Mrs Addo.

Belinda was so excited that she was going to introduce Joe to her mother. Joe's humility and intelligence had earned him so much respect among students and staff that some junior students could hardly talk to him, although he was very affable. Some of his mates called him Gentleman Joe. He was nice and friendly, but being such a poor boy, he sometimes found it difficult to mingle with these students from wealthy homes, so he kept to himself most of the time. His books were his closest friends. To him, being a student meant studying and being occupied most of your time.

His dear mother missed the driver who usually took his money to him at school on this occasion. The school was situated by the side of the main road on the outskirts of Miawani, so whenever his money was due, normally on Friday mornings, every two weeks, Joe would stand by the gate, waiting for the driver to turn up. Unfortunately, when the driver showed up that morning he told Joe he did not see his mother. Joe wasn't much worried anyway, because he had enough to last him a couple of days, if not weeks. However, he introduced the driver to the security man and said whenever the money was ready he could give it to the security man to pass it on to him.

"So, how are you going to survive, son?" the security man asked Joe after the driver was gone.

"Well, I have got some cash on me, so, I will manage until whenever it arrives," Joe said.

"If you run out, let me know so that I can loan you some cash," said the security man.

"Thank you very much. I will let you know if I need some cash. Thank you once again for your generosity," Joe said gratefully.

'If I had not met Bob and his mother, how would I have survived? Thank God for them. I know God has a hand in what I'm experiencing. He makes a way where there is none. He knew I would miss this week's cash from my parents so He provided through Bob and his mother. Thank you, Lord Jesus, for your provision,' Joe prayed in his heart as he went back to the dormitory.

For breakfast that morning, he cooked some of the cocoyam he had brought from Bob's place. The aroma attracted other students to enquire how he came by the cocoyam.

"It's a long story, if I should explain," he said to one of them.

"It smells good and I expect it to taste good too," another boy said.

"When, where and how did you get cocoyam on the campus?" asked another.

"I call it manna from on high. I went to my aunt to get some money and we had a misunderstanding over an issue, so I left her place empty-handed and...," Joe was trying to explain.

"You, Joe, had a misunderstanding with your aunt? This can't be possible. This might be the first time, if what you are saying is true," interrupted one of his room mates.

This room mate knew a bit about his aunt as having a lot of control over Joe so he was surprised to hear him say he had disagreed with her on an issue.

"Yes. There is always a first time, you know. She was trying to force something down my throat and I was not prepared to swallow it so I spat it out. She doesn't understand why, because she thought it was for my own good. But I don't believe the fact that if something has worked for someone it means it would work for everyone. Everyone is different hence we have different destinies."

"What is it that she tried to force down your throat?" asked the room mate.

"That's a private matter, you don't have to know everything," answered Joe.

"That's true. The cocoyam is now the bone of contention. How did you get it?" asked one of them.

"Like I was saying," continued Joe, "when I left my aunt's place, I roamed the neighbourhood for a while, and as I was contemplating whether to go back and beg her for some cash, I bumped into an old classmate who took me home. And as if it had been divinely planned, when we got to his house, his generous mother was just about finishing cooking so we had a wonderful home made lunch of *banku* and okro soup. When I was leaving they gave me what we are now talking about, the cocoyam, and some loose change."

"No wonder you call it manna from on high," said a room mate.

"Yes, because I was desperate and did not know what to do, just like the Israelites felt in the wilderness. They wanted to go back to Egypt because they had no food or water, but God provided manna for them, because He did not want them to go back to Egypt. He did not want me to go back to my aunt, so He miraculously provided manna for me."

"Enough of the sermon, Pastor Joe," said one of them.

"It must be ready by now. Could someone get water and I will bring it to the table for us to enjoy," said Joe.

Back in Diasempa, Joe's mother was worried that she could not get the money to him that morning. His father, however, was of the opinion that at eighteen years, Joe should be able to cope under such circumstances.

"That's what helps to make you a man, by learning to survive when the unexpected happens; because if everything works out as he expects, he will never mature. I will even suggest that we keep it for two more days before sending it to him. One day he will tell us how he managed and how it helped him to mature," said Agya Boakye.

"You don't want my son to starve to death, do you?" Darkoaa asked.

Agya Boakye laughed and told his wife that Joe would not die for going without food for only two or three days.

"Understand me, woman, I'm not being hard or trying to deny him what is due him. All I am saying and wish you understood it is that he will survive by any means possible. He will mature only through times like these, when you don't know where or when to get your next meal," he added.

Darkoaa was beginning to get upset with her husband's comments about their son, and to avoid further arguments, she walked out of the room.

PKK finished clearing the plots in two days during which he was not allowed to participate in any class work. He could have done it in less than a day, but he chose to delay to plan where to spend the following two weeks of his suspension. By the third day he hatched an idea. He would spend four days in the village with an uncle, three days with an aunt in another town, another three days with a friend in the city and then spend the last four days at home because he did not want his parents to know of the suspension.

He would lie to them that due to renovations in some parts of the dormitories, most students whose areas were affected had been asked to go home for at least three days. He came up with this beautiful, well-calculated idea on how to spend his 'holidays,' as he called it. But travelling from the school to the village and to another city required money, and he did not have enough to cover all these expenses. He needed to raise money.

The Headmaster charged the Housemaster to see to it that he completed clearing the plots and leave the campus soon afterwards. So in the afternoon of the third day when the Housemaster realised that the plot was clean as required, he called PKK to have a word with him.

"Are you leaving this evening or tomorrow morning?" he asked.

"Leaving for where, Sir?" PKK asked back.

"Well, now that you have finished the campus part of the punishment, you have to commence your two weeks suspension with immediate effect," the Housemaster said.

"Sir", he said, "if I may ask, is it your own decree or you were asked to carry it out by a higher authority? And if the latter is your answer, may I please have a word with whoever he may be?"

"Look here, young man, I'm just doing what I have been assigned to do," the Housemaster said.

"And that is why I want to speak to who assigned me to you. Because I can figure out that since you don't have the final say, you may not be of help to what I want to speak to him about," he insisted.

While this dialogue was taking place, PKK stood still with both hands at his back. He did not raise his voice, neither did he look angry. He was very composed and concise. He had the right to be heard and therefore demanded it. Since his punishment began, the reasons for it had been speculated in two ways.

The authorities, in an attempt to avoid being scandalised, peddled the version that PKK was being punished for being rude and insulting a member of staff. On the other hand, those who heard it from the horse's own mouth spread it as it was; that he had claimed to be more intelligent than some of the teachers. It was for this reason that when a student came into the office where he was demanding his right, the Housemaster changed the conversation and asked him an irrelevant question at that moment.

"So where did you say you come from, I mean your hometown?"

Seeing that he wanted to cover up, PKK pretended not to have heard what he said. He was going to say something when the Housemaster turned to address the intruder.

"What can I do for you? Next time, you should learn to knock and wait for a response before you enter."

The student had knocked but there was no response from inside, even though he heard them talking.

"Sorry for intruding, Sir. The Headmaster said you should come to 6A immediately, Sir," the student said.

"Okay, I will be there in a minute," said the Housemaster.

When the student left, the Housemaster told PKK he was going to see the Headmaster and would get back to him on his return.

"In the mean time, if you don't mind, can you tell me why you want to see who is handling your case?" he asked.

Still maintaining his expressionless composure, PKK made another statement that the Housemaster could not do anything about.

"Well, you want me to leave campus this evening or tomorrow morning, but I don't have any money for transport, so it is impossible for me to travel at this moment."

"All right, leave that to me and I will get back to you," the Housemaster said and dismissed him.

In 6A, PKK's class, an argument between two students who belong to different factions on his issue had been reported to the Headmaster because it was leading to a fight. The Headmaster's presence brought some order, but tensions were still high. When the Housemaster arrived he could see that almost everyone was tense. The Headmaster pulled the Housemaster aside and said they had to do something about the issue immediately.

"What issue?" asked the Housemaster.

"PKK's, that is what has brought about this confusion," said the Headmaster.

Outside the classroom where they were talking, they could still hear the students arguing. Those who did not support PKK's comment said he was undermining the credibility of the teacher and the integrity of the entire school.

"I've got an idea," said the Housemaster, "let's give them an assignment that will take about an hour. Let them write how they spent their last long vacation. Set someone over them to make sure no one talks to another. During the next hour, let's have a meeting with all the teachers and other staff to discuss the issue. Some solution might come out of it."

"Good," said the Headmaster. "Call the rest of the teachers to the meeting room and I will meet you there soon."

"Just before I leave, I was with PKK when you sent for me. He said he hasn't got money to travel home now, so what shall we do about that too?" asked the Housemaster.

"We shall discuss that at the meeting," the Headmaster said.

After the Headmaster had instructed the English teacher to give them the composition, Joe, who had remained silent during all this commotion, asked the English teacher to excuse him for a few minutes. He was granted the permission and he followed the Headmaster to have a word with him.

"Sir, can I please talk with you for a minute," Joe asked.

"You sure can, Joe," said the Headmaster.

"Sir, I wasn't on campus when this fracas started and I am extremely worried about where it could lead to. I have been quiet all this time and contemplating on the comments other students are making about it, and I strongly believe it could tarnish the good image of this great school."

The Headmaster was quietly listening to Joe as a child pays attention to a father's instruction without questioning. He was startled by the wisdom with which Joe was addressing him.

"I am therefore of the opinion that, to let sleeping dogs lie, call an assembly of the whole school, including all the teachers and staff, and as the head of the school, issue a statement that no one is to mention anything about it again. Whoever defaults would be expelled from the school instantly."

"You are talking as if you are in my mind, Joe," said the Headmaster. "That's exactly what I intend to do in the next few minutes."

"Then about PKK," Joe continued, "I will plead with you that since he has served the first part of his punishment, for the sake of peace and also to maintain the dignity of our great school, please pardon him and cancel the suspension. I'm done, Sir."

"Joe, I am yet to come across a lad of your age with so much wisdom and humility. I am meeting with the rest of the teachers and I will put this suggestion on board and see how it goes. Thank you very much," the Headmaster said.

In the dormitory, alone, PKK was thinking of how to raise money for his fare to the village while he awaited a response from the Housemaster. At the meeting, when the Headmaster tabled the suggestion he had received from Joe a few minutes earlier, he made it sound as if it was his own idea.

"You all know of the recent happening in the school concerning PKK's comments. Since we decided to punish him, the student front has almost split into two, or I may say three because there are others who have chosen to remain neutral. A few minutes ago there was an argument between the factions which nearly resulted in a fight if I had not intervened."

Some of the teachers were so angry about the comment that they felt PKK should have been given a more serious punishment than what he had received.

"Why are we still entertaining this boy in the school?"

One of the angry teachers whispered to another during the Headmaster's address and the Headmaster heard him so he told the teacher to wait till he has finished before making whatever contribution he had.

"I have therefore invited you all here," continued the Headmaster, "to see how best we can resolve this issue before outsiders and other schools get to know of it."

"I won't be surprised if it's already in town," said another staff member, in the hearing of the Headmaster.

"Well, wherever it has got to, we must stop it from spreading any further," said the Headmaster.

"How?" asked someone from the back.

"That's why we are here," replied the Headmaster. "So what do you suggest?" he asked them.

"I think he is too arrogant and so must be expelled from the school," someone said.

"Let us pardon him, since this is the first time such a thing is happening in the school."

"He should go home for a month, and not two weeks and this will serve as a deterrent to would-be trouble-makers."

Another angry teacher suggested PKK go home for a complete year. In that way, he added, he would learn to be humble after missing out a year in his education. The meeting room was becoming like a marketplace because everyone expressed their opinions all at once and not necessarily addressing the Head. It was at this point that the oldest man in the school, a history teacher called Mr. Adwenmoa, asked for silence and began to speak.

"I have been teaching in this school for the past twenty years. Majority of these students were not yet born and this is the first time a case like this is happening here. Edinpa is well respected and the best school in the entire district. If we don't quench the fire that someone's comment has lit, it is not just the school's image that will suffer but also some of us here will be casualties. It could create hostility among some of us."

"So what do you suggest?" asked the Housemaster when the speaker paused for a moment.

"I will suggest that we bury the issue as it is now, and let the boy off the hook, because if we send him home, it will be like washing our dirty linen in public. He will talk about why he was sent home and people would start asking questions."

"No way, he must be punished severely since such comments from a student about his teacher should not be tolerated in the school," someone said from the back.

"I am not saying what he did is right," said Mr. Adwenmoa, "what I mean is that two wrongs do not make a right. He has made a mistake, agreed, but don't let us make a mistake too."

As the atmosphere was getting tense, the Bursar of the school, Mr Atta Agyarko, added his voice.

"Point of order, point of order," he said, and when he was given the chance to talk, he addressed the house as follows:

"My fellow staff and teachers, I believe we have the Head of this school as the chairman of the meeting. He has heard all that is being said and I will suggest that he use the power entrusted to him to filter what has been said, issue a statement and close this meeting. Because if we should carry on like this, we shall leave this place without arriving at any decision; rather, like Mr. Adwenmoa said, we shall leave here with more casualties."

"Well spoken. I support what he said," someone said.

"I support him too," agreed yet another.

The Headmaster rose from his seat, placed his left hand into his trouser pocket, held his chin with his right and walked half-way across the room. He then turned back to his seat, but did not sit down. He stood behind the chair and held the back support with both hands, still thinking of what to say. The room was quiet as all eyes were fixed on him and every ear attentive to what was going to come from the Head. After a while, when his behaviour had hypnotised everyone present, he began to speak.

"Thank you very much, Mr. Adwenmoa, fellow teachers and staff. Opinions are like finger prints, we have all got some, but no two are the same, and that is what has been expressed here today. But as the Head of the school, I wish to make this statement and hope that you would back me up for it to remain as such. I have been informed that the boy has completed the first part of his punishment."

Those who were not passing comments at this time were listening attentively to what his conclusion would be. He glanced at their faces and continued.

"At 4:00 pm today, I am going to call an assembly which every individual in this school must attend, and I will repeat what I'm going to tell you now," he paused and licked his lips.

Everyone was wondering what the Head of the school was going to say because he was expecting the entire staff to back him. Already, they were divided in opinions about the issue at stake and, as some of them stared at each other and others at the Head, he began to talk again.

"PKK's comment and whatever is linked to it is a taboo in the school and anyone found discussing it will be expelled instantly. PKK will join his fellow students in class tomorrow. However, if he himself makes any more of such statements, he will leave the school immediately. Thank you for your presence," he said and closed the meeting.

"*Tweaaa,*" said one of the staff.

"Who said *tweaaa?*" asked the Headmaster.

The one who said it did not respond. He whispered to the one nearest to him that PKK should not have been let off the hook, but a verbal decree had been issued and it had to be adhered to. Some of those who were not in favour of the decree wanted to talk to the Headmaster afterwards, but like Pilate telling the people of Israel concerning Jesus, 'What I have written, I have written,' he told them that what he had said would remain as he said it. Needless to say, they left the meeting room with mixed feelings.

Before he invited PKK to his office to tell him the news of his pardon, the Headmaster had first spoken to Joe. Since he came to meet those who had been there five years and over, Joe had proved to them that there is a difference between wisdom, knowledge and intelligence. He applied his God-given wisdom to intelligence, then using the knowledge of the environment in which the incident was taking place, his carefully chosen words to the Headmaster yielded positive results. The Head wanted to show his appreciation.

"You and PKK are of equal intelligence but you don't behave like him," he said.

"Well, we may be of equal intelligence, Sir, but we are different individuals from different backgrounds," said Joe.

"You are right. Everybody is different," the Headmaster agreed. "At the meeting I have told the staff what you suggested to me and majority of them have agreed to it. I'm so grateful."

"I also thank you for giving me the opportunity to express my view," said Joe.

The Headmaster then dismissed Joe and told him to go and call PKK to his office. After he had been told that he could resume classes the next day, that he had been forgiven, PKK thanked the Headmaster, and for the first time, said he was sorry for what his comment might have caused.

"It has caused a lot of problems but, as I told you, be careful of what you say in future because the next time anything like that happens, you will be given the marching order. You may go," the Headmaster said.

PKK left the office promising that no such thing will ever happen again, not from or by him. He smiled within himself that he was off the hook. He looked for Joe to tell him of the good news and Joe told him to thank God for that. Joe also told him to be careful with his words from then on.

When Joe's money finally came, it made him feel very rich because he hadn't used much of what he had brought from Bob and his mother. He had been living on the food they gave him. Bob's mother had made sure that the bag they were giving to Joe contained a bit of every edible item that was at home when he arrived. Joe gave some to a junior student with whom he had formed friendship recently. The boy was just as humble as Joe, so friendship easily flowed between the two.

Joe had not heard from Auntie Cornie since he left her place in anger, but that did not stop her from pursuing her plans. By hook or crook or both, she wanted Joe to befriend Belinda, because according to her, if you rub shoulders with the rich, you become rich too. She was a woman who was more interested in money than moral pursuits. Cornie lied to Mrs Addo, informing her about fake plans to attend a funeral with some friends that weekend.

"Since you have already made other plans, I will go alone and give you the feedback. I asked my daughter about your boy and I was honestly amazed about what she told me about him, just as you said," said Mrs Addo.

"Are they friends already?" asked Auntie Cornie.

"Not really, but she did confirm that he is a very brilliant and gentle chap," said Mrs Addo.

"Did you tell her what we discussed?" Cornie asked.

"No. Not on the phone. I want to meet the two of them and arrange a meeting with them and my husband. We need to speak to both of them."

"That's true. My regards to them when you go," Auntie Cornie said enthusiastically.

Belinda and Joe had said 'hello', 'good morning' or 'evening' a few times casually whenever their path crossed each other while on campus, but they never engaged in any real conversation. However, since the day Auntie Cornie spoke to him about her, Belinda seemed to be opening up to him. One morning, at the assembly, after greeting Joe with a smile, Belinda asked if he had a particular Maths text book that she could borrow.

"I'm sorry I don't have it at the moment," said Joe. "I used it three years ago and gave it to a friend. I will ask him if he is through with it and get it for you."

"Thank you very much," said Belinda.

In the past two or three days, she had felt like telling Joe that her mother knows his aunt, but something inside of her had been restraining her. The same feeling showed up this morning but she decided to wait until she had introduced him to her mother. Joe, however, was suspicious that his aunt might have made a move without his consent, so he still did not show any sign of being interested in her.

'Birds of a feather flock together,' it is said. Belinda had two close friends, Eva and Vida, whose parents were also very rich and she informed Eva that her mother knows Joseph Boakye's aunt.

"How did you know that?" Eva asked Belinda.

"My Mum told me the last time she called. She will be coming here next weekend and would like to see him."

"I don't think he knows it because if he did he might have said something to you," said Eva.

"Something like what?" Belinda asked, giggling.

"Don't you know these boys? They will always want to engage you in a conversation, hoping to lead to something, especially when they know someone you know. Anyway, I'm sure when your mum comes, it will be a different story," said Eva.

Vida saw the two from a distance engrossed in conversation and ran to join them. From the look on Belinda's face, Vida could tell that she was happy and she wanted to know what was making her so cheerful.

"I hope you two are not gossiping about me," Vida said jokingly.

"Yes, it's about you," said Belinda, still giggling.

"Who else do you think we can gossip about, apart from you?" asked Eva.

"Whatever it is that you are gossiping about will certainly eat you up, if you don't tell me," Vida said.

Eva and Belinda burst into laughter. Vida knew very well that it was a joke so she also joined in the laughter and Belinda said;

"When it finishes eating us up, it will turn to you and consume you too."

"Nothing can eat me up because my mind is pure and my heart is clean. It's you two who are hiding something in you and that thing will soon explode and consume you," said Vida.

"Talk of the devil and he appears, there goes our talking point," said Eva, pointing to Joe who was entering the dining hall.

"You cheeky girls," said Vida, "so is he the one you've been talking about?"

They all laughed and Belinda told Vida what her mother had said about Joe as they also went into the dining hall. Belinda had been thinking of how to approach Joe to inform him about her mother's intention to know him. The thought had occupied her mind since her mother enquired about Joe. Each time she saw him, she shivered and wondered what it would lead to after she had introduced him to her mother. She respected Joe for at least two things - his intelligence and humility. His respect for all and obedience were second to none in the school. There was always a smile on his face and she never saw him angry.

Once, some students held a revolt against a decision by the Boys' Prefect. It was the carefully chosen words of Joe that brought calm. Belinda remembered that very well. It was his idea which the Headmaster had implemented to solve PKK's problem, but no one knew about that and he did not go about telling others, let alone his occasional break-time teaching of junior students. Above all these, it was evident that his knowledge of the Scriptures was not just to pass Bible Knowledge exams but he actually lived it. Belinda just hoped her mother would have enough time to spare so she could tell her all the good things she knew about Joe. He and PKK, no doubt, were the two best students in the school, but PKK's arrogance gave Joe the upper hand in many cases.

PKK possessed a talent for art and had taken part in designing some T-shirts for a local printing firm for small commissions. It was this firm which printed his very well-known T-shirt with the inscription, 'BRAINS AND MONEY - WHICH WILL YOU CHOOSE?', and to commemorate his waived suspension, he contacted one of the lads at the firm on the day he was pardoned to print boldly in front of a white T-shirt the words: 'TO BE A WINNER, JOIN THOSE YOU CAN'T BEAT.' Anyone who saw him in it understood what it stood for, but they refrained from commenting on it.

He used this T'shirt most of the time when he knew no teacher or the Headmaster could see him. But the Headmaster took notice of it eventually and summoned him to his office immediately to warn him not to wear it again in the school. He did not explain why, neither did PKK ask any question about it, because he knew what he was portraying was provocative. In the last two years, he had led the school to win three debates against other schools in the district so he was a force to reckon with and this somehow made it difficult for the authorities when dealing with him.

Belinda was looking forward anxiously to the arrival of her mother with presents and the formal introduction of Joe to her. She was anxious about how she would have the courage to go to Joe and tell him her mother wanted to see him. To Joe, since the day he disagreed with his aunt about the issue that was the end of it. He did not know that Cornie had been working on it relentlessly.

Mr. Addo's reluctance to asking Joe to help Belinda had nothing to do with her academic achievements; rather, it had to do with what he himself had been doing and continued to do. It was purely due to his guilty conscience, the way he had been dealing with vulnerable ladies. Despite his reservation he agreed to the idea of paying Joe for his services, to please his wife. On Saturday morning when Mrs

Addo was due to embark on her journey to the school, the two found themselves in another argument.

"So, how much are you going to pay him for his services?" he asked.

"Pay who?" demanded Mrs Addo.

"I mean the boy you are hiring to help Belinda with her studies."

"And are you asking me how much I'm going to pay him? I thought we both agreed on this issue, so why are you asking how much I'm going to pay him? I did not decide on this alone, so you don't expect me to pay him alone. According to his aunt, the boy may not even accept money, so all we have to do is give him some tips and presents, after all..."

"That's okay, woman," said Mr. Addo. "You made the contact, and you are going ahead today to make further arrangements, so there is nothing wrong in asking how much the boy is to be paid. You and I know that whatever he would be paid is not going to come from your purse, so why are you worried?" he asked.

"You sounded like you were not interested in this whole arrangement and that is why I want to put things right."

"So do we have to go and meet them in the school or you will arrange to bring them home sometime later?" he asked.

Mrs Addo began to calm down because for once, her husband seemed to be saying something positive about the arrangements.

"Well, my meeting with them today will determine the next step to take," she said.

"What time do you hope to be back?"

"I will try to be back before three because of the funeral. I would like us to go together in the 'Be My Wife'."

"In what?" asked Mr Addo.

"I mean the BMW," the woman said amid smiles.

Shaking his head and laughing, Mr Addo asked which one and how she came by that name for the car.

"The black one, of course, we can't use the white one for a funeral when everyone will be wearing black. So you did not know that the youth in town refer to BMW as Be My Wife?"

"I am hearing it for the first time. What if the white one was the only car we had?" he asked.

"If it was the only one then we would have had no choice, but here we are with a fleet of cars. We have to use the right one for the occasion," she said.

While the Addos were talking about the trip to the school, Auntie Cornie travelled to Diasempa to inform Joe's parents of her arrangements for him to help a wealthy couple's daughter at school. She told them of Joe's chances of making some money out of it.

"I'm sure they will give him a lot of presents too, because they are very rich. They have lots of cars, houses, good business, etc."

She painted such a beautiful picture about the arrangements to them that there was no way they could object to it. Joe's mother saw nothing wrong with her son putting his God-given talent to use to make some money, for that matter.

"Thank you very much, he is your nephew and I know you want the best for him so if it's within your power, go ahead and help him," said Darkoaa.

But Agya Boakye had some questions to ask. He knew Cornie very well. She would not do anything that she would not personally benefit from. And that was very true, because Cornie's sole intention of making this connection was that as soon as Joe got into the picture, she would use him as a link to milk the Addos.

"So how did you get to know this couple?" asked Agya Boakye.

31

"They are friends of Kwaku's father's brother in-law," Cornie said.

"Friends of Kwaku's father's brother-in-law, so they are not your direct friends?" he asked.

"I got to know them through Kwaku's father years ago and they are a nice couple," replied Cornie.

"Well, I'm not much bothered about how nice they may be. You said they are very rich, do you know how they make their money and the business they do?" he asked.

"Why these questions, what have they got to do with Joe helping their daughter for some pocket money?" asked Darkoaa.

"The questions I'm asking have got everything to do with the arrangement Cornie is making, Darkoaa," Agya Boakye said calmly. "As a parent, you must always be sure of where your child is heading to."

"If all goes well, who knows, they may even end up marrying in future and Joe, you and I would never lack a thing, and trust me, I can work that out," said Cornie, getting up to leave the couple to sort it out.

She had dropped the bomb and was not concerned with whatever destruction it caused. Agya Boakye continued smiling without showing his teeth. He remained silent until Cornie was out of the room.

"Darkoaa, do you think your sister is doing all this for nothing? I believe you heard her very well saying she can work things out and that you will lack nothing? I bet she has got something up her sleeve, not just for Joe to earn some pocket money."

"Something like what?" asked Darkoaa.

"Well, you wait and see," he said.

Agya Boakye did not trust Cornie due to her cunning nature. He had been among a group of elders who sat on her marital case on more than three occasions. Some of the comments she made plus those that were made by her ex-husband shocked the entire arbitration team so much so that a few of them thought it was better for them to go their separate ways. Since then, Agya Boakye had been very cautious when dealing with her. It was poverty that made him agree to allow Joe to stay with her in Kumasi. If he had had his way and the means, he would never have consented for his son to stay with her. Not even for a day. She had influenced Joe in many ways, but he had maintained his integrity over the years while he was with her.

'*But we have no choice*', Darkoaa said to Agya Boakye nearly six years ago when the decision to send Joe to Cornie was being contemplated. Now Cornie had got control over him and was trying to manipulate his life and his future. Agya Boakye had to exercise his authority as a father and stand against this whole connection by Cornie.

CHAPTER TWO

JOE MAINTAINS HIS INTEGRITY

On campus, PKK was furious about what the Headmaster had said regarding his T-shirt. He had wanted it to say what was in his mind but a higher authority had warned him not to wear it again, at least not on the school premises. The first time Joe saw PKK in that T-shirt he questioned him about it and advised that he should not wear it in the school but PKK did not listen to him.

"Now I can't even wear this T-shirt again," he complained to Joe.

"Why can't you?" Joe asked, laughing.

"The Headmaster said so," he told Joe.

"Do you remember me telling you about it? I think he is right because it is very provocative, considering the recent fracas. If he said you shouldn't wear it, I will advise you not to. Don't give them the chance to keep an eye on you constantly," Joe said in his usual humility.

For some time now since he was let off the hook, PKK had been quiet and wanted this T-shirt to speak for him but it was being banned too. Some of his close friends were beginning to keep him at an arm's length. Their actions were speaking louder than words.

On Saturday when visiting time to Edinpa Secondary School was approaching, most of the students who were expecting visitors came out from their dormitories to the entrance and stairs and some peeped through their dormitory windows to see who was visiting who. Some of them, including Joe, were not expecting visitors and were either reading in their rooms or in some of the classrooms. Others were just socialising. As soon as the gates were opened, the visitors flocked into the school's compound to embrace, shake hands and kiss their loved ones. Mrs Addo was among the first ten visitors that entered.

A couple who were visiting their second-year son with their two other children were the centre of attention, because coincidentally, it was the son's birthday. They had come with lots of presents and cards for him. They had prepared sweets including chocolates in small packets for him to share with his friends. The noise of the students and visitors singing "Happy birthday" to the boy brought those who were in their rooms and other places to the entrance and among them was Joe. Belinda was inspecting the presents her mother brought to her when all of a sudden she saw Joe going to the scene of celebration.

"That's Joe, Mum, the boy you asked about," she said to her mother.

"Where is he?" asked Mrs. Addo.

"There, the boy in the white shirt and black jeans," Belinda said, pointing to Joe.

"Quick, call him over before he gets into the crowd," commanded her mother.

"No, Mum. Let me take these things to the dormitory first. We can't have a chat here, we'll go to the common room," said Belinda.

Soon after seeing Joe and telling her mother, Belinda suddenly brightened up and her mother couldn't tell whether it was the presents that were making her so happy or the sight and thought of Joe. Innocently, Joe went for a packet of sweets and chocolates.

"If this is being done for the boy at school, then it would have been a big party if he was at home," Joe was thinking as he unwrapped the chocolate.

35

"This is what distinguishes us from the rich," he said to another poor boy.

"You are right, boy. I can't even remember my birthday most of the time, because there is nothing to celebrate it with," said the boy.

"Oh! So I'm not alone. I have never celebrated my birthday," Joe said.

Belinda packed the things her mother had brought for her back into the bag and was in the process of taking them with her to her dormitory when her mother told her to take a carrier bag from the back seat for Joe. Belinda said Joe would be very surprised because she was sure he was not expecting anything from anyone.

"I haven't once seen his parents or anyone visiting him," Belinda said.

"So how do you see him generally?" Mrs Addo asked her daughter.

"Honestly speaking, Mum, words can't adequately explain the enormity of this boy's qualities. He is humble, brilliant, neat, etc; anything you will expect from someone who has been well trained. He commands so much respect in this school. In fact, I can't tell you all about him, except what I've observed myself," said Belinda.

"That's fine," said her mother, "his aunt told me the same about him."

Belinda went to drop the bag on her bed and came back to take her mother to the common room, with the bag for Joe. She then started her search for Joe. When she found him she said hello and went on to explain that her mother was in the common room and would like to see him.

"Is that so? When did she come and why does she want to see me?" Joe asked.

Although he knew very well that his aunt was behind this connection, Joe was surprised and confused because he didn't know what his aunt had said to the Addos since the last time they talked about Belinda.

"She said one of your aunts mentioned you to her," said Belinda, smiling.

"Is that it?" he asked.

"Yes."

Joe continued to act clueless. He was trying as much as he could not to give Belinda and her mother the slightest idea that he had heard much about them from his aunt. This was the very first time he had spoken to Belinda beyond hello and good day, apart from the day she asked him for a text book. He could see that Belinda felt very uncomfortable just like him, but he tried to put on a brave face.

The common room was very large with lots of chairs and tables offering single, two or group sittings where people could sit and chat. Some, however, preferred spending their visiting time in their cars or in the park to enjoy the natural atmosphere. Belinda had chosen the common room for two reasons. Firstly, she had always spent time with her parents in the car or the park, but today she wanted her mum to have a feel of the common room. Secondly, she did not want people to be gazing at them in the open while they talked with Joe. In the room, they would only be seen by those who happened to be there. She selected a table close to the entrance so that they could sneak out without drawing attention. As soon as they entered the room and got to the table, Belinda's mother got up and with an outstretched hand, said:

"Hello, I'm Mrs. Addo, Belinda's mother."

Joe responded in like manner and mentioned his name.

"How are you?" she asked.

"I'm fine. Thank you. And you?"

"I'm very well. Thanks. So how are you enjoying life on campus"? Mrs Addo asked.

"Honestly, I would prefer the word managing to enjoying because, life on campus for some of us is a struggle," said Joe.

"I know, but sometimes we can lighten our burdens with the words that we speak, you know," said Mrs. Addo.

"How is that possible, Mum?" asked Belinda who had remained silent during the pleasantries.

"We must always talk about the things that we believe in and it shall be so," Mrs Addo said to both Joe and Belinda.

The young ones looked at each other before turning to look at the woman again, wondering if she was going to elaborate on this statement.

"Anyway," she changed the conversation, "Auntie Cornie is a very good friend of mine and when I told her the other day that I would be coming to visit Belinda, she mentioned you to me and I promised her that I would ask of you."

"Thank you very much. That's very kind of you and a surprise to me," said Joe.

"I come here almost every fortnight so I will be seeing you whenever I come. Sometimes her dad comes and other times we come together, so you will soon get to know the entire family."

"That will be very good," said Joe.

"While you are here together, and being a senior student, please keep an eye on Belinda for me, and if you could help her with her studies too, we would very much appreciate it," she requested.

"That will be no problem at all. In fact, I like to teach other people what I know, because by so doing I also learn a lot," said Joe.

"How do you want me to refer to you?" asked Mrs Addo.

"I am Joseph Boakye, as I said earlier, but everyone calls me Joe, so I don't mind if you call me same."

"Okay, Joe, I will see you again before I go, but just in case I don't, this is a token for you for agreeing to keep an eye on Belinda."

She took the carrier bag from the table and gave it to him.

"Thank you very much. This day is going to go into my autobiography. Thank you very much. And Belinda, if you need any assistance don't hesitate to let me know," Joe said.

"Thank you, too," said Belinda.

Joe asked to leave and as soon as he got to a corner where they could not see him, he opened the bag to see the contents. In it were two beautiful designer T-shirts, unlike the cheap ones he had been wearing. All his shirts and T-shirts were more than a year old, but he kept them neat so some of them still looked a bit new. With the addition of two brand new T-shirts with the tags still intact, it felt like he had been given a million cedis. At last, he was also going to wear designer clothes, he imagined. Mother and daughter also left the room soon after he was out of sight and went to sit in the car.

Naturally, those who have been in the common room and seen Joe and Mrs Addo talking with Belinda were wondering what was going on. Until now, they did not know of any link between them, so how come that mother and daughter were having a conversation with Joe? They talked about the trio, but no one was bold enough to ask Joe or Belinda what brought them together. Before Mrs Addo left, she gave some money to Belinda to give to Joe and told her they would arrange to take him home one day.

Joe scanned his mind to see if he could remember any time he had received such a gift, but he could not. Some four years earlier, one of Auntie Cornie's boyfriends gave him a second-hand pair of shoes which were too big for him. As a result he could not wear them. His aunt gave them to another man a few months later and promised to buy him a fitting new pair but she didn't. Joe did not ask for it either, because he did not like the man's present in the first place. He was still admiring the T-shirts in the dormitory when one of his room mates came to tell him that Belinda was looking for him. He quickly put them in his trunk, locked it and rushed downstairs to see her.

"My Mum wanted to see you before going but we could not find you," said Belinda.

"Sorry about that. I was in the dormitory, admiring my presents. They are such a wonderful gift. I haven't received anything like this before."

"This is just a tip of the iceberg, more will follow later," said Belinda with her usual smile.

"I am very grateful to you and your mother. Thank you very much."

"You are welcome," said Belinda. "And she gave me this envelope to give to you." (She handed the well-stuffed brown envelope to him.)

"Again!" Joe exclaimed.

"Yes, she wanted to give it to you herself before leaving but we couldn't find you, as I said."

Joe wondered if this was a shadow of the things to come as his aunt said. He told Belinda again not to hesitate in seeking his assistance in whatever concerning her studies. Upon receiving the T-shirts, he had thought of letting his aunt know, but he brushed the idea off, thinking it might encourage her to continue with her plans, plans that she said would be to his advantage. Now with this money, Joe had the feeling that Mrs Addo might tell Auntie Cornie of the visit and what had transpired. It was Cornie who had mentioned him to Mrs Addo, so if she had come to see him, she must inevitably give her some feedback, for the sake of courtesy, Joe thought. For this reason Joe decided to drop his aunt a line, informing her about the visit.

Joe wasn't being too proud or stubborn; he was only trying to protect his own reputation from the temptations that could possibly be attached to this whole connection. His aunt did not understand his refusal to befriend Belinda, instead she thought only of the financial gains that could come from the relationship. When Belinda told Eva and Vida about how her mother's meeting went with Joe, she did not mention the gifts for the poor lad.

"You will have to teach us whatever he teaches you," said Eva.

"I will be happy to pass on to you whatever I learn from him," Belinda promised.

Eva and Vida had boyfriends but Belinda didn't, so naturally they hoped this could be a turning point in their friend's life, that after a while she would be going out with Joe. On a number of occasions they had teased her about her virginity so since she told them of what her mother had said about Joe, they had been talking about it without her knowledge, that soon she would become a different Belinda. Once in a conversation about Joe, Vida almost said it to her face.

"You will soon get to know how it is when ..."

Eva quickly winked at Vida in a cautioning gesture and changed the topic under discussion. Later on, Eva said to Vida that if she had allowed her to complete the statement, Belinda would have had an idea that they've been talking behind her back about Joe. The two had been and were still in a series of relationships, but Belinda was naïve about such things. There were times she would avoid a conversation about their individual relationships. Vida had made it clear to them that she had three boyfriends, but none of them was in the school.

There was one called Paa Nii who used to visit her at a particular time every Saturday but had stopped coming lately. Vida lied to her friends that the boy was schooling in another town, and that was why they don't see him. But the truth was that the boy found out about her affairs with another boy and broke up with her. Eva also had two boyfriends. One of them was her junior in the same school, the son of another rich man in the city and the other boy was from a school in a nearby town, a poor but handsome boy.

Eva always got money from the boy in her school and sent it to the poor boy. The boy never came to the school to see her, because she had lied to him that her parents had set spies on her all over the school, including the security man. The poor boy, not wanting to lose what he was getting from Eva, accepted that as true.

They met at an inter-school sports event and fell in love and when he visited her not long after the event, she introduced him to his rich boyfriend as a cousin. She later explained to him that they knew her as a good girl, the only good girl in her class who had no boyfriend, so if at those early stages they got to know that he was her boyfriend, it would spread like bush fire in the school. She introduced her rich boy as the Assistant Head Boy. Feeling swollen-headed for this promotion, the rich boy instructed her to let him know whenever she was going to see her cousin so he could send him some gifts.

Eva capitalised on this statement and for nearly fifteen months, she was robbing Peter to pay Paul. Vida was the only one who knew about her relationship with this poor boy but had vowed never to reveal it to anyone because Eva had once helped her out when two of her three boyfriends visited almost the same time without any formal notice.

On that day the two girls were chatting with John, one of Vida's boyfriends who had arrived earlier when Vida was called to the gate house. Upon seeing Victor, she was shocked and for some time did not know what to do. She took him to a different meeting room and sent for Eva. Upon her arrival, they communicated with their eyes and hand gestures. After a while Vida told Victor they were going to get something and come back in a minute. When they got to the corridor Eva suggested that they go to stay with John for some time. The plan is that while they are there Vida would say that she needed to go to the loo and dash to see Victor to inform him of the meeting of all the girls in their department. She was not to spend a long time with him. Before her return, Eva would have told John about the said meeting.

If girls in their teens were able to device a plot like this to deceive men, you can imagine what they would be capable of in their twenties, thirties, or married. *"Fear woman,"* someone once said. The girls carried out this plot and it worked like magic. Within fifteen minutes, they sent both boys away. From that day they pledged their support for each other in such circumstances. These were the type of girls that Belinda, Daddy's innocent girl, was dealing with.

Some days after the visit to the school, Mrs Addo called Auntie Cornie to talk about the trip. A meeting involving the Addo family, Joe and Auntie Cornie was arranged to take place at the Addos' home in three weeks' time without Joe's knowledge. Belinda now had the courage to approach Joe quite often and they spoke openly and freely. It was during one of their conversations that Joe learnt about the meeting that his aunt had arranged with Mrs Addo.

"I don't know what you are talking about," Joe said, "a meeting with your parents and my aunt in your house?"

"I thought you had been informed already by your aunt," said Belinda.

"I am not aware of any such meeting. Besides, I am supposed to be at Diasempa on that day. My parents have sent me a message to come and see them on that day."

Joe was not telling the truth. He wanted to be out of the meeting, because he didn't know what was going on between the Addos and his aunt. He was willing to do as Mrs Addo had asked of him on the day she visited, a simple request that required no special meeting.

"Linda, I am willing and prepared to do as your mother requested, to help you with your studies, keep an eye on you and see to your general welfare in this school, but I don't want this to be a big family affair like you are telling me now," Joe said.

"There could be a reason for this meeting, you never know, so I would suggest you try all you can to make time for it," Belinda said.

"Of course, I know there is a reason for every gathering," Joe said, "but as I told you, my parents want to see me that day so it will be impossible for me to make it."

The two had never talked so long at any given time, and it looked to others passing by that each was trying to explain the importance of an issue. At a certain point, due to the attention they were receiving from fellow students, Joe suggested that they talk later. That evening, Belinda called her mother and told her that Joe was not aware of the meeting so her mother promised to speak to him herself the next morning. Belinda was not very convinced that the meeting would come off, and even if it would, the outcome was uncertain. Joe spent the night with many thoughts on his mind. He decided to do some reading to take his mind off the issue, but the more he tried the more scenes played in his mind of the Addos and Auntie Cornie at a meeting.

'Lord, please show me what to do and guide me through it all,' he prayed.

The next morning, instead of calling Joe as promised, Mrs. Addo called Auntie Cornie because she didn't want to bypass her when making arrangements concerning Joe. After all, if it hadn't been for her, Mrs Addo would not have known Joe.

"Maybe the man forgot to deliver my message to him," said Cornie.

"Belinda informed me that Joe would be going to see his parents on that day so I don't know whether we can arrange to meet with him on another occasion," suggested Mrs Addo.

"Why can't we meet at the school a bit early in the morning before he leaves? Cornie asked.

"That's fine by me, but you have to notify him about it before we meet," said Mrs Addo.

"Yes, yes. I will send him another message as soon as possible. In fact, I'm going to the station now to get someone who is likely to see him this evening," said Cornie.

The truth was that Auntie Cornie would have forgotten about the meeting herself, if Mrs. Addo had not called. She had forgotten to send a message to Joe earlier about the meeting. The problem with Auntie Cornie was that she talked too much, especially in an attempt to persuade so sometimes she forgets what she has said. She sent a quick message to Joe informing him about her plans to visit soon. Joe did not hear anything from anybody again for a while.

The day before the meeting, Joe sat under a mango tree reading *Twelfth Night* by William Shakespeare at the edge of the school football pitch when Belinda and Eva approached him for assistance with a Maths excercise. There were six problems, the girls has been able to solve four, but the other two, they could not get their heads around them. After reading the question, Joe asked Belinda if she had been studying the book he gave her because all the questions came from that book. Belinda giggled without responding to Joe's question.

"Which book is that?" asked Eva.

"It's a Maths book I used years ago, and it contains a lot of such problems," said Joe.

"I will show it to you later," Belinda said to Eva.

"Any way, let's get cracking on it," said Joe.

Using different figures, he explained the questions to them in such simple terms that even a child could grasp the solution with ease. Soon, the girls were solving the remaining two questions all by themselves. Joe informed them about his trip to see his parents the next day, and Belinda also said she was expecting her parents on campus the next morning. On learning about this, Joe decided that since they were coming to the school, he would use that opportunity to meet with them without his aunt.

"This guy could be a very good teacher, if he chooses to do that in future," said Eva to Belinda afterwards.

"Yes, look at the way he explained the work, so simple," said Belinda.

"He should be teaching in a classroom, not under a mango tree," said Eva. "If I were him, I would organise some time out of school hours to teach other students for a fee. He could be making some good money from it, you know?"

"That's right, I know he's been teaching a few other students, but I don't think he has ever thought of charging them as you are saying. I will suggest it to him, who knows, he might start with us and get others to join later."

"We could give him some tips to keep him going," said Eva.

"That's a very valid point because little drops of water, they say, make a mighty ocean. It could be the three of us - you, me and Vida," Belinda said.

"But would the school authorities allow him to do that for a fee?" asked Eva.

"If they do not give him the permission to do it, we could engage him privately for that purpose," said Belinda.

"What if they find out and are not happy with it?" Eva asked.

"We shall arrange for a secret place outside the school. We need to tap into his store of knowledge before he leaves here," Belinda said.

When Vida joined the two, it was a different story. She met an old boyfriend in town and the boy wanted her back.

"Imagine, after a year of incommunicado, he still wants me back," said Vida.

"Didn't you tell him you have a new boyfriend, or boyfriends, to be precise?" Eva asked.

"Why should I say that to him? This is one of the guys who used to pay so I am going to play hard to tempt him on, so that when I do give in, which will happen eventually, there shall be nothing that I will ask for which I won't get from him."

Belinda kept silent as the two girls talked about this boy. She wondered how long they had been in this business and how long they were to remain in it. From her point of view and the words she heard from these two, their main reason for having more boyfriends was to get money from them. There were about twenty such girls in the school but they were not friends, except Eva and Vida.

The other girls who were in this game considered themselves as superior girls and did not like mingling with anyone of a poor class. Their clothes, shoes and other things about them depicted some kind of competition among themselves. Some of the boys called them High Society Girls, HSGs for short. They assumed that these High Society Girls would offer themselves to anyone who would give them money, even though their parents gave them whatever they wanted or needed. They didn't care who that person was. So long as he would pay, they were willing to offer themselves.

On Saturday morning at about ten o'clock, Belinda's parents arrived at the school with her little brother, Kwame Addo, who was eleven years old. The trainers, jeans and the T-shirt he wore, though simple, showed that he was from a well-to-do home. There was another room in which students could host their visitors but that room was not used much because it was without a proper view of the outside. This was where Belinda decided to spend time with her parents and little brother.

"Have you seen Joe's aunt?" Mrs Addo asked her daughter.

"I don't know her so even if she is here I can't tell."

As they were talking, Vida came to say hello to Belinda's family. When Belinda asked her if she had seen Joe around she informed her he was with a lady in the common room.

"That could be his aunt," said Mrs Addo. "Go and find out Belinda, and if she is the one, invite them here."

Belinda left the room with Vida who was heading to the dining room.

"My Mum tells me they knew each other long before I was born," Belinda said to Vida concerning Auntie Cornie.

"Old time friends, one day we shall be talking to our children like that," said Vida.

"Yes. It will be a good time I hope, but that will depend on how we get on while we are here. Any way, let me go and see if they are there," Belinda said.

"Okay, I will see you later, then," replied Vida.

In the common room, Auntie Cornie who had arrived about half an hour earlier to the surprise of Joe, continued with her attempts to brainwash him about Belinda.

"I am willing, and I have made it clear to herself and her mother that I will help her with her studies, but having an affair with her is out of the question," Joe said.

"Well, I know one thing will lead to another so let's leave that for now," said Auntie Cornie

Joe had planned to impress the Addos by wearing one of the T-shirts Mrs Addo had given him on her last visit. He wasted no time in introducing them to each other when Belinda came to where they were.

"This is my aunt, Cornie," Joe said to Belinda. "And this is Linda, Mrs Addo's daughter."

"Nice to meet you, Auntie," said Belinda, offering her a handshake.

"My nice lady, how are you?" asked Cornie.

"I'm fine, thank you."

Belinda told Joe of her parents' arrival and their wish to see him.

"That's great, let's go and see them, Joe," said Cornie, getting to her feet before Joe.

Joe got up reluctantly and followed them. He didn't want to offend Belinda and her family so he put on a smile and pretended to be excited about meeting them. He was glad to meet the Addos, of course, but Cornie was making things too complicated for him. When they arrived at where the Addos were, Auntie Cornie went straight to hug Mrs. Addo and their pleasantries alone took about two minutes, hugging, shaking hands and stealing looks at each other.

"When good old friends get together after many years of separation that's what happens," Mrs Addo said when she saw the funny look on her husband's face.

"It's been a long time," said Cornie.

"A very long time, I think it's about six years ago when we last saw each other," said Mrs. Addo. "How is Kwaku?"

"He is a big boy now, almost a young man," Cornie responded.

"You should have brought him to this great reunion," Mr. Addo chipped in.

"I will bring him next time. You will hardly recognise him because he has grown very tall," said Cornie.

As the others looked on, the women continued to ask of some other old friends and talked of things they used to do and the places they had visited together in the past.

"When will these ladies sit down for us to talk?" Mr. Addo asked.

Looking at her husband from the corner of her eyes and laughing, Mrs Addo said:

"Mr, I know what you do when you meet your old school friends."

The youngsters could not help but join in the laughter as Cornie and Mrs. Addo talked some more. The meeting itself lasted less than ten minutes because Mrs. Addo and Auntie Cornie had already settled the scores on the phone. It was just a matter of making it known to the young people, plus a few words of advice.

Mr. Addo was not yet convinced that they were entrusting their daughter into safe hands. He remembered his own Secondary School days when he had tried to go to bed with any girl who was free and easy in her behaviour towards him. He was such a big time womanizer that some people thought he could never settle down with a single woman. Even now, after many years of marriage, he did not belong to his wife alone.

He thought every man was like him, so one could somehow understand his feelings towards the whole arrangement. Auntie Cornie had the same feeling, but she liked it that way. If anything was to happen, she would argue out that they pushed their daughter to Joe. Cornie was the type of person who always looked for loop holes with which to blame others, even though she may have initiated the problem.

"We shall hold you responsible if any bad thing happens to her while she is in your care," Mr Addo said in a jovial way, but inwardly he meant every single word.

"In my care?" Joe asked. "I thought I was just going to keep an eye on her and help her with her studies."

"Keeping an eye could be translated as being in your care," confirmed Mr. Addo.

"Mr. Addo and his jokes!" exclaimed Auntie Cornie.

"This is not a joking matter, it could be a long term keeping an eye on her," he said, laughing to lighten the weight and seriousness of his comments.

He did this just to change the atmosphere because he observed that Joe looked worried, but he wasn't joking. Every thief thinks everyone is a thief. His comments drew Joe's mind to what Auntie Cornie had been saying about having an affair with Belinda, but he wasn't interested in that. She was a beautiful girl, humble and innocent, but none of these qualities made Joe fancy her, even though he applauded them. The Addo's son, Kwame Addo, sometimes called KA, was sitting between Belinda and Joe as the adults talked and he asked Joe if he liked football.

"It's my best sport," Joe responded.

"I like it too. In fact, I play for my school," said KA

"That's good, but unfortunately, much as I like the game, I have never been very active in playing it. But I know the standing of all the teams in the country. I have been following the league since I was about your age," said Joe.

"So which team do you support?" asked KA.

"You'll be surprised to hear this, but the fanaticism aroused by football puts me off supporting any team," replied Joe.

"My Dad supports Accra Hearts of Oak but I think my team, Kumasi Asante Kotoko, is the best team in the country."

"Do you ever argue with your father over football," Joe asked.

"Yes, because he doesn't want to accept that Kotoko is the best," KA said to the hearing of all, so his father turned to him and started laughing.

"Don't start it here, KA," said Mr Addo. "Are you also a Kotoko supporter, Joe?"

"No, I don't support any team, the arguments put me off."

"Good!" said Mrs Addo.

"The next time we clash with them, I will suggest that you join the team that wins, Brother Joe, whether Kotoko or Hearts," KA recommended.

"I see football pretty much as politics and so I don't want to get involved in it. I hate arguments," said Joe.

"I wish these two were like you, Joe," said Mrs Addo, referring to her husband and son.

"But Mum you know Kotoko is the best, don't you?" asked KA. "There are some good players like Maamah Acquah, Polo, Adolf Armah and the rest playing for Hearts, but they need the scoring abilities of Osei Kofi and Opoku Nti. How many penalties has your goal keeper saved for instance, compared to Robert Mensah?" he asked his father.

Belinda, Joe and Auntie Cornie could not stop laughing as the visiting three continued to talk about football. KA, young as he was, knew the names of almost all the players in the first division. Talking about Kotoko, he knew where everyone played and who was good or weak at any position.

"Where did you get all this information about football from?" Auntie Cornie asked him.

"From the TV and newspapers, I like the game so much so that it has more or less become part of me. I watch every game, read about it and discuss it with others," he said.

Mr Addo said he had a business meeting in the evening so they needed to be on their way. He thanked Auntie Cornie for bringing them into contact with Joe and Cornie replied saying she was glad that Joe had accepted responsibility for keeping an eye on Belinda and helping her with her studies.

"If there is anything you are not happy about or want to know, don't hesitate to contact us. Or if there is the need for us to come here to see you at any time, just let us know, and mind you, you wouldn't be doing this for free. We shall reward you handsomely," said Mr. Addo.

"Don't worry about that, Mr Addo, because it is God who rewards," said Auntie Cornie.

It's true that it is God who rewards but at the back of her mind, Cornie knew that it was because of the financial rewards that compelled her to force Joe into the affairs of the Addos, and Joe knew it too. Besides, she wanted Joe to have an affair with Belinda so as to benefit more from the Addos' finances, the concept which had put Joe off at the initial stages of this connection. Before they left, Mrs. Addo invited Joe to come with Belinda to spend a few days with them at the end of term. She gave the car keys to Belinda and asked her to go with KA to the car and bring a blue bag on the back seat. When Belinda and her brother left the room, Mr. Addo asked Joe if he had a girlfriend in the school and he said no.

"Well, I was just going to tell you to let her know that Belinda is just a family friend so that she doesn't get jealous."

"Oh! Thank you. I'm not into that kind of thing as yet," Joe said amid his gentle smiles.

"So, you don't have a girlfriend at all?" asked Mrs. Addo.

"No."

"He is not that type Mr. Addo. Joe is a good boy," said Auntie Cornie.

Cornie tried to convince the Addos that Joe was not a threat to their daughter so they had nothing to worry about. She was acting like *anomaa kokone kone* who goes up stream to stir the water and comes down stream to ask why the water is dirty. She was pushing Joe into it and yet claiming he couldn't and wouldn't do that.

"Is it true that you don't have a girlfriend at all?" Mr. Addo asked again.

"No, I don't. And I don't want one at this stage of my education. I want to concentrate on my studies until ..."

Joe did not finish his statement before Belinda, holding a kind of blue sports bag fully loaded, entered the room with her brother.

"Give it to Joe," her mother instructed.

"That's from us to you Joe, for accepting to keep an eye on our princess," said Mrs Addo.

Joe accepted the bag from Belinda, looked around it and called on his aunt to thank the Addos on his behalf. Auntie Cornie, with a broad smile, stood up and walked over to where the couple were seated and offered a handshake to say thank you. Joe did the same. Before Joe got to Mrs. Addo, her husband signalled her to give Joe an envelope stuffed with cash.

"Not again," Auntie Cornie said when she saw Mrs Addo giving the envelope to Joe.

"That's okay. He is our child too, just like Belinda and Kwame, so whatever we can do to make them happy, so long as it is within our means, you can count on us," said Mrs Addo.

Because of Mr Addo's appointment, they left the campus not long after they had finished with Joe and his aunt. Joe's happiness upon receiving the money and bag was short-lived. No sooner had the Addos left than Auntie Cornie demanded a share of the cash. The Addos had wanted to give her a lift to a town closer to where she could get another car to her destination without hassle, but she refused the offer. She said she had some family issues to discuss with Joe, but in actual fact, it was unfinished business that she wanted to sort out with him. She had an eye on the envelope.

"This is my connection, don't forget, so I am entitled to a percentage of whatever comes out of it," she said.

Joe was shocked to hear these words from his aunt but kept his cool, as always. He reached for the envelope from his back pocket and stretched out his hand to give it to her.

"This is the entire envelope," he said, "take what you want from it and give me the rest."

"No. I can't do that, you just give me some of it," she said, without taking the envelope from him.

"I don't know what percentage you want from it so you take it and I will have what is left. And the bag too, I don't know what is inside so I might as well open it while you are here," Joe said calmly.

"I mean the cash, not the bag and its content. The content might only be for men or boys. They may not be of any use to me," said Auntie Cornie. "All the same, let's see what it contains."

Joe slowly unzipped the bag and asked her to empty the content herself. The look on Joe's face spoke a lot to her so she told him to zip it up again which he did without saying a word. He then opened the envelope, checked how much it contained in front of her and asked her how much she wanted from it.

"Give me one-third of it and take the rest. You know I have to pay for my transport fare," Auntie Cornie said.

"I think it's better to tell them that anytime they want to give me something, they should pass it through you. In that case, you can deduct your percentage before it gets to me."

"Why?" asked Cornie.

"Because it could bring some misunderstanding if it should come to me first."

Her true intentions about trying to bring Joe and the Addos together reflected in this first meeting. Mrs Addo, in consultation with her husband, had given Auntie Cornie more than enough for her transportation without the knowledge of the youngsters before they left. It was therefore, out of greed that she demanded and collected a third of what was given to the poor boy, claiming she had to pay for her fare back to Kumasi.

"You don't need to worry about that, you just have to let me know that they have sent you an X, Y or Z amount then we shall sort it out," Auntie Cornie said.

"This is becoming the kind of business which I am not prepared for," said Joe.

After putting the money into her purse, she dropped it in her hand bag and she was all smiles.

"Don't worry, Joe, if you remember what I told you on the first day I mentioned them to you, they are in the money so we must find a way to help them spend it. I thank God for giving you such a good brain. You must put it to good use."

Joe looked at her as she talked but said nothing. He was very surprised by her, regarding the money and her general behaviour.

"Most importantly," she continued, "if you start having an affair with her, you will be swimming in money very soon."

"That is the bit I don't want to hear or do, Auntie, to have an affair with her," Joe said.

His mood was changing at this time, and Cornie could sense that so she tried to change the topic.

"Well, it would come naturally because one thing leads to another, as I have always said. By the way, have you heard from your parents lately?" she asked.

"I would have gone to see them today, had it not been for this meeting."

"So when do you hope to go?"

"Maybe next weekend, I'm not very sure."

"If you go don't tell them about this new development, because if they get to know that you are getting money from other sources, they may adjust your remittances," said Cornie.

She was telling Joe not to tell his parents about the Addos, meanwhile she had already told them herself. Joe had always been suspicious of his aunt when it came to money issues, but her behaviour that day seemed a bit extreme. Shortly after her comments she sent Joe to get Belinda. He did not know what she had in mind to tell Belinda, but knowing who she was, he envisaged that she could plant something evil in the girl's mind.

Joe went round the campus, not looking for Belinda. He came back to tell her that Belinda's friend said she had gone to town with her parents. Before Auntie Cornie finally left, she shamelessly reminded Joe to let her know anytime he received something from the Addos. Meanwhile, Belinda told her two friends of the outcome of the meeting.

"Why did she come?" asked Eva, when she heard that Auntie Cornie was there too.

"It might be a coincidence, but I will find out from Joe later. She seems to be very influential," Belinda said.

"Does she?" Eva asked.

"Yes," answered Belinda.

"So what's going to happen to what we discussed the other day about asking him to give us some tutorials for a fee?" Vida asked.

"He has promised to help me so you have to wait for me to start with him, and then as time goes on, I will speak to him about you. I know he won't say no," Belinda assured them.

"And you should let him know that money and other essentials won't be a problem at all," Eva said.

In these last few weeks, Joe had received so much money and gifts that he began to wonder if it wasn't the beginning of a turning point in his life. He still had much of the money from Bob and his mother plus food when Belinda's mother came the first time to give him some more. Since he was not used to having so much money, he was not used to spending so much either. He had enough before the Addos visited again.

If his greedy aunt had not taken a third of that amount, Joe would have considered himself one of the rich boys on campus at the time. Among the things in the bag which the Addos gave him were a pair of blue and white trainers, two pairs of jeans, three shirts and two T-shirts, so besides improvement in his finances, his outward appearance was also going to be enhanced.

There were some text-books which he had been borrowing from other students because he could not afford to buy them. Now that he had been so blessed, Joe decided to buy most of these books, if not all, to enable him lend them to those who may need them in future. Some two years earlier, in his former school, Joe borrowed a book from a mate who had borrowed it from another student. He accidentally spilled palm oil on some pages of the book. When the book was finally returned to its owner, he got so angry that it caused a big problem between these hitherto good friends.

Joe got between them saying he was to blame, and pleaded with the owner to forgive him. Unfortunately he argued that his friend should not have given a borrowed item to a third party. Due to the words that were spoken in the heat of the moment, the two friends' relationship took a different turn. They were still friends, but not as close as before. *'This was my fault,'* Joe kept saying to himself for as long as he was in the school. Although he had no need of that book at this point in his career, it was this book that he decided to buy first, as a memorial. In the evening of the day he bought the book, PKK saw him and asked what he was doing with it.

"Don't tell me you are still learning something from that book," said PKK.

He knew there wasn't a topic in that book Joe did not understand, so he was surprised to see him with it.

"It is a memorial," said Joe.

"What sort of memorial?" asked PKK.

When Joe explained to him what had happened in his former school concerning the book, PKK simply said he could not be friends with people who can't forgive and forget such trivial issues like palm oil on a few pages of a book.

"That guy must be very mean," PKK said and walked away.

He had taken it lightly, but to Joe, it was a big issue which still bothered him. If it had not been him, the two friends and their relationship would not have been strained. At some point, he thought of going to look for the owner of the book so as to give him this brand new one in exchange of the palm oil stained one. But when he considered all that had gone on between the friends as a result of his mistake, he called it off because it would have been like opening a healing wound. He decided to keep it and lend it to Belinda.

After waiting for some time without Belinda coming to him with any problem to help her solve, Joe thought it wise to test her with some Maths questions to assess her progress. By evening, Joe had prepared ten questions and was in search of Belinda to hand them to her.

"Linda," Joe called when he spotted her with some of her mates. "I want you to try your hands on these questions to see which one you may find easy or difficult. They are problems I dealt with earlier when I was at your level so they will be of great help."

"Thank you, Brother Joe. I like the way you call me *Linda*. Eva and Vida have started calling me that now."

"Is it because I'm calling you Linda that they have started calling you same?"

"Yes."

"Personally, I can't remember the last time anyone called me Joseph. Everyone calls me Joe, as you know, and I like it that way too."

"I prefer Joe to Joseph myself. It's simple and straightforward," said Belinda

"I like that, *'simple and straightforward.'* I want everything about me to be like that, simple and straightforward. Anyway, try your hands on these and let me know if you get stuck," Joe said while Belinda gazed at the sheet of paper.

"I am going to try my best," she said.

As they departed, both of them looked back and their eyes met so they smiled at each other and moved on. Joe was just glad to help Belinda become one of the best students in her class.

CHAPTER THREE

THE TURNING POINT

One Friday evening when Bob returned from work, his mother asked him if he had heard from Joe. When he said no, she suggested he find some time to go and see him.

"At least you can take some *gari* and a few foodstuffs to him. He was saying life on campus was a bit hard if you don't have a constant supply of some essentials," Bob's mother said.

"I've made plans for the next four Saturdays, apart from tomorrow. I wanted to stay at home and do some tidying up in my room and also to do some work in the backyard garden."

"If you decide to go on the fifth Saturday, they may be on holiday, you know. Why don't you make a quick trip to the school tomorrow," said his mother.

"I think it's a good idea. It will be a surprise to him since he is not expecting me," said Bob.

In Bob's house, there was a room which was reserved for farm produce and other things that were not frequently used. They called it the food room, some kind of a storage facility. Mother and son went into the room to see what Bob could take to Joe, and as usual, there was a variety of food stuffs. It really deserved its name because it never run short of food. If the family chose not to go to farm for a whole week, there would be enough in the food room to depend on, plus what they could get from the garden at the back of the house. A selection was made quickly and a bag, full of raw food and some smoked fish, was ready to be taken to Joe the next day. Bob's mother added some money to the food.

"When you go, tell him to come home whenever he needs some food or anything that we could provide," said the woman.

"I'm going to see Kwabena Boye, one of our mates, before I embark on the trip tomorrow," said Bob.

"Why do you need to see him before you go?" she asked.

"Because when I told him Joe visited the other day, he wished to have seen him too, to show his appreciation for all that he had done to help us when we were together at school."

Kwabena Boye was also working and staying in the family house, so in a way, his situation was the same as Bob's. He was earning without spending. In both his former school and the present one, Joe had never refused anyone who needed his assistance. In fact, that is his nature, always willing to help. He learnt this attitude from his parents since childhood. Bob went to tell Boye about the intended trip the next day. Boye explained that if he had known about it a day or two earlier, he would have gone with him.

"This is an impromptu trip, actually. It was my mum who suggested it a few hours ago, but since I have other commitments in the coming weeks, I have decided to make it tomorrow," Bob said.

Boye gave him some cash and *gari* to take to Joe. He had other obligations and so could not go with Bob.

"Tell him we shall visit him in full swing one day, that this is just a token to show my appreciation for everything he did for me while we were together," said Boye.

The *gari* which Boye gave Bob to take to Joe was enough for about twenty servings, if Joe was to eat it alone. *Gari* can be preserved for a very long time, so almost every student in a boarding house has some with them all the time. The good thing about *gari* is that you could eat it raw, eat it with stew or soup or better still add water, sugar and milk and eat as a snack. It is popularly known as soakings. No student on campus will refuse soakings with roasted ground nuts. Some called *gari* 'the students' companion'.

After buying all the books he needed and other things, Joe still had an enormous amount of cash on him and wondered what to do with it. You see, when you are used to scarcity and you suddenly have so much, it becomes a worry to you. This was a poor boy living from hand to mouth over the years and all of a sudden, has become rich! What was he going to do with the money? The fact that he had more than he had ever needed filled his mind everyday, hour, minute and second but he could not discuss it with anybody. He needed advice, but asking for people's opinion on what to do with the money would reveal his wealth, so he devised a plan.

One afternoon, in a group of some of the best brains in the school, including PKK, in an attempt to find an answer to his money worries, Joe invented a story. He said there was this poor boy, so keen about school and who wanted to do everything he could to get the highest level of education in the country. Unfortunately, his parents were struggling to keep him in school because of insufficient finances, and out of the blue, this poor boy found some gold which he converted into cash.

"I couldn't finish reading the article because it was from a magazine which someone was reading on a tro-tro. This person got off the tro-tro after a few stops," Joe said.

His friends were waiting to hear what he was going to say next when he paused for a moment.

"What would you have done with the money, if you were the poor boy," he asked them.

"I would have fun, do all the things that cash have deprived me of in the past and save the rest," someone said.

"I would live as I have been living over the years and dip into it occasionally," said PKK.

"Since my parents are struggling to keep me in school and I'm going to school in order to get a better paid job, I would quit school and go into business so I could make my parents comfortable," said another boy.

"What if you are too young to do any big business?" someone asked the boy.

There was no response before the bell rang for assembly. As the group dispersed, Joe felt excited from within because he had already found an answer to the question. Henceforth, he was going to save all the money that would come his way. Then after Upper Six, if things did not work out well for him to go to the Polytechnic, he would go into buy and sell business with whatever capital he had accumulated.

'I hope my parents will live long enough for me to make it in life so that I can look after them very well,' Joe said to himself.

One thing about Joe was once he made plans he prayed about them and acted on them. He did not procrastinate. The next morning, a Saturday, he headed for the post office to open a savings account. No sooner had he left for the post office than Bob arrived on the campus. It was his first time there so everything looked strange to him. At the gate house, Bob asked to see a Sixth Form student by the name Joseph Boakye.

"I know a lad called Joe in Lower Six but I don't know if he is the Joseph Boakye you are looking for," the security man said.

"He is just about my age and height, and comes from Diasempa," said Bob.

"Oh! It's Joe, the boy with brains," the security man said.

"Yes, Joe, he is a very bright boy, we used to be in the same school before he came here," said Bob.

"You have just missed him, he said he was going to the post office, probably to get some stamps or post a letter," the security man said.

"Is he expecting you today?

"No," said Bob. "I wanted to give him a surprise so I didn't notify him."

"OK, you sit here and wait for him because this is the only entrance," said the man, pulling a chair for Bob to sit on in the gate house.

"Thank you so much," said Bob.

"Joe is such a clever and popular student. I believe that he is from a good family and has been brought up very well," the man said. "If all the boys were like him in this school, there would be no complaints at all."

Bob sat there, absorbing all the good things being said about his friend. He wasn't very surprised, because what the man was saying about Joe was true. At the post office, all that they required of Joe was proof of identity. Fortunately, he always had his school identity card with him so he showed it to the clerk who took some information from the card and told Joe he could deposit any amount at any time into his account and take whatever amount he needed from it, provided it didn't exceed what he had in the account.

He had gone there with all the money he had, so he kept a few Cedis as pocket money to last him until his next remittance and deposited the rest. Armed with his yellow savings book measuring four inches by six, Joe went back to campus. Bob was the first to spot him and announced to Abu, the security man.

"Just wait here and see what I will do," Abu said.

He was a nice, funny old man who always shared jokes with the students. Some of them took advantage of his jovial nature to be rude to him sometimes, but he considered them as kids and so did not take any of that to heart. He got out and apprehended Joe while Bob listened from inside.

"Hey Joe, I didn't know your full name is Joseph Boakye!" he said laughing.

"Yes, that's my name, and there is Kwadwo in between, Joseph Kwadwo Boakye from Diasempa!" Joe said.

"Okay, Mr Joseph Kwadwo Boakye from Diasempa, now at Miawani, do you know a lad called Robert Kwarteng?"

"Yes, Bob. He was a very good friend in my former school. How did you know him?" Joe asked.

"Do you owe him anything?"

"No. Why?"

"Well, he came here to look for you and he didn't look very nice. He was kind of angry when I told him you were not around."

"Bob angry? Did he tell you why he was angry?" asked Joe.

He was wondering what it could be that made Bob angry or why he had come to look for him on campus. Joe's smiling face turned into a serious one beccuse the last time he saw Bob, it had been all smiles and fun. Within those few seconds, scenes of his last encounter with Bob played in his mind; the food they had eaten together, the money and food stuff from Bob and his mother, etc. It had been a very happy moment that day. Why then had Bob come to look for him in anger? Initially he had taken it to be another of Abu's jovial tricks but when he considered how he came to know Bob's full name, it baffled him. Bob in the meantime was listening to the conversation from the gate house.

"Did he say he was coming back?" asked Joe.

"No. But he left a bag to be given to you. It is in the gate house so you may go for it," said the man.

Feeling perplexed, Joe headed toward the gate house for the said bag when Abu confessed he was only joking, that Bob had left the bag for him. After releasing a heavy sigh of relief, Joe went into the gate house to see not only the bag, but the bearer as well whose sides were hurting from the laughs that he had been forced to engage in. You can imagine the jubilation, hugging, the shaking of hands, etc.

"I didn't know you were coming here today, Bob!" exclaimed Joe.

"Yeah, I wanted to give you a surprise, like the security man had just done."

"His name is Abu and he is always playing funny jokes but this one was more than funny. I was beginning to take him seriously at some point, you know. Anyway, how are your parents?" Joe asked.

"They are both fine and send their greetings."

"Thanks pal. Thanks for coming."

Turning to the security man who was watching the two friends with a smile, Joe said:

"This is a very good friend. We were together in my last school and lived in the same neighbourhood..."

"Don't tell me the history because I know it all already," Abu said.

"You haven't been doing your detective work on him. Have you?" Joe asked.

"Of course, I have. What else do you expect me to do with someone I don't know looking for someone I know? Surely, I have to know who he is, where he has come from and for what purpose."

"And if you are satisfied with your interrogation, will you now give him an entry permit?" asked Joe.

"I will give him a three-hour entry visa which will expire at 2:25," Abu said, looking at his wrist watch.

They all laughed as Bob reached for the bag but Joe grabbed it from him.

"Let me help you, Bob," he said.

"It's all yours, any way," Bob said.

"All for me?"

"Yes, from my mum, Boye and myself."

"You mean Kwabena Boye? Where did you see him?" asked Joe as they headed to the common room.

"He is in town and working, too. He could not go any further after Form Five, just like me."

Joe kept introducing Bob to everyone as they went along and so it took them a while before they got to the common room. Being a Saturday, there were a lot of visitors and it was not until they had settled in a corner that Bob gave him the money from his mother and Kwabena Boye.

"And this is from me too. Just a little for other essentials," said Bob.

"Don't call it little, Bob, this is too much for me. And your mother, I wonder why she still bothers herself about me," said Joe.

"In fact, it was she who suggested that I come to see you today. She said she has heard so much about life on the campus; how sometimes some students will run out of food and cash. She said if the distance from Miawani to our house was one that one could walk, she would have asked you to come home for dinner every evening," Bob said.

"May God bless her for such thoughts about a poor boy like me," said Joe.

"She is always talking about you," Bob said. "She said I should tell you to come home whenever you needed something that she could provide."

"I'm happy to hear that. So how is Boye doing?" Joe asked.

"He is very well and said he would come with me next time. The other *gari* in the green bag is from him."

"Eh, *Akete* Boye, I can't wait to see him. You know I've not seen him since I left there," lamented Joe.

Kwabena Boye was a very small fellow hence most of the people in their locality used to call him *Akete*, literally meaning small or little.

"Yeah, he said so, and he is also hoping to see you before long."

"That will be great," said Joe.

He was apparently missing the company of friends he used to have in Kumasi as Bob told him of old friends and what some of them were up to. Bob asked him how life in general had been on campus so far.

"It's been tough on the campus, Bob, but the good Lord has always been kind to me, providing all my needs through people like you."

"It is because you are depending on him, that's why He is providing for you. And also because of who you are; your humility, sincerity and the way you deal with people will always draw good people to you," Bob said.

"Well, I think that is the way we all have to live, treating people the way we would like to be treated. It's as simple as that," said Joe.

"Unfortunately, sometimes when you try to treat people fairly, the same people turn around and stab you in the back. This is the reason why some people find it difficult to do good these days," Bob said.

Joe agreed to what Bob said, because he had witnessed a number of such cases himself. They were still discussing the issue of trying to do good and its opposite results when Belinda came to the room looking for someone. When she saw Joe and Bob, she went to their table to ask Joe if he had seen the student she was looking for. Joe had not; however, he used the opportunity to introduce Bob as a former classmate who had come to visit, and Belinda as a family friend and fellow student.

"You are welcome to our school, Bob. I hope we shall be seeing more of you in future," said Belinda.

"Yes. I shall be coming to see you every now and then," Bob replied.

"Okay, I will see you guys again in a minute," Belinda said and walked out of the room.

Bob wanted to know how Joe got into contact with Belinda and he told him how it all began, starting from the day his aunt mentioned her to him, the very day they bumped into each other and had *banku* together at Bob's place. Joe was careful not to say anything about his aunt's suggestion of befriending Belinda. At the mention of his mother's delicious *banku* on the day, Bob's face brightened and Joe asked him why the sudden facial expression.

"I'm going to tell you a secret and this is to be between you and me," said Bob. "My mother did something that day which added a lot to the respect and love I have for her."

"What was it?" Joe asked.

"It was the food. It is my dad's favourite and he had specifically asked my mum to prepare it for him before he left for work that day. You know, it's just the three of us there, so she had made it for three. But with you around, she had to sacrifice her part for you and she told me later on that she felt very happy and satisfied for what she had done," Bob explained. "And it has brought a change into their marriage life!"

"How?" asked Joe.

"They eat together now, from the same bowl," said Bob.

"What do you mean by that?"

"You may not believe it, but it's true, I had never seen my parents sitting and eating from the same bowl before until that day. I don't know whether it was due to my dad's work schedule or not. But from the day you visited, because the food was so small ..."

"Because of me?" chipped in Joe.

"Yes, because of you," Bob said.

They both burst into laughter, but inwardly, Joe was embarrassed that it was his fault that Bob's mother did not have her share of the family meal that day.

"Not long after you had left," Bob continued, "my Dad returned from work and Mum told him you came in just as she was about to finish cooking so she gave you her part."

"What a shame!" Joe exclaimed.

"No. Don't say that. It was good you came," Bob said, "my Dad did not wait for Mum to finish explaining when he told her to lay the table so the two of them could share his. As they ate, talked and laughed, they seemed to have found some joy in eating together and so since that day, that is what they have been doing. If Mum finishes cooking, she will wait till my Dad is back from work before they eat. It has offered both of them the opportunity to talk over certain issues and particularly, I have also noticed that their love life is blooming again."

"I really should have said no to the food," said Joe.

"Well the rest is history, and she felt happy doing what she did," Bob said.

When Belinda left them, she rushed to her well stuffed bag to fetch some snacks. She had observed that the table before them was empty. A few minutes later, she came back to them with some soft drinks, biscuits and hand tissues on a tray.

"This is to welcome you to our school, Bob," Belinda said and placed the tray on their table.

"Thank you very much", said the two friends simultaneously.

"You have to tell me more about this angel, Joe," Bob requested as they began to eat and drink when Belinda left them.

"Like I told you earlier, I've been helping her with her studies and her parents are very generous to me. She herself has been a blessing to me too, as you are witnessing now," Joe said.

"Such people are very hard to come by these days, you know."

There was a mango tree at the edge of the school's football pitch. This was where Joe spent most of his quiet time. He suggested to Bob that they go there to enjoy the fresh air as well as escape the common room which slowly became over-crowded. Joe put the empty tray at a safe place where he could come for it later to give to Belinda. Bob noticed that everyone was friendly with Joe and he commented on it. Joe in turn said it was his way of life to be friendly with all and to give everyone his or her due respect. Although they were deep into conversation, Joe's mind was on another trip to the post office on Monday, to deposit what he had received from Kwabena Boye, Bob and his mother. In his heart, he praised God for His provision.

There was no branch of The Church of Pentecost in Miawani, so on some Sundays Joe worshipped with the Assemblies of God, the only Pentecostal Church in the town. Bob wasn't much into church activities and Joe knew that. Once when he invited him to church, Bob told him in plain words that he wasn't ready. Several further attempts proved futile before Joe left Kumasi so somehow he gave up on him with anything regarding church.

"Do you still go to church?" Bob asked.

"Yes, I do. Have you now started or you are still not ready yet?" Joe asked.

"Not yet. But very soon, I'm going to start."

"If you start now, I bet you, it will be the best step you would ever take in your entire life," Joe said.

Joe had learnt about tithing years ago but due to the fact that he had never had enough to keep him going, he had not been tithing. But as he spoke to Bob about church, it occurred to him that now that he had got enough to put some away, he ought to tithe. Immediately, he made a mental calculation of all the cash that had come to him in the past few weeks to know the right amount to tithe.

By the time Bob was about to return, Joe had persuaded him to go to church and he promised to do that. To make sure Bob did as he had promised, Joe gave him a note which he wrote when Bob visited the Gents to take to one of the deacons at his former church.

The deacon was someone with the gift of evangelism. No matter how hard your heart was, the convincing message about Christ, His death, resurrection and second coming from Deacon Bismark Debrah would melt it. With these qualities in mind, Joe felt he was the right person to handle Bob. In the note, Joe spoke about Bob as a good friend whom he wanted the deacon to do all he could to recruit to the fold. Joe stated in the note that Bismark should not give Bob the impression that he had asked him to do that.

When Bob boarded a lorry at the lorry station Joe chatted with him through the window. He told him how grateful he was for the visit and the gifts.

"Extend my most sincere gratitude to all, especially your parents and Akete Boye," Joe said as the vehicle began to move.

On his way back, Bob thought of how fortunate Joe was, having such a beautiful girl like Belinda to serve him. Could this be a one off kindness or had she been doing it every time Joe got visitors? Joe had introduced Belinda to Bob as a family friend, but could she Joe's girlfriend and he did not want him to know?

Joe felt happy and worried at the same time about the influx of money into his hands lately. Never in his life had he handled so much money, all for himself, and no one even knew about it. He also recalled the promise from the Addos about treating him as one of their own. But his major worry was Cornie's involvement. She had asked for a third of whatever came from the Addos. If she ever got to know that he had opened an account, there would be trouble. Joe prayed for wisdom to handle the situation.

Eva and Vida were becoming friendly with him. Once when he was going through some science questions with her, Belinda said in passing that she wished Eva and Vida were there also to learn what he was teaching her.

"You can explain it to them later," said Joe.

"Yes, I can," Belinda said, "but you can do it better so I will be glad if you could let them join us next time."

"Okay, I will think about it and let you know," said Joe.

"You won't be doing it for free, keep that in mind. The girls are loaded with cash and they would be more than willing to part with some money to get a little bit of your knowledge," said Belinda.

"Linda, that won't be a big deal but I need to think about it first, so just give me a little time," replied Joe. "We need to be careful the way we go about it because of what is going on in the school these days."

"What is going on?" asked Belinda.

Joe refered to PKK's incident and told Belinda to give him some time. He liked the idea one hundred percent; *'they would be more than willing to part with some money to get a little bit of your knowledge,'* that meant more money in his coffers! How could a poor boy like Joe refuse money? He would not, but he had to play a bit hard to get. Good thinking! When Belinda informed her friends of Joe's response they were very excited. The girls' parents were loaded with cash and they always had more than they needed on them. They were desperate due to the fast approaching mock exams.

"I'm sure you want to get more marks in the mocks than us and that's why you don't want him to teach us," Eva said, jokingly.

"Don't think that way, Eva, I've just discussed it with him and he asked that I give him a little time. I can't push him. Who knows, he might come back to say let's start tomorrow. Let's just wait and see," said Belinda.

"Don't take her seriously, she is only joking," Vida said.

"I will be with him tomorrow so I will remind him and let you know what he says," Belinda promised.

"Tell him we will fix him right," Eva said.

"I've already told him that."

Later that day, Belinda called to inform her mother about how Joe was helping her and said she wished she had started studies with him earlier.

"He is really good! He explains things like a real teacher and I'm benefiting a lot from him," she said.

"Get very close to him at all times so that you can learn more from him," said Mrs Addo.

"That's just what I want to do now. Some of my friends want him to teach them too after I had explained something he taught me to them."

"Good. And another thing is you should always try to give him some tips from your pocket money to entice him. If you do that, he will always be willing to teach you whatever you need to know," advised Mrs Addo.

"I will, Mum. Thank you so much. I love you," Belinda said to end the conversation.

Mrs. Addo advised her daughter to get very close to Joe, but for a beautiful sixteen year old virgin to get too close to an energetic young man inevitably meant something more than just teaching and learning. Belinda took the advice at face value but when her mother also called to tell Auntie Cornie about what she had said to her daughter, Cornie was over the moon and said things would happen naturally.

Cornie was hopeful that Joe would take some initiative to make a proposition to Belinda, as long as she got closer to him. She noticed during their meeting that Belinda looked very innocent in terms of relationships. This observation had been a bit of a worry to Cornie because her main reason of arranging this was to pave the way for Joe to get into the girl's life and into the frame of the Addo family, because of their money.

She was the kind of woman who will do anything to get money. She got it sometime, but it never stayed. Being so much into fashion, she was always buying new things, clothes, shoes, jewellery etc. Her wardrobe was full of such things and only a fraction of them were bought with money from her wages. The rest had been generated from unexplainable sources and through dubious means. And now she was trying to use Joe's intelligence as another source of generating funds to feed her addiction to fashion.

Her thinking was that one day Joe would see some sensitive parts of Belinda that would serve as a trigger. So, to help expedite this process, she purposely bought her a pink V-neck blouse that she knew would reveal her cleavage. It was a short blouse, which meant that part of her stomach would be bare, revealing the hair below her navel.

Cornie had used this kind of outfit to lure a lot of boys and men during her school days so she knew that Joe would be enticed. She parcelled it nicely and posted it to Belinda as a surprise gift, with a mission, of course. The day Belinda received this blouse, she called to tell her mother how kind Joe's aunt was, for thinking of her to send her such a beautiful blouse. Her mother then called Auntie Cornie to say a big thank you on behalf of Belinda. Cornie said it was okay and was just glad that Belinda and Joe were getting on well.

She was praying for the blouse to serve its purpose. Two weeks later, Auntie Cornie paid a surprise visit to Joe. By this time Joe had sorted things out with the girls and was teaching them twice a week. They met every Wednesday evenings and on Saturdays. On Wednesday evenings the girls brought their problems and on Saturdays Joe gave them work and helped them to explore other subjects and topics he felt were necessary at their level.

This Saturday afternoon, when they were about to go to their usual meeting place, Auntie Cornie arrived. After Joe had settled her in the common room, he quickly went round to the girls to cancel the day's programme. To make her feel good, the girls organised a nice snack for her and Joe. Belinda introduced the other two girls to Auntie Cornie and they all thanked her for Belinda's present.

"We all like pink, but she likes it most so you got her right colour. It's such a beautiful blouse," Eva said.

"The next time I come around, you will all get something like that," Cornie promised.

"Thank you. Thank you very much," said the girls.

They talked about school life and general things for a while before leaving Joe and his aunt. Belinda did show the blouse to Joe the day it arrived but he had not seen her wearing it so when Auntie Cornie asked him how he found her in that blouse he told her the truth; that he has not seen her in it.

"Tell her that you want to see her in it one day," she told Joe.

Joe didn't say anything, but laughed.

"Why are you laughing?" Cornie asked.

"How can I tell her what to wear, Auntie?"

Cornie shook her head and swallowed the drink that she was sipping.

"Oh! Joe, my Joe, don't you know that if you tell her that it will draw her attention to the fact that you are noticing her appearance? Then she will be trying to impress you with what she wears," she said.

"Impress who? Me? What for?" he asked.

"Joe, try and understand that all that I am doing is for the good of your future. Money is the reason for all our struggles in life. We all work hard in order to acquire wealth, and here you are with the only daughter of a wealthy couple in your hands. Do you want someone else to come and take her away from you? Don't you want money?"

"Of course, I do. I want more of it, but not through the means that you are recommending."

"I have said it before, Joe, and I am saying it again that many are looking for an opportunity like this and you want to kick it away. What else do you want me to say about this issue to make you understand that you could be rich in no time, you could become ..."

"Nothing, say no more about it, please," Joe cut her short.

"By the way, have you received anything from her parents lately?" she asked after a few seconds of silence.

"Yes," answered Joe.

"How much was it?"

"It wasn't money, two T-shirts and a greeting card."

"Nothing else?" she asked.

"No, you can find out from them if you want."

Joe decided not to give her any money and he knew she could not go to the Addos to enquire if they had given him something. So, although he had received money on two occasions from the Addos and occasionally from Belinda herself, he told his aunt no money had come from them, apart from the card and the T-shirts which Belinda brought to him from a weekend visit home.

Besides cash from the Addos, the two girls also contributed so Joe was rich in his own right. But he still continued wisely to live a low profile life. Cornie's first trip had been very profitable, a heavy envelope from the Addos and a third of what Joe had received from the same source, but this time round she went back to Kumasi empty handed.

Joe put a tenth aside from any money that came into his hands for tithing, used a bit of it and saved the rest. His visits to the post office became more frequent, to avoid the temptation of wasting the money. While helping the girls he did not, for the sake of the money he received, neglect his own pattern of study. It was as if the first and second positions in their class had been reserved for himself and PKK. In all their fortnightly trial exams, it was either PKK at the top, followed by Joe or vice versa. Neither of them ever took a third position but in the coming mock exam, Joe was determined to outdo PKK by a greater margin.

PKK's punishment and threatened suspension, coupled with events relating to them had made him a bit reserved, and this was telling on his studies. He neither fully participated in group discussions nor put up his hand to answer questions in class. Being a concerned friend, Joe had a word with him one Friday after class.

"Don't let the issue dampen your spirit so much because it could affect your academic output," Joe said.

"I'm no longer happy in the school, Joe."

"You see, if you had apologised for your comments from the start, it would not have come this far. And if you had not gone for that T-shirt, matters would have died naturally," said Joe.

But PKK, being who he was, prone to arguments and always claiming to be right, had given way to emotion and now he was paying the price. Most of his friends kept their distance for fear of being branded as a threat to authority like him. With all this negativities working against him, Joe hoped to outdo him in the mock exams. Belinda and her friends were also determined to do better, as a result of what they were learning from Joe.

Joe was looking forward to the exams and continued to pray that he would remember everything that he was studying. He also prayed that through Deacon Bismark, his friend Bob would convert to the Christian faith. Being an experienced evangelist, Deacon Bismark kept the note he received from Joe, thanked Bob and got a few details from him.

He prayed that God would minister to Bob before he made a move. A few days later, he went to Bob's house, pretending to thank him again for the note. He then engaged him in a conversation about general issues of life before asking him if he would accept an invitation to church the next Sunday. To his surprise, Bob did not make any excuses at all.

"Yes, I really want to. When do you start and what time do you finish?" Bob asked.

"We start at 9:00 and at the latest by 12:30 you will be home. We finish at 12:00 if there is no special activity like a naming ceremony, dedication, etc," Bismark explained.

"Okay, I will come to your place for us to go together," Bob promised.

"No. Since your place is closer to the church, you just get ready and I shall be here at about a quarter to 9:00 so we can go from here," said Bismark.

Many a time, people have said to him, *'yes, I will be there. I will come to church,'* but they never turned up, so Bismark wasn't leaving anything to chance. He would pick Bob from his house and take him to church. If he is able to take him once or twice, he would relax and see whether Bob would show any interest. Bismark gave him a few leaflets before leaving his house. He continued to pray that Bob would be faithful to his word and accompany him to church on Sunday.

Of all the members of his local congregation, Bismark was considered the number one soul-winner and if you ever asked him how he went about it, he always said the Holy Spirit did the job. If you had him on your team as a campaigner, you would always win your elections! He knew how to talk to convince people. Once a ruffian himself, Bismark effectively combined elements of his sordid past with prayer and fasting to evangelise. That evening, after Bismark's visit, Bob's mother asked him the reason for the visit.

"He came to invite me to church. He is a member of Joe's church."

"Invite you to church! That's good, my son," said Bob's mother.

"Joe gave me a letter to bring to him when I went to see him the other day and he came to thank me and..."

"And invite you to church?"

"Yes."

Bob's mother might be religious, but not a regular church attendee. She loved people, and was very open and generous, qualities that are required of all religious people. When Bob told her he would be going to church the next Sunday with Joe's friend, she was very happy. She had attended Deacon Bismark's local Church of Pentecost once when a friend was christening her child, but no one took notice of her, nor followed her up so she did not go again. She knew many people in that church and had some of the members as friends. She also appreciated the lifestyle of these friends and was therefore very happy when Bob told her he was going to Pentecost.

On campus, ten Maths questions in the girls' class boosted their confidence so much that they could not wait for the real mock exams to take place. A few days earlier Joe had expounded a similar problem to them to their full understanding. He had given them five questions and they solved them quickly, all three of them had correct answers.

When similar questions came up during one of their classroom sessions, the girls looked at each other with a smile from the separate places where they sat. They used different formulae and

arrived at the same answers. Vida, especially, had not been very good at Maths, but she was surprising her teacher and mates lately, thanks to Joe. She called her parents that day to tell them of it and mentioned Joe to them.

"Is he in your class?" her father asked.

"No, he is my senior, he is in Lower Six. He finished Form Five in a different school and had just come here. He is a brilliant mind," said Vida.

"I would like to see him when we come over next weekend," her father said.

Belinda's parents were paying Joe for his services but Eva and Vida did not know about this. So the girls bought presents for him and gave him tips regularly. When Vida's parents came to the school the following weekend, a similar meeting like the one with the Addos was held with Joe. He was charged to keep an eye on Vida and to help her with her studies for a fee.

"How much would you like us to pay you, weekly or monthly, to teach her what she needs to know?" asked Mr Ansah.

"I'm sorry I can't charge you for it, Sir. But whatever you offer me, I would gladly accept," Joe said.

This was another wealthy couple asking Joe how much he wanted them to pay him and he throwing the ball back into their court.

"Okay, we shall think about it and get back to you. In the meantime, try to teach her all that she needs to know at her level since you have passed that stage already," Mr Ansah said.

"I have already started and I will continue to do my best for her," Joe promised.

To show their appreciation for the job done so far, Vida's parents gave Joe a substantial amount of cash with a promise to hear from them soon.

"Where do you come from, Joe?" asked Mrs Ansah.

"I'm from Diasempa in the Eastern Region," Joe answered.

"Oh! Diasempa, I once attended a funeral there," said Mrs Ansah. "That's where our Chief Accountant comes from."

"You mean Mr. Osafo Ampomah?" asked Mr. Ansah

"Yes," she answered

Joe did not know Mr. Osafo Ampomah at that time so he told them Diasempa was too big to know everyone, besides, since he left the town at the age of thirteen he had not spent much time there.

After all that needed saying had been said, Joe left their presence, thinking of this next source of income as Vida's parents were getting involved. What about Eva? Should he continue accepting tips from her or involve her parents? Before he got to his dormitory, Joe had decided to allow nature take its course. He was not going to say or suggest anything to Eva. She would surely know from her friends what's going on and advise herself, Joe assumed.

News about the three girls' excellent marks in the Maths questions was fast spreading round the campus. It was suspected that there was something strange about it but no one could pinpoint what it was. Some of their mates were bold enough to ask and they attributed their success to Joe's brilliant teaching techniques.

All this while, Eva and Vida eagerly awaited the day Belinda would tell them that Joe had proposed to her. Each of them wished Joe belonged to her but they reckoned it would look like snatching their best friend's boyfriend, even though there was nothing between Joe and Belinda. They therefore planned to push Belinda to make the move, if Joe would not. Belinda was a very shy girl, too shy to make such a move and Joe too had made up his mind not to get into any relationship.

Joe received a message from the driver who brought him money from his parents that they wanted to see him whenever he could come to Diasempa. They added extra money to his normal remittance for his fare but when Joe received the money, he smiled and thought he probably had more than they had. However, his plan to keep his financial position a secret remained. Whatever money came into his hand went into his account at the post office after taking a tenth for church plus what he needed. When he had the chance to go to Diasempa to see his parents, he went with a bag full of goodies like sugar, salt, smoked fish and meat and several other things that he knew his parents would need. His mother was particularly surprised to see him bring such provisions.

"How did you get the money to buy these things," asked Darkoaa.

"I have been saving a little of what you sent to me for this purpose. I always think of you and hope that one day I would be in a position to supply you with all that you need," Joe said.

"Don't starve yourself, Kwadwo. Don't bring back to us what we send to you. We are okay here, by God's grace," Darkoaa said.

"He is going to be a man very soon so he is learning how to provide for his family. He is practising something good," said Agya Boakye.

"I want to go and see some of my friends in town so we shall talk later, when I come back," Joe said to his parents.

"We invited you here for a reason, Kwadwo," said Agya Boakye, "you haven't even asked why we invited you and you want to go out to see your friends. Are you being changed by the life on campus?" he asked.

"No, no, no, Paapa. I'm sorry about that," Joe said, dragging a chair to sit down close to his father.

"How is life on campus?" asked his mother.

"Fine, Maame. I'm experiencing the best part of my education at this time, honestly. One of my friends visited me from Kumasi the other day with a lot of foodstuff."

"Have you heard from your aunt lately?" asked Agya Boakye.

"Yes."

"She came to tell us about a girl in your school that she has arranged for you to help with her studies," said Agya Boakye.

"That's true, Paapa," confirmed Joe.

"My concern is that she said she could work things out for you to marry her in future, and that you shall lack nothing if it so happens because of her parents' wealth," Agya Boakye said.

Joe shook his head in disbelief, wondering what Auntie Cornie might have told his parents about him and Belinda.

"I'm not against you using your intelligence to make some pocket money, but my fear is the involvement of your aunt in the unfolding drama," said Agya Boakye.

"How do you see the girl yourself, Kwadwo?" his mother asked.

"She is beautiful and her parents are rich, but I've made it clear to Auntie Cornie that I'm not interested in her. I have told her I don't want to involve myself in any such relationship until I complete my education. So don't worry about that. She is not going to make me change my mind this time," Joe said.

"The moment you get involved with girls, you are doomed, especially the way your aunt wants you to go about it. I suspect that she wants to use you as a bait to get something from the girl's parents, so be careful," said Agya Boakye.

"Initially, I didn't see anything wrong with it, but as we talk, I am getting to understand your views," said Darkoaa. "Teach her what you can, be nice to her but be careful as well."

"I will, Maame," Joe promised.

CHAPTER FOUR

BACK TO DIASEMPA

Eva received a letter from one of her boyfriends. She showed it to Vida and the two decided to use it on Belinda.

"Let's show her a line at a time and pretend Joe asked us to give it to her," said Eva.

"Good idea," said Vida, "so which line should go first?"

"There is something he wrote in the second paragraph, let's look at it again," Eva said, unfolding the sheet in her hand.

'Each time I set my eyes on you I shiver,' Eva read it out.

"That's a good one, that alone will do," said Vida.

"Wait, there is another one here," Eva said.

"What did he say again?" Vida asked.

'I don't know how to tell you how much I love you,' read Eva again.

"Mmm, I think that one should come first, I bet this guy has got words. You know what? You go and wait for us under the mango tree, Joe's favourite resting place and I will go and bring her there," said Vida.

"That's why I like your way of thinking. You understand every step in my plan," Eva said.

"If I have to strip her for him, I am prepared to do that. I will make sure it happens before the end of this term."

They were both giggling as Vida made this vow and left to look for Belinda. The innocent girl was in the middle of research for a history assignment Joe has given her for the weekend when Vida approached.

"What are you up to, lucky girl?"

"Doing some research on the Second World War, I have an assignment to complete before Monday. And why do you say that I'm lucky?" asked Belinda.

"You are indeed a lucky girl," repeated Vida.

Vida did not tell Belinda the reason for calling her a lucky girl; rather, she invited her to see Eva under the mango tree. They had conversations with Joe under the mango tree most of the time hence Belinda assumed he was there with Eva. The two girls had already rehearsed what to say or do at each point in the plot so as soon as Vida and Belinda got to Eva, they started laughing.

"Here I come with the lucky girl," said Vida.

"What others are dying for has just landed on your lap without a struggle," said Eva. "You are a very lucky girl indeed."

"Some girls are going to be jealous of you from now on," said Vida.

Surprised and not knowing what was going on, Belinda asked them what it was all about.

"It's all about someone who is infatuated about you," said Eva.

"Me? Who is that person?" asked Belinda.

"He said it's hard for him to come straight to you so he chose to use me as a go-between," said Eva.

"He is someone you cannot say no to," added Vida.

"Whoever he may be, could you please tell him kindly, that I, Belinda Addo, am not ready for such things."

"If you had said you were not prepared I would have understood you, but if you are talking about readiness, girl, you are more than ready," said Eva.

"Look how shapely you are! In fact, I think it was that pink blouse you wore last weekend when we were playing around the park that drew his attention," Vida said.

"Look here, if this is a joke, you girls must stop it now. But if you mean what you are saying, then pass on my message to whoever sent you that he has picked on the wrong person." Belinda turned to walk away.

"Let her read it herself," said Vida.

"Read what?" asked Belinda.

"The guy's own words," answered Vida.

"Oh, so that person sent an open love letter to be given to a girl by another girl. He must be a fool," said Belinda.

"Stop insulting him because you may love him too if you get to know who he is. Come on, read this sentence," said Eva.

She showed her the carefully folded letter, revealing only the parts they had planned to let her read. She wanted to get the whole letter to check the undersigned but Eva would not let her.

'I don't know how to tell you how much I love you,' it read.

"Who is this person talking about, and who is he?" Belinda asked.

"About you, of course," replied Vida.

"Wait, there is another line here."

Eva turned her back to Belinda and got the other sentence ready for her to read.

'*Each time I set my eyes on you, I shiver.*'

"Who could this be," Belinda asked, smiling.

"Promise us that you won't let him down and we will tell you who he is," said Vida.

The girls were still pulling Belinda's legs when all of a sudden people began rushing to the gate house. One of the students had been knocked down by a passing vehicle as he alighted from another. The commotion from the accident had disrupted the girls' plot and set Belinda's mind imagining who this boy could be. She joined the others at the scene, but her thoughts were on what she had read a few minute ago. '*Who could this boy be? Is he in the school or outside? How did he get to know me?*'

Belinda kept imagining answers to these questions. She suspected that the person might be in the school because Vida mentioned the pink blouse. She did not take it outside the campus so the person may have taken notice while she washed or in the afternoon as they played around, if what Vida said was true. She did not feel comfortable when the hair on her tummy above her skirt line was exposed. She pulled her skirt up most of the time to cover her bare stomach, but the hair still showed each time she raised her hand as they were throwing a ball around, just having fun.

As they mingled with the crowd, Belinda lost sight of her friends. She knew some of their boyfriends and so somehow, she thought that a friend of one of their boyfriends might have spotted her and felt so tongue-tied that he decided to make his feelings known through them. Joe was out of the picture because she had noticed that he wasn't interested in such things. He had not shown any interest in her, and if at all he fancied her, Belinda didn't think he was such a fool to make it so public by telling her friends first.

Vida and Eva pulled away from the crowd to discuss what they had done. Both girls were sure Belinda would be in the dark as to who this boy might be and Vida suggested that they look for her and tell her the letter was written by Joe to see her reaction. When they found Belinda in a secluded place, the look on her face showed how confused she was.

"Who did you say wrote the letter and why did the person ...?" Belinda was asking them but Eva interrupted her.

"It was written by someone you know very well but for reasons known only to him, he chose to let you have it through me," said Eva.

"The guy loves you and I'm sure you can't say no to him. I felt the same way with my first boyfriend. He sent me a letter through one of our friends and I nearly cursed him for doing that, but in the end I really, really loved this boy," Vida said.

"It's about time you broke that line, Belinda," Eva said.

"Which line are you talking about?" asked Belinda.

"Are you going to remain a virgin forever?" Eva asked.

"What's wrong about that? Until I marry, I will not do any such thing."

"What about us who are doing it and enjoying it?" Vida asked.

"Well, that's your choice."

"You don't know what you are missing. If you do it once, you will know what it feels like and ask for more," Vida said.

"She will become like Oliver Twist, asking for more," Eva said amid laughter.

Eva held Vida's hand and said, "Okay, okay, now listen, sweet sixteen, virgin Belinda, the letter was written by, by, by, by ..."

"By who? asked Belinda, impatiently.

"By Joe!" said Eva

There was complete silence. The pen Belinda was holding dropped to the ground and she kept her eyes on the pen for a few seconds as the girls looked at her. For those few seconds her mind went blank. She did not know what to say or how to react to it. She considered what a 'YES' or 'NO' response to this could bring to her hitherto cordial relationship with Joe. What others would think and how her parents would react to it if they got to know that she was having an affair with Joe bothered her acutely. When she finally raised her head and blinked, the tears that had welled up in her eyes dropped down to her cheeks. Speechless, she turned to walk towards the dormitory.

Academically Belinda had improved greatly and everyone, especially her teachers, testified to this. She felt more confident now in the midst of her mates who were witnesses to her breakthrough. Her parents had for sometime now been giving her more than she asked for because her results had improved so much, and she owed all that to Joe.

'So Joe has secretly been in love with me all this while and he never showed it even once?' Belinda soliloquized as she headed for the dormitory.

Just like Joe, Belinda had decided years ago, that she would not have a boyfriend or have sex while still a student. Most of her friends, both on campus and in her home town had been in a relationship at some point in their lives. Some still had more than one boyfriend, like Eva and Vida, but it had never bothered her nor occurred to her to try and see how it felt to be in love. Now, the boy who was transforming her academic life was also proposing to her!

'Is this for real or is he just trying to take advantage of me? I will hurt him if I say no, and saying yes means breaking my own vow,' she thought.

91

Almost two years back, one of her friends back home got pregnant and in an attempt at abortion, she nearly lost her life. It became big news in the town and the girl's education came to an end as a result. She was a brilliant girl, but one bad step jeopardised her future. This girl's predicament played on Belinda's mind as if it had just happened. It seemed so fresh to her. The same could happen to her too if she decided to follow this route. Joe was like a big brother to her now and even among the students, some of them saw them as such, a brother and a sister or cousins. She called him Brother Joe and he called her Linda, sometimes, Lin. Would life ever be the same for the two of them if they started having an affair?

She could not complete one thought that came into her mind as she kept skipping from one to the other. She was confused as she paced to and fro in the dormitory, hitting the wall with both palms, biting her lips and scratching her hair until Eva and Vida knocked at her door. She was on her bed by now and sprang to her feet in a flash. She was shaking and did not know who was at the door. The tears had not stopped flowing since she left their presence as one could tell from looking at her face.

The friends did not wait for her to open the door which was not locked. They pushed to open it, alarming her even more. The girls themselves were shocked to see the state she was in and so decided to tell her the truth. They feared she may either harm herself or do something worse. Eva put her hand on her shoulder and tried to talk to her but Belinda pushed her away and turned to face the wall.

"Take it easy, Belinda. It's just a joke. Here is the letter, it's my own letter. Not from Joe. Please don't be upset," Eva said.

Belinda heaved a heavy sigh of relief and turned to face them. She wiped her tears with the back of her hand and said to Eva,

"Why did you do this to me?"

"We just wanted to have fun with it. We thought Joe may be interested in you, and that is why we picked on him," said Vida.

Belinda got the letter from Eva, looked at the undersigned and gave it back to her without reading the entire content. She was still too traumatised to make any comments so she just sat on her bed and listened to them as they talked about the sender of this letter that had caused her so much heartache in the past few minutes. It was addressed from Kukurantumi, Eva's home town, written by a boy she met there when she went on holiday. Vida knew about this boy but not Belinda.

Because of Belinda's innocence and her personal standards, although the three were very good friends, there were certain things that the two did not talk about when Belinda was around. It took some days, almost a week for Belinda to get over the shock that the letter gave her. She felt very uneasy each time she was with Joe, thinking that one of them might have mentioned their plot to him.

With time, Eva's parents also got to know Joe and started sending him money and presents regularly. At some point, he had so much money in his account that the manager of the post office, Mr Marfo, arranged a meeting with him. On the appointed date, Joe sat in front of the manager and answered his questions like a full adult. He asked Joe about his background, how come he had so much in his account as a student and his plans for the future. When Joe told him of the source of his income, the manager was amazed.

"I can offer you two more candidates, my own children," said Mr Marfo.

"I would have loved to, but I can't teach them on campus. The authorities would not allow that. But if I could get a private place, I wouldn't mind teaching them what I know on weekends, Saturdays to be precise."

"You can do it in my house. I have a spare room, large enough to accommodate close to twenty students," said Mr Marfo.

"Okay, we shall talk about that later," Joe said.

Something that had started as a one to one with Belinda was

turning into big time business for Joe. During this conversation, the manager advised Joe to transfer some of his funds to the bank where he could buy shares and have other benefits plus a greater interest, compared to the post office.

"If you do as I am recommending, by the time you leave school, you would have enough money to venture into some kind of business," he said.

"Thank you very much. Like I said, when I come next time we shall talk about it," said Joe.

He left Mr Marfo's office, promising to come back to see him in the next few days so they could discuss his children's lessons in detail. The man's advice had profound impact on Joe. He started envisaging the future and how it could be with him having so much money. Not long ago, he could hardly feed himself but now he was seeing himself as a future businessman. Back on campus, Joe told Belinda about this new development, but in order to keep his account at the post office a secret, Joe said the man invited him upon someone's recommendation.

"The man said he wanted a part time teacher to help his children who are in a different school and someone from this school mentioned me to him."

"Who could that be, that mentioned you to him?" asked Belinda.

"I don't know, but the man is willing to offer one room in his house for this purpose," Joe said.

"That's a very good opportunity, because some of their students may join and you could charge them to earn some more money," said Belinda.

"Yes, that's true," Joe said.

"Some students from this school might be willing to join, if the man would allow that," said Belinda.

"That's the snag, *if the man would allow that,* I will be seeing him again before the weekend, any way."

It was just the next day that Auntie Cornie sent a letter to Joe, inviting him to come and see her at his earliest convenience. When he told Belinda of this invitation she gave him more than enough for his fare and after Belinda had informed Eva and Vida of the trip, they also gave him some cash. Joe was becoming a magnet. Everything he did and wherever he went, he was attracting money.

Eva and Vida realised the effect their plot had on Belinda and so apologised to her one morning. Since the day of the plot, they saw that Belinda was not very comfortable when they were together with Joe, but when at last they came forward to say they were sorry, she forgave them and let go of her feelings.

At their second meeting, Joe told Mr Marfo that he would not charge him for the services to his children but he would accept whatever amount he would offer him. Initially, Joe had thought of asking him if he would allow other students to take part in the lessons in his house, but as the conversation continued, he did not say anything about it. He decided to keep that to himself and see what would happen when they start.

Auntie Cornie was still eager to get a percentage from whatever cash Joe received from the Addos. Joe's reaction on the day she requested for a third of the cash from them should have put her off, but she was not the type to throw in the towel so easily. If Cornie wanted something, she would do anything to get it. Joe assumed that her reason for inviting him was to demand her percentage from the profit of the contract she had awarded him. Joe went to see her and, as he had anticipated, Cornie's motive was cash.

"How much have you received from them again?" she asked.

"Mr Addo came to the campus last week and gave me a few Cedis."

"How much was it?" asked Cornie.

Joe gave a polite smile while he dipped his hand into his pocket.

Cornie also smiled and looked attentively at Joe's hands. She didn't bother to look at his face because her interest was in what was in the pocket and not his expresstions. Joe took out a few Cedis from what was in his pocket and put the rest back.

"This is a third of how much he gave me," he said and gave it to her.

"You see what I told you, they will supply you all your needs," Cornie said. "How are you getting on with Belinda?"

"She is fine," Joe said without looking at her face.

"I mean, have you said something to her yet?"

"Something like what?" he asked.

"Don't wait for someone to come and take her away from you, Joe."

"Auntie, I would be very happy if you stopped putting pressure on me to do something that I'm not interested in. In fact, if it continues like this I will have to tell Belinda about it and stop helping her because I don't..."

"That's OK, Joe. It's fine. Just teach her what you can."

Cornie decided not to press him any longer, at least for the time being. She was hoping that it would happen naturally. Things were taking a different turn now. Previously, if Joe came to Kumasi it was to ask for some cash from his aunt, but this time he had come to give her her contract fee. She told Joe to let her know as soon as they sent him some cash so she could secure her share. Joe promised to do as she had requested and left.

On the way back, Joe planned how to approach the Head of the school about the Saturday teaching appointment so that he could be given permission to leave campus at a certain time. He gained approval from the authorities straightaway. So long as it was not going to interfere with his personal school work they saw nothing wrong with it. Later on, in a personal one-on-one discussion about it with the Headmaster, he told Joe to be mindful of what he was going to do and what he would say to his students. He cited PKK's issue as a typical example.

"I don't want history to repeat itself, so be very careful," said the Headmaster.

"Thank you, Sir," said Joe.

"You are a witness to the implications that his comments brought to the school so you have to be careful."

"Sir, I'll not do or say anything that could jeopardise this opportunity."

"I trust you would not give the other staff any opportunity to complain about these classes, because not everyone of them was happy with it when I told them, considering PKK's issue."

"I'm glad you were able to make them agree to it. Thank you very much, Sir," said Joe.

The Headmaster made it clear to Joe that because of PKK's issue, some of the teachers didn't want to agree with his request, but because of how he had comported himself since coming to the school, he, the Headmaster, had put in word for him, securing him the opportunity. Mr Marfo also spoke to other big shots in town about Joe and three weeks after the conversation in his office Joe was teaching eighteen students from the two Secondary Schools in Miawani in Mr Marfo's house on Saturdays, including Belinda, Vida and Eva.

Mr Marfo provided five benches in the room without tables. They wrote with their books on their laps. These were the children of very rich parents paying specific amounts to Joe, besides the gifts and food items that they gave him. He did not need to buy anything because whatever he needed was provided by students or their parents. Every one of them wanted to impress him with cash, gifts and other services.

Because he was not buying anything, the bank account which Mr Marfo helped him to open was in a very good state. When the branch manager of the bank realised how much was coming in regularly without any going out, the bank wrote to Joe. He was advised to buy shares which could yield a lot of dividends in a very short time. They reasoned that being a student he may not be able to run a business properly so they considered the shares to be the best option. Joe adhered to this advice and bought shares in the bank.

Everything was going well for Joe. The results from his students in their school work were amazing. Each of them had made significant progress since they came into contact with him. He had stopped his parents from sending him money and he sent them some from campus instead. Once during an English lesson with his students, Joe told them a story and asked them to report it to someone who wasn't there in their own words.

"There was a young boy called Kujo," he started, (he was talking about himself, his sister Brago sometimes called him Kujo, a name she coined by joining Kwadwo, his middle name, to Joe), "the second of two children of poor peasant farmers. He topped his class in every exam until the age of thirteen when he passed the Common Entrance Examination. With his good grades, his first choice school wrote to him immediately, offering him admission, but his parents could hardly afford to send him to school in the city. They could not afford the boarding fee and life in the city in general for this bright boy."

Because Joe had told his students that they would have to write the story he was telling them in their own words, they were all very attentive and making notes. He wanted them to take in every word and statement, so he spoke as if he was just speaking to a friend. That was the secret of his teaching abilities. Joe taught in such a conversational way that you couldn't forget what he said to you.

"This was a family that could not afford three square meals on some days," he continued, "Kujo had been helping his parents to pay for his fees by rearing chickens and selling eggs. He also took up some manual jobs on his days off school to subsidise what his parents were earning from their farm produce. A very hard-working child,

Kujo was always on the go, doing something to generate some funds to help his parents and himself."

Joe told this story in such an emotional way that some of the students felt sad. These were a group of children from wealthy families who had never experienced hunger or want. He said Kujo sometimes saved his pocket money and went to school on empty stomach, so as to add up to what his parents could raise for his education.

"It was getting to exams time and they were revising what had been taught from the beginning of the term," Joe continued. "But Kujo had to spend a whole week at home, crying his heart out, until the next market day when his mother took some of his chickens and eggs to the market for sale. Fortunately he got just a little more than the fees, so the very next day, he went back to school to pay his fees and join his mates."

A boy sitting by the window raised his hand to ask a question about where Kujo was at that time but Joe told him to wait till the end of the story. He explained that what he wanted to know would be in the story.

"One of Kujo's aunts worked in the city so his mother suggested that he stay with her, to be a day student. For some reason his father objected to it initially. When the closing date for admitted students to send in their forms was drawing near and no alternative had been found, his father consented to his mother's suggestion. After spending five years with his aunt and coming out with flying colours in every exam, he gained admission into one of the best schools in the country to further his studies. With these harsh conditions and peer pressure, Kujo was determined to study hard with the hope of becoming someone special in life. This is a part of the life story of Kujo."

Joe then told them to use the next twenty five minutes to write the story in their own words. He also reminded them to pay particular attention to their punctuation. A real perfectionist, Joe wanted everything to be as it should.

"If anyone wants some clarification about what you have heard so far, just ask me and I will be glad to explain it," he told them. "You could lose some marks if you don't cross your '*t*'s or dot your '*i*'s properly."

"We know that for sure," said one of the boys.

Belinda knew a little about Joe's past, so as he told the story of Kujo, she was the only one who suspected that he might be talking about himself. There was a statement in the story that convinced her that he was talking about himself- '*After spending five years with his aunt.*' She knew Joe had stayed with Auntie Cornie for five years in his former school, but she kept her suspicions to herself. As they were writing, one of the boys raised his hand for attention.

"Did you say Kujo stayed at home for a whole week or month?" he asked.

"A whole week," Joe replied.

The boy was the only one who had laughed at the end of Kujo's story. He was someone who always sought attention so most of them suspected he asked the question just for the others to know he was present. He sat at the back that day because he came late. The benches were arranged in such a way that their backs were toward the entrance, so if you were late you had to sit at the back. Joe had made it clear to anyone who joined that if they came and the front benches were not full yet, they were to join those in front until there was no space for another bottom.

Kujo's story was so emotional that most of them had their eyes glued on Joe and did not realise that Kwame Darko, the attention seeker was at the back. Twenty-five minutes later, Joe collected the sheets they had written on and told them they would discuss and continue from there the following Saturday. Kwame Darko asked another question before the end of the session regarding the story of Kujo.

"Didn't Kujo's parents have any properties they could have sold to see him through school?"

"You will find the answer in the sequel," Joe answered politely.

Besides the fact that Joe was teaching them to progress academically, he also instilled discipline into them. Each day, before they started classes, he would either say a short prayer or ask someone else to pray and at the end, he did same. That day, he asked Kwame Darko, for the first time, to say the closing prayer and he prayed as follows:

"God, we thank you for bringing us to the successful end of yet another session. We pray that you help us to remember whatever we are taught each day. Please give Brother Joe more wisdom, knowledge and understanding so that he can also impart them to us. And whatever Kujo, our subject-matter for today is doing now, God, we pray that you will go to his aid and let him be successful and a blessing to his parents and other people. We ask this in the name of Jesus, Amen."

Everyone was surprised to hear him pray this way. Taking him for how he behaved, no one thought he could pray the way he did. When Joe called him to pray, the others started giggling because they thought he was going to make a joke of the prayer but he surprised them all, especially Joe, who took the guy's prayer to be a prophecy into his life.

There was such a loud resounding '*Amen*' and noise from the students at the end of the prayer that Mrs Marfo had to come in to see if everything was okay. From that day on, Kwame Darko was called 'Pastor' by those present. You can never tell what is in someone until the time has come for it to be revealed. There are a lot of ordinary people you meet every day who can do extraordinary things when given the chance. In the same way, there are a lot of people whose real potential is overshadowed by circumstances.

At the end of the term, when exam results were sent to parents and guardians of Joe's students, things took a different turn. His students did so well that other people began asking questions as to how it happened and all fingers pointed to the once poor boy who was sent home many times for not being able to pay his school fees, Joseph Kwadwo Boakye. As his popularity increased, so did his finances. He had so much at the bank and the post office that he was taking care of his parents.

There was nothing he needed that he could not afford. The news got to Auntie Cornie that Joe was now a teacher with many students so she invited him to Kumasi to hear it from the horse's own mouth. Joe went with his chest out and head held high.

Auntie Cornie was happy and jealous at the same time with the changes in Joe's circumstance. Happy because he no longer came to her for cash and jealous because she envisaged that if it continued that way Joe would soon be having more money than her. In fact, Joe had more money than her at the time.

During the long vacation, students were scrambling for a place in his class, but the maximum the room in Mr Marfo's house could accommodate was eighteen and that he already had. Some parents were prepared to pay twice the amount that the old students were paying for a place. Mr Marfo gave Joe money occasionally for his children but with time, Joe stopped taking the money and told Mr Marfo to use it as collateral for the rent of the classroom. The man had taken Joe as one of his children and he sometimes called him Dad.

At a point in time, Joe was being sought for by all the rich parents in Miawani. Those from other towns who had their children in schools at Miawani were trying to lure him with money. Among the rich parents in Miawani was Mr. Osei-Asibe whose son was doing well but he thought if he came under the canopy of Joe, he could do better. He invited Joe to his house one day for a chat.

"I hear you are teaching some students in the town and their parents are testifying about their progress," said Mr Osei-Asibe.

"It's the Lord's doing, Sir," Joe said with a smile.

"Are you from this town?" Mr Osei Asibe asked.

"No. Sir, if I were I would have preferred to be a day student. I'm from Diasempa in the Eastern Region."

"Well, the reason I invited you here is about my son. He is doing well at school but from what I hear, I believe that if he came to you, he could do better.

Joe began to smile whilst he doodled on the back of the book he was holding. He thought the man was going to ask him to add his son to his class, but Mr. Osei- Asibe had other plans.

"I want to help you so you could also help my son. I don't mind erecting a shelter at the corner of the compound so you can get other students to join on Sunday evenings. I won't charge you a thing for using my premises; all I want is for my boy to be as good as you are in order to help his siblings, and I would pay you a good amount," Mr Osei-Asibe said.

"Thank you very much, Sir, but I need to think and pray about it. I will come back to give you a feedback." Joe said.

"That's fine. So when do you think you can come back? I'm a very busy person and I don't want you to come in my absence."

"By this time next Sunday, if God spares us our lives."

This statement from Joe impressed Mr. Osei-Asibe so much so that he could not say anything else to make him decide on his request there and then. After they had talked over a few social issues, Joe asked permission to leave. As soon as he left, Mr Osei-Asibe talked to his wife about Joe's response.

"He isn't an ordinary brilliant boy. The fear of the Lord is in him. He is extraordinarily mature for his age," said Mr. Asibe, to the agreement of his wife.

"That's why he is so clever, the fear of the Lord is in him," said his wife.

"I hope our children will copy his example by being with him," said Mr Osei-Asibe.

Mr Osei-Asibe was determined to get Joe close to his children so he told his wife that he would invite him again if he did not turn up as he had promised. Mr Osei-Asibe happened to know Mr. Marfo so he called him that evening to tell him of the outcome of his meeting with Joe.

"My son heard about him from school and told me what he was doing," said Mr Osei-Asibe

"I've never come across a boy of his age with that kind of intelligence and humility," said Mr Marfo.

"How did you get to know him?" asked Mr. Osei-Asibe.

"Once I was going through some files of our customers and I saw his records. Money seemed to be coming in always but there were no withdrawals, so I invited him to my office one day to ask how he came by that much money, being a student," said Mr Marfo.

"And what did he say was the source of the money?" asked Mr Osei-Asibe.

"At that time," said Mr Marfo, "he was teaching three of his junior students and their parents were paying him good money so I introduced my children to him and as we speak now he has eighteen students who meet in my house every Saturday."

"I want to engage him on Sunday evenings but he says he needs to think and pray over it."

"Yes, that's Joe, he wouldn't take a decision without first taking it to God in prayers," said Mr Marfo. "My older boy used to be in the tenth position but now he is always in the first five."

"That's great," said Mr. Osei-Asibe.

They continued to talk about Joe and Mr. Osei-Asibe hoped that

Joe would come back to him with a yes to his proposal. Two weeks later, the Addos invited Joe to come home with Belinda. While they were there Mr. Addo questioned his daughter secretly if Joe had ever made any advances towards her and she said no. He had been monitoring Belinda's progress and Joe's gentle attitude and had come to the conclusion that, after all, they would make a good couple in future but he did not tell anyone about it. His initial objection to Joe helping Belinda was making it difficult for him to come out openly to talk about his observations or opinions. He only said to Joe that Belinda was doing well lately.

The Addos, especially Mrs Addo, treated Joe like their own son, as they had told Auntie Cornie the day they met at the school. Belinda called him brother and treated him just like that. Her younger brother, Kwame Addo, also struck up a close friendship with Joe.

"Dad, would you please allow Brother Joe to come home with Belinda for a holiday?" asked KA.

"Why?"

"I just want to be with them, Dad," KA said. "Or if the driver can take me to the campus at least once every month."

"Okay. I'll discuss that with your mother."

KA pressed his father so much that arrangements were made for the driver, Ntow, to take him to the campus once every month. Belinda felt on top of the world whenever they were with Joe without their parents. Joe was like a big brother to them.

Ntow took the opportunity to do his own thing, driving around the town, having drinks and socialising until it was time to take the boy back to his parents. Sometimes while in Miawani on his own, Ntow acted big as if he owned the car. He got himself a girlfriend in the town. Taking him for a rich man, the girl's friend advised her to get pregnant by him so he could take her as a second wife but Akoto, the girlfriend, didn't like the idea. She was only interested in the rides in town, the gifts and the cash he gave her. After Ntow had had enough fun with her, he told her one weekend that he was travelling overseas and would come to see her on his return. That was the last she saw of him.

Even at the climax of his popularity both on campus and outside, Joe never gave up praying constantly at a particular time of each day and fasting on every Monday, the day he was born, till 6:00 pm. He was also faithful in his tithing. No one knew about this because it was something between him and God. By the time they got to Upper Six, he was leading PKK in every exam, but Joe never boasted about it.

Upon the advice of a couple whose child he taught, Joe erected a kiosk in Diasempa for his mother to sell a few things. The couple were traders themselves in Kumasi so they supplied his mother with everything she needed to start with. In order to silence his aunt, Joe sent her a specific amount of money every month. Money was coming in from three avenues-his Saturday classes, the Sunday classes which he had started lately in Mr Osei-Asibe's house and profits from the shop his mother was operating. His share of dividends also remained untouched at the bank. He never spent any of this money, because his numerous wealthy students and their families supplied all he needed.

By the time he finished studying Business Management in Upper Six Joe had acquired so much money that he bought a plot of land at Diasempa. The only person who knew about it was his very good friend, Kwasi Amfo. He was about six years older than Joe but the respect they had for each other made it easy for them to get on so well.

During Joe's last few days on campus, everyone in the school wanted to talk to him so as to know how to contact him when he was finally gone. Those he was teaching were trying to do everything possible to persuade him to stay at Miawani and assured him that they would see to his welfare.

Mr. Osei Asibe, especially, said he could help him set up a private school in the town but Joe did not give an immediate response to this proposal. He told him he had other plans and would get back to him later if that was to be his chosen option. The Head and other masters of Edinpa Secondary School also encouraged him to take further courses, get a degree and so on. He was confused because everyone seemed to be so concerned about what he would do when he left campus, giving him a variety of ideas regarding his future.

Two days before the send-off party for the final year students, Joe sat Belinda down and for almost thirty minutes encouraged her to be serious with her books and also to select a few of the junior students to teach them all that she knew. He said by so doing she would broaden her personal knowledge on a lot of subjects and possibly become like him by the time she was in Sixth Form. He also told her not to hesitate in contacting him for further one-on-one teaching, if she needed to.

The party was scheduled for a Saturday and most of his students had informed their parents of Joe's last day in school, so some of them came to wish him well in whatever he would be doing next. The gifts they brought to him that day were more than he had ever had in his entire life, plus money and other promises. The large common room was converted to a party hall and a platform was created in the centre to cater for those who loved doing justice to their dancing shoes. A shy Joe did not do much of dancing, but he was always engaged, talking to almost everyone.

Some two hours into the party, the Headmaster called for attention and, as was the practice of the school, some of the outstanding students were honoured with trophies, various certificates and prizes. For his outstanding contribution to the school, Joe was the last to be called and given a special award.

In the Headmaster's address, he said if the school was to have ten such students as Joe, the authorities would not have half of the problems they have been dealing with over the years. At the end of his statement, there was a rapturous applause in the auditorium. Responding to the applause, Joe thanked everyone and said they have made his stay in Miawani and the school a memorable one. He received a standing ovation for this comment.

"I don't want to mention names, but I can say that some of you have been pillars to my survival in the two years that I've been in this great school. The first day I came here I thought my stay was going to be lonely, because I didn't know anyone, but now you have all become like brothers, sisters and parents to me."

Joe was in high spirits as he spoke but towards the end, he made some emotional statements regarding his poor family background and how sometimes it had been tough for him to stay in education. The manner in which he spoke caused some of the students to fight back tears, especially when he said they may not see each other again. He saw the reaction his words were causing and switched to the future, so as not to dampen the party mood.

"I appreciate all the pieces of advice most of you have been giving me to aim for the university, but the results of the exams will determine what I do next."

He joked by saying the gifts he had received would take him more that two trips to take them to Diasempa but one of his students shouted from the crowd that he would take care of that in one go. The student later told Joe that he had already sorted things out with his parents for their driver to take Joe to Diasempa whenever he was ready to leave campus. Before the party came to an end Joe had spoken to everyone in the school and shook hands with them.

"Why did you say we may not see you again?" asked Belinda when she embraced Joe instead of shaking his extended hand.

She had her head on Joe's shoulder for a few seconds and her firm breasts pressing against his chest might have aroused many young men, but Joe had no such feelings towards Belinda. She was like a small sister to him.

"You know we don't own our lives, Lin, so anything can happen to any of us at any time. Some of us, who knows, might travel to places where..."

"I know but the way you said it sounded like you don't want to see us again," Belinda cut in, after they had disengaged and looked into Joe's eye.

"Far from that, that's not what I meant," Joe said with a smile as they were joined by PKK and another student who was also considered as a sharp brain.

"That was a good speech, Joe," said the other student.

"Thanks," said Joe.

In a low voice, PKK whispered to him that both of them would always be remembered in the school.

"That's for sure," Joe agreed.

For the many debates and quiz contests that he had helped the school to win, PKK had also been given an award. As the crowd broke up, Joe looked for the student who had promised to transport his presents and personal belongings to Diasempa and when he found him he took him to his dormitory.

"Are you sure the car can carry all these?" Joe asked.

"Don't worry, Joe. The driver will come with a pick up, and I will go with you because I want to know where to find you, if I need you."

Joe was very happy with this offer because when the gifts started pouring in from the morning, how to get them home had become a worry to him. He had already spoken to all the people who mattered to him in Miawani so the next day when the driver arrived he was ready to go back east, to Diasempa, the land of his birth.

"I'm going back home to cool off for a while," he said to the few students, including Belinda, Vida and Eva who had gathered around the truck to see him off.

He hugged them one after the other and some, especially Belinda, who could not hold back their tears and had to be consoled by her friends, left the scene before the car started to move. At the gate house, Joe got off the car to shake hands with the security man and thanked him for being so nice to him.

"It was good knowing someone like you, Joe," said the man. "Good luck!"

During the journey, the student assured Joe that if he needed anything or help that he could provide, Joe should come and see him on campus and he would sort him out. The boy's father was a Minister in the ruling government and had other private businesses so money was not a problem to him at all. As they neared Diasempa, Joe told the driver and the student that he was from a very poor home so they should not be surprised about anything they might see on arrival. The driver said he was born and raised in a village himself so Joe should not bother about his background.

When they arrived, because his home was not accessible by car, they parked by the side of the road, and Joe quickly took two bags home while the driver and the other boy unloaded the rest of his belongings. The dash home was to tell his mother to get some cups ready to serve the visitors with water and also to invite anyone who was at home to help with the luggage.

Everybody was surprised at the things Joe had come home with. They would have been more surprised if they knew the amount of cash on him, and what he had in his account. Neighbours came to welcome him and commented on how he had matured. His father was not at home so he missed the wonderful welcome that greeted his son. Brago, Joe's elder sister, kept a close eye on all the things that he had come home with.

"How did you come by all these things on campus?" asked his mother after the visitors were gone.

"We'll talk about that later, Maame," said Joe.

Things looked a bit strange to him because he had not been living in Diasempa for the past seven years, apart from the occasional short stays during vacations. But this time he had come to stay with no immediate plans to travel anywhere. Unlike his old days at home when he had to struggle to get whatever he needed, this time he had come home with a lot of cash, perhaps a little too much for anyone of his age in the entire town. He spent the next few days visiting some old school mates and friends and going to the farm with his parents. He told everyone who cared to know that he would be in Diasempa until his exam results were out before deciding what to do next.

In the mean time, Joe had informed his father about his intention of having a shop in the town. Initially, Agya Boakye was also of the opinion that if he had good grades he should further his education, but when Joe told him of his reasons of wanting to operate a shop in Diasempa, Agya Boakye gave him his blessing. He told Joe to tread cautiously because of what some of the shop keepers were rumoured to be doing. Some were believed to be using their shops as a cover up to engage in illegal activities that Agya Boakye was not happy about. A particular case was a shop-owner who was sleeping with other men's wives in his shop until he was caught red-handed one afternoon.

Joe was not at Diasempa at the time of the incident but he heard of it and told his father not to worry about anything like that because he would not do anything that could possibly bring shame to the family and himself.

CHAPTER FIVE

KEPT BY THE POWER OF GOD

When Joe's results were in, everyone thought he would go to the polytechnic and further to the university, taking into consideration his intelligence and wonderful grades, but he had a different idea, an idea he got on the day he quizzed his friends at school about the poor boy who found gold. He reckoned that if he acquired all the degrees in his chosen field, he would still end up working for somebody or some firm for money. Someone who had studied under his feet and thought he was the best teacher he had ever come across said to a friend that Joe would surely go into teaching. He had the ability and techniques to explain things for even a primary school child to understand.

He had become friends with very influential and wealthy people in society, including bank managers and businessmen and so he decided to put into practice all the theories he had learnt at school about business. He contacted a few of these tycoons about his business ideas and most of them were of the opinion that he should go to the university to acquire a degree when he showed them his results. But after explaining his family background and other intentions to them, almost all of them agreed to his plans. He wanted to be close to his people in Diasempa, especially his parents who were now advancing in age.

Some of these business people did not want to invest in the rural area, for fear of not gaining any profit and possibly losing their initial capital outlay. Mr. Addo, Belinda's father, was one of them. Nothing would make him 'throw away' money in the village where goods could sit in the shop till they were dusty and looked old.

"Things don't move fast enough in rural areas," he said to Mrs. Addo when she tried to convince him to help Joe.

"But he says he wants to be close to his people so I think we can support him," said Mrs Addo. "Besides, Diasempa is more of an urban status, being the capital of the Awkaetnaf District.

"If he decides to come to the city, I would agree to help him, not in the village," he insisted.

"Diasempa is not a village, and remember that we have promised to help the boy in any way that we can. If he starts operating from there and things don't work out well, no one would blame us. But refusing to assist him completely is not right," said Mrs Addo.

"Woman, understand me, you can't do business in the village. What do the people have and what can they buy?" asked Mr. Addo.

She did not respond to his question, rather she decided to stop persuading him for the time being, thinking he might have a change of mind later on. When Mrs. Addo informed Joe about her husband's stand, he told her not to worry, that he would reconsider the situation as to whether he had to invest in the city. But inwardly, Joe was happy that things had taken this turn. Because of his aunt's incessant pressure on him to have an affair with Belinda, he was looking for an opportunity to break away from the Addos, and this seemed to be the chance. Belinda, however, assured Joe when she heard of her father's refusal to help him that she would speak with her father.

"Don't worry, Brother Joe, I will speak to the old man," she said. "He won't say no to me. But tell me, why don't you want to stay in the city?"

"It's simple, Lin, I want to go back to my roots. I want to be with my people, especially my parents, so that I can help them in my own small way," Joe said.

113

Joe had made his intention perfectly clear to Belinda, to get close to his parents, but specifically, he was planning a get away from her, and her father refusing to assist him was a nice escape route which no one was aware of.

It is said that when one door is closed, many more will be opened. Another wealthy couple whose son has been topping his class since he began taking lessons from Joe agreed to his idea of establishing in Diasempa and promised to give him a small quantity of every item they sold in their shop for a start. They would not require any money from him, until he had sold out. To this couple, Joe's modesty and determination to succeed needed a push. He had changed their son's academic abilities and so they were prepared to help him in whatever he wanted to do to make his own life easier and successful.

All that Joe needed was a vacant shop, and they were in abundance in Diasempa. Most of the shops he had known during his primary school days in Diasempa had been shut down because the children of these shop owners who had become old or had died had either migrated to the urban centres, or they were just not interested in the buy and sell business.

Joe's father accompanied him to Mr. Amoako, an incapacitated elderly man who used to own the largest shop by the lorry station. None of his children was able to take care of the shop when the man was struck down by a mild stroke. It had been about six years since the man became disabled. His wife had tried seeking medical help to revive him but it had all proved futile, draining all their resources. Every item in the shop was sold to buy medicine, food and their general up keep until the shop became empty and so the wife had to close it and stay at home, caring for the man. They were living on the rents from three of the rooms in the main house and remittances from some of their children who were themselves finding it hard to make ends meet.

Mr Amoako's children had lived for the moment without any plans for the future because they thought Dad was always there, loaded with cash to provide what they needed or wanted. Now, although

Dad was there, he was not even able to fend for himself properly. When Agya Boakye explained their mission to them, Mr. Amoako asked Joe how soon he wanted to move in and he said he would have to see the state of the shop in order to know what needed re-fixing before he could tell when to move in.

"That's true because I haven't been there myself for over three years now so I will let Kwame go and open it for you to assess it," Mr. Amoako said and called in his son.

"When we have had a look at it, we shall come back for us to talk about the rent and other conditions," said Agya Boakye.

Mr. Amoako was so desperate that he asked them if they were coming back the same day. He needed cash, and soon, at that. His wife gave the shop keys to Kwame and instructed him to go with Joe and his father. Kwame was about two years older than Joe and although, they knew each other, they were not friends. Years ago, when their father's shop was booming, only a few lads could associate with them. Now he and his other brothers and sisters wanted to be friends with everyone, in order to fit into the society that they had once shunned. Kwame knew Joe as the son of ordinary, poor local farmers, so when he got to know that it was Joe who wanted the shop, he was completely shocked. As he watched Joe making notes of things that needed doing, Kwame could not believe his eyes.

From their estimation, it wasn't going to take more than a week. The major work was the painting but even that could be done in half a day. They went back to see Mr Amoako and his wife and a deal was concluded in about twenty minutes. He was renting it to Joe for a renewable period of one year. In the mean time he asked for six months rent in advance and two months refundable deposit, should Joe decide to vacate the shop after the first year. Joe whispered into his father's ear that they would bring the money the next day and take the keys to start work. When they left the house, Joe asked his father if he knew any reliable workman who could do the job as soon as possible.

"Papa Nar is there. He can do all the work in no time," said Agya Boakye.

"Can we go and see him now?" he asked

"Yes, we can, but it wouldn't do any good till we get the key, then we can take him there to evaluate the work," Agya Boakye said.

Papa Nar was a Krobo man who had come to live in Diasempa many years before Joe was born. He undertook all kinds of carpentry work including the building of coffins. He always had some on display in front of his workshop which was at the back of the market. Because of the coffins that he built, most children were scared of him. As a child, Joe had always been afraid when walking in front of his workshop and this was the man his father had recommended for the job.

Joe went to the bank the next day for the cash and also to see the man who would supply him with the goods. In the evening when he returned from the city he went for the key with his father. Because the shop faced the main lorry station, the place is always full of people and when they saw the shop which had been closed for a long time open with Joe and his father inside, they wondered what was going on.

It happened to be a Monday and so, as he always did, Joe was fasting and praying. He committed the whole building of which the shop was a part into the hands of God. That evening, before he ended his fast, he went to walk in front of the building, touching the very doors of the shop, and asking God to touch them as he had done. He asked God to protect him and the shop from all the powers of darkness.

Here was an inexperienced young man of twenty-one years going into business to compete with people who have been at it long before he was born. The best thing to do, Joe envisaged, was to invite God to take control of the entire business. Like young King Solomon, asking God to give him wisdom to rule the people of Israel, Joe asked that God himself be the owner of the shop and manage it as He wished. He also prayed for the man who was going to supply him with the goods and asked God to sanctify all that the man was going to give to him. Lastly, he prayed that God block any instances that will not be to His glory. No wonder in the Addos' house, Belinda was trying to convince her father to help Joe but Mr. Addo would not give in.

God has a way of sorting things out for those who trust and commit their lives into His care. Judging from the transformation that Joe had brought to Belinda's progress in education, Mr Addo should never have refused a request from him, and his wife, as she had done many times, should have been able to convince him to help Joe, but this time around she could not. God knows the end from the beginning of every matter. He knew that if Mr. Addo offered Joe any assistance in his business, another phase of bonding would be established which the young man would not be able to break away from with ease. It could also give Auntie Cornie a firm grip on Joe's business, life and future and so the Almighty God hardened the heart of Mr. Addo, like He did to Pharaoh during the time of Moses.

"Dad, how could you say no to Joe, someone you have promised to help, someone who has turned my life around in terms of education? You are a witness to what I have been achieving since Joe came into my life."

"I thought you told me you were not having an affair with him?" Mr Addo asked.

"I'm not having any affair with him, Dad. I just feel you can and should help him," Belinda insisted.

"What do you mean by him coming into your life, then?" he asked.

Belinda looked at him from the corner of her eyes without saying anything for a while. Most of the time when she talked with her father about Joe, he had made comments which seemed to suggest that something was going on between them. There wasn't any such thing, so this time, she decided to ask him one question to find out how he would feel if at all there was something going on.

"Dad, what is wrong about me going out with Joe? Do you want me to go out with him or not?"

"Oh! So you've been in love with him all this while? You could not maintain your virginity as you said. You are going after that poor village boy," ranted Mr Addo.

He was raising his voice and this attracted his wife to the living room where father and daughter were arguing. Mrs. Addo wanted to know from Belinda the facts of what her father was accusing her of.

"So who broke your virginity and when did this happen?" asked Mrs Addo.

There was silence as Belinda and her father looked into each other's eyes.

"I am asking you a question, Belinda," said her mother.

"Ask Dad, Mummy, because he is saying it. I haven't done anything with anybody, yet he is accusing me of it," Belinda answered.

"Who told you about it?" Mrs Addo asked her husband.

"Nobody told me about it, but I strongly suspect that she has done it."

"Done it with whom? And what makes you suspect that? Is there any proof to it?" Mrs. Addo asked.

"No. But ..."

"But what?" asked Mrs Addo.

He picked the phone which had rung three times already without answering his wife's question. Guilty conscience has led to suspicion. Mr. Addo has himself violated many young girls, some as young as Belinda, so he suspected that for his daughter to get so close to a boy like Joe, definitely he must have slept with her as he would have done. He always said to his friends that if a fowl is close to you, it's not difficult to catch it. While he was on the phone talking about business with one of his friends, Mrs Addo pulled her daughter to the corridor and asked her to confide in her if she has slept with anyone.

"I haven't done anything with anyone, Mummy, but Dad is always suspecting me of having an affair with Joe. And now he is accusing me of losing my virginity to him. Joe has not for once done or said anything to show that he is even interested in me, so why all this suspicion?" Belinda asked in tears.

"I don't know."

"If there is any way that my virginity can be tested to prove him wrong, I'm prepared for the test. I want him to take me for a test to show whether I'm still a virgin or not. I'm going to ask him to do that, if that would make him stop accusing me of something I haven't done," she said angrily.

"Personally, I don't know why he is still suspicious," said Mrs. Addo. "I spoke to him about this before you and Joe came into contact and when he raised it again a few months later I told him you have assured me of keeping your virginity till you marry. Any way, you leave it with me and I will sort it out with him."

Belinda had a very soft spot for Joe, no doubt. She respected him so much and might have said yes to him if he had asked her to sleep with him, but like she rightly said to her mother, Joe had not once done or said anything to show his interest in her.

Meanwhile, Joe was moulding his own future in Diasempa. About six days after he had got the key from Mr Amoako, he acted as an apprentice to Papa Nar and completed everything that needed doing in the shop. As they worked, many people came in to ask them what they wanted to use the shop for and they did not fully believe when Joe told them he was going to sell hardware.

"Is that not Agya Boakye's son?" an inquisitive elderly man asked a driver at the lorry station when he saw Joe putting finishing touches to the front door.

"Yes, he is," the driver responded. "I hear he is going to operate the shop, but I suspect that he is going to run it for someone."

"Whoever the owner may be, it can't be a member of his family," said the elderly man.

"We all know his father's family as well as his mother's, who among them can own a shop?" asked another man standing by.

'Isn't this the carpenter's son? Isn't his mother's name, Mary?' Matthew 13:55-56. People asked these questions when Jesus began doing miracles among his own people. They had even gone further to state that they knew his brothers, how then could he be doing those things he did in the midst of his own people? When, by God's grace, you begin to rise above your peers, it is your own people who will be the first to doubt your ability to succeed. Your own people who are supposed to rejoice over your success would sometimes try to undermine you.

'Is that not Maame Darkoaa's son, the boy who used to be sent home from school for his fees?'

'Isn't that Joe, Agya Boakye's son, who used to carry people's luggage from this very station for tips?'

The questions and rumours were endless and the observers were agog with curiosity. They were in for a shock, if they knew where he was coming from. Spending forty days and forty nights of fasting in the wilderness made Jesus powerful and filled with the Spirit of God. It had been over seven years when Joe used to carry people's luggage for tips at the station. Now, however, no one knew the preparations he had been through from that time and what he has come back to this very station to establish.

Yes, it was Joe, the son of Agya Boakye and his wife, Maame Darkoaa of Kristom. The people of Israel knew Jesus too well to believe what he was doing among them. To them, the carpenter's son should have become a carpenter under normal circumstances and not a miracle worker. So it was with the people of Diasempa, Kwadwo Boakye should have taken after his parents and go into farming, but when you find favour in the sight of God, the impossibility becomes possible.

When everything was completed, ready for business, Joe locked himself up in the shop for one whole day. He has heard some of the negative comments being made by people and he was determined not to let them have any effect on what he has planned to achieve. But he could not do it on his own. He knew that, *'Unless the Lord builds the house, its builders labour in vain. Unless the Lord watches over the city, the watchmen stand guard in vain' (Psalm 127:1-2)* Joe wanted the Lord himself to build the shop and manage it. So that day when he locked himself up in the shop, he based on the above scripture and committed the shop fully into the hands of the Most High God.

He made arrangements with the man who was going to supply him with goods to send the delivery on the day before the next market day. He bought other items that he could not get from his supplier's warehouse but were in high demand in Diasempa. Before the truck arrived Joe had already spoken to six porters who would help him unload the goods so they were waiting when the driver parked right in front of the shop. The strange, big truck attracted a lot of people to the station to watch what it contained.

Agya Boakye was there, standing by as a security guard to make sure all the boxes went into the shop and no other place. Spending the rest of the day and greater part of that night to put the items where they should be in the shop, Joe was helped by his parents and good friend, Kwasi Amfo.

Joe opened the shop on Friday, which happened to be the market day in Diasempa when the town was full of people, especially farmers who have come from the surrounding villages to sell their farm produce. There were also people who have come from the other big towns to engage in trade and other matters. Like the day of Pentecost when people from all walks of life had come to

Jerusalem, that was the day the promised Holy Spirit descended on those in the upper room, and the whole town was in a state of confusion- *Acts 2:1-12*

'What's going on?' That was the question on many lips.

The once most popular shop in the town which has been shut down for a long time has suddenly been opened. Apart from the United African Company (UAC) and the Ghana National Trading Corporation (GNTC), it was the next largest store to be owned by an individual in the town, so it had indeed been a very popular shop before it was shut due to the owner's ill health. Both UAC and GNTC were also shut at that time.

'Who is running it now?' they asked.

In order to be one hundred percent sure that they were not being lied to, people went in there in their numbers to ask Joe if he really owned the shop and everyone was surprised when he confirmed that he was the owner. Being the first day, he had expected it to be a window shopping day, but he sold so much that never before in all his life had he counted that much money in any single day. People had been travelling to other nearby big towns like Koforidua to buy most building materials and other items, but Joe has brought them to their door steps. Whatever material one needed to work on a building, he had it in his shop. He made a thorough research before presenting a list of items to his supplier that he knew would sell.

He arranged the items in such an orderly manner that it was easy for him to take stock every evening before he closed the shop. Each evening, he knew what he had sold, how much money had come in and what he needed to order. The small kiosk which his mother was operating was also doing very well. He did not need to pay rent for the shop for the next six months but he looked after Mr. Amoako and his wife like he would his own parents. Some of his friends with whom he attended primary school and had remained in Diasempa all their lives came to him for a chat. He visited others too in the evening when he closed the shop and there was never a time when Joe acted superior to any of his old time friends.

One Friday afternoon, Belinda told Vida and Eva that she wanted to visit Joe in a few weeks time to see how he was doing and the two girls said they would like to go with her. Joe had given them such a good foundation that by the time they got to Form Four the three of them were always occupying a place in the first six after every exam. Each of them was also teaching some junior students, something that Joe had told them to do. He decleared to them that the more you teach the more you learn and don't forget things easily if you continued doing it. They have all been writing to Joe once in a while, but Belinda's corresponding with him was more frequent. She promised to get in touch with Joe so they could fix a date for the trip.

Auntie Cornie was also going to Diasempa more than she used to do in the past, and it was always to get some cash from Joe. He never denied her anything that she asked for. Her son, Kwaku Odame, was in his first year in secondary school and, apart from Joe paying his school fees, he always sent him money and other essentials whenever his mother was in town. One weekend, Cornie went to see Mrs. Addo for a discussion about Belinda and Joe. She told Mrs Addo tha Joe was doing very well and she did not want him to go and marry any of those girls from Diasempa.

"Of course, I would not expect a young man of his calibre to marry an illiterate or a rural girl," Mrs Addo said.

"I don't know what plans you have for Belinda, but I am wondering, should Joe be willing to wait till she finishes her education, would you allow him to marry her?" she asked.

Mrs. Addo laughed and took a sip from the orange juice she had in her hand.

"Did Joe send you on this mission or you are only making your own enquiries?" she asked.

"In fact, I fear that the ladies would soon begin knocking on his door because of his success but I don't want him to marry someone that I don't know," said Cornie.

"Well, if Joe had sent you, it would have been a different thing, but as it is now, you don't know his plans and neither do I know my daughter's. She may choose to go to the university, go to live abroad or something. So I will suggest you ask Jos's opinion first. After all, he may not even like someone like Belinda?" Mrs Addo said.

"Who would refuse a beautiful girl like Belinda?" Cornie asked, giggling.

Mrs Addo insisted that both of them may have different choices; besides, she did not know what her husband would say about it. They agreed to meet at a later date after both the young people had been contacted on the issue. Since Cornie connected Joe to the Addos, she had received so much money and other things from them that, breaking the link, she feared, could mean the end of those benefits. So, she was determined to convince Joe that of all the ladies in the world, Belinda Addo was the best one for him.

When Cornie left, Mrs. Addo was in a fix as to how to present this matter to her husband, because of his suspicion she did not want a situation where he would say, '*I said it. I knew there was something going on.*' So to tell him now that Joe wanted to marry Belinda would give him an upper hand in the yet-to-be-abated argument about the youngsters. After days of hard thinking over the issue, Mrs Addo decided to ask Belinda first and based on her response, she could then discuss it with her husband or forget about it. So one day, on their way back from shopping she asked Belinda in the car to tell her of her plans towards marriage. She beat about the bush for a while, telling her when and how she got married to her father and then chipped in:

"So when do you intend to marry?"

"Why this question, Mummy?" Belinda asked.

"Oh, I just want to know so we can plan in advance."

"That's my private life."

"It is your private life, but don't forget that your life is connected to mine."

"You're right, Mum, but marriage is not something that I have even thought of, honestly."

"You will soon be a grown-up, so you should start thinking and making preparations toward it. Now tell me, what type of man would you like to spend your life with?"

Munching her biscuit, Belinda did not answer her mother's question. She looked out of the window, watching some young boys selling dog chains in the vehicular traffic. Her mother called her attention and asked her again to tell her the man she would like to marry.

"But you've just told me to start thinking less than a minute ago and now you want an instant answer. Please give me some time, some days, weeks or months to think about it and I will give you an answer. This is a question relating to a lifelong journey, you know?"

They continued to talk about this issue until they got home without Mrs Addo mentioning the discussion she had with Auntie Cornie. Some weeks later, Belinda and her friends visited Joe at Diasempa as planned and although they did not spend much time there, it was a great reunion. They were very surprised to see Joe managing such a large shop on his own. He had wanted to take them home to meet his parents but the girls said they had to go to Kukuruantumi, Eva's home town before returning to Miawani, so they promised to come again. On their way back, the girls talked so much about Joe and said he was surely going to be someone great in future.

A month after speaking with Mrs. Addo, even though she had not heard anything from her again, Auntie Cornie went to ask Joe about his plans on marriage. On arrival in the shop, she congratulated him for the progress he was making and said he should be careful in dealing with some members of the family, especially Brago. While the conversation was going on Cornie chipped in the main purpose of her visit.

"You see, now that you are prospering, most of these local girls would like to show that they love you, but the fact is they would only be trying to suck your money. So I will suggest that you get married. As soon as you do that, all those who would be making plans towards you will back off," she said.

"You are right, Auntie, some have already started making moves, but you know me too well that I'm not into that kind of life," Joe said. "When I'm ready to..."

"You see? That's why I want you to marry now. And not just anybody, it should be someone known to both you and me. For your information, I was with Mrs. Addo the other day and we talked about it, you and Belinda. It's been over three years now since I've been talking to you about her and ..."

"Belinda isn't someone that I would like to marry, Auntie. I would like to marry from Diasempa and no other place," said Joe.

"Her parents could help you expand this shop and have branches in other towns if you are married. I bet you would not have to spend a dime on the marriage arrangements. She is the only daughter, as you know, and so they would like to make her wedding splendid."

"I don't want to marry Belinda, Auntie. She is not someone I want for a wife."

Cornie tried to convince Joe with what Belinda's parents could do for him, but no amount of words would make Joe change his mind. If he wanted someone to choose a wife for him, it should be his own mother and not Cornie of all people. Joe told her that Belinda visited him with two of her mates sometime ago and if he was interested in her, he could have mentioned it to her himself.

"Can you give me just one good reason why you don't want to marry her," asked Cornie.

"It's that simple, Auntie. I want to marry from among our own people, here in Diasempa."

126

"Well, like I have said many times before, I say it again, think about it and let me know your final decision."

Joe had already made his final decision, but in order to make her go away, he promised to think about it and get back to her later.

"Kwaku's mates will be going to Akosombo on excursion but I don't have enough to pay for his fare so he asked me to tell you about it," said Cornie.

"I hope he is doing well at school," Joe said as he put his hand into his pocket for some cash.

"Think about me too, not just your cousin," she said.

"I'm fixing both of you," Joe said and gave her a lot of cash. "Pay for his fare, give him some pocket money and keep the rest."

"Eh, Joe, you will live long to look after me very well before I die," Cornie said.

In about thirteen months, Joe was able to pay for all the goods that were supplied to his shop and so everything in the shop belonged to him from then on. His treasury bill was yielding so much at that time but his plot on the outskirt of the town was still undeveloped. Amfo, his friend, had been farming on it all the while. No one, not even his parents, knew about this plot.

Three months after sorting out his accounts with the supplier, he planned with Amfo to engage a mason to lay the foundation of a four-bedroom house on the plot. Fortunately, the plot was in a remote area so not many people noticed the job that was being done on it. Before this time, Joe had renovated the family house and built a basic bungalow for himself on the small available space at the edge of the compound. He became the sole breadwinner for his entire extended family, that is, cousins, nephews and nieces, etc. and he helped anyone outside the family who needed his help.

While some girls of the town were trying to force themselves on him, those 'holier-than-thou' ones at the local church were also trying hard to be noticed by him but Joe maintained his equanimity. One of the deaconesses approached Maame Darkoaa that if Joe had not arranged marriage with anyone, she would like him to marry her twenty-year-old daughter, but Maame Darkoaa lied to her that Joe said he had someone in mind.

At funerals and other gatherings many ladies desired to share his table with the hope that they may be lucky, but Joe only moved with his male friends and elementary school mates. Among his mates there were a few girls, but he showed no interest in any of them. Once, during a social gathering at church, he was advised by his Pastor to marry in order to avoid the temptations that some ladies could give rise to.

"I know you are a man of very strong will-power, but no matter who you are, no matter what your morals may be, there are three things which could bring any rising or successful man down - money, pride and women," said the Pastor.

Joe looked at the Pastor as he paused to take a drink. He was wondering if anyone had contacted the Pastor with marriage proposals in connection with him and that was why he was talking to him about it.

"Everyone, including myself, can testify of your modest behaviour in this town and beyond, so pride is out of the issue here, but the money that is coming into your hands and the absence of a woman in your life could be a temptation. It is therefore important that you find yourself a woman and when you are settled with her, the two of you could then control the money, instead of it being in your sole control."

"Thank you very much, Pastor," Joe said.

"Well, I am talking to you from experience. I don't want any answer from you for now. I want you to pray and think about it."

Joe thanked him again and again as they mingled with the others. About a week later his parents called him one Sunday when they returned from church and added their voice to the pressure on his bachelorhood. It was then that Joe realised from his mother that it wasn't only the deaconess who had approached her but four other people in the town wanted Joe in marriage to their daughters or nieces. Joe was seen as a shining star and everyone wanted to associate with him. His father asked him if he had anyone in mind to marry and when he said no, they advised him to look for someone to settle down with, just as the Pastor had said. Joe thanked his parents and made a very passionate appeal to them.

"You know I have spent many years outside Diasempa and so although I know a lot of people, I don't really know their background and I don't want to take a wife whose family history I don't know. I therefore want you to look around town to find me someone who would be an ideal wife for me and daughter-in-law to you. Whoever God leads you to find and you recommend, I would accept."

"What about the lady your aunt talked about?" Darkoaa asked.

"Which lady are you referring to?" asked Agya Boakye, as if he did not know.

"The one his aunt came to tell us about," said Darkoaa.

"Forget about that lady. I wouldn't like Kwadwo to marry her because of your sister," said Agya Boakye.

"What exactly do you have against Cornie that makes you feel negative about anything that she is involved in?" asked Darkoaa.

This question nearly brought about an argument so Joe had to jump in to save the situation immediately.

"I have already made my mind clear to Auntie Cornie about her so I thought this lady's name would not surface at all in a discussion about my marriage. I am surprised that she still came to talk to you about her. I'm just not interested in her."

"There you are. What else do you want to hear?" Agya Boakye asked his wife.

In the end, they agreed to Joe's request and promised to find him somebody from a well-respected family in Diasempa.

"I want a good Christian, please," said Joe.

According to Joe, marriage must be based on love and understanding so whether the partner was highly educated, illiterate, beautiful or ugly was not a matter of prime importance to him. All he wanted was someone who shared his beliefs and would understand him. He says if you marry a very beautiful woman who does not share your values, you are in for trouble. He added that he had always wanted someone from a lowly background like himself.

During their deliberations, Joe told his parents that he wanted to get a small shop for one of the members of the family whose husband was dead and was finding it hard to care for her children. He has been helping this lady financially and in other ways, but he wanted to give her something that would constantly provide for her. He said he might not be able to take care of her and the children indefinitely, so the shop could give her some source of income to manage her own life. His parents were glad about it and encouraged him to go ahead. He had already made all the feasibility studies on the shop, so three weeks after discussing it with his parents, the lady was running her shop.

Joe's good intention was criticised by her older sister, Brago. She complained that the shop should have been for her instead of this relative. Brago accused her of using witchcraft to win Joe's favour. Joe heard this accusation through the grapevine, but for the sake of peace, he turned a deaf ear to it.

Brago was the wayward type who could give you real trouble if you crossed her path. Together with about ten other young women in their mid-twenties, they formed a clique called Company C. Whatever the C stood for was never revealed. They were hard core young women who lived their lives as they wished. Neither their own parents nor members of their respective families could reason with them. Bad company, it is said, corrupts good morals.

Agya Boakye and his wife had tried their best to keep her under their wings, but Brago sneaked out and went her own way. Almost all of the girls of Company C got pregnant at one point or the other. Some terminated a number of pregnancies and carried on with their lives and a few of them chose to have their babies.

Their male counterparts were the fun-loving Borle group. These were lads in their twenties who had been long time friends during their elementary school days at Diasempa. Some of them were at that time in various higher institutions in Accra, Kumasi, Koforidua, etc. Others too were working outside Diasempa and came home whenever there was some special occasion. As earlier stated, they were fun-loving and womanisers who were in a sort of competition as to how many girls each could 'bed' when they were in town.

Each of them had more than one steady girlfriend some of whom belonged to Company C, but they were always determined to lay hands on as many new girls as they possibly could. This more often than not caused fights among the girls.

The local boys could not compete with the Borle boys because of their exposure to life in the cities and they took advantage of that to paint the town red whenever there was an occasion. If not all, most of them engaged in smoking cigarette and cannabis just for the fun of it and some of them gave up later but to others, it became an addiction.

One of them, a very tall lad who also had long front teeth which always made him look as if he was laughing was the worst of them all because when it came to women, he would 'bed' anything in a skirt, young or old. He happened to be Brago's boyfriend and so there was constant friction in their relationship.

Known as the black sheep of the family, Brago could behave nastily, and in order to forestall the possibility of her bringing the entire family into disrepute, Joe invited her to his room one evening and asked her if she could begin some trading because he wanted to give her some money.

"Yes, Joe. I can go to Sekune to buy plantain, cassava, etc and take it to Koforidua or Accra to sell," she said.

Joe did not mention any of the things he had heard her saying about the shop he got for the relative. He told her to find out how much she would need as a capital and let him know.

"If I get about three million Cedis I would be fine with it," she said.

Joe laughed and advised her to find out from the people who were already in the business. He told her never to base a business venture on assumptions but on thorough research on the type of business she intends to undertake. The amount she asked for was not a problem to Joe, but he knew that every business requires a plan.

"This is the reason why most people fail in their businesses," said Joe. "Instead of doing proper research, they just assume that if I had so much and used 'x' amount to buy twenty of these bags (he pointed to a bag by the door), I could sell them at 'y' amount and have 'z' profit. So they put in all they have without taking into account the cost of carting the items to the sales destination, the rate at which these items could sell and if at all they are needed in that environment."

Joe was lecturing his older sister as if she was one of his students. Whether in good faith or not, Brago took his advice and said she would let him know the results of her research in a few days. She started telling her friends that she would soon be trading between Diasempa and Accra.

As soon as Joe had laid the foundation of his house, he began working out the cost of each level of the project. He made such good arrangements that the project never got stalled at any point. By the time one phase was completed, he had made provision for the next. Amfo and his wife did not discuss the project with anyone, as they had agreed with Joe from the time he bought the plot.

His shop was so stuffed with goods that whatever one wanted, one could get it there. Most of the other shops in the town were losing their customers to Joe. Everyone was sure of getting what they wanted from his shop, so some people would go straight there instead of trying other shops first. If anybody came to look for something that he did not have, Joe would make sure that item was available in a matter of days.

As this trend continued, a few of the old time shop owners started complaining that Joe was using voodoo to attract customers. They said the church that he seemed to be so serious with was only a cover up. Two of these shop owners, Akwankwaa and Akonoba, conspired to contact a spiritualist to do something for them to halt the progress of Joe's business. If they had known the powers that were behind Joe's success, they would not have dared. But their hearts and minds were pregnant with wickedness and since no pregnancy lasts forever, whatever they were pregnant with had to be given birth to some day.

The spiritualist whom Akwankwaa and Akonoba contacted gave them *mortor*, some smooth, black powder to sprinkle in front of Joe's shop so that whoever walked on it into the shops and came out would never go back there to buy anything. Their source of livelihood was at stake so they were prepared to pay the heavy amount which the man charged them. Each of them paid a quarter, making up half of the charge and it was agreed that the remaining half would be paid in a few days' time.

So one Sunday night, when Joe was at church, they went to sprinkle the medicine in front of his shop. They had a drink together afterwards, happy that at last all their lost customers were going to come back to them. They opened their shops all the seven days of the week but Joe did not open his shop on Sundays so as to make time for church. When they got to their respective homes, they went straight to bed and slept throughout the night because of the effect of the drinks. Around the middle of the night it started to rain, and it rained so heavy that many places in the town were flooded and the entire medicine was washed into the drains. It was at dawn that they realised what had happened.

That morning, staff from the Local Council whose duty it was to see

133

to it that the streets and pavements were kept clean at all times had a field day, cleaning all the debris that littered the streets. When they got to the front of Joe's shop which was still closed at that time of the morning, they did extra work there. Joe had always been very kind to them, giving them tips several times and, unlike other people, speaking nicely to them whenever they were there to work. Some of them used to call him Master which Joe has actually begged them to stop.

When they found the front of Master Joe's shop in a mess, every hand was put on deck. They scrubbed, washed and cleaned every bit of foreign material away. While the cleaning was in progress, Akwankwaa and Akonoba, as if drawn by some force to the station, stood at different spots and watched in shock. It had not rained in the last few weeks, the weather had been clear the day before without any sign of rain, how come this heavy down pour? They just could not understand why it rained or why it should rain that night.

They were still hanging around to watch what was going to happen to their plans when Joe came to open the shop. He was a little late today because he had to attend to a part of the backyard garden fence which the wind that accompanied the rain had ripped apart. Because he was late, many customers were waiting for him to open, so as soon as he appeared nearly ten customers gathered around the door before he opened the first padlock. He apologised for keeping them waiting.

That day, in less than two hours, he sold more than he did on some full days. The windy rain has caused some damage so people needed to do a lot of repairs on their properties, and the only place they were sure of getting whatever they required was Joe's shop. Akwankwaa and Akonoba should have been at their respective shops to make some few Cedis, but here they were, wasting time and absorbing all the humiliation silently.

Being a Monday, Joe was fasting and praying, a bad time to attack the child of God. They had picked on the wrong fellow at the wrong time. Akonoba approached Akwankwaa from his vantage point and they arranged to meet again at the bar where they had the drink to discuss what had to be done next. They knew this plan has failed. They had been knocked out in the very first round and could hardly believe what was going on before their eyes.

That day, Joe's shop was like a bee hive as customers kept coming and going and the guy was all smiles. Some customers lamented about the wreck the rain had caused, but no one can blame God for what He chooses to do at any point in time. Akwankwaa had brought up the idea of contacting a spiritualist, and Akonoba had suggested which one they should go to. So when they met again for further strategies, Akwankwaa also mentioned another powerful man he knew.

"I am sure he can do something about this situation."

"What about what we owe the first man?" Akonoba asked. "I think we have to go back to him and tell him what has happened, maybe he can try it again."

"In fact, I wanted us to try somewhere else, but as you said, if we explain that this one has gone down the drain, he may consider us, forget about the balance and do it again," Akwankwaa said.

"Yes, instead of trying somewhere else, it's better to let him know what has happened," Akonoba added.

It was therefore arranged that they go back to the man at a later date. This was an embarrassing situation that they could not discuss with anyone. They were both very moody throughout the day and the few people who went to their shops could tell that they were not themselves. A friend asked Akwankwaa if he was all right and he lied to him that he had had too much drink the night before and blamed his mood on a hangover.

Meanwhile, Auntie Cornie had not given up on her plans to get Belinda for Joe. She did not know about the discussion Joe had had with his parents regarding marriage. His mother contacted their District Pastor on the matter and a search for a suitable partner for Joe was started. Darkoaa told the Pastor what Joe had said, that whoever the Lord leads them to find for him as a wife he would gladly go ahead to marry that person.

Auntie Cornie contacted Mrs. Addo again to find out if she had come to any decision with her husband and daughter about her proposal. The tutorial Belinda had received from Joe had boosted her confidence so much that she was sure of making it to the university. She had told her mother that she would not mind getting married to Joe, if only he could wait for her to obtain a degree.

This decision was not known to her father because he would not like the idea of his golden girl going to spend the rest of her life in a rural area after having a taste of the good life in the city. Mother and daughter planned to keep this a secret and wait to see what the future would be like. When Mrs. Addo told Auntie Cornie of this decision, she took it as a step in the right direction. Her duty now was to convince Joe to wait till Belinda was ready for marriage. When Belinda was talking to her mother about marriage, she remembered how she had reacted on that day when Eva and Vida pulled her leg that Joe had written a love letter to her.

'What would they say if they got to know in future that I'm married to Joe?' she kept asking herself.

Auntie Cornie went to Diasempa again to speak to a few relatives to support her plans. She told them of the wealth of Belinda's parents and the possibility of them turning their lives around for the better if Joe got married to Belinda. This time she decided not to talk to Joe about it, instead she arranged it in such a way that the four relatives she had spoken to would talk to him individually. The idea she sold to them was that Joe should wait till Belinda was ready for marriage. Some of them said it was a good idea for Joe to marry the child of a rich man.

Mr. Amoako, the landlord, whose shop Joe was renting, had a very beautiful daughter, Akua, about the same age as Joe who was living in Tema. She came to Diasempa once to see for herself if what she was hearing about Joe was true and was indeed short of words when she saw what Joe had done to the shop. Joe knew the girl when they were children but had not seen her since he went to school at Kumasi.

"Is he married?" Akua asked her father.

"He is not married yet so I can speak to him if you like him," said the old man.

"I don't mind," said Akua.

"Okay, I will invite him here tomorrow and introduce you to him."

"He knows me already, and I know him too."

"I still need to talk to him about you," said Mr Amoako.

Some ten years back, Mr. Amoako did not want his children to associate with the likes of Joe but now he was personally willing to introduce his daughter to him. That's the way life goes. When the going is good everyone wants to be your friend

Joe had given Brago some money to trade with and as her business was going on very well, she started buying expensive clothes, shoes and living big. Her mother once advised her to be careful of her extravagance but she wouldn't take any of that. She told her mother in plain words that even though Joe had provided the capital, she was the one who was spending her time and energy to make the business flourish, so she had the right to enjoy it. There were rumours that she had boyfriends at the places where she bought her stuff and where she sold them, but no one dared to confront her about it.

Akua, Mr Amoako's daughter, could not wait for Joe to be invited to the house. She went into the shop to have a chat with him, flashing her eyes and smiling all the time she was with him.

"I haven't seen you for about ten years now," she said.

"Yes, it was around that time when I went to school at Kumasi," Joe said.

"When I heard that you were running the shop, I did not believe it. I never thought of you coming to do something like this here in Diasempa."

"Well, that's me. I had always wanted to be around my people. I love this town of ours so much so that I couldn't think of going to establish anywhere else."

"That's a good idea. Home sweet home, they say," said Akua.

"It's true. Seeing your own people and talking with them like we are doing now, to me, is very inspiring. Home is where the heart is, you know."

"Yes. Any way, I will be spending the weekend here so I hope to see you again before I go back to Tema."

"That's fine. I haven't seen the old man today. I hope he is fine?" asked Joe.

"Yes, he is. He was telling me all that you've been doing for him and my mother. Thank you very much," said Akua.

To this, Joe only smiled without saying anything. As Akua was leaving the shop, she swayed her waist to impress Joe that she could be a good bed mate, but Joe turned a blind eye to that. Some girls had tempted him in the past by asking if they could bring him some food in the shop and to keep them away, he always told them he brought food from home.

One such girl who had been refused many times before was the daughter of one of Mr Amoako's tenants. Alice was about three years younger than Joe and was a final year student in the only secondary school in Diasempa. Once when she was going to the stream to wash her clothes, she visited the shop to ask Joe if he had anything to wash that she could take with her. Joe thanked her and said he did his washing over the weekend.

"I always do my washing on Monday afternoons after school, so you can keep your laundry and bring it to the shop for me to come for it, if you like," said Alice.

"Thank you very for the offer, but washing is one of the things I enjoyed doing as a form of exercise," Joe said with a smile.

"You just don't want me to do anything for you, I know," said Alice.

"No. That's not the case at all. I'm sure that one day or at some point, I will need you to do something for me," Joe said.

Disappointed, Alice left the shop thinking of what to do next or when Joe would call her to do something for him and use that as a springboard. Joe did everything he could to avoid all those girls who tried to impress him.

The relatives whom Cornie had tried to work through to persuade him to wait for Belinda did not succeed. He told them he had found someone and would introduce her to them soon. They wanted to know who this someone was, but Joe wouldn't tell them. In fact, there was no one yet, he just wanted to put them off with their unwelcome suggestions. When Mr Amoako invited Joe to the house, Akua tried to engage him in a conversation but Joe was in his usual taciturn self, giving her only 'yes' or 'no' answers. Upon Mr Amoako's enquiries, Joe lied to him that he was engaged to someone.

On the night before Akwankwaa and Akonoba went to see their man, a different opinion emerged, bringing about a sharp argument between them. Akwankwaa wanted them to try someone else as he had earlier suggested because the spiritualist would surely demand his balance but Akonoba insisted they go back there because that was where they had started. They could not agree on the next step to take so they left the bar in anger, without any plans to meet again over the issue.

After a long time without any of them showing up, the spiritualist sent someone to go and demand the balance from them. When the messenger went to Akwankwaa's shop, he told him to go and see

Akonoba. Akonoba also told him to go back to Akwankwaa. What made the messenger so angry was that Akonoba insulted him and drove him out of his shop, telling him not to come to him again because he, the messenger, knew nothing about their connection with the spiritualist who sent him.

"I know everything, and I will tell everybody if you don't give me the money," the messenger threatened.

"Go on, tell the whole town if you are really a man," said Akonoba, thinking the messenger's words were an empty threat.

The messenger became impatient because they kept tossing him to and fro like a ping pong ball until he started explaining the situation to the onlookers in front of Akonoba's shop. Bretuo, who was a friend to Agya Boakye, pulled the man aside and tried to calm him down, and also to get more information on the issue.

"So, do you know the name of the man they were targeting?" asked Bretuo.

"I don't know him but I learn he is a young man who has opened a new shop in town and everyone seemed to be patronising his shop," replied the messenger.

The man's anger made him talk louder and some of those who had gathered there from the beginning of the argument knew that Joe was the one these people had wanted to destroy. In a fierce anger, Akonoba, at one point pushed the messenger to get away from the front of his shop and the man returned the push with a blow to Akonoba's temple, resulting in a real fight. The messenger was younger and stronger so he gave Akonoba quite a beating before some people managed to separate them.

One of the eye-witnesses rushed to inform two police officers who were patrolling the area and they came to the scene straightaway. The assailants were taken to the police station with quite a crowd following them and after taking their statements, the police went to arrest Akwankwaa for his involvement in the case. They were forced to pay the messenger what they owed his master.

While all this was going on, Joe was still making money in his shop. He had heard of the uproar in the town about an argument leading to a fight and the subsequent arrests, but he was not the type of person who could not wait to find out more. He would rather wait for the news to come to him than dig for it, if it did not directly concern him. So he did not show any interest in the rumour until his father sent for him to close the shop and come to see him immediately.

It was very unusual for Agya Boakye to order his son in this way so Joe knew it must be about something important. Without any questions, he closed the shop and went to see the old man at home.

"All the uproar in the town is about you, Joe," Bretuo said to Joe as soon as he got in.

"Why, Agya Bretuo?" asked Joe.

Bretuo looked at Agya Boakye without saying any more. He had already narrated everything to Agya Boakye and was expecting him to tell Joe what was going on.

"Do you remember the conversation we had before you started operating the shop, Kwadwo, about some people using voodoo to run their shops?" asked Agya Boakye.

"Yes, Paapa," said Joe.

"Akonoba and Akwankwaa were trying to destroy you and your business with juju," said Bretuo.

Joe was beginning to smile as Bretuo told him what was going on in town. He explained to him just as the messenger had said.

"This confirms what I told you, Kwadwo," said Agya Boakye.

"Don't worry, Paapa. Trust me," said Joe. "Whatever they have planned will come back to them as it is happening now."

Darkoaa was so terrified that she told Joe not to go to the shop for a while. She said they needed to pray and fast for God's protection but Joe was not shaken at all. After reassuring his parents and Bretuo that there was no need to panic, he went back to the shop. The news spread around town so quickly that many people came to the shop to ask him what he was going to do about it. He said he only wished to thank God for not allowing their plans to succeed.

During the following days and weeks, people were waiting to see if something evil would happen to Joe, but after many months had gone by without anything happening to him, most people of the town believed that God was with him. Meanwhile, the two disgraced elderly shop-owners had shut their shops completely. People began to talk about them as using voodoo to operate their shops over the years and so stopped buying from them, which led to the closures. They and their family members were disgraced, many of their friends disassociated themselves from them and Akonoba had since gone to live in his village, while Akwankwaa hardly came out of his house.

To tell the whole town that he was under God's protection, Joe wrote boldly in front of the shop, KEPT BY THE POWER OF GOD and COME WHAT MAY underneath it. Some people started calling him, 'Kept by the power of God' while others called him, 'Come what may,' 'The Miracle Man,' etc. and he always smiled back, giving glory to God.

People were patronising his shop even more than before the incident, giving him more money to complete his house. Alice, who had been trying for so long to win Joe's love without success was contemplating black magic, but when the men's attempt failed and the news kept spreading, she also had a change of mind. She never approached Joe again with her inviting eyes, tempting gestures and hints.

CHAPTER SIX

KWAKU IS CAUGHT IN THE ACT

On the day that Amfo finished painting the house, Joe took his parents there to see it. They were impressed, and thanked Amfo for everything that Joe told them he had done. They knew them to be very good friends but not to the extent that Amfo could handle such a project from start to finish without any complaints from Joe. By that time, the marriage plans with Evelyn, the young woman his parents in collaboration with the District Pastor had found for him, was at advanced stage. Joe told his parents that he would move into his house on their wedding day. In the meantime, he begged them not to go telling people about it because he wanted to surprise everyone.

Evelyn was a twin and two years younger than Joe. A committed Christian, she was a chorus leader at the Odumase branch of the church and her twin sister, Bevelyn was a Sunday School teacher. They both played the tambourine very well. Their parents were not as serious with church activities as the girls, although they did attend the Presbyterian Church. When Joe went to tell Auntie Cornie that he was getting married to Evelyn, she was very upset and expressed her disappointment. Joe didn't tell her anything during the arrangements because he didn't want any interference from her.

"What can you get from that girl, Joe? Her parents are common farmers, they have got nothing to offer you," she said.

"Well, that's what I've decided. She is the one I want to marry," said Joe.

"What am I going to tell Mrs. Addo, Joe?"

"Just tell them the truth. As a matter of fact, I am going to send them an invitation if they could make time to attend the wedding," Joe said to her confused aunt.

Auntie Cornie had been working things out behind the scenes with Mrs. Addo in the hope that Joe would one day give in to her plans to marry Belinda, so the introduction of Evelyn into the picture came as a big shock. She did not like the idea of Joe marrying Evelyn whom she referred to as a village girl, but what she felt was not going to change anything. She and Brago were of the feeling that Joe should have married someone of some high social standing, not a village girl like Evelyn.

But what they failed to realise was that Evelyn wasn't a village girl, she had attended secondary school in Takoradi, the harbour city. After leaving school, when it became difficult for her to get a job in Takoradi, one of her uncles got her a position at the Local Council at Diasempa and that was why she had come to live with her parents at home. She was well educated and had good manners. Beautiful and modest, Evelyn was known in Diasempa as someone who lived according to her beliefs, a perfect match for Joe, so whatever his aunt or anyone else said about her was irrelevant to him.

At that time Brago's business had started nose-diving because of Yaw Donkor. Everyone in the family knew that Brago was having problems financially, but nobody could talk to her about it. After the breakdown of her previous marriage, Brago had been in and out of relationships with no intention of marrying again until she met Donkor, a widower with two grown-up children, who promised to marry her. Jude, her son, was about three years old when Brago separated from his father.

Donkor owned a lorry and drove it himself, transporting foodstuff from villages to the city. It was in his business that he met Brago

144

and started dating her. Some four months into their relationship, Donkor's lorry was involved in an accident. He used all the money he had to carry out repairs on it, but the more work he did on it the more faults were found. When he ran out of money completely, he borrowed some from Brago and said he would pay her as soon as the lorry was back on the road.

Brago trusted her man and gave him money time and again until her own capital was exhausted and she started trading with her savings. When things did not work out as Donkor had expected, he started distancing himself from Brago. It was when she asked him to find her some cash to save her business from total collapse that she became suspicious that the guy was up to something funny.

Brago could not discuss it with anybody, nor could she go back to Joe for more money. Eventually, she managed to track Donkor down at his home town and demanded her money from him in a manner that did not go down well with Donkor. Brago tried using her Company C attitude but Donkor would not take any of that.

"I don't know why you've been avoiding me, but if it's because of the money, then that's why I'm here. I need the money now," said Brago with a frown.

"How do you expect me to get money for you when the lorry is still at the workshop? From where can I get the money? You just have to wait till it is back on the road, and I will sort you out," said Donkor.

"I don't care how or where you would get it from. I need to run my business, so I need it, and I need it today. I mean now," Brago demanded.

"Brago, I don't have any money to give to you today, that's the bottomline. You still have to wait till I get the lorry back on the road," said Donkor.

"I'm not going anywhere until you give me the money."

"From where? How?"

"I don't know. All I want is my money."

"OK. You may search the room, if you get enough to make up what I owe you, take it and go. I can't take this attitude of yours any longer."

"You can't take my attitude but you could take my money; is that what you mean?" asked Brago.

They argued over the issue until Brago got very angry and left for Diasempa. After this, she stopped going to him for a while, thinking he would eventually send her the money or some of it, at least. Then one afternoon she met someone from Nkwanta, Donkor's town, who told her that he was dating another woman in his neighbourhood. This information hit Brago like a tornado.

The man she had spent all her business money on was cheating on her, and possibly going to dump her for this other woman. No way! The Company C aggressive nature bubbled up in her. She thought of what to do to this man to get her money back. Their relationship had become a secondary matter to her now. All she wanted was her money.

Company C was not as active as it used to be a few years back. Some of the members were married or had left town but the leader and two other members were in Diasempa, so Brago went to talk to them about Donkor and the money. At the meeting, it was decided that Brago should question Donkor about this other woman. If he denies the allegation, she was to continue moving with him cautiously, for the sake of the money or until the lorry was back on the road because that way she could get her money back. All the same, they were going to investigate and if it was found to be true, Company C would storm the said lady's house to warn her to stay away from Donkor. If she failed to back off, then they would show her that she was trespassing because Donkor was Brago's man.

One of them, Asantewaa, knew a lot of people in Nkwanta, so she took it upon herself to investigate and in less than two days she got all the information they needed. Donkor was really going out with another woman by name Odaamea. They went to Odaamea's house to scare her into believing that if she valued her life she should stay away from Donkor. Odaamea had heard of Company C and what they were capable of, so she quietly pulled away from Donkor. After that Donkor himself was warned that if he did not want any trouble, he should refund Brago's money to her before a given date. With these threats, Brago managed to get some of the money, enough to keep her going with her business, although on a very low scale.

Brago then broke up with Donkor, having caused him a lot of headaches. She made it clear to him that no one used a Company C lady for free, let alone make her bankrupt, without paying dearly. The history of Donkor's relationship with Brago, before and after the break-up would make a whole book. She made life hell for him as she could not get back to full business. For some time Donkor was scared of going to Diasempa and Brago too could not go to the villages to buy anything. She bought them from other retailers in Diasempa before taking them to Tafo or Koforidua.

Meanwhile, Joe was being assisted by Amfo and some family and church members for the preparations towards the engagement and wedding. On their last day of counselling at the mission house, both the Pastor and Evelyn were astonished when Joe showed them pictures of his house.

"After we've been joined together, we would go to our own home," said Joe.

Evelyn gave a sigh of relief, apparently indicating that she dreaded going to live in the family home with her in-laws, especially Brago, known in Diasempa as a hard lady.

"I'm so impressed, Joe," said the Pastor, still examining the pictures.

"From my childhood, I have always thought that it is better for a man not to stay in his family house when he marries. If I had not been able to finish my own, I would have rented a place, rather than live with my family," said Joe.

"It's a good thing to do, so that you can live in peace as a couple," said the Pastor.

"Yes, but please do not tell anyone about it for now," Joe said to both Evelyn and the Pastor.

It was a Thursday and the engagement was to take place on Saturday morning followed by the wedding in the afternoon of the same day. At that time it was known by a lot of people in Diasempa that Joe was going to marry Evelyn. At home that evening, Joe told his parents that he had made Evelyn aware of the house.

"It's a good thing you have kept it till this time," said Agya Boakye. "It would make your wife respect you more as a husband, capable of dealing with situations in a responsible way."

"Thanks, Paapa. That's the way I wanted it."

"Like we've been telling you always, try not to hide any of your plans from her, now that you are going to live as a couple," said Darkoaa.

"And do not allow anyone to interfere with the plans you make with your wife, especially your aunt, Cornie," said Agya Boakye.

At the mention of Cornie, Darkoaa looked at her husband without making any further comment. Joe could have made both the engagement and wedding big because he had the means, but together with Evelyn, they decided to keep it simple. It was, however, considered one of the best and well organized weddings in the town. Nearly everyone who was invited turned up, including those who had only just heard that the successful young shop owner was getting married. Some had come only to see who the lucky woman was and to wish her all the best for married life.

There were two branches of The Church of Pentecost in Diasempa at that time, Central and the Odumase branches. Joe worshipped at Central and Evelyn, Odumase, where the wedding took place. The building could not contain the congregation so a lot of people had to listen to what was going on from loud speakers which had been placed outside. Among them were those ladies who had tried to win

Joe's love but failed. Alice was biting her upper lips as the Pastor blessed the marriage, wishing she was Evelyn.

When Joe bought the plot, it was a farming area but it had become part of the town due to rapid developments by Diasemparians who had moved to the cities and abroad. People whose houses were around the area had believed it when Amfo told them that the house belonged to one of his friends abroad. Everyone in Diasempa knew somebody of the sort so when they tried to find out who this friend was Amfo told them that his friend did not want anyone to know his identity at least for that time.

Many times during the construction, Amfo had gone to Joe's shop when other costumers were around with a list of items and pretended to buy materials like other customers. When they met in town, they talked like any normal friends would do, but deep down a lot was going on between them.

When the convoy left the church to follow the car carrying the bride and the groom, they wondered where exactly they were heading after passing the route that led to Joe's family house. Amfo, leading a group of selected family members and friends, left the church early to make sure everything was in place before the convoy arrived.

The large space in front of the house had been cleared of every twig that could cause someone to stumble, and tables and chairs had been well arranged for an ample reception. On arrival, everyone was asking whose house it was and some were of the opinion that Joe might have rented it for the occasion. After everyone was seated and food was about to be served, Joe made his first ever long speech to such a large audience.

"Most of you here today are very much aware of my background, that my family was one of the poorest in Diasempa. My parents had no money at all and so on many occasions during my early days at the Anglican Primary School, I was sent home because they could not pay my fees."

Agya Boakye, sitting by his elegantly dressed wife, Darkoaa, was nodding his head as his son reminded him of the past gloomy days. Life was hard indeed in those days for the couple and Agya Boakye had to go and borrow money sometimes to keep his children in school.

"Many times my sister and I went to bed hungry, it was very hard but I was determined to make it with the help of God," Joe continued. "Sometimes in my tattered uniform, I hurried up to school just to find the others laughing and making fun of me. But I managed to make it through hard work, and most of my mates are here now to testify to this fact."

His speech seemed to be touching the hearts of the gathering so most of them were silent but one young man who had been in the same class with Joe years ago stood up and shouted,

"Joe, you were the best in every subject!"

Joe turned to the direction of the young man and smiled.

"Yes, that is Kwame George, one of my classmates in Form Five," he said, still smiling. "Someone may ask, 'How did you get to where you are today?' I began teaching some of my fellow students for a fee to top up my pocket money when I started Sixth Form in Miawani. At one time I was teaching two full classes of eighteen and twenty students on Saturdays and Sundays respectively, and that was when money started coming into my hands. I managed the money well and decided to start my shop after Upper Six. I would like you all to thank my friend Amfo for me, because it was he who tipped me off about the land we are standing on and helped me to buy it. He also helped to put up this building for me, making the best use of the resources I could afford to spend on it."

At this revelation those who thought he had rented the place for the reception were all silent. Those whose houses were around the area and had constantly questioned Amfo about the ownership of the building praised Amfo as a faithful and trusted friend. Everyone was amazed that Joe had been able to build such a house. He went on to tell them that if you were endowed with some God-given talents you must make good use of them to your advantage and that of others.

"Now, on behalf of my beautiful wife, Evelyn, and my family, I will like to once again thank everyone here, and most especially those of you who contributed in various ways to make this occasion a success. Thank you all and may God bless you."

Belinda was there with her family and so were Auntie Cornie and all those that she tried to work through to make Joe wait for Belinda. Pretending to be in support of the marriage, Auntie Cornie went to hug Evelyn who was chatting with Bevelyn, her twin sister.

"If any member of our family tries to give you trouble, let me know to sort them out. I brought Joe up so he is more attached to me even than his biological parents," said Auntie Cornie.

"Joe tells me that," Evelyn said with a smile.

"May God bless your marriage and give you wonderful children," said Auntie Cornie.

"Thank you very much, Auntie," said Evelyn.

Cornie left Evelyn and her sister to join the crowd. At the end of the celebration only five people were left with the couple, namely, Amfo, Joe's friends - Bismark and Bob - the best man and the bridesmaid. Joe had requested that they spend the night with them. The reason why Joe asked them to stay was that he was going to organise a half-night prayer meeting with them to commit their marriage and the house into the hands of God. Normally, on the first night of every couple being joined together, most people think they should be left alone to enjoy themselves, but Joe had a different agenda.

For a very long time, Joe had never done anything without first seeking the face of God and the directions he had had from Him were always the best; so this life-long journey deserved the same approach.

Joe had personally worked things out with Bismark to lead Bob to the Lord about five years earlier and the latter had become a firebrand when it came to prayers, just like his mentor. Bismark had become an Elder in the church at that time. Amfo was also very prayerful and these were the people that Joe wanted to help him and his wife on their first night. They prayed for a very long time, thanking God and asking him to protect their marriage and the house from every kind of harm.

At about midnight when they brought the service to a close, Bismark and Bob shared one room close to the living room, the best man and Amfo shared a room and the bridesmaid used a separate room. The couple finally went to share their first night together as man and wife in the master bedroom.

They did not sleep much actually, because Joe had a lot to tell Evelyn about himself. Evelyn did not talk much, she was a good listener and when she had something to say she said it lovingly. Her words were well seasoned and Joe was grateful for her contributions. Joe told her his likes and dislikes and Evelyn did the same, telling him of her school days in Takoradi, friends and so on.

The shop was closed for a week for them to get used to each other and enjoy the peace of their new home. Joe had not been going to the house openly during its building stages so now that he was living in it, he saw a few things that he wanted to be done differently. He wanted some flowers at certain places in addition to what Amfo had planted already, a hen coop under the mango tree and other things. They visited family and friends during that week, getting to know each family member well.

Occasionally, they went to the shop to pick something or just to have a look around. Evelyn never went to the shop to see Joe while they were courting because she did not want people to suspect that they were in a casual relationship. They spent most of their time at home arranging and rearranging things, a habit they both enjoyed. Neither of them left anything where it should not be and expected the other to sort it out.

Another habit that was to help them a lot was the study of the Bible and prayers. Both of them had been very good at Bible Knowledge in school so it was easy for them to blend. Sometimes they chose a particular book in the Bible to study for a month, then each of them would set a number of questions for the other to answer.

Some six months into their marriage they decided that Evelyn should resign from her job to join Joe in running the shop. They had arrived at this decision because most of the time when Joe had to go to the city for business or make any trip, the shop had to be closed. If he had to spend all day on such trips, it meant the shop had to be closed that day. Secondly, he wanted Evelyn to know everything about his business, to introduce her to his business partners, customers, etc. In fact, he wanted the shop to move on whether he was there or not, and there was no other person to take that responsibility better than his better half.

Not very far from Bosompra, the area designated for the guiding spirits and ancestors of the town of Diasempa, lived Hagar, a young girl of fourteen years. She had dropped out of school due to some harsh circumstances after her father's death and wanted to learn sewing, but she could not afford the enrolment fee or a sewing machine. She therefore decided to sell iced water to raise some money for that purpose. But selling iced water also required some capital and to get this capital, Hagar decided to go into the *aworom* business.

Aworom, a kind of broad leaves in the bush, was used in wrapping most things sold in the market. There were particular places where the leaf survived and so one had to go searching for them, but where they grew, they did so in abundance.

Hagar joined girls much older than herself who were already in the *aworom* business and started saving the pesewas to buy the wares she needed for the iced water business. Upon her mother's advice, instead of waiting till her savings became a lump sum, Hagar started buying the items one at a time. Maame Nkansaa's advice to her daughter was based on the fact that whenever Hagar brought home some money there was always something they needed to buy, salt, soap, cream, etc, so she could hardly save the money she was making from *aworom*. But with determination, she was able to buy all that she required in less than four months.

Hagar was very happy on the day she bought the last item, a rectangular, grey tray measuring about sixteen inches by twelve. She chose the grey colour to match her cups and washing basin. But then, there was another hurdle to be jumped, which is where to sell the iced water. Some people sold theirs at specific areas and in front of shops. They had tables and chairs so people came to buy from them, but you needed permission from these shop owners to sell in front of their shops.

It was during this time that Hagar became friendly with Afrakoma. They lived in the same neighbourhood but they were not friends. The girls knew each other but they only greeted one another when they met face to face. Afrakoma was selling oranges and cooked eggs in front of the shop next to Joe's, so Hagar approached her to have a word with the shop owner if he would allow her to put a small table next to hers to sell iced water.

"I don't think it would be a problem at all, but let me speak with him first thing tomorrow morning," said Afrakoma.

"Okay. I will come back tomorrow evening to hear what he says," Hagar said and thanked Afrakoma.

Hagar went back home to tell her mother what Afrakoma had said and they concluded that should the man refuse to allow her sell in front of his shop, she could always carry her iced water around the station and people would still buy it. But Hagar was praying that Afrakoma would come back with some positive response. The next morning, as soon as the shop owner came in, Afrakoma asked him if it was okay for her friend to come and sell iced water next to her table.

"So long as the place is kept clean and tidy, I don't have a problem," said the man.

"Thank you very much," said Afrakoma. "I will come and introduce her to you tomorrow."

"Okay."

Hagar had been brought up in the fear of the Lord and her mother had shown her that cleanliness is next to godliness, so from a very young age she had always made sure that her environment was as tidy as it should be. When she went to see Afrakoma again and was told what the man had said, Hagar returned home to her mother with smiles. She was confident that her attitude towards cleanliness was second to none. So was it that in a matter of days, Hagar started selling iced water very close to Joe's shop. Each morning, she went to buy ice block from the manufacturers about five minutes' walk from the station and carried it to her table.

She knew the other girls who were already doing petty business there. These girls were handling money everyday and so could buy whatever they wanted and whenever they wanted, but Hagar's case was different so she kept to herself most of the time. She had gone into this business with a target in mind. It is natural for people who have no one to help them to be more focused than those who have everything going for them. Hagar's father had always worked hard to look after his family so now that he was no more, she had to face the future all by herself, and she wasn't going to take any chances.

When Hagar joined the other girls at the station, most of the shop owners in the area, including Joe and his wife, could tell that someone new was there. At first, they thought she was behaving that way because she was new, but when after two months they still saw her as someone with a unique character, they concluded that she had come from a very good home. Hagar was very respectful, humble and always ready and willing to help anyone who needed her help.

Once one of the girls spoke rudely to Hagar in the hearing of all but Hagar just turned and walked away from her. That day, Joe said to Evelyn that if Hagar had been any other girl, she might have responded in like manner. Evelyn in turn said the incident reminded her of when she was in her first year at secondary school when another girl had wanted to pick up a fight with her for accidentally stepping on her shoe.

"I just looked at her, said sorry and walked away to join another group," said Evelyn.

"It's always good to walk away from trouble, if you can," said Joe. "I just can't understand why the other girls are so rude to each other and do not behave the way that new girl does."

"Well, everybody is different, you know," said Evelyn.

The couple saw Hagar's humility and modesty and wished that in future their children would become like her. By the time they celebrated their first anniversary, both Joe and Evelyn were looking very well, they had gained some weight. Generally, everything was moving on fine, but they had some thorns in their flesh. They had observed that Auntie Cornie and Brago were not in favour of the marriage. Joe tried every means to get them to accept his wife, but they wouldn't.

Joe decided to try another strategy to see if Auntie Cornie would open up to Evelyn by sending her to Kumasi occasionally to give her money and other presents. Many times, Evelyn herself bought presents for her and her son, Kwaku, thinking it would make her change her attitude towards her, but nothing worked.

Once when Evelyn took to her some clothes that she bought for her, Auntie Cornie told her that she had been served a notice to be made redundant in the following three months. This was a great worry to her because she had not been able to complete the two bedrooms and a large living room which she started building some years earlier in Diasempa. From her estimation, her redundancy benefits would not be enough to complete it, so she would have to come and stay in the family house.

Evelyn saw this as an opportunity, because some few months earlier Joe had discussed with her his intention to help Cornie complete the building, if she changed her attitude towards their marriage. Evelyn knew that her husband would not promise anything that he could not or would not do, so even though his aunt had not changed one bit, Evelyn was sure of Joe helping her if she was retrenched.

Evelyn told Cornie not to worry and that whatever level she could build up to with her redundancy benefit, she would speak to Joe so that together, they would support her to complete it. She emphasised on the word *together* to let Cornie know that it was not just Joe who was going to help her but she would also contribute to make her dream come true. Cornie's face suddenly changed when Evelyn said those words.

"Are you sure of what you are saying, Evelyn?"

"I trust Joe will agree to help you because I am personally going to play a part,"

"Thank you very much, Evelyn. Your words have lightened the burden on my mind. Now I can sleep in peace, perfect peace. Thank you. But promise me that you will not tell any member of our family about this," said Cornie.

"Why should I do that, Auntie?" asked Evelyn.

"You know some of our people are difficult and talk too much, that's why I don't want..."

"Don't worry about that, Auntie."

Evelyn assured her that no one would know about it and on her way back to Diasempa, she was happy that at last Auntie Cornie would change her attitude towards her. She knew how influential Cornie had been in the affairs of her husband. Even though Joe was trying to distance himself from Cornie, on several occasions she found a way of making him do as she suggested.

When Evelyn informed her husband about the discussion she had had with his aunt, Joe said it was fine because that would bring a change in her actions. He said he would provide the money and materials but would prefer that Evelyn dealt with her, in order to build a cordial relationship between them.

Auntie Cornie's son, Kwaku, was in his third year in secondary school and with his mother's retrenchment pending, he decided that if he was able to complete Form Four, he would look for a job to support her. Joe had been helping with his fees and other things, but Kwaku knew that if his mother became redundant it would be difficult to go beyond Form Four.

His father was married to another woman who was tougher than Cornie and so Kwaku had never bothered to go and ask him for any assistance since he started secondary school. His father did not care about him either, because of the way Cornie had treated him. Kwaku was in correspondence with Joe and Evelyn and when he expressed his fears about his education to them, they assured him that if he wanted to go further, they would support him.

Evelyn and Joe had all these good intentions, not only for Cornie and her son, but also the entire family. Unfortunately, however, Evelyn's inability to conceive was becoming the talk of the town, especially among their own relatives. She had earlier lied to some of her relatives when they questioned her after the first year that they had decided to wait awhile. Some of her own relatives, her mother, in particular, suspected that Joe was impotent. Cornie and Brago, among other members of Joe's family blamed it on Evelyn, suspecting that she was infertile. Bevelyn, Evelyn's twin sister, had also married Amponsah Kakabo, a man from the town one year after she and Joe had got married.

Evelyn's father wasn't very well before they married and the sickness got worse every day. Joe took it upon himself to look after his father-in-law financially and in other ways, taking him from one doctor to the other and so on, but death did not let go of its grip on the man. Two years into their marriage when the couple's childlessness had become big news on the lips of most people in Diasempa, Evelyn's father passed away. Their father's funeral was organised so well that people talked about it for a long time.

Joe and Evelyn footed all the expenses and told the family on the final day of the funeral rites that if there was any more debts to be paid, they should not hesitate to let them know, referring to himself and Evelyn. During the funeral, he had actually handed cash to most of the family members to do what he felt needed doing. With regards to Kakabo, Bevelyn's husband, Joe gave him a lot of money and told him to use it to play his part as a son-in-law.

Joe knew Kakabo's financial situation and didn't want their mother-in-law to think that he did not do much to help. Kakabo was very appreciative to Joe because when the death occurred he lamented to his wife that people may compare what he would do to Joe's. Joe had anticipated this scenario and acted wisely. Sometimes he gave money to the family and said it was from himself and Bevelyn's husband. The two were on very good terms and acted like brothers, making life easy for the sisters also, but because of their situation their own people were making life hard for Joe and Evelyn.

When Auntie Cornie finally came to settle in Diasempa after her redundancy, as promised, Joe and his wife wasted no time in helping her to complete her house. Sadly, soon after that, she started talking to Joe about taking a second wife so as to have children because she suspected that Evelyn would not be able to bear him any. Joe did not take her seriously at first and brushed it off, but Cornie kept whispering into his ears to get rid of Evelyn.

Around that time, there was a pretty lady in her late twenties in Diasempa called Serwaa. She used to work as a secretary to a businessman in Accra and was flirting with her boss, a married man. Serwaa was a very insatiable lady who capitalised on her beauty to lure every man she came into contact with. While having an affair with her boss, she was secretly dating one of her boss's friends, also a married man. When this other man's wife got a hint of the relationship through one of their staff, she acted like a wounded lion.

The informant had monitored Serwaa for a long time and so told the woman of her affairs with her boss too. The woman went to fight with Serwaa in the office which led to the revelation of other secrets. She lost her job as a result and had come back to Diasempa to stay while she looked for another job. Nobody knew about this in Diasempa, although it was big news around that part of Abeka Lapaz where she used to work.

Serwaa lied to everyone in Diasempa that she was made redundant. She was introduced to Cornie by another friend at a party and they became friends too. Cornie always talked about how redundancy had affected her life and kept assuring Serwaa that with her age, she had a better chance of securing another job. She considered Cornie as a big sister and most of the time discussed issues with her and asked for her advice.

Kwaku came to Diasempa on vacation and decided not to go back to school for no apparent reason. Evelyn and Joe spoke to him on separate occasions, assuring him of their support but Kwaku just did not want to stay on at school. Food wasn't a problem in Diasempa at all, but money was, because there was not much opportunity to find a job, apart from farming.

One day Evelyn met Kwaku with a certain group of lads who were in the habit of smoking and drinking so she read between the lines that he could be influenced by them. She therefore spoke to Joe that in order to get him off the street and away from the company of those boys, they should let him come and help in the shop, since he had decided not to go back to school.

"The shop is getting busier everyday and it's apparent that very soon we might need someone to help us, so instead of employing someone from outside, I will suggest that we take Kwaku," said Evelyn.

"His mother is very domineering and so I don't want to involve him in this business. She could use him as a decoy to disturb us," said Joe.

"You know her too well this time so I think we can deal with that aspect. From what Kwaku would be paid he could also support his mother. Who knows, that may give us some breathing space," said Evelyn.

Joe agreed with his wife and two days later invited Kwaku, Auntie Cornie and his own parents to his house to tell them that they wanted to employ Kwaku in the shop. During the meeting, they all advised Kwaku to behave well because whatever he did while he worked in the shop could open other avenues for him and other members of the family

"Since you are going to be in the shop with Evelyn more often than Kwadwo, I will suggest that you consult her before you do anything there. Also, beware of your friends. Do not entertain them in the shop at all because they could give you trouble," Agya Boakye advised.

"I will personally like to thank Evelyn," said Darkoaa, "because some women would not allow their husbands' people to know about their business, let alone employ them."

"In fact, it was Evelyn who suggested this to me. She said he saw you with some boys that could be of bad influence and that was when she started talking to me about getting you away from their company," Joe was addressing Kwaku.

"And the only way we can do that is to keep you occupied," Evelyn added.

"Thank you very much, Evelyn, because like Maame Darkoaa said, it's not every wife who would do what you have done," said Auntie Cornie rubbing her palms together and fiddling with her knuckles.

"I also thank you for thinking about me and giving me something to do," said Kwaku. "I promise to do as I would be told."

Deep down in his heart Kwaku knew it was the best opportunity that could ever come his way as a dropout so he determined to work hard to please both Joe and Evelyn. His mother also saw that as a nice way of getting more money from the couple, and of course

Kwaku. To her, the shop was going to be a gold mine, so long as Kwaku was there.

Two weeks after the meeting, Kwaku started working in the shop and moved in to stay with the couple who already had Jude, Brago's eight-year-old son living with them. Jude had been there for nearly a year before Kwaku joined them. They ate breakfast and dinner at home and were provided money for lunch. Jude was a very rude boy but Evelyn dared not complain because of his mother.

Bevelyn, Evelyn's twin sister, had a child eighteen months after her marriage and this made the pressure from their mother on Evelyn very intense. The contrast between Joe's parents and Evelyn's mother was that Agya Boakye and his wife were devout Christians but Evelyn's mother was like a piece cut from Auntie Cornie. She had not much to do with the things of God. Joe was looking after Evelyn's mother like he would his own, which she enjoyed greatly, but she wanted more than that, a grandchild. Joe had refurbished his in-law's old house to look almost new, but Evelyn's mother kept nagging her that if they were unable to give her a grandchild, whatever they were doing was of little importance to her.

While Joe's parents were praying for them to have a child, Evelyn's mother wanted them to separate. She talked to everyone she met about Evelyn's condition and constantly suggested that she divorce Joe. Some of her friends supported her but others did not agree that divorce was the solution. In Joe's family, his own sister Brago and Auntie Cornie were putting pressure on him either to take a second wife or divorce Evelyn and marry another woman. Initially, these two had tried to stop the marriage but Joe had not given in to their suggestions that Evelyn was a poor village girl who had nothing to offer him, and now they were capitalising on her condition to prove to Joe that she was no good.

At a certain point some people outside the two families were beginning to ask the source of Joe's wealth. He had worked very hard for it, no doubt, spending sleepless nights in preparing notes to teach his students and being faithful to God in tithes. This was the source of his wealth, but it is said that when there is a gap on the anthill every animal can enter it at will. Being unable to have children had created an avenue for speculation. Some people were saying that Joe might have given away his manhood in exchange for money and so could not make his wife pregnant. Others said Evelyn was barren. Even some people from their church who were expected to help them with their prayers were among those greasing the rumour mill.

Once at a night club Kwaku heard some people talking about the couple's condition and felt very bad. These people did not know that the guy whose back was towards their table was Kwaku. He was sad about the comments they were making, but in order not to cause a stir, he just kept silent and listened. He was out with a new girl on their first date and tried not to embarrass her by picking a fight with these gossipers. Kwaku was chatting with the girl but his attention was on the conversation that was going on behind him. His serious girlfriend, Doris, who was known to his mother, would not go to a night club with him because she said only bad girls go to such places.

Doris constantly warned Kwaku to stop 'clubbing', but he didn't listen to her. Kwaku decided not to interrupt these gossipers until one of them, a woman in her early twenties, said Evelyn might have damaged her womb with a series of abortions before they married. This made Kwaku turn around gently to look at their faces, sternly. They all saw him but he said nothing, rather he turned back to face his girl and took a sip from his glass of beer.

If Kwaku had been with his male pals, it would surely have ended in a fight, because whenever he went out with his friends he bought all of them drinks so they did his bidding. He sometimes even dictated who should sit where in the clubs. But this night, he was being gentle to impress this new girl. Of all the five gossipers, it was only one who was visiting and did not know Kwaku. The visitor asked one of them in a whisper why Kwaku had looked at them so sternly. The other four looked at each other and the one sitting next to the visitor said quietly that they would talk about it later.

"Play us some reggae, Mr. DJ," said one of the gossipers, trying to change the conversation.

Kwaku was being well paid and looked after by Joe and his wife so if anyone dared to say something negative about them it was like attacking him personally. Apart from the new girl, another reason why he did not respond to the gossip was that if it resulted in a fight and the matter got to Joe, Kwaku knew that Joe would not be happy with him going to the club. He decided that at a proper time when he met any of the gossipers in town he would confront them about what they said concerning his cousin and his wife. Joe and Evelyn had been trying to persuade Kwaku to attend church with them but, like his mother, he showed no serious interest.

On top of all the money that he earned and the tips from the couple, Kwaku was still not satisfied and stole from the shop every now and then. He was living a very 'fast' life. If his mother had not been greedy, she would have questioned him about the kind of life he was living and all the money she received from him. He was paid only at the end of the month, so his spending was questionable, but Auntie Cornie saw nothing wrong with it.

Evelyn had seen Kwaku pocketing money from the sale of some items a number of times but found it difficult to tell Joe. She feared how Auntie Cornie would react to it if Joe took some action. Once Evelyn caught him red-handed and Kwaku apologised to her after giving the money back to her. He begged Evelyn not to tell Joe about it. Evelyn did not mention it to Joe then, but it was happening so often that she suspected that he could drain their accounts if not checked. So one morning after Kwaku left for the shop Evelyn told her husband about it.

"Joe, I would like to tell you something that is bothering me," said Evelyn

"What is it?" asked Joe.

"It's about Kwaku and the way he's going about things in the shop."

"What is going on that I know not about?"

Evelyn hesitated for a while because she did not know how Joe would take what she was going to tell him. Joe stopped the shoe he was polishing and looked at Evelyn in the eye and asked her again to tell him what the problem was.

"He's been stealing from the shop."

"What?" he asked, as if he did not hear her well.

"Sometimes when he sells item he does not take the money to the till. He puts it into his pocket."

"Why haven't you told me about it, Evelyn? Don't you know he can make us go bankrupt by so doing?

"I know, but you see…"

"No 'buts' in a case like this. What if he …"

"Hold on, Joe, calm down for now and keep an eye on him whenever you are in the shop with him."

Joe was furious that Evelyn had not informed him earlier and vowed to sack Kwaku instantly, if he caught him stealing. Joe gave Evelyn authority to expel him from the shop, if she caught him again.

Kwaku went to his mother one evening to tell her that he wanted to come back to stay with her. Auntie Connie asked her son if he was having any problem with Joe or his wife and Kwaku said everything was okay. Kwaku did not want Joe to see the extravagant life that he was living. He assured his mother that if he came back to live with her, he would be able to look after her better and so Cornie consented to the move. Kwaku just did not want to be supervised by the couple.

But young Hagar, although not being supervised by anyone in particular, was doing all she could to keep the place where she traded as clean as possible. Most of the time, when she arrived early and there was any mess in the area, Hagar swept it before setting up for the day. One day when she was sweeping in front of Joe's shop she was questioned by one of the girls called Dufie.

165

"Why do you bother to sweep the front of other people's shop?" Dufie asked.

"What's wrong with that?" Hagar asked back without looking at her as she continued to sweep.

"How much do they give you for doing that?"

"No one gives me anything. I just can't operate in the dirt. I hate the sight of filth and that's why I always want to clean here."

Dufie was joined by another girl who thought it was useless doing such a thing for the rich couple. Laughing, the other girl also asked Hagar if Joe and Evelyn had been giving her some of their wealth to do that job for them. The couple did not even know that it was Hagar who had been cleaning there most of the time. It was the responsibility of the Local Council and so they had no idea whether someone else was doing it sometimes.

A few days after telling his mother about the move, Kwaku told Joe he wanted to go back to his mother's house. His reason was that if he stayed with them and they continued providing for him like they were doing, he would never grow. Knowing how his mother reacts and her attitude regarding Evelyn and their marriage, Joe did not want a situation where Cornie and some family members would think that it was his wife's fault that Kwaku was moving out of their house, so he tried to dissuade him from moving. But Kwaku told him he had already informed his mother and she said it was okay so if Joe would let him, he would like to move out the coming weekend. Joe then said if his mother was okay with the move, he had no problem with it either.

Joe decided to find out from Auntie Cornie that evening and she confirmed that if Kwaku did not start managing his own life from that time it would be difficult for him in future. Evelyn was not happy with the move because, as Joe had anticipated, she felt people might blame it on her. She also tried to persuade Kwaku to stay, but he had already made up his mind and had his mother's approval. He moved out the following weekend.

It was a very worrying period for Evelyn because she did not know what her in-laws would think about her, considering her condition and the state of their marriage. From that time whenever she was with Kwaku in the shop she tried to talk to him to come back and stay with them but he said he was fine at his mother's place.

In Accra, Kate, one of Evelyn's class mates, was looking into an album on the sofa with her husband when they came across an old school picture. She started calling names and putting her finger on their faces until she came to Evelyn.

"And that is Evelyn, the quiet one," said Kate. "I hear she is married to a rich man and runs a shop with the husband."

"When did you take this photo," asked her husband.

"It was a day before we wrote our Middle School Leaving Certificate exams. We had gone to view the hall where the exams would take place and on the way back we met John, the photographer, and decided to take a shot."

Her husband was smiling as he looked at this old black and white picture. There was a lad in there that resembled someone known to the husband.

"Who is this guy?" he asked.

"That's Nicholas, a very gentle boy. He loved arts and reading a lot. The guy was always doing something."

"He looks like one of my mates at ABUSCO," said the husband.

Kate had something to say about each individual she pointed at. On Daniel, she said he was the school boy businessman who used to sell key holders and other things during weekends. He was more mature than the other boys.

"Those days are long gone," Kate said as she turned another page.

"Have you seen any of them lately?" asked her husband.

"The last time I saw one of them, Ampem Darko, was about four years ago, at the Kaneshie market."

"There are some of my mates whom I have not seen since we left school," said the husband.

"Me too, that's life, you know. Some people come into your life for a while and disappear, you don't see them again," said Kate.

"That's very true."

They continued to talk about their mates and hoped to see some of them in future. Kate said there was one of her mates who was always late for school and got lashed almost every morning.

"I was once lashed for being late and..."

"Why were you late?" asked Kate.

"I had gone to farm at dawn with my parents to take some fuel wood home before school time," said the husband. "It wasn't the first time I had done that, but on that day I was distracted by a small bird which I thought was a baby learning to fly. It was in the bush by the side of the road so I put my load down to go and catch it."

"Was it indeed a baby bird?" Kate asked and giggled as her husband narrated his ordeal to her.

"No. It was a fully grown bird."

"How did you know that?

"My uncle told me when I described it to him later on. He said that was its nature. Each time I got close to the bird, it jumped onto another branch."

"Why didn't you just let it go its way?" asked Kate.

"The problem was that it never flew far from me so I thought I was eventually going to catch it and before I realised I had followed it deep into the woods."

Kate burst into laughter again as her man was reliving the experience.

"I only gave up on it when I stepped on some sharp thorn and started bleeding. Walking back home with my load and injured foot was not easy."

"Where were your parents?

"They were working on the farm. They always returned after three in the afternoon. It took me a while to get home and prepare for school, late."

"And got lashed," chipped in Kate.

"Yes."

"My mate's case was different," said Kate. "He lived with a couple as a househelp and had to do a lot of chores at home before coming to school but the teachers would not take any of that as an excuse to be late."

"Poor lad," said the husband.

"On top of that, because he worked late into the night, he was caught most of the time dozing during classes and got a few canes for that too."

Kate's husband only shook his head without saying a word while they flicked through the album and considered how fortunate he had been to be raised by his own parents.

When Kwaku used to live with Joe he had his freedom, not like Kate's classmate. Some days Joe allowed him to go ahead to open the shop first before they joined him later. These were his happiest days because if there happened to be any sales before the couple arrived, the money went into his pocket. Not just a part of it, but all the money. It was difficult to detect that something was missing from the shop because there were so many items, unlike the early days when Joe was operating the shop alone and knew where everything was.

Now the shop was so full with goods that Joe was taking stock once every month and Kwaku took advantage of that to pocket the cash from items sold out of the sight of Joe and Evelyn. One morning he went to the shop early and sold one of three painting brushes that arrived the previous day when he was not around. The money, as usual, did not go to the till where it belonged.

"This will do for the evening," Kwaku said and put the money in his pocket.

Moments later, when the couple arrived, Joe went round inspecting the items on display and realised that one of the brushes was missing. He walked to the till to see if the money was in it. When he did not see any money, he asked Kwaku if he had sold anything and he said no. Joe made him aware that when the brushes arrived the day before they were three, so they began searching for the missing one, in case it had dropped somewhere. Even though Kwaku knew the brush was out of the shop and the money was in his pocket, he *helped* Joe to search in vain for it. The look on Joe's face showed he was angry but he said nothing because he did not see him sell it.

While Kwaku was draining the couple's finances in this manner, his mother and Brago were also trying to destroy their marriage. Brago told Cornie that Joe had already made a mistake by marrying an infertile woman and they, being concerned aunt and sister, must find a way to help him get rid of her or take a second, productive wife. Auntie Cornie agreed with Brago, but their worry was that in spite of their childless state, Joe and Evelyn were so much in love and united that it was difficult for anyone to penetrate their relationship.

"I don't think they have heard what people are saying about them," said Brago.

"I'm sure Joe will be thinking of Belinda now," Cornie said.

"Can't we contact her again?" asked Brago.

"No. It's too late now, because I hear she is married."

As they talked, looking for an opportunity to accuse Evelyn or get rid of her, Brago asked Cornie if she was sure that Evelyn had not given Kwaku any cause to make him go back to live with her and Cornie said no. Cornie said she was happy to be living under the same roof with her son, because Kwaku kept her company in the house. But the real reason for her happiness was the money and other things she was receiving from her son.

That evening, before Kwaku went night clubbing, Serwaa visited Cornie and when she was introduced to Kwaku, he was infatuated by her beauty. Kwaku could spend a whole night in the club and when he returned home, his mother would never say a word to reprimand him. At the night club Kwaku discussed his plans about Serwaa with Dan and he told Kwaku to forget about her and stick to Doris. He went home late that night. In fact, it was dawn so he could not get up early the next day. Evelyn and Joe got to the shop before him to see Hagar sweeping the front of their shop.

"Thank you very much, Hagar," said Evelyn.

"It's my pleasure, Madam," said Hagar. "I like to brighten the corner where I am."

"God bless you for such a thoughtful act," said Joe.

As Joe opened the shop, Hagar collected the rubbish she had gathered to put in the rubbish bin a few metres away and went back to her table to get her cups and other things ready to start the day's work. Her mother, Maame Nkansaa, was not very well on that day and could not go to the farm. She therefore had to go and buy *gari* on credit from a petty trader close to their house. Maame Nkansaa asked the woman to give her a hundred Cedis worth of *gari* until Hagar, the breadwinner returned home to pay. She had some left over soup which they were going to use in the evening and she knew Hagar would bring some food home, as she normally did.

In the shop one morning, when there was no customer around, Joe had a chat with his wife about a househelp. Kwaku had been doing a few things to help when he was there, but since he moved back to his mother's, Joe and Evelyn did the things that Jude could not do. It had always been difficult to get someone reliable as a househelp, because even your own people can let you down sometimes.

During their deliberations, Evelyn mentioned Hagar and they decided that Evelyn will talk to her before the close of the day. They saw Hagar as being very respectful and hard-working, even though they did not know anything about her background.

When Evelyn saw Hagar that afternoon washing some of her cups, she told her to come and see her in the shop whenever she had some time. Hagar was not that busy so she wiped her hands and went to see Evelyn almost immediately, thinking Evelyn wanted to send her on an errand.

"You have not been here for that long but I can see the difference you are making in this environment," said Evelyn.

Hagar smiled for this compliment and thanked her.

"How old are you?"

"I'm fourteen years, Madam."

"Okay. Keep up with the way you go about things. You are a good girl."

"Thank you, Madam."

"Are you living with your parents at the moment?"

"I'm living with my mother. My father died about ..."

"Oh, I'm sorry to hear that. Where do you live?"

"Our house is not very far from Bosompra at Oboase, near Obuorho Station."

"Well, I was talking to my husband about you this morning and he said I should ask you if you would like to stop selling here and come to stay with us and help us at home."

Evelyn was at this time looking straight into her eyes. Hagar's smile was no longer visible. Momentarily, she was thinking of what to say in response to this request. She was very much aware of the couple's childless condition and had on a few occasions heard the negative comments that others were making about them. How would life be to live with this couple? The question seemed to be coming out of her mouth.

"We are living with one of my husband's nephews, younger than you, so you can take him as your small brother," said Evelyn.

"I will have to speak to my mother about it, Madam," said Hagar.

"That's fine. Have a word with her about it and let me know what she says tomorrow. I would like to meet her, to explain matters better to her."

"OK, Madam. I will let you know tomorrow."

"Thank you," said Evelyn.

Hagar also thanked her and left the shop. In the meantime, she did not discuss their conversation with any of the girls. She was still wondering what would come out of it. She had always stayed with her parents until her father died and she had never spent a day outside of her mother's life, so she was not very sure that it would be possible for them to live apart, although in the same town. When Hagar told her mother about the request from Evelyn, Maame Nkansaa asked her if the couple were Christians.

"They are very good Christians," said Hagar.

"I don't want you to be led astray after all my efforts to show you the proper way of life."

"They are such a nice couple," Hagar said to her mother, "unfortunately they don't have a child of their own."

"Oh no, that is sad. Such people are very sentitive so one has to be careful in dealing with them."

"She said she would come and see you."

"Why are you the only one among the other hawkers that they want to come and stay with them?"

"I don't know why, Maame," said Hagar. "The only major interaction I've had with them was when they came to see me sweeping the front of their shop some days ago. It's something I have been doing most of the days when I reach there early and the place is in a mess."

"Well, if you like them then you can go and stay with them, so long as I will be seeing you once in a while."

Maame Nkansaa had always said to Hagar that whatever she could do to help others, no matter who it is, she should do it and God will reward her. She kept telling her that whenever she saw someone in need of help and she was in a position to help, she should help them, not considering whether the person was poor, rich, wretched, disabled or mentally infirm, because in life there is always a time when someone needs a helping hand. Throughout the rest of the evening they talked about Joe and Evelyn and Hagar's possible move to their place.

Around that time, The Church of Pentecost which Joe and Evelyn fellowshipped with was the fastest growing church in Diasempa, even though other churches had been in existence long before Pentecost was introduced to the town. The church was planning a fundraising event in aid of a playground for the children in the town. The aim was to keep them away from going to the streets to do things that street children do. When the announcement was made, the couple decided to offer a lot of money towards this project, even though they had no children to benefit from such a facility.

The entire congregation was happy and showed their willingness to raise the funds.

In Diasempa, there was a mentally disturbed man who was found wherever there was a gathering with music, drinks and food. His family had given up on him and so he had become a vagrant, eating whatever he found and sleeping wherever he found comfortable. Whenever there was a gathering, he would be there, begging for food and drink. He wasn't a violent man at all. Sometimes he could chat with other people as any normal person would, except that he looked wretched and often said things that people thought were funny. He went to the stream to wash occasionally and if there happened to be any children around, they made fun of him. He was one of the most popular people in the town, almost everybody knew him.

Historians in Diasempa said he was born that way. He was in his late fifties and was always roaming the streets and whenever he passed by Joe's shop he gave him some money or food.. He was called Yaw, the Akan name for a Thursday-born boy and his surname was Appiah, but from childhood, instead of Yaw Appiah, some people omitted the 'w' in Yaw and the capital 'A' in the surname and replaced them with a small 'a' to join the two names as one, so they called him Yaappiah.

A few people, like Joe, were nice to him and offered him food when he asked them. Whenever he walked by the station, he went to the front of Joe's shop where he was sure of getting something from Joe or his wife. One day when he passed by the shop, Evelyn gave him part of the lunch she had prepared for Joe who had gone to the city and had called to say he would be late in returning. The man was very happy and sat right there in front of the shop to eat. He did not stop blessing Evelyn as he ate.

On this trip, a business partner told Joe he was selling his car to buy a new one and asked if Joe knew anyone who might want to buy it. The car was just four years old and well maintained so it looked almost new. He had not budgeted for it, though, yet when the man told him of the going price, he said he might want to buy it himself.

Joe had learnt to drive and got a licence long before he married because he had plans to buy a car in the future. He therefore asked the man to keep it for him for a few days because he had to discuss it with his wife. Joe controlled the money, but he wouldn't use any of it without his wife's knowledge, especially when it had to do with a property.

When he returned and told Evelyn about the car, they agreed to buy it. The owner said he could not sell it to Joe for the amount he would have sold it to someone he did not know, so he reduced the price by about twenty per cent.

The day Joe brought the light blue Toyota Corolla to Diasempa, it was a huge surprise to all. No one had ever seen him driving and he had never discussed his plans to buy a car with anyone. He taught Evelyn the theory of driving in two weeks and put her behind the steering wheel on the third week. A born teacher, if Joe taught you something you understood it straightaway. He had a way of teaching and explaining a point so that even the slowest person could understand quickly.

So in no time Evelyn was also driving in the town. What Joe liked to do most of the time was to sit in the passenger's seat and allow his wife to drive. One day Evelyn told Joe that she had not seen or heard of any of her women friends driving a car and praised him for giving her that opportunity.

Not long after that, Evelyn met Kate in Accra one afternoon and they resumed the close friendship they had enjoyed at school. Kate had got married two years after secondary school and started having children right away. The youngest of her three children was two years old and when Evelyn told her that she was desperately hoping for just one child, Kate felt sorry for her. They were calling each other almost every day since their first contact and one day Evelyn told Kate the problems she was facing with her in-laws and other people as a result of her inability to conceive. Evelyn was almost in tears when she was speaking and Kate promised to talk to one of their doctor friends on her behalf.

"I've been to a lot of doctors, Kate, but none of them seemed to know what's wrong."

"Don't be so disturbed because there is always a way, where there is a will. I will get in touch with the doctor as soon as I can and get back to you," Kate promised.

"Now I can hardly face my in-laws because of what they are saying about my situation."

Kate could tell that her friend was sobbing as she spoke so she decided to end the call, promising to call her again later on. To add to her problems, Jude was being rude to Evelyn and gave bad reports about her to his mother. Evelyn was trying to train the boy in the washing of plates and other household chores but he took it to be a kind of punishment. He came back from school very late one day and when Evelyn asked him where he had been, he got upset and reported it to his mother the next day. Brago asked Jude what time he had come home from school and knew it was too late, yet she said Evelyn had no right to question her son. She told Jude that if Evelyn knew how to bring up children she should produce her own.

Ayibey, one of Darkoaa's friends, had come looking for her and heard Brago and her son talking about Evelyn so she rebuked Brago for saying such things to Jude.

"If the boy was my child, I would just keep quiet and allow Evelyn to train him for the good of his future," said Ayibey.

"If she presumes she knows what is good for children, she should wait till she gets her own, then she could train them," insisted Brago.

"That's rude, Brago. You shouldn't be talking like that about your sister-in-law to your son."

Jude went out of the house as Ayibey was still talking with his mother, promising to come again and tell her whatever Evelyn did or said to offend him.

"You see, you have given him wings to fly," said Ayibey.

Brago ignored her and went into her room. During their conversation, Brago said to Jude that Evelyn was no use to his uncle so she was looking for an opportunity to dress her down. What Evelyn had said to Jude was that he should wash the dishes they had used for dinner before he went to bed and also to come home straight from school after it had closed for the day. But Brago wanted her son to be like a Company C member that no one could tame.

Because of business, Evelyn was at home with the boy more than Joe and she never complained to him about the boy's behaviour for the fear of his mother. So Joe was not aware of what was going on at home. Evelyn did not want to have any confrontation with Brago so she had to stomach all that the boy was doing. There were certain things in the house that a boy of his age could do and that was what Evelyn had wanted to help him learn properly but the boy and his mother saw it differently.

Evelyn was very careful in her choice of words when instructing the boy to do anything in the house. At a certain point, she didn't want to let him do anything for her, but at the same time she felt that would not help him, and again, her own conscience would not judge her right for neglecting the boy. She kept praying and hoping that one day there might be a change.

As planned, Evelyn and Joe went to see Hagar's mother at their home at Oboase to talk about the move. Hagar had told her mother the day before that they would be coming to see her so she waited for them expectantly. Maame Nkansaa made sure the porch was tidy. From that afternoon, she kept dusting the two wooden stools which the visitors would sit on. She used the corner of her cloth to wipe them again when they arrived and after the pleasantries she opened the floor for talks.

"Hagar has informed me about your request and I have no objection to it," said Maame Nkansaa. "All I ask for is that you treat her well, like your own child."

"We shall treat her well, Maame," Evelyn promised.

"She has been my only companion since my husband died. She was doing well at school but I could not bear to see her being sent home many times for lack of school fees so she had to stop her education at a certain point."

The woman was blinking, trying to conceal the tears welling up in her eyes as she spoke. Joe observed it and turned away his gaze for a moment but Evelyn kept looking at her. Maame Nkansaa turned to look at her daughter and said in some sort of vibrating voice;

"She is my only friend and comforter now."

"Is she your only child?" asked Joe.

"No, I have an older son who is in Accra, but life is not treating him well, either."

"Don't worry because there could be a change very soon," said Joe.

"I see Hagar as a wonderful girl with a bright future, and like my husband said, it is my prayer that God would soon bring a change to your circumstances," said Evelyn.

With many words of encouragement and comfort, they assured the woman to trust them with the welfare of her daughter.

"Please let us know when you are ready and we will come to pick you up," Joe said.

"I will tell you tomorrow when I come to town," said Hagar.

Before they left, Joe had given the woman some money and simply said he had been in a similar situation before and knew how it felt like to be sent home from school for fees. However, he felt it was wise not to talk much about his own past at this time. He knew how his parents, especially his mother, had felt in those days. But God had turned things around for him so he was hopeful that He could do the same in Hagar's case.

On the way back home, they passed by Joe's parents' and while

Evelyn and her mother-in-law talked Joe called his father aside and informed him about Kwaku stealing from the shop. Knowing the way women talk, he had chosen to discuss it with his father to seek his advice.

Agya Boakye told him to be vigilant till he caught him red-handed one day. Joe said he wanted to give him some money and send him away from the shop but his father suggested that he should wait till he was caught in the act and then the circumstances would determine the action to take. A few weeks later when they were eating, Agya Boakye hinted to his wife what Joe had told him about Kwaku, and Darkoaa said she had also heard how Kwaku spent so much money on friends.

The kind of people Kwaku associated with were those that he knew had no link whatsoever with any member of his family or Evelyn's. But the fact that they lived in the same town should have made it clear to him that someone, somewhere would realise what he was doing and speak to somebody about it. Many times when he met someone new and was introducing himself he would say he was the cousin of the guy who owned the biggest shop by the station and worked with him.

The only person who usually questioned him about his spending and how he came by so much money was Doris, his girlfriend. She had often told Kwaku not to do anything that could tarnish his reputation in Diasempa, because she suspected that he was not spending from his wages. One day she spoke to him seriously about it and Kwaku stopped giving her money as often as he used to do from that day. He kept from Doris how he got the extra cash, and pretended to be spending within his means.

When Kwaku used to live with Joe, Evelyn had treated him just the way she treated her husband in the hope that his mother would consider that and accept her into the family fold, but Cornie and Brago just wanted Evelyn out of Joe's life. Once, in a crowded area in town, Evelyn spotted Brago and said hello to her but she ignored her. Thinking that Brago did not hear her, Evelyn walked close to her and attracted her attention.

"How are you, Sister Brago?"

"Who is your sister? Am I one of your mother's children?" Brago asked with a frown as she walked away.

Those who did not know the relationship between them wondered why Brago behaved in that manner. Someone said even if they had had a fight in the past, the fact that Evelyn has managed to approach her should have settled everything, and that Brago should not have acted the way she did. As people looked at Evelyn, she felt so embarrassed that she bowed her head and walked in the opposite direction. Brago then went to tell Auntie Cornie that she had snubbed that good-for-nothing girl in town. The two vowed to make life so unbearable for Evelyn that she would walk out of the matrimonial home herself.

That evening, when Evelyn narrated the incident to Joe, he reassured her and told her not to worry so much. He told her that everyone in Diasempa knew Brago as being arrogant and disrespectful. Joe had every right to confront his sister about her action towards his wife in public, but he kept his peace. Besides, Evelyn said she did not want him to have any problem with his sister, for the sake of their marriage. Joe and Evelyn valued their marriage so much so that, for the sake of it, even though people were threatening their happiness, they refrained from hitting back.

They were supposed to go for Hagar the next day, so to get their minds off Brago's behaviour, they decided to put the room where she would be staying in order. While they were preparing the room for her, Hagar's mother was also preparing her daughter's mind for the turning point in her life.

"Don't ever give them any cause to complain. Take his nephew as your younger brother, and be humble and respectful to all as you have always been."

"I'll try my best, Maame," Hagar promised.

Mother and daughter hugged as they cried on each other's shoulder for the separation that was to come. When you have lived with your parents all your life and suddenly circumstances force you to leave them, emotions always come into play. In the case of Maame Nkansaa, she saw Hagar as a friend and comforter. Her husband was dead, her son was also struggling in the city and now the only one left with whom she shared ideas was going away. Her breadwinner was going to leave her alone. Though she was crying, Maame Nkansaa continued to advise her daughter.

"Do all you can to make your stay with them something that would make me proud," said Maame Nkansaa.

"I will, Maame."

"Don't take any of your friends to the house but, if at some point you have to, make sure your master and his wife are aware of it first."

Hagar was nodding and imbibing in all that her mother was saying to her.

"If brother Kofi comes let him know where I am," said Hagar.

"I will tell him whenever he comes home again. I don't know when that will be, any way."

Hagar went round the few friends she had to tell them that they would not be seeing her around so often because she was going to stay with the couple who own that big shop at the station. On their way back from the shop that evening, the couple went to pick Hagar to their home. They took Maame Nkansaa with them to know where her daughter was going to begin her new life. After chatting for a while in the living room, Joe drove the woman back to her house while Evelyn showed Hagar around the house.

"This is your bedroom so you may go for your bag and get settled in," Evelyn said when they got to the attractively furnished room.

"This is the first time I am going to have a room all to myself," Hagar said with a smile.

Evelyn smiled back and told her that they would not in anyway restrict her movements so if she wanted to go out to see her mother or anywhere else and that she should just let them know in advance. Until her father's death, Hagar, her parents and big brother all shared one room, with their belongings, of course. When their father died the three of them had some space, then her brother left for Accra, giving mother and daughter more space. But to have a whole room with a wardrobe, a bed, a dressing mirror, etc to herself was enough sign to a brighter future. She was introduced to Jude and they were both told to live in harmony as brother and sister.

She had already informed some people of her relocation to Joe's, but when Hagar had not gone to town a number of days to sell iced water, some of the girls began to talk about her. Some thought it was a good move, considering how kind the couple were, but others would not like to be maids, especially in their own town, or to some of their own people. Yet another group thought her stay would be a flash in the pan.

They expected that something would happen to bring Hagar back to her table to sell with them. But to the surprise of the observers, Hagar was coping very well in her new environment. Her only problem was Jude. He was very disrespectful, not only to Hagar but also to neighbours who respected Joe and his wife so much so that they found it difficult to complain to them. Instead, they reported Jude's truancy and misdemeanour to Hagar and told her to speak to her little brother to change his ways.

When school closed at 4:00 pm, knowing that his uncle did not come home till about 6:00 pm, Jude would play around until about ten to six before coming home, even though the school was only ten minutes walk from the house. Evelyn and Hagar had been telling him to come home straight from school but he refused to listen to them. One evening, Joe left Evelyn in the shop and came home a little earlier than usual to prepare for a meeting. Jude had not arrived home from school. When Joe inquired from Hagar, he learnt that Jude always came home late, refused to do what he was supposed to do and when Hagar complained, he got upset.

Just as they were talking, Jude came in and shouted for Hagar. Joe signalled to Hagar to remain silent. The kitchen was closer to the main entrance than the living room where Joe and Hagar were, so Jude dashed to the kitchen to look for something to eat. They waited awhile and then tiptoed to the kitchen. Jude was about to open the fridge when he saw Joe at the door and Hagar behind him.

"What time did school finish, Jude," Joe asked?

There was no response, instead, Jude bowed his head and could not look at his uncle. His hand was still on the fridge door handle. He could not open the fridge and neither could he let go of the handle.

"Did you hear me, Jude?" Joe asked, this time in a raised and authoritative voice.

Jude straightened up and said:

"We finished at 4:00 pm."

The clock on the wall showed 5:54 pm. He had come home about the same time the day before. Joe raised his head to look at the ceiling, he looked down at the floor, then the ceiling again and took a deep breath without saying a word and left the kitchen. He thought hard of what to do or say to the boy, but when he considered his marriage and the boy's mother's attitude towards Evelyn, it was difficult for him to take any decision at that moment.

"You see why I have been telling you always to come home straight from school," said Hagar.

"Leave me alone," replied Jude in anger.

The way Jude reacted to situations went a long way to prove that he was indeed a product of a Company C comrade.

"Many days for the thief, one day for the owner," Hagar said and left for her room.

Yaappiah, the vagrant, knew where to look for food when he was hungry; the refuse dumps, dustbins and the marketplace. There was always something for him to eat from these places. He drank from the gutters and would rather go to beg for food in the market place than from his own house or people. Lately, he had stopped going to the stream to wash so he was looking very dirty. Some people, especially those who knew his family, often gave him food when he asked them. Others, however, hurled insults at him and drove him away from their sight, chasing him with brooms and sticks and that was when the children joined in to humiliate him.

One afternoon, a boy pulled at the hem of his already tattered clothes as he was running away from a woman chasing him with a stick. He bumped into a young lady who was carrying several crates of eggs and they fell and shattered. He kept on running from the scene, caring nothing at all about the fight that erupted between the chaser and the owner of the eggs.

Hagar and Evelyn had with time become like a mother and her daughter. Joe also treated her like a daughter, and Maame Nkansaa had become like a real mother to the couple. They treated and cared for her like their own mother.

One Saturday, before leaving for the shop, Joe gave Evelyn five hundred thousand Cedis for Hagar to do some shopping for her mother the next day. She was to use a proportion of it for the shopping and reserve some cash for her, just in case she needed to buy something for herself. On top of that, Hagar was free to spend the whole day with her mother. Hagar was so thankful for this kind gesture. She never expected something like that, not that much money. They had been sending her few items and money in the past but not to this magnitude.

By this time Kwaku was enjoying his freedom in his mother's house. One night his friend Dan called on him to ask for a loan of two hundred thousand cedis which he hoped to pay at the end of the month. At the mention of two hundred thousand, Kwaku jumped from his seat and heading towards the bedroom, said:

"I am sorry to tell you that I can't give you a loan of two hundred thousand Cedis tonight."

Surprised at his behaviour, Dan wondered if Kwaku had someone in his room that he did not want him to know about.

'At least he should have stayed here to tell me he could not afford it, but he has left me here just like that,' Dan thought.

Kwaku has always had time for Dan when they talked about girls, drinks and music. Why then has he left his good friend in the limbo when he needed his help most? As Dan sat there confused and contemplating on this, he wondered if he had asked for too much. When Kwaku reappeared, he was holding the money and smiling.

"Like I said, I can't loan you two hundred thousand Cedis, but I can give you two hundred thousand Cedis for free," Kwaku said and gave the money to Dan.

"How can I thank you, Kwaku?" Dan asked, looking shocked.

"Don't to worry because I owe you so many favours. That's what friends are for."

Kwaku had a box in his room on top of which he had arranged some other things, and it was in this box that he kept his money. He came home each day with some cash, at least enough to spend with his friends every evening. Apart from Doris that all his friends and mother knew, Kwaku had several other girls in addition to hit-and-go ones. It was this kind of lifestyle which he did not want Joe to know about that made him move to his mother's place, leaving Jude who had become vey insolent. His insolence towards Hagar required a lot of patience to deal with as it happened on the Sunday morning when Hagar was going to her mum's with the shopping and cash from Joe.

"Jude, would you like to come with me to my mum's?" Hagar asked.

"Why do I have to come with you?"

"I just felt we can have some fun. We have a mango tree there..."

"Don't forget that I also have a mother. If you want to go to your mother, go and I will go to mine."

That was how cheeky Jude was, but Hagar was not very surprised because she knew who she was dealing with. Not long after Hagar was gone, Evelyn called Jude to the living room and asked him to get a duster to clean some dust on the window sill but the boy told her that it was Hagar's job.

"I know she does it but there is nothing wrong if you do it too. What if Hagar was not here? Who would have done it?" asked Evelyn.

"I don't know," said Jude, shrugging his shoulders.

"Ok. Now I am asking you to do it because Hagar is not at home."

"Is it by force? I will tell Hagar to clean it when she returns."

"No, Jude. I want you to do it now," said Evelyn.

"Fine then, I will clean it for now, but I won't do it next time because it's her job, not mine."

Jude went for the duster and started cleaning the window sill with such anger that he pushed down a small vase which got broken in the process. Evelyn had to tell him to stop the cleaning. He stopped without showing any remorse. She collected the broken pieces and finished cleaning the sill herself.

Jude talked to Evelyn like one would with his or her mate. He showed her no respect whatsoever. Evelyn dreaded any confrontation with Brago so much so that it was difficult for her to keep reporting the boy's behaviour to her husband. Once, Evelyn told Joe that the boy was being rude to her and when Joe rebuked him, the boy went to tell his mother that Evelyn was giving his uncle bad reports about him. Luckily, Joe's parents were at home and heard about it and intervened to silence Brago because she got angry. Jude was rude, but Evelyn had to accommodate him, anyway.

When Hagar arrived at her mother's, Maame Nkansaa had just returned from the market with a little shopping. From the last time she saw her and now, Nkansaa realised how much her daughter had changed.

"You are looking good, Hagar," she said.

"Yes. Maame, I am being well looked after. They are a wonderful couple to live with. They asked me to bring these items to you," Hagar said, pointing to the three carrier bags she came with.

Hagar's mother could not believe her eyes as she looked at the bags with her mouth and eyes opened wide. As she moved closer to inspect the items, Hagar gave her the money.

"Money as well?" Nkansaa asked, demonstrating her delight.

"Yes. It is two hundred thousand Cedis," said Hagar.

"Do you remember what I said to you on the night before you left here, that if you served them well, they would be good to you too?" asked her mother.

"I remember those words very well, Maame. Do you have any washing to do?"

"No. You should be on your way to your mistress, that's where you belong for now and that's where you should be."

"Madam said I could spend the rest of the day with you, Maame. She said she would come and see you next weekend," Hagar said.

Her mother was so thrilled on hearing about the proposed visit and also for having her daughter to spend the rest of the day with her. She had not eaten rice for a long time and Hagar had brought some among the shopping so she asked her to cook some for them to eat. As soon as Hagar set the rice on fire, she started doing some cleaning in the kitchen while they continued to talk.

On that Saturday when Joe left home early, he had been in the shop all day, but Kwaku managed to sell some key locks for 1.2 million Cedis and pocketed the money. Unfortunately, the customer brought them back on Monday morning because they were the wrong type. Kwaku tried to deal with the customer in front of the shop.

"Bring them back tomorrow morning for an exchange," said Kwaku.

"I need them now, or you give me back the money," demanded the customer.

"You come. Come here for us to talk," Kwaku said, trying to pull the customer to a corner where Joe would not see them.

"Why that side? This is where I bought them. Why do you want us to sort it out somewhere else?"

The man's raised voice reached the ears of Joe who thought he was trying to pick up a fight with Kwaku so he went closer to calm the customer down.

"What's the matter, Sir," Joe asked the customer with a smile.

"I bought these locks here on Saturday but the person whose job I was going to use them for wants a different type so I brought them for a change and he is telling me to bring them tomorrow," said the customer.

Joe could not remember having any records of the locks sold on Saturday so he collected them from the customer and told him to calm down. He then told Kwaku to go and call him Sam, one of the shop-owners, two shops away. These were locks that were being sold at five hundred thousand Cedis apiece.

"Where is he going?" the customer demanded and tried to grab Kwaku's hand.

"Don't worry, he is not running away. He will be back in a minute," said Joe.

"Are you sure?"

"Yes. How much did you pay for them?" Joe asked.

"I paid 1.2 million Cedis for the four of them."

Joe smiled and shook his head. He walked into the shop to drop the locks on the desk as the man followed him, demanding the right locks or the money back because he was far behind time with the job. Besides, he had seen the type he needed in a different shop. When Kwaku returned with Sam, Joe was standing at the same spot with the customer. The man asked Kwaku for the money; this time he was very angry and was talking louder, attracting others' attention.

"When did you sell the locks, and where is the money, Kwaku?" Joe asked him while Sam looked on.

"On Saturday and the money is at home," he said.

"OK. You go and sort it out with him and don't come back to the shop again,"

"Can I have the locks back until I get my money?" asked the man.

"They belong to me and that is why I said he should go and sort it out with you, since he said the money was at home. I am sorry about that," Joe said.

Sam just watched as Joe dealt with them but he did not utter a word. He followed Joe into the shop, leaving Kwaku and the customer. Most of the people who were witnessing the scene were agog and wondering what was going to come out of this. Kwaku walked away from the area, followed by the customer demanding his money.

"This is a bad day for him," said Sam.

"It's been going on for a long time and I just can't take it any longer," said Joe.

"Sometime ago I tried to help a friend by employing him to assist me in the shop and had a similar experience," said Sam.

"Well, that was a friend to a friend, but when your own cousin does such a thing to you, it hurts a lot," said Joe.

Away from the scene, Kwaku told the customer that he could give him some of the money that day and the remaining in two days, but the guy wouldn't take any of that.

"Look, if this is a joke, you had better stop it now," said the man.

"I'm serious. I can give you the rest on Wednesday."

"If I don't get the full amount today, there would be a serious trouble between the two of us," said the man.

Between Saturday evening and Monday morning, Kwaku had squandered nearly one million of the man's money. He had about two hundred thousand at home and had already made plans as to how he was going to spend that money in the coming days. But now, he had to think of a way to raise this man's money. He decided to go and borrow the required amount from one of Joe's business partners. Some people at the row of shops wondered whether Joe would allow Kwaku back into the shop or not.

Two men whose shops were close to Joe's talked about the incident and one of them said each time Kwaku bargained with a customer at a particular corner in front of the shop, it was for his own gain. Whatever he sold at that corner, the money never reached the till. They had seen him many times bargaining there, but his luck ran out that Monday morning.

When Evelyn came to the shop and Joe told her about the locks and his decision, he had to make another decision there and then. Evelyn had not done anything wrong to anyone in Joe's family but she had been at the receiving end since they got married. So in order not to make her situation worse, she opted to stay away from this issue right from the start.

"Please, can I go to Tafo now as you sort the issue out, because I don't want to be entangled in it?" Evelyn asked.

"You may go tomorrow morning," said Joe.

"Please it is better I leave now because in that case I would be completely out of the picture."

Joe looked at his wife as she pleaded for permission to leave Diasempa as soon as possible. Evelyn was worried about what could become of Joe's decicion as she persisted for him to let her go.

"OK. You may go. Let's keep in touch every two hours, if possible," said Joe.

"That's fine. Please take it easy and don't do anything that could bring more problems," Evelyn advised.

"Don't worry, Evelyn. I won't do anything reckless, you know me," said Joe.

"Don't tell Hagar of the incident for the time being. Also, you have to be very careful in dealing with Auntie Cornie in this matter because it is most likely that she wouldn't be happy with your decision."

"I don't care how she takes it, Evelyn. I'm just glad that you were not around when it happened," said Joe.

Evelyn left the shop as soon as she could and called her cousin at Tafo on the way home to tell her of the impromptu visit. At home she told Hagar that Joe had sent her to Tafo and Accra and she would be away for two days.

Kwaku had been giving his mother whatever she asked for, especially money. Some few weeks earlier Cornie bought some clothes on credit and when the dealer came to demand the overdue payment that morning, she told her to come back in the evening because Kwaku was going to give her money on his return from work. She was confident of having the money in the evening because Kwaku had promised her before going to work but now he was on his way home to take the remaining money.

One of their uncles came to Joe's shop not long after the incident and when he asked for Evelyn, Joe told him she had travelled to Tafo. He also asked about Kwaku as they talked and Joe shook his head, forced a smile and looked at his wrist watch without responding immediately. His uncle read between the lines and suspected that all was not well with that smile, so he asked for Kwaku again.

"Hmm, Uncle, you are the first to know about this issue."

"What issue, Joe?" Uncle KK asked.

"Uncle, I've taken a decision, and nothing would make me reverse it."

"What decision is that, and what led to it?"

"Kwaku has been stealing from the shop for sometime now and what he has done today is a bit over the top, so I have sacked him about an hour ago."

"What did he steal today?

"He sold these locks on Saturday without my knowledge and took the money. Unfortunately for him they were the wrong type so the costumer returned them. A few days ago he did the same to some paint brushes and I can't take it any longer.

"Well, you have to do what is right for your business," said Uncle KK.

"I've had enough of him, Uncle. He is becoming a pain to me now."

"It's your business, Joe, no one can force you to go against your will. When is Evelyn coming back?"

"Wednesday, maybe."

Meanwhile, the customer was threatening to take the matter to the police because Kwaku was delaying him. By this time they were close to the shop where Kwaku intended to borrow the money, so he begged the man to wait in front of the shop while he went inside to negotiate. This was the first time Kwaku had come for help from Kwame Boafo and because of the latter's connections with Joe it did not take long for him to be convinced by Kwaku's lies. He told Boafo that he was off duty that day and had come window shopping.

"There is something that I've been looking for since last year and I've just seen a man who has come from Koforidua with one for someone. But he says if I can pay him a million Cedis now, he would let me have it. Unfortunately, I don't have any money on me at the moment and so I was wondering if you could lend me one million cedis. I'll bring it back to you tomorrow morning."

"I will be a bit late tomorrow so you may bring it in the afternoon, around mid-day," said Boafo.

"That's fine, I will be on my lunch break at that time so I will rush to come and give it to you."

Kwame Boafo pulled open a drawer and counted out the money for him. The customer was keeping an eye on the entrance to the shop through which Kwaku had entered, thinking he may escape. He heaved a sigh of relief when he saw Kwaku reappear with an envelope in his hand. Kwaku told him he was going to give him the full amount in a few minutes. From there he took a taxi home with the customer.

They all behaved like the strangers that they were on the way to Kwaku's place. No one spoke a single word to the other, not even the driver. Normally, three young men in a taxi would have talked at least about current affairs in the country or something else, but the body language, as the two entered the taxi, was clear to the driver that there was some tension so he minded his business and drove on.

When the taxi dropped them off near the house, Kwaku told the man to wait outside as he went in to get the money for him. His mother was surprised to see him come home at that time of the morning. She assumed that he might have forgotten something and had come back for it.

"Did you come to get something?" asked Cornie.

"Yes," he replied.

He went into his bedroom to unpack the gadgets on top of the box in which he kept his money. He counted two hundred thousand Cedis to add to what he had gone to borrow and packed the box back as it was. On his way out to settle with the man, he told his mother that someone was waiting for him outside, but he would come back soon. Kwaku handed the man the large envelope he had received from Boafo and asked him to check it. The guy counted 1.2 million Cedis and said;

"You are lucky. It would have been bloody between us."

"Okay, mate. Let's leave it at that," Kwaku said and walked back into the house.

His mother was waiting, expecting to get some cash from him. Kwaku had not yet decided how to tell her about what had happened so he went into his room for some thinking, but his mother won't allow him to think.

"Can I have the money for the woman?" she asked.

"Not today, Mum."

"I have promised the woman that I won't disappoint her this evening, so please..."

"Mum, I'm sorry you can't have it today," Kwaku said as he came out of his room.

"Please, can I have at least half of it because she said she had to go for some fabric tomorrow and needed the money as soon as possible," pleaded Cornie.

"It's not a lucky day, Mum. I can't afford any money today."

Cornie told him that she would be in deep trouble because she had assured the woman she owed that she would not disappoint her, and she had no money herself to give to her. For sometime now Auntie Cornie had been depending on Kwaku for most of the cash she needed and he was able to meet her demands.

She never questioned how he got all the money to give to her. Surely, it was not from his wages, she knew that, because sometimes she demanded and got from him more than his monthly wages in one month. Kwaku was getting bored with his mother's persistent lamentations so he left the house. When he had gone for several hours, Cornie decided to take some money from her friend, Serwaa, which she used to pay for the clothes later in the evening when the woman came by.

Kwaku's friends were aware of how extravagant he was and had been taking advantage of it. If Kwaku saw something that he liked, no matter how expensive it was, so long as he had the amount, he would pay to own it. This was another reason why he chose to go back to live with his mother. His room was full of gadgets and some expensive ornaments. His friend Dan supplied him with most of these items and where he got those things could be anyone's guess. Dan connived with one of his friends who had a sound system for sale at three hundred and fifty thousand Cedis to sell it to Kwaku for one million Cedis.

"The most expensive one I've sold was four-fifty," said the friend.

"You just watch me do the talking when we go. I'll make him pay one million." Dan said.

"Well, if you say so," said the friend.

"If you are in doubt, I want us to make a deal. If he pays more than four-fifty, the extra amount would be mine, plus my commission," said Dan.

"Agreed," said the friend.

The friend agreed because he was sure no one would pay that much for the system. Dan had no idea that Kwaku had been sacked, so they went to the shop to ask for him and Joe told them he wasn't around. Dan and the friend went to ask Auntie Cornie and she told them Kwaku had been leaving home very early lately. After four days of trying to locate Kwaku without success, the young man with the sound system found a new buyer, to the disappointment of Dan.

CHAPTER SEVEN

OUT OF THIS PLACE

Evelyn returned from Tafo after two days but with Joe's consent, decided to take a few more days off. During those days at home, she observed how rude Jude was towards Hagar and told him to show her some respect because she was older than him. Besides, Evelyn told the boy that it was not good to be that rude to anyone, young or old. Another time he left a plate he had used the previous day in the sink without washing it and when Evelyn saw it the next morning she questioned him.

"Why didn't you wash your plate last night, Jude?"

"I was tired," Jude said and turned to walk away.

"Jude, Jude," Evelyn called but the boy refused to turn back.

"I will wash it when I return from school," he said and kept going.

"You have to wash it before you leave for school, Jude."

"I can't do it now. I will be late for school," he said in a very rude manner and slammed the door behind him.

"Jude, are you walking out on me?"

There was no response. The boy was gone, and as he always did, after school he went to report the incident to his mother. Brago was very angry and said that Evelyn was taking her son for a houseboy.

As soon as Jude left, Brago went to discuss the issue with Auntie Cornie.

"I suspect that she was doing the same to Kwaku and that is why he has moved back here," said Auntie Cornie.

"Yes. I strongly believe that it was because of her that he left the place," agreed Brago.

"It's about time someone dealt with that unproductive barren girl harshly to make her know that Joe had a family before marrying her," said Cornie.

"That's just what I intend to do," said Brago. "I will make her see my true colours this time around. I'm going to deal with her in a very serious way."

The next day Evelyn was at home alone in the afternoon weeping and praying about her childless condition when she heard a knock on the door. She quickly wiped her face, put on a smile and went to open the door to see Brago standing there with a face that told her all was not well. Evelyn ushered her into the living room and offered her a seat but Brago refused to sit down. She would not even accept a drink from Evelyn.

"Look here, Evelyn, I have come to tell you what you have to know, if you don't know it already that, when Joe is not around, my son Jude is your head of family. You must therefore treat him the way you would treat your husband."

"What is the matter, Sister Brago?" Evelyn asked, confused.

"I've told you not to call me your sister because I'm not one of your mother's children," said Brago.

"Please, what is the matter? Why are you so angry?"

"I don't like the way you are treating my son, he is not your house boy. That's the matter," said Brago. "If you have anything good to put into bringing up children, wait till you get your own, if at all that is possible. And don't experiment with my child. He is not your slave so don't treat him as such, period. If I ever hear you mistreating him again and I come here it will be the worse for you. I don't even know why Joe is still keeping you here, anyway."

Evelyn was trembling as the words gushed out of her sister-in-law's mouth like a stream. When Brago finished what she had to say, she walked out of the room, slamming the door just like her son had done the day before. The bang from the slam of the door shook Evelyn and made her heart skip its beating. Too traumatized to talk, she sank into the sofa behind her like a falling sack of corn.

"For how long can I bear this, God?" Evelyn asked.

Evelyn wept like a baby. In her tears, she begged God to look down on her and wipe the tears from her eyes. Coincidentally, Joe needed something from home so he closed the shop to go and get it only to be met by his wife crying, and it took him a while to make Evelyn talk. And even when she started to talk the tears would not let her complete one statement at a go. After hearing all that Brago had come to say to his wife, Joe comforted her and promised to go and have a word with his sister. He had been trying to avoid any situation that would look confrontational where Evelyn would be involved, but this act of his sister was the last straw. He couldn't remain silent anymore.

In the mean time, Kwaku was also trying to avoid a lot of people, especially Kwame Boafo. He had promised to take the money back to him the next day but it had been a while now with no sign of him. Kwame Boafo discussed his loan to Kwaku with a friend who informed him that Joe had sacked Kwaku for stealing. Boafo was surprised and said he would find out from Joe himself.

As promised, Joe went to the family home to have a word with Brago that same afternoon but did not meet her. His mother was at home so he told her a part of what had taken place. There were other people in the house and for the first time, Joe decided to talk to his mother about Brago's action in the hearing of those present. He spoke so angrily that his mother had to beg him to calm down. The people around started blaming Brago for what they were hearing from Joe.

They knew very well that for Joe to speak in that manner meant something significant was likely to happen afterwards. But if Brago was there, they might not have been able so say all that they were saying, knowing who she was and how she reacted to situations. Every member of the family was scared of her. As they talked, Agya Boakye walked in and asked Joe why he was so angry.

"Paapa, Brago has been going round spreading scandal about Evelyn and me and this afternoon she had the audacity to walk into my own home to pile insults on my wife in an attempt to excuse her son," said Joe.

It was the first time both Agya Boakye and Darkoaa had seen their son speak so angrily. Joe invited his mother to come to his house with him to hear it from Evelyn herself. It had been a very bad day for Evelyn. Her tears had never ceased since morning when she told Hagar to go and spend sometime with her mother. Her plan for the day was to appeal to God for a child. She believed that if she were able to have a child for Joe, part of her misery would come to an end, if not all. But her focus had shifted from crying to God to worrying and crying about Brago's abuses and threats. What made her problems more worrying was that she could not share them with anyone.

Her own mother who, under normal circumstances, should have comforted her at times like this was rather insisting divorce. Bevelyn was the only one who could understand what her sister was going through. When Joe arrived with his mother Evelyn was still crying. Darkoaa put her hand around her neck and drew her closer to herself on the sofa.

"What is it, Evelyn? What happened?" Darkoaa asked.

Evelyn could hardly speak as Joe paced to and fro, hitting his forehead with the palm of his hand. Whatever was going on in his mind was yet to come out.

"Maame," Evelyn began, "I was here this afternoon when I heard a knock on the door. I went to open it and there stood Sister Brago with a frown on her face."

She began to sob again and this time Joe pulled out one of the coffee tables and sat on it opposite them. He tapped Evelyn's knee and urged her to talk.

"She would not even sit down," continued Evelyn, "then she started telling me that in Joe's absence, her son, Jude, was his next of kin so I should treat him like I would treat Joe. She said if I had anything good to put into children, I should wait till I got my own, if at all that was possible."

"Did Brago say that?" asked Darkoaa.

"Yes, Maame. She says she does not know why Joe is still keeping me here, that if I mistreat her son and she comes here again, I won't be able to take what she'll do to me. I asked her what the matter was but she..." Evelyn paused to blow and wipe her running nose.

"Did you hear that, Maame?" asked Joe. "I'm not going to wait for her to come and insult my wife again in my own house. The boy will have to go back."

Evelyn begged Joe not to let the boy go, but he was determined to. He had yet to tell his mother about Kwaku and now he was going to take Jude also back to his mother.

"Joe, please let him stay. I will only have to be careful the way I deal with him. Please don't throw him out," begged Evelyn.

"It's for me to decide, this time around. He must go. I've had enough," Joe vowed.

"Sometimes, the best solution is separation," added Darkoaa in support of Joe's decision.

Evelyn stopped crying for a while but she looked traumatised, having in mind what Brago could do if Jude was to be taken back to her. She was scared of Brago, but Joe felt it was about time he demonstrated to his sister that she had no right to keep interfering in his marriage.

"Don't worry about whatever happens next, because everyone knows her as a trouble-maker," Joe said to Evelyn.

"If he remains here his mother will never change. This should serve as a lesson to her," added Darkoaa. "I will always stand by you, so don't worry about her."

When someone says, '*Let me tell you about my mother-in-law,*' we expect some kind of negative statements or humorous anecdotes because the mother-in-law caricature has been a standard centrepiece of ridicule or comedy. But Evelyn's experience, however, told a different story. Her mother-in-law was very supportive and stood against anything or anyone that threatened their marriage. Evelyn had become like a daughter to Darkoaa. There were some things she could discuss with her mother-in-law which she could not with her own mother. Accepting people as they are was one of Darkoaa's many qualities which Evelyn loved.

Darkoaa told Evelyn that while it is often wise to give thought before coming to a decision, sometimes the decision you take in the heat of the moment is the best. Joe had decided that Jude should go back to his mother, and that was that. While Darkoaa was still trying to comfort Evelyn, Joe went to the kitchen for a glass of water and after drinking he repeated that Jude will have to go back to his mother.

That afternoon when school finished, instead of going straight home, Jude went to the family home and Brago told him she had gone to deal with Evelyn. She said she was sure that Evelyn would not give him any more trouble. The boy felt happy and said he would report to her in a day or two.

Joe knew what his sister could do and he was not going to wait for her to cause any havoc so he did not go back to the shop; instead, after taking his mother back to the family home, he came to pack everything that belonged to Jude into a bag and put it into the boot of his car. As soon as Jude got home, Joe told him to get into the car, still in his uniform, without telling him where they were going. He did not say a word to the boy as he drove, but as they got close to the family home Jude became suspicious.

"Are we going to see Grandma?" he asked.

"No. You are going to stay with your mother from now on," Joe said without telling him why or even turning to look at him.

"Why?" Jude asked.

"Because your mother wants to bring you up her own way," said Joe.

It then dawned on the boy that the trip may be linked to his mother's action. When Joe parked the car and opened the boot, he took the big bag and told Jude to take the other one. Jude began to sob, but Joe started walking towards the house and asked Jude to follow him.

Darkoaa was telling Brago that she had gone too far when Joe and Jude entered the house. Joe dropped the bag and said to them that Jude was then coming to live with his mother so she could bring him up the way she wanted. Jude cried and said it was his fault that his mother behaved that way but Joe said if he changed his ways and his mother changed hers as well, in future he and Evelyn might have him back. But for then he would have to stay with his mother so that she could give him the kind of training that she felt Evelyn was not capable of. No one said a word on behalf of the boy because of what his mother had done.

"You are my elder sister," Joe said to Brago, "I give you all the respect due you but I will no longer tolerate your attitude towards Evelyn. You are my sister and she is my wife. She had never been rude to you or any member of this family. You've been abusing her many times; you even snubbed her in public, and now you had the audacity to walk into my own house to abuse her. Let this be the last time."

When Joe had finished saying these words, he walked out of the house. Jude was still crying and begging to go back with him but Brago stood there without saying a word. She didn't expect Joe to act in that manner. She thought she was going to get away with her actions as it had happened many times before. Some people in the house commented on Brago's action as Maame Darkoaa explained Joe's decision to them. They had heard what Joe said and they were all of the opinion that no one could blame Joe for bringing the boy back to his mother. Brago could not utter a word to defend what she did or refute any of the things Joe said. She did not think that Evelyn would tell Joe of what she had gone to say to her that afternoon.

Evelyn was always worried about what her in-laws would think about her, but she had done her best. She had taken care of Kwaku just like she did Joe, until he moved out of the house and Joe had to sack him later. Now he had sent Jude back to his mother and she feared that people would blame her without considering what could have been the reason. She worried a lot in the days and weeks that followed, but as they say, time is a healer, so in time she got over it and said what has to be must be.

Kwaku did not save any of the money he made from the shop because he thought it was always going to be like that. After all, it was his cousin's shop and Joe might even leave the shop to him in future. He had this notion at the back of his mind, but now, some of the people he used to treat nicely sometimes were those that gave him pocket money. At last, he told a few of his pals that he was out of job because of Evelyn. His best friend, Dan, was helping him to get a job at a saw mill at Asuofuo and on their way to the place one morning, Kwaku saw Kwame Boafo coming towards them.

"Dan, wait, wait," Kwaku said and took cover behind a kiosk.

"Why, what's going on?" asked Dan.

"It's that man in the blue T-shirt. I don't want him to see me?

"Why?" Dan asked.

Dan opened the newspaper he was holding wide and pretended to be reading, giving Kwaku more cover. When Boafo passed by, they walked fast in a different direction.

"Isn't he the man who sells hardware?" Dan asked.

"Yes. He is one of Doris' uncles and he has been inviting me to come and see him at home but I haven't been able to go yet," Kwaku was panting as he lied to Dan.

"You had better go and see him because he could give you some business," he told Kwaku."

Dan believed what Kwaku told him about Kwame Boafo and was even willing to go with him to see the man at home, but this was the last person on earth that Kwaku wished to see, until his money was ready. Alas, for a jobless man to raise one million Cedis in a few days in Diasempa was an illusion.

Kwame Boafo supplied Joe with shovels and he also got some building materials from Joe. He went to Joe's shop to look for Kwaku and pretended not to know that he has been sacked.

"I've not seen you for a long time," Joe said on Boafo's arrival.

"Maybe you don't want to do business with me again that's why you don't contact me these days," Boafo said in the same jovial manner.

"No," said Joe. "As you can see, some of the shovels are still not sold."

"How is Madam?" asked Boafo.

"She is at the back there," Joe said and whistled to call Evelyn.

"Is that how you call her?" Boafo asked, laughing.

"That's how we call each other," Joe said as Evelyn emerged.

"You are looking sweet, as always," Boafo said.

"It's the Lord's doing and thanks also to Joe, who is taking very good care of me."

"This is the best compliment I've heard from a wife about her husband," said Boafo.

Evelyn laughed and asked if Boafo would like something to drink but he said he was fine. She then moved away from the men, thinking they were going to talk business.

"Where is Kwaku?" Boafo asked Joe when Evelyn was going.

"I no longer work with him. He was not being honest so I sacked him."

"When?" asked Boafo.

"It's been almost a month now," Joe said.

The shock on Boafo's face made Joe ask him if there was any problem and he told him of the money Kwaku had come to borrow from him just around the time when Joe said he sacked him.

"Well, you can check on him at his mother's place," said Joe. "You see, when you have a cup in your hand with some drink in it, you can sip it in bits or gulp it at one go. You can also tell people it contains water, soft drink, tea or coffee, when in actual fact the content is whisky. But when the cup is full and it is running over, whatever it is will be revealed for everyone to see."

"You are right, Joe. I'll go and look for him. But what actually happened?"

"He was stealing from the shop until I caught him red-handed one day so I decided not to work with him again."

"He could have drained your finances, you know," said Boafo.

"That was why I gave him the sack."

"I don't blame you. Anyway, I will go and look for him."

"Good luck," said Joe as Boafo was leaving.

Kwaku had lied to his mother that it was Evelyn who asked Joe to sack him from the shop. Poor Evelyn was always bearing the brunt. Auntie Cornie went to complain to Joe's mother that Evelyn had finally succeeded in forcing Joe to sack her son from the shop.

"Have you found out from Joe why he sacked him?" Darkoaa asked.

"No, but Kwaku tells me Evelyn is the cause," Cornie said.

While the conversation was going on, Agya Boakye was listening from the living room so he joined them on the veranda.

"Since you have not investigated the facts of the case, you should not go about blaming Evelyn. I'll find out what happened from Joe," said Agya Boakye

"I'm sure she is the reason, just as Kwaku said," insisted Cornie.

"There are two sides to every coin, Cornie. I want to get Joe's side of the story, so come back in the evening with Kwaku and let's see if we can get him reinstated," said Agya Boakye.

"I'll go and find out from Joe what made him sack Kwaku," said Darkoaa.

"Leave that to me, Darkoaa," Agya Boakye said, insisting that Cornie should come back in the evening with Kawku.

The real cause of all this hostility towards Evelyn by some of Joe's relatives was that she had not conceived as yet. Her own mother was also thinking that Joe was not 'man' enough to make her daughter pregnant, even though no one knew whose fault it was. But someone was working on this on her behalf in the city. Kate, her friend, contacted a doctor about Evelyn's case and the doctor suggested that Evelyn herself should come and see him. So arrangements were made for Evelyn to travel to Accra one Monday.

As soon as Auntie Cornie left the house, Agya Boakye started making arrangements for a meeting with a few members of the family who were free that evening. It was at this meeting that Joe, for the first time, told them the facts about Kwaku stealing from the shop. The last straw was the locks which he said if they had not been returned, two million Cedis would have gone from his accounts, because the locks were worth five hundred thousand cedis each. But Cornie was still insisting that Evelyn had a hand in Joe sacking Kwaku.

"Evelyn was not there when this happened," said Joe.

"I went to the shop on the day of the incident and saw the locks myself," said Uncle KK. "Evelyn had travelled to Tafo that day so she wasn't around to have a hand in it as you are insisting, Cornie."

"Ask Kwaku himself if there is anything he can say to dispute what I'm saying," said Joe.

"What I told my mother about Auntie Evelyn was made up," said Kwaku, with his eyes glued to the floor.

"You should be ashamed of yourself," said one of the elders. "Why are you trying to damage Evelyn's name? What has she done to you?"

They all rebuked Kwaku and said Cornie should not blame Joe for sacking him. One of the people said Kwaku should return all the money he had stolen from the shop since he had been there but Joe said he wasn't demanding that. Another person said Joe should forgive Kwaku and take him back.

"I had wanted to build a business that would remain in the family but that dream is being shattered by recent events," said Joe. "Kwaku is my cousin and will forever remain one, but to take him back is something I cannot do. When Auntie Cornie heard that I have sacked him, she should have come to me to find out what happened, instead of her going about telling people that it was Evelyn who persuaded me."

"You should not always believe what people tell you about others," said Agya Boakye. "If I had not called this meeting, no one would have known the truth about the issue and Evelyn would have been blamed."

Agya Boakye promised Cornie that he would have a word with Joe later to see if he would change his mind about taking Kwaku back. He knew very well that it was not going to work; that when Joe made up his mind he stuck to it. Evelyn did not attend this family meeting so during that time when she was being defended by her husband and others, she was making preparations to travel to Accra to see Kate and the doctor. Kate's husband reminded her to show Evelyn their old school picture and Kate said she already had it in her handbag.

When Joe went back home, he did not tell Evelyn the full details of the meeting, especially Kwaku's allegation against her. He only told her that the meeting offered him the opportunity to tell his family what made him sack Kwaku.

Joe and Evelyn had contributed a good deal towards the playground fundraising at church because they thought it was a good cause. Alas! Some people talked negatively about their contribution. Among them were two female members of the church. One said if Joe and Evelyn had children, they would not be able to spare so much money.

"What a waste! If they were paying school fees and buying books and uniforms, they would not waste such money."

"Don't consider their contribution a waste. It was for a good project which in future our own children could benefit from," said the other.

"It is a waste, a complete waste. If I had money like them, I would live like a queen with lots of help in the house and enjoy myself. They cannot produce children. That's why they are wasting money like that."

This lady could not understand why the couple should spend so much money on something that was of no use to them. But to the couple, it was a pleasure to help others. Being a modest couple Joe and Evelyn always dressed simply, and that was another area where they suffered abuse from some people. Evelyn liked to design most of the *kaba* which her seamstress sewed for her and a group of ladies copied her designs.

They were always looking out for what was new that she wore. Yet these same people saw her as an unproductive woman in society. The way they looked askance at her in the streets was enough to make Evelyn cry. She always tried to be helpful to everyone, but her good intentions sometimes landed her in trouble.

Once she saw that an older boy had pinned a younger boy to the ground and was hitting him like a punch bag near the shop, so she ran to the rescue of this younger boy and brought him to her shop. The older boy reacted by throwing stones and sticks at her in the shop. A young man came from behind the boy and grabbed his hand, seized one of the sticks which the boy was going to throw at Evelyn and started whipping him with it. He said he was going to take him to the police for the damage done to some items on display in front of the shop.

Someone who knew the boy's mother rushed to their home which was just two houses away to tell her and she came rushing to the scene. She was just like her son, very arrogant. She went straight to the young man and told him to let go of his grip on her son. The man tried to tell her what the boy had done but she was not ready to listen. Evelyn came with the small boy to tell her what her son had done and she told Evelyn to shut up as soon as she began to speak.

"People like you should not talk about incidents involving children because you don't have what it takes to bear one," she said to Evelyn.

"How dare you talk like that to her? Instead of apologising for the damage caused by your son, you are insulting her," said the young man, who had now let go of the boy.

"Who is she to correct my son?" asked the woman.

"I am not surprised at your son's behaviour. He is just like you. One day you will pay for what he has done and what you have just said," the young man said.

Evelyn stood there speechless as the man exchanged words with the boy's mother. Within a few seconds, what the woman said to Evelyn sank deep into her whole being and tears rolled down her cheeks. Trying to control her emotions so as not to let others see that she was crying, she turned away, bit her upper lip very hard and wiped away the tears, but it was too late, everybody there saw the tears and their faces changed at once. She took the small boy back to her shop.

"You are a very stupid woman for talking like that," someone said to the woman.

"Your son is just like you, a stupid fool," remarked another woman who wanted to fight with the woman for behaving the way she did.

The young man had support from others who were standing by and when the woman could no longer cope with the verbal attacks from the crowd, she left with her son.

"You are a disgrace to the family you belong to, and a very bad example of a mother to others," the young man said.

Evelyn closed the shop not long after she had sent the boy on his way. Joe had gone on a business trip that day and when he came home that evening, Evelyn told him she had not been feeling very well so she closed the shop about three hours earlier than usual. She could not tell him about the incident. She was not sick physically but the words of the boy's mother had really hurt her, making her feel very low in spirit. It was difficult for her to go back to the shop to face the people around there who heard what the woman had said to her.

All the other shop owners and hawkers around the station knew that Joe and Evelyn had no child, but because of how they comported themselves and dealt with people, they were highly respected.

Some of their own people had been talking a lot about them but for an outsider to say that to her face in public was too hard for Evelyn to bear. For nearly a week, she could not go to the shop and Joe sensed that there was something emotionally wrong with his wife.

He had heard a lot himself about what some members of his own family were saying about their situation, but no one had been able to say to his face what the woman said to Evelyn. One day Joe mustered the courage to ask Evelyn if she had been hearing the rumour that he was hearing.

"About what?" Evelyn asked.

"It's about our childlessness. You and I know that people have been asking questions but now they seem to be making statements, even among my own family. The rumour is that one of us is infertile," said Joe.

"I have been avoiding most of my friends because of the questions they ask me about it," said Evelyn.

Evelyn was beginning to wonder what the future held for her if they were making such statements. But Joe, a man of great faith, assured her not to lose heart because no matter what they did or said he would always stand by her. Evelyn began to cry as she thought of what the boy's mother had said to her and her own mother's pressure on her to divorce Joe. The fact that it had been over six years since they got married gave people the opportunity to complain, and they were not getting any younger.

"Let's brave the storm, Evelyn, because I faithfully believe that God can change our situation in His own good time."

"I know, Joe, but for how long do we have to go through this," Evelyn asked, still crying?"

Joe had no answer to this question so he kept quiet and looked up the ceiling as Evelyn buried her face in both hands. Hagar called Evelyn from the corridor and as she could not control her tears, she got up and rushed to the guest room which was closer to where they were. Evelyn had gone out for a walk during the afternoon to ease some of the tension and in her absence, her mother phoned. Hagar told Joe that Evelyn's mother called and had asked that she return her call. She came out of the room as soon as Hagar left and when Joe told her of her mother's message, she promised to call her later but Joe insisted that she call right away, and she did.

"She sounded a bit cold and said she wanted to see me urgently," Evelyn said to Joe afterwards.

"You had better go and see her now, to find out what the matter is," said Joe.

"OK."

"If you go and there's a need for me to come over, call me and I will be on my way."

Evelyn left immediately to hear why her mother wanted to see her. That evening, by chance or whatever you call it, Kwame Boafo met Kwaku in town after several attempts to get him at home. They met face to face at a corner where he could not escape, even though he tried to turn around.

"Why are you trying to hide from me?" Boafo asked. "As the saying goes, you can run but you cannot hide. You've been running for far too long."

"No, I'm not running away from you. I am only in a hurry to meet someone," said Kwaku.

Kwame Boafo was with a friend who was aware of the one million Cedis. Kwaku lied to Boafo that he was rushing to go and collect money from someone who owed him and this person was due to travel that evening.

"I will send it to you this evening or at the latest by tomorrow morning," said Kwaku.

"I cannot trust you because you promised to bring it the next day after borrowing and it has been over six weeks."

"I swear on my mother's life that I will let you have it as soon as possible," said Kwaku, always looking over his shoulders to see who else was watching them.

"How could you trust someone who has evaded you for over six weeks that he will indeed come and see you tomorrow? I would not let him go, if I were you," said Boafo's friend.

"Who are you, and what do you know between the two of us?" asked Kwaku.

"I am a friend and I know about you and the money," the man responded.

"Hey Mister, mind your words," warned Kwaku.

"I'm not a stranger in this town, if you don't know. I know you," said the man.

"If you fail to bring it this evening as promised, I will report it to the police," said Boafo, after asking his friend to stop arguing with Kwaku.

"You have met a good man," the man said.

Because of Boafo's relationship with Joe, he didn't want to get tough with Kwaku and allowed him to go, but Kwaku knew that was not the end of it. Boafo would surely come to his house again or meet him in town one day. He had not told his mother about the money he owed Boafo. In fact, none of his friends or Doris knew about it, because it was so embarrassing for him to tell people that he owed someone that amount. He who used to give out money to friends without thinking of what to get from them in return was now in need, but there was no one to help him out.

By the time Evelyn got to her mother's house, a lot of thoughts had battled in her mind. *'Mother may be sick, she may need some money.*

Maybe there is something wrong that she needs to discuss with me alone. Or has she already invited Bevelyn? Surely, it's not going to be about my marriage.' But that was the exact reason for this invitation. For no sooner had Evelyn sat down opposite her mother than she began to hit the nail right on the head.

"This is not the first time I'm talking to you about this issue, Evelyn, nor is it going to be the last. I have decided, after a very hard thouht, that you divorce Joe for his inability to make you pregnant. I have learnt from a very reliable source that he is either impotent or sterile," said Konadu.

Evelyn was looking straight into her mother's eyes as she spoke. She said if she did not divorce Joe, she would regret in future, when she was old and had no children to look after her. Evelyn had wanted to say something but as soon as she opened her mouth, her mother told her to hold on.

"Look at your twin sister, you married long before her but she has already got a child," she said. "Joe just can't make you pregnant, even his own people are aware of that. He is not capable."

"There is nothing wrong with Joe, Mum. If there was something wrong with me, would you advise Joe to leave me for someone else? You are compounding my misery, Mum."

"Listen to her. Am I compounding your misery for suggesting ways and means to have your own children?" Konadu asked.

"Yes, you are. Because being a mother I expected you to support me in times like this and not to..."

"The only support I can offer is what I'm doing, to help you out of this mess."

"You are not helping me one bit. I'm going to spend the rest of my life with Joe," Evelyn said amid tears.

Evelyn shed tears the rest of the time she spent at her mother's. Konadu said that she wanted the best for Evelyn and not what she was going through. She made Evelyn feel stupid for sticking to a man who could not make her pregnant, but Evelyn decided not to let her husband know of how her mother was nagging her for a divorce. So back at home, Evelyn told Joe that her mother needed some money and she had sorted her out.

Kwaku was still going round telling everyone that it was Evelyn who forced Joe to sack him from the shop, even though he had asked Joe to forgive him for lying about his wife.

But Doris liked Evelyn a lot and wished to be her sister-in-law in future. She had not really interacted with Evelyn that much but she always said good things about her to Kwaku. The way Evelyn spoke to people and dealt with them, the way she dressed and her modesty in general was something that appealed to Doris greatly. Kwaku knew that, so when at last he was telling Doris that he has lost his job, he simply put it that Joe said he could no longer employ him because the business was not doing well. Doris was suspicious of what Kwaku said but she couldn't go to Joe or anyone to find out the truth so she accepted what he told her, somehow.

Evelyn travelled to Accra to see Kate who took her to the doctor. After the introduction, the doctor asked Kate to excuse them so he could get some detailed information from Evelyn.

"How long have you been married?" asked Dr Ankrah-Badu.

"It's been over six years, doctor."

"Have you had any miscarriages or abortions in the past?"

"No."

"You know some girls do silly things before they get married and those things sometimes affect them in later years," he said. "Some do terminate pregnancies without considering the consequences of their action in future and most of the methods they use are dangerous."

"I haven't done any such thing, doctor," said Evelyn.

"Are you on any medication at the moment?"

"No"

"You will have to go for some laboratory tests to see the condition of your womb, blood, hormones, etc. The results of the test would determine how to deal with the situation. It could be a simple or complicated issue, but with current developments in the field of science, almost every scientific problem is solvable. Let's just hope this is not something ordained by God," he said.

This statement made Evelyn straighten up in her chair and look into the doctor's eyes, expecting to hear more from what he had just said. But he said no more because he could read shock on her face.

"You mean it could be something I have to accept?" asked Evelyn.

"It could be, but I believe that God can reverse every situation," he said. "He who brings the dead back to life is capable of anything."

Evelyn was taken aback at these comments from the doctor and he kept assuring her that with God all things are possible. While he prepared the note for the test, he asked Evelyn to invite Kate back into the office. Dr Ankrah-Badu added a note addressed to one Joel to attend to Evelyn immediately. However, he said the results would take three to four days to get to him. Kate told Evelyn it was a good start as they headed for the lab.

Evelyn had been granted permission to go to Tafo on the day Kwaku was sacked and went to borrow the one million Cedis from Kwame Boafo. And again, while he was out of town seeking medical answers to the condition that had made her a laughingstock in the town of Diasempa, Kwaku was being sought for to pay his debt. Boafo went to his house two days after his encounter with him when Kwaku was still in bed but Auntie Cornie lied that he was not at home because, Boafo looked angry.

"What should I tell him when he comes back?" Cornie asked.

"Just tell him it is the man he promised to come and see two days ago," Boafo said.

"Sir, what did you say your name was?" Cornie asked.

"Just tell him what I said and he will know who I am," Boafo said as he walked away.

Auntie Cornie stood there to make sure Boafo was out of sight before going to call Kwaku from his room.

"A man came looking for you. He seemed to be angry so I told him you had gone out. He said you promised to come and see him two days ago."

"Oh yes, I'll go and see him this afternoon," said Kwaku.

Kwaku knew it was Kwame Boafo but pretended it was nothing serious and went back to his room. There was no way he could raise one million Cedis that afternoon to go and see him, but that's what he had said to his mother. Auntie Cornie did not question what was between him and Boafo so Kwaku did not explain to her either. Boafo decided to call in the police the next time he was going to look for him.

Everyone wants to protect and care for their loved ones, so on that day when Auntie Cornie had protected her son from an unknown man who seemed to be angry, Bevelyn was also discussing her twin sister's issue with her husband, Kakabo. Bevelyn was worried about the way their mother was going about her sister's situation, her persistent pressure on her to divorce Joe was something that had become a burden to her.

"I've been talking to her to leave them alone but she wouldn't listen," said Bevelyn.

"I believe love trumps everything, so for as long as they love each other, I don't see why she should tell Evelyn to divorce him," said Kakabo. "If one of them was complaining, that would have been a different issue, but since they are happy together, irrespective of their situation, I think it is better to leave them alone."

"I feel the same way, but my Mum thinks..."

"If she ever mentions it to me, I will tell her straightaway that she should leave them alone," Kakabo said.

Bevelyn and her husband were witnesses to the good changes that Joe had brought into the family since he became a part of it. Yet, their mother wanted him out of it because she thought he could not make her daughter pregnant.

Kwame Boafo knew almost all the police officers in Diasempa, including the Inspector, so together with his friend, he went to lodge a complaint that someone had defrauded him of one million cedis. The Inspector immediately dispatched a uniformed officer to accompany Boafo to get Kwaku. On the way, it was planned that Boafo's friend would pose as Kwaku's friend while he and the police lay in wait. Just as they had anticipated, when the friend knocked at the door, it was Cornie who opened the door.

"Good morning, Madam," the friend greeted with a smile.

"Fine morning," Cornie responded.

"I'm Kwaku's friend and one of our friends informed me that Kwaku has lost his job and fortunately, there is a vacancy at my place of work so I've come to ask him if he would be interested," the imposter said, still smiling.

"Kwaku really needs a job so he would be interested. What is your name, young man?" Auntie Cornie asked, making her way back inside to call Kwaku.

"Tell him One Touch," the man replied.

"Ei! One Touch, Kwaku really needs a One Touch from you for a change in his circumstance."

As soon as Cornie entered the door, the man signalled for the police and Boafo to approach. Kwaku's previous lifestyle had attracted so many friends to him that sometimes when they called him in town it took a while for him to recollect how he got to know them. He could not remember anyone by the name One Touch, but he thought it could be one of those that he used to buy drinks for in those good old days. Better still, he thought it could be a friend of some of his friends who wanted to reciprocate some of his generosity when the going was good.

He was only wearing trousers so he grabbed a shirt and put it on and led the way with his mother following. When Kwaku saw the officer and Boafo, he tried to rush back into the house, pushing his mother down in the process, but he was held by the officer with the help of the impostor and Boafo.

"Play it cool, mate, because now you are like a gold fish in a glass bottle with nowhere to hide," said the officer.

"What is it, Kwaku? One Touch what is going on? What has he done?" Auntie Cornie asked as she struggled to her feet to follow them outside.

"You will know when you come to the station," the officer replied.

Kwaku was handcuffed and driven to the station in Boafo's car. His mother limped back to the house, wailing. She was approached by one of the neighbours who witnessed the arrest to find out why.

"I was indoors when one of them came to say he was trying to get a job for Kwaku, so I went in to call him and the rest is what you have just witnessed," said Auntie Cornie.

"You had better go and find out from the police station now," advised the neighbour.

The neighbour wasn't very convinced with Cornie's explanation of the arrest because, considering Kwaku's lifestyle some few months back and his recent loitering in the neighbourhood lately, she smelt a rat.

At the station, Kwaku's charge was put to him as fraud. He was asked to pay the one million Cedis immediately and be released or go to court to plead his case the next day. After taking off the handcuffs, the officer in charge asked him to take off his shirt, watch, belt, slippers and wallet from his trousers pocket because he was to join the other inmates. An inventory was taken of the items before he was pushed into the narrow cell measuring about six feet by eighteen, holding eleven prisoners at that time.

Without any enquiry as to what brought him there, at the command of one of the inmates, they all started beating Kwaku. Areas around his head were the preferred target by majority of them. Only a few chose to hit the torso. They beat him until he started bleeding from his nose and mouth. The morning sun was at its peak so it was very hot in the cell. Sweat, tears and blood were all over him, especially around his face.

After a while, the one who ordered the beating asked what brought him there but he would not believe anything Kwaku said. The guy himself did not lay his hand on Kwaku. He just sat at a corner and amused himself with what was going on. Kwaku cried for help but the only people who could hear him were those beating him. The guy ordered them to stop when he felt Kwaku had had enough. He then told Kwaku that what he had just experienced was part of the welcome package, so he should prepare for some more later on. Auntie Cornie went to the police station and was told of Kwaku's charge and the demand or a court action the next day.

"Please can I see him for a few minutes? Maybe he could direct me to get the said amount from somewhere," Auntie Cornie pleaded.

"He would not be allowed to speak to anyone outside the cells unless the Inspector authorised that, and he is out on a mission," said the officer in charge.

Much as Cornie pleaded, the officer refused to let her talk to Kwaku so she had to leave the station confused and angry at the same time. In less than an hour after the arrest, someone came to ask Joe in the shop if he was aware of it and he said no so the informant said it might be a rumour, then. About an hour later, another person came to confirm to Joe that Kwaku was in the hands of the police. Joe decided not to do or say anything about it until he had been informed by Cornie or someone from the family. When Evelyn came to the shop later, Joe told her about it.

"I hear Kwaku was arrested this morning," said Joe.

"Oh Kwaku! So where is he now?" asked Evelyn.

"Honestly, I have not been told by anybody who knows the details, so there is not much I can say. A customer told me about it a few minutes ago."

"Please don't hesitate in helping him if you have to," said Evelyn.

"I will gladly help, if there is the need for me to do so," Joe said.

Since the day Agya Boakye organised the meeting to know the facts of what led to Joe sacking Kwaku from the shop, neither Joe nor Evelyn had seen Kwaku again. From the police station, Auntie Cornie went to see Doris for help. She told Doris that the police were demanding the full payment of the amount or else he would be taken to court the next day.

"So what do we do now?" asked Doris.

"That's why I've come to see if you could help, because I don't know where to get one million Cedis right now," said Cornie.

"I'm not so concerned about the money, but Kwaku's reputation. To have a prison record is not good at all," said Doris.

"Not at all, but that's what is going to happen if we are not able to get the money today."

"Why didn't he tell me that he owed someone?" asked Doris.

"I didn't know about it either, otherwise I would have made some arrangement to get it paid, rather than wait to get him arrested," Auntie Cornie said.

Doris had eight hundred thousand Cedis at home so she gave it to Auntie Cornie. She was saving this money to help her mother acquire a plot of land, but she would suspend all other things to seek Kwaku's freedom first. Cornie thanked her and said she was going to go round to look for the remaining two hundred thousand Cedis.

"I will have to go to the station at about 6:oopm so I'm wondering if you could meet me there around that time." requested Cornie.

"I will," said Doris.

In the cell, when Kwaku was thinking of how or where to get the money, his thoughts were interrupted by an authoritative voice.

"Where is one million?"

Kwaku heard the voice but he did not answer because he did not know that he was the one being referred to as One Million. An inmate told him he was wanted and he replied through his broken and swollen lips that his name was Kwaku.

"Come here quickly for your exercise," said the same voice.

Reluctantly, Kwaku ambled towards the man who by all indications was the boss of the inmates.

"Is that how you walk at home? Quick, kneel down. Raise your hands up and come to me here on your knees."

Kwaku did as he was commanded because he wanted to avoid further beatings.

"Now, do the same and go backwards, quick!"

He slapped Kwaku for not walking on his knees fast enough, and the drill continued for about five minutes with kicks and slaps.

Auntie Cornie and Doris were trying to avoid this kind of treatment, but until they were able to raise the remaining two hundred thousand Cedis, Kwaku had to endure it. Cornie went to Joe to inform him of the arrest in the hope that he would give her part of the money. Evelyn had gone to the market and Joe pretended not to know anything about it so after the normal pleasantries, he asked his aunt about Kwaku.

"I'm just coming from the police station because of him," said Auntie Cornie.

"Why?" Joe asked.

"The police refused to let me talk with him but according to them he owes someone one million Cedis and unless he pays the money, he will be taken to court tomorrow for judgment. He can even be imprisoned for that," she said.

Joe suspected that it might be Kwame Boafo, but he kept that to himself. He did not want to get involved in any negotiation with whoever the creditor may be so he gave one million Cedis to Cornie to go and get her son out of the cell. Under normal circumstances, Cornie should have told Joe that Doris had already given her eight hundred thousand Cedis and needed only two hundred thousand, but the greedy woman was taking advantage of his son's condition to make money.

She thanked Joe and promised to let him know of the outcome. Joe told her he should have accompanied her to the station but he was expecting some deliveries and did not know when Evelyn would return from the market. Cornie was glad that Joe could not go to the station with her because of the money given to her by Doris, since the latter was to meet her there.

People are different and so while Cornie was being dubious at the expense of her son's predicament, young Hagar was carrying out every advice her mother gave her to the letter. She saw an old lady carrying a bag and seemed to be struggling with it so she decided to help her.

"How far are you going, Nana?" Hagar asked.

"I am going to Kristom, near Opanin Kwaku Dampare's house," replied Nana Seimaa.

"You mean where they park the State Transport Corporation bus?" asked Hagar.

"Yes."

Hagar smiled and took the bag from the old lady.

"I am not going that way, but I can take it there for you, Nana," she said.

Hagar kept to the old lady's slow pace and the two talked as they went along. The old lady kept blessing Hagar till they reached her destination.

"God bless you all the days of your life. I pray that you get a good husband who will love you and care for you whenever you are ready to marry. May you bear children who will fear the Lord and be obedient to his word," Nana Seimaa said and pointed to her door.

Hagar thanked her for the prayers and wished God's blessings for the old lady too. On her way back home, Hagar felt so happy that she had been of help to someone and more so for the old lady's prayer and blessings for her. In her heart, she prayed for God to provide such opportunities to her always, where she could be of help to those who needed it.

Just before 6:00pm, Doris went to the police station with the two hundred thousand Cedis which she had gone to borrow from a friend. She was asking the officer in charge about Kwaku when Auntie Cornie arrived and called her aside.

"Did you get the rest of the money?" asked Doris.

"No, but I'm going to give them the eight hundred thousand cedis and plead with them to let him out to look for the rest," Cornie lied.

"I've gone to borrow from a friend to make up the one million," Doris said and gave the money to Cornie.

Cornie had left Joe's one million home before coming to the station. She wanted to use the eight hundred as bait for the cops to let Kwaku out to sort the rest out by himself. When they approached the officer to present the money for Kwaku's release, things turned out differently.

"The Inspector is not available and may not be back till about midnight," said the officer.

"OK, we have got the money so we want to pay for his release," said Auntie Cornie.

"I'm sorry, Madam, but you have to come back tomorrow," said the officer.

"Why?" asked Cornie.

"The Inspector wants to investigate his background, in case he has already got some criminal records."

"He is not a criminal. He has not got any criminal record. This is just an unfortunate incident with someone without patience," Cornie said angrily.

Kwaku heard his mother shouting at the officer but there was nothing he could do or say from where he was. He did not know of Doris' presence and, if at all he did, he would surely not have liked her to see him in that state.

"Please can we have a little chat with him?" Doris calmly asked the officer.

"No. Please come back tomorrow," the officer said.

When they realised that no amount of words would persuade the officer to let them speak to the prisoner, they left the station. Kwaku of all people, known as being the most generous guy among his friends, was now behind bars, among criminals and unable to communicate with the outside world, not even his own mother or girlfriend. He was considered the most generous because he spent as freely as the money came to him.

If Joe had not taken that bold decision to get rid of him, Kwaku might have sent his business crumbling in future and his own people might have blamed poor Evelyn. They would have said Joe was doing well before he got married and then his business took a nose dive afterwards. But it was the complete opposite. Evelyn had been a source of inspiration to Joe and a great supporter of his business ventures. He always discussed issues with her and sought her good opinion in managing the shop. Watching television in the living room that evening, Joe told Evelyn he had an idea that he wanted to share with her.

"What is it? You know I've always trusted your good ideas," Evelyn said.

"It's about moving to Accra," said Joe.

At the mention of Accra, Evelyn began to laugh and Joe asked her why she was laughing.

"I am not laughing because it's a funny idea. I am laughing because today, I mean now, this very moment, I know and believe that we were made for each other," she replied.

"Why do you say that?" asked Joe.

"My answer to that question is in my little notebook in the car," said Evelyn. "In fact, I had wanted to discuss something with you too on Sunday."

She called Hagar and told her to get the book for her. While Hagar was going to get the book, Joe asked Evelyn time and again to tell him why she made that statement but she insisted that the answer was in the book. In that little notebook Evelyn had made a list of things to discuss with Joe on Sunday, after church.

Like her husband, Evelyn had developed the habit of praying over every issue or idea before acting on it and she chose Sunday as the best day to discuss it with Joe, because it was their most relaxed day of the week. It was on rare occasions that they went out on Sundays after church, so it was the best time to talk. She had four items on the list. As soon as Hagar brought the book Evelyn opened a page and gave it to Joe to read what she wanted to discuss with him.

1. A teacher to help Hagar at home with Maths and English.
2. To teach Hagar how to drive.
3. A specific amount for our parents on regular basis.
4. A possible move to the city, preferably, Accra.

Joe was smiling as he read the items on the list and when he got to the last one he asked Evelyn when she had those ideas.

"The first three were about two or three weeks ago but the last one was on the night you told me what some of your relatives are saying about our condition," said Evelyn.

"I also decided on relocation when I heard about the rumours," Joe said.

They talked at length about these things. The first two were considered as future issues, the third one could be initiated immediately but the fourth one needed a lot of planning, because of the shop. Evelyn was of the opinion that they could get some reliable person from the church to run it and visit regularly for auditing, but Joe won't buy that.

"What I mean is a complete move from this environment which is somehow becoming hostile to us. I don't want a situation where our people would be seeing us every now and then to talk about us. We shall take everything from the shop and give the keys back to its owner," Joe made himself clear.

"That's right. Out of sight, they say, is out of mind," Evelyn added.

That wasn't how Joe had planned it initially. He wanted to be close to his people and that was why he came to establish in Diasempa,

229

but the same people were being hostile to him and his wife, so he was being compelled to move. He decided to go to the city to make some feasibility studies in the coming week. With attacks on their marriage coming from some of their in-laws and even outsiders, one couldn't blame the couple for getting out of the environment of their own people.

Had Joe been any other person he would not have listened to Cornie at all with regards to Kwaku's issue but he had given one million Cedis for his release. Sadly, greedy Cornie has kept the money.

"The President wants to see you," an inmate said to Kwaku, pulling him by the ear as instructed.

Knowing what could happen to him if he put up any resistance, Kwaku did not tell the guy to leave his ear. He endured the pain and calmly followed his lead. He asked the inmate if it was the national President who had come to Diasempa and wanted to see him.

"Why would the national President want to see a thief like you?" asked the inmate.

"I am not a thief. I only owed ..."

Kwaku wanted to explain to the guy that he wasn't a thief but the guy slapped him on the face and told him to shut up. He held his left ear again and pulled him to the boss. It was then that Kwaku realised that the guy who had been giving instructions and drilling him was referred to as the President of the cell. He was the longest serving prisoner and a hardened criminal. It was he who wanted to see Kwaku, not the national President. The inmate had pulled Kwaku's ear so hard that it hurt him. He covered the ear with the palm of his hand as he stood before the President.

"Boss, do you have a fan at home?" asked the President, addressing Kwaku as Boss

"Yes," Kwaku answered.

"What brand is it?" he asked.

"Toshiba," said Kwaku.

"Okay, go on and *Toshiba* me because it's too hot inside this empire," said the President.

He then turned to the inmate who had brought Kwaku to him and asked him to show Kwaku how to *Toshiba*. The inmate asked Kwaku to remove his trousers which he did, not daring to complain. The inmate collected Kwaku's trousers from him, held the waist and began to fan the President with the legs of the trousers from left to right and vice versa a number of times.

"That's enough. Give it back to him to do it. He's got to learn fast in this empire," said the President.

Kwaku grabbed the trousers from his trainer and began to *Toshiba* the President who was seated on the floor, close to the entrance of the cell with his legs stretched. He asked Kwaku again what brought him to the cell and Kwaku told him the truth as he had earlier tried to explain. He said he had borrowed one million Cedis from someone and lost his job just around that time so he was not able to pay back.

"The creditor got impatient and reported me to the police," said Kwaku.

"So you were brought here because of one million Cedis?" the President asked.

"Yes," he answered.

"Poor Mr One Million. You will be called Mr. One Million for as long as you remain in this empire," said the President.

"My name is Kwaku."

"Shut your dirty mouth and don't challenge the President of the empire."

From that sitting position, the President hit Kwaku with his foot and said if he wanted to know his name he would ask him. Kwaku looked about two or three years older than the guy, but as it were, he had become like a small boy and had to be obedient to him.

"You had better obey my commands and never talk back when I'm talking to you. Is that clear?"

"Yes," said Kwaku.

It was the duty of the last entrant to the cell to *Toshiba* the President whenever he felt he needed it, so the guy who was doing it before Kwaku arrived was happy when he took over his job. Kwaku kept on *Toshibaring* the President until he dosed off and Kwaku went back to the corner where he was.

Just around that time, Joe went to Auntie Cornie to find out if Kwaku was allowed home and she told Joe she would have to go back the next day because the Inspector was out on official prison business and would not be back till about midnight. Doris was with her and listened as Cornie talked with Joe.

"Did they take the money?" Joe asked.

At the mention of money, Doris looked at Auntie Cornie, wondering which money Joe was referring to. Was it the one million Cedis she had given to Auntie Cornie? Or was Joe going to thank her, show some appreciation for giving Cornie the money to get Kwaku out of prison? Will Joe give her back the money and say she didn't need to pay for it when he was around? She felt happy within that she had been able to play a part in an attempt to set Kwaku free, but Cornie was playing smart.

"No. They said I should bring it in the morning," said Cornie.

"Did the police tell you to whom he owed the money?" asked Joe.

"No. All they said was that he may be taken to court if the money was not paid in time. I didn't know that he owed anybody that amount of money, else I ..."

"Well, let's just wait and see what happens tomorrow when you take the money to them," Joe said, getting on his feet.

He gave Auntie Cornie some more money for a taxi back home from the police station if Kwaku was released. To cover up and change the subject of money, Auntie Cornie lamented that she could not tell if Kwaku was given any food since the morning that he was picked up, shedding some crocodile tears as she spoke. Apart from responding to Joe's greeting when he arrived, Doris remained silent till Joe departed.

"Oh, I'm sorry, I forgot to tell Joe that you gave me the money for him to thank you," Cornie lied to Doris.

"That's okay. We can talk about that later," said Doris.

Doris wasn't very convinced of Cornie's statement because she had taken notice of how the latter's face changed when Joe asked if the police accepted the money, but she could not comment on it. She only hoped that one day Joe would say something to her about the money and possibly reimburse her. She knew Joe as a benevolent man who would not want a poor girl like her to pay one million Cedis for his cousin's release from prison.

A few weeks earlier, Bevelyn had given birth to a second child and when she came home from the clinic, Efiemponi and Wohonipa, two distant cousins of Joe, paid her a visit. These two were among those spreading rumours about Evelyn and Joe. During their conversation at Bevelyn's, Efiemponi asked if Evelyn had been there and Bevelyn said it was Evelyn and Joe who brought them home from the clinic. When Bevelyn became pregnant with this baby, rumours about Evelyn and Joe's condition intensified. Efiemponi said she heard people saying that Evelyn was marrying money and not thinking of having her own children.

"Whoever said that is a liar. They have been trying over the years so I will suggest that you pray for them too," said Bevelyn.

The two cousins had other perceptions and laughed at Bevelyn's comment. They had believed a lie from Cornie years back and so didn't accept Bevelyn's truth.

"People are saying Joe might have used other means or all his energies to acquire wealth, otherwise how could he start from nowhere and suddenly become so rich?" Wohonipa said.

Bevelyn did not expect any of Joe's people to talk like that about him, at least not to his sister-in-law, so she tactically changed the topic.

"Some of our church leaders were here to see the baby and to pray for our family this morning and they said the Pastor would be coming here in the evening," said Bevelyn.

"I hear you've got a new Pastor. Is he like the former one? I hear he is..."

Bevelyn could not wait for Wohonipa to finish before she made a statement that was to silence her for a long time.

"You are always hearing from other people. I wonder what others hear from you and about you," said Bevelyn.

Efiemponi took a quick look at Wohonipa, their eyes met but none of them said a word. If all the family members would support and defend Evelyn like her twin sister had been doing, things would not have gone this far. Bevelyn was proving to be a real blood sister in this wise. Evelyn's problem was getting out of hand, and she was having sleepless nights as she cried her heart out to the Lord to bless her with a child. She tried to wear a smile during the day but at night, almost every night, it was a different story. One night she woke Joe up to tell him how she was feeling. She had been crying for a while before she shook Joe's shoulder for his attention.

"Joe, I love you and I know you love me too, but I don't think we can continue like this," she said with tears in her eyes.

"Continue like what?" asked Joe, half awake.

"Our childlessness is giving me sleepless nights and worried days. Now I can't face my family and friends anymore, and the way people look at me in town speaks volumes of what is on their minds."

Joe was fully awake now and sitting on the bed while Evelyn lay on her back, staring at the ceiling. With tears streaming down her temples, she said sometimes she wished the ground would open and swallow her when she was with mothers and their children.

"I can't take it any longer, Joe. I wish I were dead or out of this place."

Joe obviously did not know what to say to make his wife stop crying. He tried to console her but the tears just kept flowing onto her pillow.

"Don't speak like that, Evelyn. There is time for everything and don't forget also that God's time is the best," Joe said, tenderly.

"But Joe, you know what people are saying about us, especially, some of your own people and some of mine..."

"Let them say what they like, sweetheart. If we have had six children since we married, the same people would have gone around making other comments. Let them talk."

Joe was angry, not at his wife, but the entire situation was getting too much for him. The words that their own people were saying were making him mad. He continued to comfort Evelyn but she could not stop crying. As she cried, she pictured most of her school friends and ladies of her age group she knew in the town who had two, three or even four children. What was wrong with her that the doctors could not tell? Was anything wrong with Joe as people, including her own mother, were speculating?

She knew that she had not indulged in the corrupt ways that some girls were in the habit of doing. She had never had sex before getting married, so to suspect her of any sexually transmitted disease that could affect her fertility was unthinkable. Joe sat on the bed thinking while Evelyn cried her heart out. As he thought, the words *out of this place* hit home.

"Out of this place!"

Unconsciously, Joe said it out loud. Evelyn turned to stare at him. She opened her mouth slightly, wanting to say something but she stopped.

"We are going to get out of this place as soon as possible, Evelyn. I was thinking of us moving out slowly but, from the look of things, I think we've got to move out quickly."

For some time the couple had been making arrangements to move to Accra where they had already rented a shop. They were yet to finalise the tenancy agreement with the landlord of the flat they had gone to view near Banana Inn. They were planning to move the items in the shop to the city shop in bits, but that night, they decided to hire a truck that would cart all of them out at once. By the morning, Joe had suggested that they tell only their parents, the shop owner and a few very close friends about the move.

Joe had not made any plans to travel, but their decision as they talked throughout the night led to him having to go to Accra to arrange for a truck the next morning and also see the landlord at Banana Inn. Evelyn had said she wished she was dead or *out of this place* so Joe thought that so long as it was possible to get *out of this place*, he must do so quickly. Evelyn was at her wit's end and could even commit suicide if she remained in this place, Joe feared, so the earlier they moved, the better.

Meanwhile, Efiemponi and Wohonipa who had been talking negatively about Joe and Evelyn had almost come to blows sometime after they visited Bevelyn. Efiemponi accused Wohonipa of spreading scandal about Joe and his wife but Wohonipa denied it. As fate would have it, Darkoaa was visiting Efiemponi's mother and she heard them shouting at each other about her son. She waited patiently outside the gate to hear all that they had to say. Efiemponi explained to someone who was trying to calm her down that Wohonipa told her sometime ago that Belinda, Joe's girlfriend during his school days, had confided in someone that all her attempts to make Joe sleep with her had failed.

This story had, in fact, been part of Cornie's fabrications years ago during her initial opposition to Joe marrying Evelyn. She told some of the relatives that she had arranged for Joe to befriend Belinda but for some strange reasons, Joe did not sleep with her for the two years that they were together. Based on this false information, some of them had concluded that Joe was impotent. Over the years they had talked about it in secret but now Joe's mother has heard it all. Efiemponi and Wohonipa stopped the argument instantly when Maame Darkoaa burst in and threatened to tell Joe about it to find out the source of this rumour.

CHAPTER EIGHT

CORNIE INTENSIFIES HER PLOT

In a matter of days, Joe and Evelyn moved to Accra with Hagar and all that they needed there, after going with Agya Boakye to hand the shop's keys back to Mr Amoako. To show his appreciation, Joe gave Mr Amoako a lot of money and promised to come and see him whenever he was in Diasempa. Mr Amoako and his wife sobbed when receiving the keys because, since he started running the shop, Joe made sure that they lacked nothing in their home.

When Joe married, he had discussed the man's plight with Evelyn and together they treated the old couple as they did their own parents. In the last few years, the man's health had improved a little. There was always a smile on his face, all because of how he was being cared for by Joe and Evelyn. But now that his benefactors were leaving, how was he going to cope? This question was alarming to the couple, but Joe assured them of his continual providence.

On the first day when Joe opened his shop in Accra, a young man who owned a mattress shop opposite his came over to introduce himself to him as David Darko, called DD by friends. He said he was operating the shop with his wife who had just given birth to a baby girl and so was at home. Joe told DD he was new in the city and would introduce his wife to him later. He congratulated Joe on his relocation and with the passing of time the two were to become good friends.

Before they moved to Accra, Efiemponi and Wohonipa had always felt butterflies in their stomachs when they saw Joe. Although they lived in the same compound, the cousins had not been on good speaking terms since Darkoaa overheard them.

What made them even more scared was that they thought Joe must have been told about it and that soon, they were going to be called before the elders of the family. They wondered why Joe had not shown any sign of being angry with them. Efiemponi wanted to go and tell him that it was Wohonipa who had passed on the rumour, but on a second thought, she realised that her approach could awaken old memories. Wohonipa was likewise determined to shift all the blame on Efiemponi, should she be questioned.

Guilty consciences gave these two many sleepless nights, but Darkoaa had not said anything to Joe. It was only after Joe and Evelyn had moved to Accra that Darkoaa told her husband about what she had heard from the cousins.

"I want to tell Joe about it because it's a shame when your own people say such things about you after all the help he has been giving them," Darkoaa said.

"Let sleeping dogs lie, Darkoaa, don't ever let Kwadwo or Evelyn hear about this; it would shatter their already fragile dreams," said Agya Boakye.

"If anybody would talk like that about him, it shouldn't be his own cousins. Outsiders might have been unkind enough to say what they said," Darkoaa pointed out.

"Don't be surprised, because those who are close to you, I mean those who know you very well, are the ones who can hit you the hardest," said Agya Boakye.

Eventually, he persuaded Darkoaa that to avoid the malicious gossip spreading further, she should not let Joe know about it but Darkoaa insisted on talking to the girls' mothers.

"Well, I won't stop you from doing that, but be careful the way you go about it," he said.

Agya Boakye was a man of few words but they carried a lot of weight, so he managed to persuade Darkoaa to keep the encounter with the cousins to herself. Meanwhile, Joe and his household were settling well in their new home in the city. He told Evelyn and Hagar that they would all have to make a lot of changes to fit into their new environment. Hagar was told to be careful who she opened the door of the house to, if she was at home alone.

When Kwaku was released, Auntie Cornie told him that Doris had paid the one million Cedis, so he did not bother to look for Joe to say thank you to him before he moved to the city. Cornie reasoned that after a while, when Kwaku's prison experience had been buried, all that was connected to it would be forgotten as well. But in Diasempa, where everyone knew someone, would her action remain a secret forever?

One afternoon when they were at home alone, Cornie told Kwaku that Dan had come to look for him but he was sleeping, so Dan promised to come back. Kwaku had told his mother that prison is like hell on earth, and he would avoid anything that could possibly take him back there.

Dan met Doris in town one day and out of their conversation came a question from Dan that raised her eyebrows. Auntie Cornie, Joe or Doris might have somehow mentioned the money to someone and it had leaked. It was being rumoured in town that it was good of Joe to have paid for Kwaku's release after what he had done to him and his wife. Others, however, said the money was paid by Doris. This rumour got to Dan and being a concerned friend, he decided to find out the truth from Doris.

"By the way, do you know anything about the money that was used to pay the man whom Kwaku owed?" Dan asked.

"In fact, I wanted to get him out the same day he was arrested so I gave his mother all the money I had and went to borrow some more to make up what he owed," said Doris.

"So you paid the entire amount?"

"Yes. I used the money which I was saving to help my mother buy a plot and I'm still paying what I borrowed."

"I hear Joe, his cousin, paid for it," Dan said.

"That's not true," said Doris with a smile. "I went to the station together with his mother but..."

"Are you sure you were the one who paid it?" interrupted Dan.

"I did," Doris confirmed.

"Well, I heard it being said that it was Joe who gave his mother the money to go and get him out the next day," said Dan. "Any way, I'll see you later. I'm going to Koradaso."

Doris was surprised to hear this and as they went their separate ways, memories of Cornie's action on the day Joe visited her to find out if Kwaku was allowed home that day began to unfold. She remembered Cornie's reaction on that day when Joe asked whether the police had accepted the money or not. Whatever money Joe was asking about, she could not ask him or Cornie. She suspected something, but could not complain. Again, after Joe had left, the way Cornie explained that she had forgotten to ask Joe to thank her made her more suspicious, but she still could not ask for a better explanation.

Kwaku had not seen or heard from Joe since he moved to the city and he did not want to see him, certainly. Once when they were talking about Joe's move to the city, Kwaku brushed it off and said they could live their lives in the city while he lives his at Diasempa.

Indeed they were living their lives in the city, away from their own people and close to the doctor whom they were seeing. When their next visit was due and they went to see the doctor, he asked them how they were finding life in the city. Joe told him they were still trying to settle. At this visit it was revealed that because of their desperation for a child they had been making love constantly. Evelyn said most of the time they felt so tired that they didn't derive any pleasure from it, but because they did not know which occasion might make her pregnant, they were making love whenever and wherever they found the opportunity to do it.

"In fact, we do it more frequently than you would imagine, sometimes in a single day," Evelyn said.

"Well, besides my profession as a medical doctor, I'm an Elder of The Church of Pentecost and I believe that there is nothing God cannot do," said Dr Ankrah-Badu.

Joe and Evelyn looked at each other in amazement when the doctor mentioned The Church of Pentecost, so he asked them why they were surprised.

"We are also members of The Church of Pentecost," said Joe. "We used to worship at Diasempa but we have not been to church since we moved here."

"You need to come to church, then."

"We will, Elder," said Joe.

"Now going back to what you said earlier," said Dr Ankrah-Badu, "making love every now and then makes the sperms weak and that could possibly pose a problem."

Evelyn was thinking whether it was right for her to have said that to the doctor. She turned to look at Joe, but the doctor continued.

"Secondly, anxiety, being too desperate for a child, coupled with what others are saying of your condition could affect you hormones and make it difficult for conception to take place."

"So what can we do, Elder?" Evelyn asked.

"You see, whenever you make love it is just for pleasure, but there are some three days within a woman's menstrual cycle when she is most fertile and it's during these three days that you are most likely to conceive if intercourse takes place."

"And when are these three golden days?" asked Evelyn.

"They are the 13th, 14th and 15th days before your next period. Conception is most likely to occur when you have intercourse within these days. I will therefore advise you to abstain from sex a few days before these three days to strengthen the accumulated sperm and make them more active."

Joe was nodding as the doctor explained the situation to them. Dr Ankrah-Badu recommended that they relax, take a holiday, if possible, and fill their minds with hopeful thoughts. Evelyn's surprised expression soon turned into a smiling one. In her mind's eye she was already seeing herself pregnant as she looked at Joe and held his hand.

"You should imagine yourselves with a child. Stay positive!" said Dr Ankrah-Badu.

Doctor Ankrah-Badu invited them to the New Mamprobi Assembly of the church the following Sunday. Evelyn was beginning to feel happier and she never stopped smiling as they were leaving the doctor's office. He had given her some hope that all was not lost yet.

Evelyn's mother, however, was still insisting on her divorcing Joe. She had gone to Bevelyn to tell her that it was better for Evelyn and Joe to go their separate ways so that at least part of the money she had helped Joe to acquire would be Evelyn's.

"Mum, is it because of the money that you want her to divorce Joe?" Bevelyn asked.

"It's a factor, of course, so that she can keep what she has acquired so far in our family."

"That's wrong, Mum. And I say it again, it's a wrong thought," said Bevelyn.

Bevelyn almost told her mother not to come to her again to complain about Evelyn's childlessness, but she managed to swallow those words. She could not imagine why her mother should want to force

Evelyn to leave Joe. When Konadu realised that she could not get Bevelyn to support her, she left in anger, vowing not to give up until they had separated.

When Joe and Evelyn attended the New Mamprobi Assembly the next Sunday to see Dr Ankrah-Badu on the platform, they felt excited and also enjoyed the service. They had missed the church atmosphere for some time so they were very glad. On the platform also was Elder Antwi who resembled the father of one of Joe's school mates at Miawani, so after the service Joe approached him to ask if any of his sons had attended his former school. Elder Antwi said no, but they however became friendly and Joe sometimes visited him at home because they lived in the same locality.

As their friendship developed, Joe started sharing some thoughts with Elder Antwi. By that time, the shop was well established, but occasionally Joe had to shut it if he had to go to business meetings and Evelyn had other things to do. Once, Elder Antwi met Evelyn in town on her way from a hospital appointment and when he enquired of Joe she told him he had gone to Tema to order some cement.

"So who is in the shop?" asked Elder Antwi.

"There is no one there. It's shut."

"That's not good enough, I think you should keep the shop open during business hours," Elder Antwi suggested.

It was a casual suggestion, but Evelyn took it to heart and discussed it with Joe later in the day when they were going home. Joe had already made it clear to Evelyn that due to Kwaku's action, he did not want to employ anyone again but Evelyn said no matter what had happened back home in Diasempa, a time would come when they would need another hand in the shop, considering the trend of things.

As was her usual character, whenever they were discussing an issue and Joe seemed not to be agreeing with her point, Evelyn would rest the matter and take it from another angle at a different time.

She changed the subject and talked about the driving lessons for Hagar. When they got home, they told Hagar about their plans for her, concerning driving and on hearing from Joe that they had already discussed with an instructor, Hagar jumped with her hands up in excitement.

"Me, driving?" she asked herself, looking up to the ceiling as if she was expecting an answer from up there.

"Don't go telling people about it till they see you behind the steering wheel one day," said Evelyn.

"When would that be, Maam?" she asked.

"You will start lessons in two weeks' time," Evelyn said.

"The instructor will let us know the exact day and time by Friday," Joe added.

"Is it very difficult to drive?" asked Hagar.

"It's like any other skill. All you need is determination and the will to make it," said Joe. "You can, if you really want to."

"I want to, so I will make it."

Hagar's excitement was beyond what words could describe. Her entire life was going to take a different turn, because no one expected a school drop-out like her to drive. Since moving from her mother's house, her appearance had changed for the better, and now she was going to drive. It was a great joy for her.

The following Sunday, at church, Elder Antwi spoke to Evelyn again about getting someone to help them in the shop. He went on to suggest Rexy, a young man of reputable character in the church to her. Elder Antwi said he had known Rexy for a while and considered him to be someone reliable. With what she heard about Rexy from the Elder, Evelyn managed to persuade her husband to give the young man a trial, so in a matter of weeks, after Elder Antwi had spoken with Joe also, Rexy started working with the couple as a shop assistant.

The one million Cedis issue involving Cornie, Joe and Doris had not been solved yet, and Dan was eager to find out the truth. He had been to Kwaku's the day before and learnt that Doris was at home with a cold so he decided to visit her and also to enquire about the money. Doris told him that she had decided not to ask Kwaku about it. She said since every rumour had a source, she believed that one day the truth would come out. Before leaving Doris's place, Dan told her that whenever the truth did come out, it would erupt like a volcano.

Serwaa's lie to the people of Diasempa that she had been made redundant went down very well with Auntie Cornie who had genuinely come home for the same reason. They had been good friends since they met and when Cornie told her about Joe and his wife and made some suggestions, Serwaa was willing to become a second wife, if they could not get rid of Evelyn. Anytime the two were together, Joe became their talking point. Cornie had planned to introduce Serwaa to Joe whenever he was in Diasempa but Joe had not been home for a long time.

"If the mountain does not come to Mohammed, then Mohammed must go to the mountain," Cornie said to Serwaa one day. "So as a first step plan, I want to send him a letter of invitation through you."

"You mean to go to him in Accra?" asked Serwaa.

"Yes. And must you go looking SAS (Simple And Smart) because he is the kind of man you cannot impress with flashy things," said Cornie.

Serwaa smiled but said nothing to this suggestion of looking great when meeting Joe. She knew she could always dress to entice men, so going SAS was not a problem to her at all.

"What if his wife is in the shop with him when I go?" she asked.

"Don't let that bother you because you are not going to discuss anything with him. Your mission is to give him the letter and walk out of the shop. That's the more reason why you must look smart so that as soon as he sets his eye on you, he will be thinking of you after you are gone."

"When do you want me to go?"

"Tomorrow morning, if that's fine by you."

"That's perfect, I can make it tomorrow," Serwaa said with pride.

"If you go and he tries to engage you in a conversation pretend to be in a haste and do not show any interest," said Cornie.

"Okay."

The next morning when Serwaa started the journey that she felt could change her entire life Joe was in his shop awaiting the arrival of some goods that he had ordered. The shop was among a group of others on Quartey Papafio Avenue in Okaishie which made the place busy at all times during the day. The Central Fire Service Office, Central Police Station, Motor and Traffic Union, Striking Force, Kantamanto, Makola 1 and 2 markets were all close by, so it was indeed a very busy area.

Porters, both female and male, were always around looking for work. Most of these porters slept in front of the shops after work each day. Whenever the porters saw a loaded truck in the area, they would run after it, each one hoping to be among those to offload it and this morning was no different. They had followed the truck from the T-junction opposite the MTU and the Striking Force and as soon as the driver parked, the truck was surrounded by not less than twenty of them.

Among the order were some roofing sheets which were due for collection by a customer that morning, but unfortunately, the item was not on the invoice. Joe asked about the sheets and the driver said if they were not on the invoice, it meant they had not been included. The driver advised him to call the office but Joe said it could be a mistake on the invoice, so he would wait till they have finished offloading the truck.

In Rexy's house that morning there was an accident. David, his twelve-year-old son, had fallen on the steps and dislocated his ankle. Akyaa, Rexy's wife, was cooking in the kitchen when she heard David screaming in pain. When she rushed to see what had happened, she also shouted for help and everyone who was at home that time rushed to the scene.

A young man in his early twenties carried David on his back to the main road as his mother wailed along, asking for help from the passing drivers to take them to the clinic. Most of the drivers drove past unconcerned and others peeped through their windows but offered no help. However, one Good Samaritan stopped to pick them to the Mamprobi Polyclinic.

Joe needed four porters to offload the truck, so he called one who had worked for him before and told him to select three others that he felt were capable of helping him. He instructed the leader to get on the truck with another one and the other two to cart the goods to the warehouse at the back of the shop. While Joe and the driver checked the goods at the back of the truck, Rexy was in the warehouse with a pen and paper, cross-checking as the porters brought them in.

The roofing sheets were not on board and Joe was worried, because he didn't want to disappoint his customer. When they had finished Joe paid the porters, closed the shop and joined Rexy in the warehouse to reposition some of the goods which had been dropped haphazardly.

"We must try to get ourselves ready before customers start coming to the shop," Joe said.

"What did the driver say was the reason for not bringing the sheets?" asked Rexy.

"He didn't even know that they were part of the order. I will call the office soon after we have put things where they should be."

They were still talking about the sheets and arranging the goods when a messenger came to inform Rexy of David's accident. On hearing this, Joe told Rexy to close the warehouse while he got the car key from the shop so they could go and see the boy.

"Boss, let me go in a taxi so you can sort the roofing sheets out," Rexy said.

"We both have to go, Rex," insisted Joe.

"Your wife has taken him to the Mamprobi Polyclinic," said the messenger.

"Boss, let me go and see him first and if there is the need for you to come over I'll send you a message," said Rexy.

Rexy was worried that the shop would be closed because of his son, but Joe told him not to worry and as he was going to get the car he said:

"I have to be there with you, Rex. What if he was my child?"

This question silenced Rexy from expressing any more concerns about the closure of the shop because he was very much aware of Joe's desperation for a child. In their easy moments, Joe had often talked to him about their situation and how that had forced them to move from Diasempa to Accra. Rexy knew that Joe would do anything or pay any amount to get a child of his own and he had always referred Joe to Abraham. He told Joe not to give up, but keep on trusting the God of Abraham who gave him a child even at a time when it was humanly, logically and medically impossible for Sarah to conceive. So when Joe asked, *'What if he was my child?'* it reminded Rexy of some of the intimate moments they had shared.

Joe called to tell Evelyn of the accident and said they were on their way to the clinic. Joe's house was closer to the clinic than from the shop. Besides, at that time of the morning in Okaishie, the traffic hardly moved, so Evelyn told him she could get there before them. For some five minutes before they got to the clinic neither Joe nor Rexy spoke and it was apparent that they were praying for the boy in their hearts.

At the reception, they were told that the boy was being attended to and when Rexy asked of his wife the receptionist said she and another lady were with the boy. Evelyn had arrived some ten minutes earlier. They were allowed to go and see the boy for a few minutes. Rexy held David's hand and asked him how it happened and he said he was trying to catch his falling plate of porridge when he missed his step on the stairs. Akyaa was standing close by with one hand on the boy's pillow.

"I was in the kitchen when I heard him screaming in pain so I rushed there only to see him at the base of the stairs, holding his ankle. He said he went to take a book from the bedroom, while holding his bowl of porridge," Akyaa was explaining to them when the doctor appeared from the adjoining room.

"The x-ray shows no fracture, that's the good news," the doctor announced, pointing at the film which he was holding. "It's going to be sore for a while, though, and that could cause him some pain, but he would be given some pain killer to ease it."

They were all silent as the doctor made some notes in a small book which he later placed in his breast pocket.

"Could you please wait outside while we work on the leg? One of the parents could stay with him for a while," he said.

Rexy told his wife to wait outside with the others and when they got to the corridor, Joe called the messenger who was standing at the entrance to join them and Joe said a short prayer for David's speedy recovery. After waiting for sometime, Joe left for the shop to sort out the roofing sheets with the suppliers. He told Evelyn to stay with them a little longer, so as to lend a helping hand just in case there was something to be done.

When Serwaa arrived at Okaishie and saw that Joe's shop was shut, she thought her trip had been in vain and was thinking of taking the letter back because she could not leave it with anyone. Auntie Cornie had instructed her to deliver it to Joe by her own hand as a part of the plot, so after hanging around for a while she decided to enquire about Joe from Akowuah who owned the next shop.

"Good morning, Sir," greeted Serwaa.

"Fine morning, lady. How can I help you this morning?" asked Akowuah, thinking Serwaa was a customer.

"Please do you know if the owner of this shop would open today?"

"Yes, in fact, it was opened this morning but the owner had to go and see someone at the hospital. I'm sure he would soon be back," said Akowuah.

"OK. Thank you very much," Serwaa said.

Serwaa, smartly dressed in black skirt and light green blouse, looked astonishing, even without make-ups. Akowuah, a well-known womaniser in the area, offered Serwaa a seat to wait for Joe but she refused to sit. She told him she was going to buy something and would be back shortly. He wanted to engage her in a conversation, hoping she could be a prey, but Serwaa had got the information she needed from him so she thanked him again and walked away.

She crossed the road and walked a little further away, heading towards the MTU. When she got to the neem trees at the T-junction on Kinbu Road, she turned left as if she was going to Kwame Nkrumah Avenue. Before she got to the junction to make the left turn, each time she looked back, she had seen Akowuah looking at her. She walked on a little further, but before she got to Kwame Nkrumah Avenue, she turned back and went to stand under the trees at the junction where she could see Joe's closed shop.

Serwaa decided not to go closer to the shop so as to avoid Akowuah because from her experience with men, she could read what was on his mind. She came for Joe and so she wanted to see Joe and not any other man. Even to Joe, as part of Cornie's plot, she did not have to talk with him for a longer period. About thirty minutes later Joe came to open the shop but she waited for him to settle down before going to introduce herself to him as Serwaa, from Diasempa.

"I saw Auntie Cornie at the station this morning and she gave me this letter to give to you," she said, as she handed the letter to Joe.

"Thank you," said Joe. "Do you live here in Accra?"

"No. I have come to collect some documents from the Ministries and would be going back in the afternoon."

"Can you please pass by on your way back for a message to her?" asked Joe.

Serwaa had tried to remain as casual as possible but this time she punctuated her composure with a mild smile.

"Yes, I can. I will come and see you before I go back."

"If you come and I'm not around, my wife would be, so just introduce yourself to her."

Evelyn was the last person Serwaa ever wished to see, so she decided that if she returned and Evelyn was alone in the shop, she would hang around like she had done earlier until Joe showed up. Joe watched her impressive figure as she left the shop, but he did not allow his eyes to transfer what he had seen of her to his mind. He thought of what the woman he had been trying to avoid had to say in the letter. Many times, Cornie had sent people to him to ask for money, so initially, he imagined that she was once again in need of some cash. He put the letter on the counter to go and do something else first, but a small voice told him to read it as it may contain a different matter, so he picked it up to open and it read;

> Dear Joe,
>
> I hope you are fine and business is also going on well. Lately, I have been thinking too much about your

marriage and the condition in which it is now. I have therefore consulted a few of our relatives as to how to handle the situation and I will gladly appreciate if you could rush down to see me for some discussions. Let me know as to when you will be able to come.

Yours,
Auntie Cornie.

"This woman is getting on my nerves. When will she ever stay away from my marriage?" Joe asked himself as he tore the letter into pieces.

Serwaa had no business whatsoever at the Ministries, so she went window shopping in another part of the city where she was sure no one knew about her past life at Abeka Lapaz. That same morning, Cornie went to see Joe's mother and suggested to her that it was about time Joe got rid of Evelyn because she felt nothing good was going to come out of her. She tried to convince Darkoaa into believing that six years was a long time to stay in a marriage which, to her, seemed unproductive.

"Don't you want to see your grandchildren or a grandchild, at least?" she asked.

"Well, I'm concerned too, but I can't do much in the situation. The best I can do is to pray for God's mercy on their behalf, and that I have always done," Darkoaa said.

"For how long would you continue to pray? We must find a way to help him out of this mess. Don't you think he needs a second wife who can be productive? Or divorce this good-for-nothing-girl?" Cornie asked.

"Why do you have such a thought, Cornie?" Darkoaa asked. "Don't forget that God has a plan for everyone's life. If this is their own cross, we have to help them carry it, instead of trying to manipulate God's plan."

The conversation turned into argument and Cornie said she would have a word with Joe about the issue, as if she hasn't been doing that already. Darkoaa got upset and told her never to make any attempt of sowing that kind of evil seed into Joe's conscience.

"You never know, maybe he is thinking the same way, divorce or a second wife," said Cornie.

"Never! Joe will never think of doing such a thing. I rebuke such a thought in the name of Jesus!"

"There she goes, *'in the name of Jesus,'*" Cornie said and got up to leave.

How could any mother trust her son so much? How could Darkoaa have so much confidence in her son that he would never do such a thing as divorcing the woman he has wedded? That he would not even think of it, let alone do it? The Bible tells us to train a child the way he should go and when he is old, he will not depart from it. Darkoaa and her husband had instilled godly way of life into their son as a child and brought him up the way he should go. So now that he was old, she was bold enough to trust him that he would not depart from the way in which he had been instructed.

Joe had also learnt from the good book that he had to be faithful to the wife of his youth. He had taken an oath before God, in the assembly of the people of God, that he would love and cherish Evelyn at all times, that nothing but death would separate them. How then could he turn around to do the opposite? Joe was well respected by all and considered to be too humble a man to divorce his wife or take a second wife.

In the shop, after Joe had spoken to one of his business partners about certain goods on phone, he asked Evelyn if she could go back to the clinic to check on Rexy and his family.

"Can I call this telepathy?" Evelyn asked, smiling.

"Why?" Joe asked.

"I was just waiting for you to finish and tell you that I wanted to go and see them."

"Off you go then. Please do get them some snacks on your way."

"I've already got some in the car," said Evelyn, picking her car keys to leave.

Great minds think alike, they say. It is also said that even in the midst of a crowd, every mother could identify the voice of her child. So in the compound where a lot was going on, it wasn't a surprise that Akyaa might have been the only one who heard the screams of her son when he fell. When she rushed to the scene, she left what she was cooking on the stove and forgot to turn it off. Some of the tenants left for work afterwards and the rest of them were either in their rooms or engaged in other activities while the busy-for-nothings talked about the incident.

The shared kitchen door was closed and whatever Akyaa was cooking caught fire. Someone passing by noticed the smoke from the kitchen window and raised the alarm. So while David was in pain at the clinic, their kitchen was also on fire! By the time it was brought under control, the fire had already caused some damage, including a co-tenant's fridge.

"She will have to pay for my fridge. How could she be so careless?" fumed Dede, the co-tenant.

"Rule out carelessness because even someone with an elephant's memory would have done the same thing, considering the pain in which the boy was," said another tenant.

"You can say whatever you want and cite all the excuses, but my fridge must be replaced," Dede demanded.

It was turning into a kind of confrontation so a third tenant told the sympathiser to stop and she did, but that didn't stop Dede from calling Akyaa all sorts of names. Being a very disrespectful woman, most of the tenants decided to leave Dede alone as she tried to clear some of the debris, cursing Akyaa and saying that she would not take it lightly with her.

Rexy was at the reception when Evelyn arrived at the clinic again. David's leg had been put in plaster and they were waiting for the completion of the paper work.

"Have you informed his school?" asked Evelyn.

"No. But I will do so as soon as we get home," said Rexy.

Moments later, Akyaa came out, pushing David in a wheelchair. Rexy went to take over the pushing and Evelyn handed the bag of snacks to Akyaa.

"Let's go to the car and I will drop you off at home," Evelyn said.

"I'm going to miss school," David said to his mother.

"Never mind," said Akyaa. "You'll soon be fine."

In the car, Rexy said to Evelyn that he would return to the shop in the afternoon but Evelyn told him not to bother until the next day. She had not discussed this permission with Joe but she knew that her husband would be fine with it.

When Serwaa came back to the shop, Joe was attending to a customer, so she waited until he was free before approaching him. Joe had already seen her and apologised for keeping her waiting. In a very sweet, melodious voice, Serwaa said with a smile:

"That's okay, business first."

"My assistant's son had an accident this morning in which he dislocated his ankle so I'm going to be very busy today," Joe said.

He went back to the till to bring a parcel for Auntie Cornie and told Serwaa to tell her that she would hear from him. He also gave Serwaa an envelope containing some money. That was one of the things that made most people from Diasempa who came in contact with Joe respect and like him a lot. He will always do something for you to remember him by, especially if he was meeting you for the first time.

"This is to say a big thank you for the trouble of having to come back here," he said.

"Thank you so much. This is a great surprise," she said.

"My regards to the people at home," Joe said.

"Okay, thanks a lot."

As she left the shop, Serwaa swayed her waist in her well fitted skirt that showed her guitar-shape figure. Joe took notice of it, but he was not impressed one bit. Over the years, Joe had mentally blinded his eyes to all the antics of other women. His mind was so conditioned on God and Evelyn that, in the whole wide world no woman could ever entice him. Evelyn knew this fact and felt so assured that no woman could take Joe from her.

As Evelyn's car approached the house, they could see people gathered on the road that led to the house. At first, Rexy thought they were there to sympathise with David, but as they got closer, the look on their faces made Rexy ask no one in particular what was going on.

"Your wife did not turn off the stove when she was rushing David to the hospital so your kitchen is burnt," someone responded from the crowd.

Perplexed, Rexy almost left the boy in the car with Akyaa and Evelyn, but he came back to help him out of the car and unto the wheelchair which the ladies had set up. All of them, except David, went into the kitchen to check the damage and came back to the boy who was now crying, not from the pain in his leg this time, but from what he was seeing and hearing.

"It's my fault," he said.

"Don't say that, Dave, it's an accident," said Evelyn, with her hand on his shoulder.

Dede had gone out of the house before they arrived, but someone told Rexy what she had said about wanting her fridge replaced as soon as possible. Evelyn heard it but she said nothing until she went back to the shop and told Joe about it. Rexy's own fridge was partly burnt too, but not as bad as Dede's and replacing both fridges required a lot of money.

Because of Dede's arrogance, Rexy dreaded her return to the house. He was very quiet for the rest of the day, thinking of David and the fridge. Rexy told Akyaa that if he had the money, he would have gone to town to get the fridge before her return.

When Dede left the house during the confusion that was going on, she went to inform her husband at work about the accident and the fridge. From the way she spoke and acted her husband suspected that she might have made a demand for the fridge.

"So how is David?"

"They were not back from the clinic when I left home. I'm going to make them pay for the fridge."

"What? Don't think about doing that," said the husband.

"Well, if you don't need the fridge, I need it," said Dede.

"Forget it, it's only a fridge."

"Oh, you want me to forget about it, do you know how I manage in the kitchen?"

"I know it's not going to be easy but we can do without it for the time being, I believe," said the husband.

"Until when?" asked Dede. "Don't tell me to forget it because I have already demanded a replacement," she said and left the office in anger.

'Money talks,' it is said, so when you don't have money you tend to live your life on the quiet, slow lane, just like Kwaku. He had no job and none of his so-called friends bothered to know how he was coping, except Dan. But he could not help Kwaku financially, because he too was a struggling man.

The name Mr. One Million which the President of the cell had given to Kwaku was known only to himself and those who were in the cell. He had talked about what he went through in the cell, including the *Toshiba* experience but not about his new name. He knew the power in a name and thought that if other people got to know about it, it would be big news in the town so he kept that to himself. But one day, unfortunately, he met another ex-convict.

"Hey! Mr. One Million," the guy called Kwaku from behind.

Kwaku turned and recognised him but said nothing and kept going.

"How is the going Mr. One Million?" he asked.

"Man, don't ever call me that again" said Kwaku, apparently not happy being addressed by his highly kept secret name. "My name is Kwaku."

"I came out last week and I'm going to see a friend at Zongo," said the ex-convict.

Kwaku turned to walk away from this guy who was getting on his nerves by trying to engage him in conversation.

"Ok, I will see you later Mr. One Million. Oh no, sorry, Kwaku."

Kwaku turned to look at him again without saying a word and walked away. As he went, he kept looking back to see if the guy was following him. During the rest of the day, the name Mr. One Million haunted Kwaku constantly. He wondered how many people have got to know about it and when or where another person would address him by it. He should have warned this ex-convict sternly about it, he thought.

Not long after Kwaku got home and into his room, Serwaa returned from Accra. She told Cornie that Joe said she would hear from him, but did not say exactly when that would be. She gave Auntie Cornie the parcel from Joe but she did not tell Cornie that Joe gave her some money too. Cornie assured Serwaa that Joe would surely come to see her.

"I will send him a reminder if I don't hear from him in the next few days," said Cornie.

"Do I have to go there again?" Serwaa asked.

'No. We have to be tactful and not let it look so obvious that you are being pushed to him. Let us play it cool till he bites the bait."

Talking in a low voice so as not to attract Kwaku's attention, Auntie Cornie said she would scheme the whole plot in a way that would involve some of their relatives giving their support. As they planned this evil towards Joe, he and his wife were also thinking of the good they could do to help Rexy and his family.

"When troubles come, they come in chains," Joe said to Evelyn.

"Yes. Otherwise, how can all these happen to a man in a single day?" asked Evelyn.

They thought so much about Rexy and his troubles that they decided to do something to ease the tension on him. Evelyn recalled what the other tenants told Rexy about Dede's demand. She suggested to Joe that if they could sort out the fridge for Rexy, it would take away a sizeable chunk of his problems. It was agreed that Evelyn would go and buy one in the morning and take it to them. She was also to tell Rexy not to come to work until he had sorted things out in the house.

Just like the way trouble comes, help could also come when you least expect it. Rexy and his wife had David's injury to think about, but the demand from Dede far outweighed that. It was infringing on their peace. Dede had earlier told them in plain words that she wanted the fridge replaced latest by the weekend. So during the night, Rexy told Akyaa that in the morning, he would plead with Dede again to give them some more time to deal with David's injury first.

"What if she insists on having it by the weekend as she said?" asked Akyaa.

"In that case, we would be left with no other option than to go and borrow money from God knows where," replied Rexy.

The couple talked at length about the fridge but they could not think of where to turn to for help. Deep within himself, Rexy was thinking of going to plead with Joe for a loan to sort out the fridge but he decided not to voice out his thoughts for the time being. Joe and his wife had been doing him a lot of good and Rexy felt it would look like taking advantage of their generosity. D.D., Joe's friend, was also very nice to Rexy and he was considering going to ask for a loan from him instead of asking Joe. But again, he did not know how Joe would feel if he got to know about it later. While all these thoughts raced in his mind, he fell asleep.

The next morning, before going to school, one of David's friends came to inquire of him. He said he had heard of the accident at school the previous day and had come to see how his friend was feeling before going to school. Unfortunately, he could not see David as he was still asleep. Akyaa told the boy that David was in pain during the night and had only managed to sleep at dawn so she would not like to wake him up.

"I am very sorry to hear what has happened to my best friend. I will come back during break time to see how he is feeling," he said.

"Thank you very much. What's your name again?" asked Rexy who had just come out of the room.

"Jonathan."

"Oh! is that why you two are friends? Do you know the story in the Bible about David and Jonathan?"

"I know they were friends but I don't know much about their friendship," said Jonathan.

"I will explain it to you from the Bible when you come back," Rexy promised.

"Okay, Sir. Thank you."

Good friends always share ideas and whatever affects one concerns the other, so at the time when Jonathan went to check on his good friend, Serwaa and her friend Betty, on the way to the market, were also discussing marriage.

"I'm trusting God to send the right man into my life one day. I don't want to rush into any relationship which could disturb the peace I'm enjoying in the Lord at the moment. You are lucky for Kay," said Betty.

"I'm not going to marry him because he hasn't got the kind of money that I'm looking for."

"Eei, you and money!" Betty exclaimed.

"What can you do without money?" asked Serwaa.

"Money is not everything, you know," said Betty.

"I know, but you've not answered my question. What can you do without money?"

"Money is good, but there are thousands of people having a lot of money but they don't have peace."

"When we are talking about money, you are talking about peace," Serwaa said with a cunning smile.

Serwaa was having Joe in mind and the assurances she had received from Auntie Cornie made her so confident that come rain or shine, she was going to marry him. Her plans were that even if Joe did not divorce Evelyn, she was prepared to go in calmly as a second wife, then later treat Evelyn in a way that would make her run away from the marriage.

It looked like Serwaa was being controlled by some external forces that she herself was not aware of, because she had always gone for rich men or those at top positions for their money. This had often ended on a bad note, but being blinded by money, she never learnt her lessons. Her relationship with her former boss and his friend should have made her turn a new leaf, but fools never learn until they are crushed, when it is too late to learn. She had set her eyes on Joe and Evelyn and was determined to get between them at all costs, with Cornie's assistance.

Serwaa had not had any interaction with Evelyn before but from what Auntie Cornie had told her, she knew Evelyn was a humble lady who would not put up a fight. Once when they were talking about getting rid of Evelyn, Cornie told Serwaa that Evelyn was too soft to compete with as a rival.

In the morning, as they had decided, Evelyn went to an electrical shop at Kokomlemle where they sold both used and new electrical appliances to buy the fridge. As she headed for Rexy's house at Aboloo Junction, Evelyn wondered how to get the fridge off the truck if Rexy happened not to be at home.

At break time, Jonathan decided to go and see David again and some of their friends went with him. David was sitting in the open with his leg on a low chair. His mother sat close by and Rexy was in the kitchen cleaning some leftover debris. David was the first to see his friends coming but he said nothing until his mother saw them too.

"That is your friend coming with others," Akyaa said.

"Yes, I've seen them," David replied.

They were four: Jonathan, Daniel, Kofi and a girl called Esther. Akyaa went to bring a bench for them to sit close to David. Jonathan asked David how the accident happened, although they had been given the details of it at school the previous day. The other boys started talking before David could respond to the question.

"Maybe he does not want to play football again," Daniel said with a smile.

"No, he just wants some days off from school," Kofi added.

As they cracked these boyish jokes, Esther felt very uneasy. A shy girl, she was not used to these types of jokes, not when someone was in pain.

"Would you two stop that joke," she said.

They all burst into laughter, including David as he used both hands to hold above the knee of the injured leg. He could feel the pain in the ankle as the muscles tightened because of the jerk from the laughter. Rexy came out to see the visitors on hearing the noise.

"Hi Jonathan! Are you back?" Rexy asked.

"Yes, just as I promised. I came with Daniel, Kofi and Esther."

"Queen Esther," said Rexy.

"Eei, I'm not a queen," said Esther.

"You could become a queen in future. Esther is a queen to me as stated in the Bible," Rexy said.

Jonathan had forgotten the promise Rexy made to him but when he mentioned the Bible again he asked:

"Sir, can you please explain the friendship between Jonathan and David in the Bible to us?"

"Yes, Jonathan was the son of the first king of Israel called Saul," Rexy began. "And David was one of the sons of a man called Jesse. When a Philistine giant called Goliath was taunting the people of Israel at war front, it was the young boy, David, about seventeen years of age, who was able to kill him to bring glory to God and saved Jonathan's father from shame. So Jonathan, who was about the same age as David became friends with him."

Rexy could not continue as Evelyn appeared, looking as gorgeous as always. The house was not accessible by car so she left it where she had parked the previous day.

"Hello, everyone!" said Evelyn.

They all responded as Evelyn put her hand on David's shoulder and asked how he was feeling. Rexy introduced Evelyn to the kids as his manager's wife and them to her as David's friends from school. Akyaa went to the kitchen as they talked.

"How is Uncle Joe?" David enquired.

"He is fine. He has gone to the shop and he asked me to bring something to your parents which I hope your friends would be able to help your Dad to bring from the car."

"Sure they can. Jonathan, can you please go with my Dad," David said.

"David and Jonathan," said Evelyn, "you remind me of the story of the two friends in the Bible."

"I was just telling them the story when you came in," said Rexy.

"I'm always delighted to see children at one place like this, showing concern for one another," Evelyn said in a whisper to Rexy.

Akyaa returned from the kitchen with some chopped pineapple on a tray for David's friends. Jonathan, who seemed to be the leader in every way, reached for the tray and decided to share it, but Daniel and Kofi were impatient as they picked a piece each with laughter. Evelyn could not help and so joined the fun, picking a piece herself.

"How happy, delightful, pleasant and joyful it is to be with innocent children," Evelyn said to Akyaa.

Again, her statement was a whisper, but Jonathan heard her and asked Evelyn if she ever played with her children like that at home. The question instantly provoked a lot of thoughts in her mind. *'Play with your children like that at home?'* If she had even one, she would do all she could to spend a lot of time with that child. But is she ever going to have one at all? This was the question that she had been looking for answers to over the years. She turned to Akyaa and pretended not to have heard Jonathan. She was saved by the taste of the pineapple which was very sweet but not enough. The boys kept scrambling for the pieces. It wasn't the right time to be gentle. One had to be fast to get the most.

As the scrambling continued, Evelyn asked if they could go to the car and leave the remaining few pieces for poor Esther who was chewing like a real lady should, slowly. Many times, Joe and Evelyn had brought bags of rice, *gari,* cooking oil and other essential commodities to Rexy and his wife which Dede had often benefited from, but Rexy was in suspense as to what they were going for this time. Intentionally creating a few yards' gap between them and the boys, Evelyn told Rexy about the fridge. She said although the burnt one was old, they were replacing it with a brand new one to silence Dede.

"When the dust settles, we shall replace yours with a larger one," Evelyn promised.

With a few other words to comfort him in those difficult times, Evelyn assured Rexy that they would stand by him at all times. So moved with emotion at the turning of events, Rexy wiped tears from his eyes.

"Do I deserve this kindness?" asked Rexy.

"You deserve more than this, Rex," she replied.

"May the Lord we serve look down from heaven and reward you for what you have done for me and my family."

Evelyn said a big Amen to that. Near the pick-up, the boys also talked about Evelyn. Daniel asked if the others could smell the perfume on her.

"It's wicked!" said Jonathan. "As soon as she arrived the whole place smelt like heaven."

"Have you been to heaven before?" Daniel asked him.

"No, but I hear the place is like..." Jonathan was saying.

"I can still smell it from where they are," Kofi interrupted.

"I bet her children are living well," said Jonathan.

To their young minds, every adult must have children or a child so they expected Evelyn to have one or two. Jonathan said he would ask her which school her children were attending so they could befriend them. Kofi was of the opinion that they use David as a link to get to know her children. He was seconded by Daniel but Jonathan insisted that it was good to strike when the iron is hot. Besides, there was no point beating about the bush when Evelyn was there with them.

"Let's get that box down and into the kitchen," Evelyn said, when they got to the truck.

The boys did not know what the box contained as they watched Rexy get on the truck to push it down for them, but outspoken Jonathan told him to get down and watch them do it.

"Let me give you a hand. It's a man's job," said Rexy.

"We are little men, you know," Daniel said.

They were all laughing as Rexy pushed the box down for them and by the time he got down from the truck, the *little men* were heading to the house with the box. Evelyn told them to come back quickly so she would drop them off at school. Rexy followed the boys and directed them to put the fridge in the open where everyone in the house could see, but he said nothing to anyone except his wife and son.

"They are replacing Dede's fridge with a brand new one so we can have our peace."

"Where is she?" Akyaa asked, surprised.

"She says she wants to drop the children off at school so they won't be late," Rexy told her.

The boys and Esther rushed to the truck to join Evelyn. Akyaa later asked her husband if they should give the fridge to Dede immediately and Rexy said they should wait till the evening when everyone was at home.

"Good idea," said Akyaa.

It was still break time and so the other children were playing around when Evelyn parked near the playground for them to get off. It was quite unusual for cars to park at that place and time, so some of the children stopped playing to look who was going to get out of the car. Evelyn asked them to wait as she opened her purse to give them some money to share. She also advised them to continue to be good children and study hard so as to achieve goals in future. As they stepped out of the car, they all thanked Evelyn and Jonathan asked her again if she had any children about their age. She said no and another question followed from him.

"Are they younger or older, and which school do they...?"

Just as some boxers are saved by the bell at the end of a round, Evelyn was saved by her phone ringing. She picked it up, engaged the gear and drove off, smiling at them. Jokingly, Kofi told the on-lookers that they had gone for a ride.

'We went to see David," Esther said the truth.

Some of the children wanted to know who the woman that dropped them off was, but Jonathan was more interested in the cash than offering explanation to those inquisitive kids.

"Now, let's divide the amount by four," he said.

"Two fifty each," said Daniel.

"Let's go and see the woman who sells *koliko* for some change," said Kofi.

As they were going to the *koliko* seller, Jonathan whispered to Daniel and asked him what he thought about the two of them getting to know Evelyn's children. Daniel liked the idea, because according to him, the woman seems to be living very good and so the moment they get involved with her children, things will be fine for them too. But unknown to them, they were only aiming at an unachievable target. Jonathan promised to go and see David again after school to make more enquiries. Daniel told him not to make it look so obvious that they wanted to get involved with Evelyn's children.

"If David should ask why you want to know about the woman, just say we want to go and thank her for the money she gave us," said Daniel.

"You can trust me for such negotiations," Jonathan said.

"Okay, it's between the two of us," said David.

"Sure."

Many times in life, if you desire something with bad motives, you won't get it, but if your heart is clean and your mind is pure, what you need sometime comes to you without you struggling for it. These boys' motives in trying to get to know Evelyn's kids were not right, but Hagar's condition in Diasempa needed a change and so God worked through her clean environment to bring about that change. Since they moved to the city, Hagar had been sending gifts and cash to her mother through a particular driver. But one day when she went to the station, the driver had already left for Diasempa so she gave them to someone else who knew her house.

When the bearer arrived and knocked at the door, it was Hagar's mother who answered.

"Please, I'm looking for Maame Nkansaa," the bearer said.

"I'm Nkansaa."

"I saw Hagar this afternoon in Accra and she gave me this parcel and money to bring to you."

"Oh Hagar," Nkansaa said, beaming with smiles as she accepted the presents. "Is she okay?" she asked.

"She was looking very well and she asked me to tell you not to worry so much about her because she is okay."

"Thank you so much, *Krakye* (gentle man)."

CHAPTER NINE

THAT'S MY OPINION – TAKE IT OR LEAVE IT

Serwaa, the city girl whose greed had sent her to Diasempa, had not given up her manipulation of men. She was helping Kay, her graduate boyfriend, to spend every pesewa that he could have saved to become rich. She went to Koforidua to collect money from him whenever she needed some and pretended to be in love with him but it was the complete opposite. Once during conversation Betty asked her if she had introduced Kay to her mother but Serwaa laughed it off.

"I'm looking forward to something great, not that poor thing," she said. "I'm just keeping him to pass time till I hit the jackpot."

"Serwaa, I will advise you, like I have done many times before, to settle down with Kay because we are not getting any younger."

"I'm not interested in him, it's that simple," said Srewaa.

"Fine. Why don't you leave him then? Maybe someone wants him, but because of you he..."

"Whoever wants him can go for him. Or if you want him I can pass him on to you."

"Don't be silly," said Betty.

Serwaa was considering Joe as a jackpot and keeping Kay in the dark, somehow. But Rexy and his wife decided to present the fridge to Dede in the open through Mr. Aki, an elderly man in the house. Rexy told Mr Aki that his boss's wife witnessed the incident and had sent him a new one as a replacement. Mr. Aki inspected the fridge and shook his head in surprise.

"Can I tell you a story before we go ahead to present it to her?" Mr Aki asked.

"Of course, you can," replied Rexy.

"Once upon a time," began Mr Aki, "long, long ago, the sun shone so much that Mr. Shear Butter was melting and his neighbour, Mr Salt, laughed at him. Mr. Shear Butter said nothing to Mr. Salt, rather, he braved the scorching sun until the evening when it became cold and he pulled himself together. They lived together in the same neighbourhood but their relationship was strained due to Mr. Salt's behaviour in Mr. Shear Butter's hard time."

Rexy and Akyaa were very attentive to the story. As he spoke, Mr Aki made no gestures at all. He only turned to look at David who was sitting at the same place at the time when the fridge was brought in. They smiled at each other as Mr Aki continued.

"Several months later, the owner of the universe turned things around and, like the days of Noah, it rained so much so that everywhere was flooded. Mr. Salt dissolved into the ground and even after it had stopped raining he could not get his fragmented pieces together. That is why today you have to search hard to get a bit of salt here and there. This is the end of my story."

"What is the meaning of this story, Mr Aki?" Rexy asked.

"You will understand it one day."

Mr Aki helped Rexy to take the fridge to the front of the kitchen where everyone could see it and went to call Dede himself. Due to the previous day's incident, Dede's comments and demand and how others had reacted to her action the entire house was tensed. All discussions in the house had some element of David's accident and the aftermath. Most of the tenants imagined what could happen in the next few days, because they knew for sure that it was impossible for Rexy and Akyaa to afford a fridge by the weekend as demanded by Dede. They also knew that Dede was arrogant and a hard woman to deal with.

When Mr. Aki knocked on her door, Dede came out with an expressionless face and he invited her to come to the kitchen. Mr. Aki headed back to the front of the kitchen where Rexy and his wife were standing by the fridge and Dede followed him. Mr. Aki went straight to the point.

"Everyone in the house is aware of what happened here yesterday and your demand that your fridge be replaced," Mr. Aki said to Dede. "Although yours was old and over-used, they are replacing it with a brand new one."

Some co-tenants who were at home at the time looked on as Mr. Aki made the presentation.

"I didn't mean a new one," Dede said.

"Whether an old, second hand or brand new one, you wanted your fridge back, didn't you?" asked Mr. Aki.

"Yes, but if ..."

"You can have it now, no buts or ifs," said Mr. Aki.

Rexy thanked Mr. Aki and the men went into the kitchen to take the damaged fridge out while Dede stood by the new one. She never expected that Rexy and his wife could afford the fridge and she was prepared to taunt them for as long as the burnt one remained in the kitchen. Each time she went to the kitchen to see the fridge, she said something that was very abusive to Rexy and his wife, but they did not talk back. So she was extremely surprised and ashamed to see a brand new fridge in place of her second-hand over-used one. Those watching said nothing, but a lot went on in their minds and they were all surprised at what was happening.

Rexy and his wife now had their peace and it was down to his employers who were always looking for an opportunity to help others. With time, Hagar got to the advanced stages of her driving lessons. Her instructor told her what she was doing right or wrong. She could drive on her own at this stage, but there were a few things that she needed to pay particular attention to.

"You are doing well, but your major problem at the moment is the way you apply your brakes. It is always abrupt, and it should not be so. The only time you brake abruptly is in an emergency."

They had parked by the side of the road and Hagar listened attentively and nodded as the instructor continued to tell her the right way to drive safely.

"Secondly, do not stop for any pedestrian to cross the road, unless at a zebra crossing. You seem to be too caring and always want to give people the chance. It is a very good attitude, but you can't do that with driving all the time. You can only do that when you know for sure that it is safe, that there is no car behind you, or coming from the opposite direction. The reason is that, if you stop and the oncoming driver is not aware of the pedestrian, he could hit him or her, or the one behind you could hit your car. So you have to be very careful the way you apply your brakes or stop for others."

"Thanks," Hagar said.

'Think of others' welfare,' this was one of the statements Maame Nkansaa made to Hagar on the night before she moved to join Joe and his wife and she was always considering other people's good before herself. The instructor had observed that each time someone made an attempt to cross the road in front of her Hagar would stop for the person.

He asked Hagar to drive him back to their home which was opposite where they were heading. There was no immediate connecting road so she had to do a three-point turning right where they were. She did it so well that the instructor applauded her. When they arrived in the house, the instructor told Evelyn about the three-point turn and encouraged Hagar to keep it up so that she could pass her test at the first attempt. Evelyn was happy the way things were going so far with Hagar's lessons.

Meanwhile, Jonathan, determined to find out where Evelyn's kids were schooling in order to befriend them, was pressing for further information about her. He had told Daniel to trust him for such negotiations so he was going to play it diplomatically. He went to David's house and started by telling him about the things they were studying at school.

"We learnt about the five great lakes in North America that are almost joined together, and their initials make up the word HOMES," he said.

"What are their names?" David asked.

"They are lakes Hurron, Ontario, Michigan, Erie and Superior. I will leave the notes with you to copy and come back for it later," said Jonathan.

"Thank you very much."

"By the way, have you seen the lady who drove us to school the other day?"

"No, she has not been here since," replied David. "It was her husband who came here yesterday."

"Do you know her children?" asked Jonathan.

"Why do you want to know about her children?"

"I was wondering if we could go and thank her, because she gave us some money. Besides, her children must be very happy indeed, those up-town children who do not know what hunger is," said Jonathan.

David listened to his friend's comments and smiled. Knowing Evelyn's childless condition, he did not know exactly what to say to his friend. Fortunately, his father came in at that time to ask

Jonathan how he was doing. He told Rexy half truth that he had come to brief David on school work.

Auntie Cornie was also doing all she could to bring Serwaa between Joe and Evelyn. Once when Joe was out of the shop, someone brought a letter to Evelyn from Diasempa addressed to Joe. Being suspicious of some of their own people's behaviour towards her, Evelyn decided to read the letter. The contents made her more worried than she had ever been.

In the letter, which had come from Auntie Cornie, she stated that she wanted to arrange a meeting with Joe and someone that she had spoken to. Secondly, she urged Joe to think seriously about something that, in her opinion, may never happen. Reading between the lines, Evelyn concluded that whoever Cornie had spoken to would be another lady and something that may never happen was about her having a child.

While tears streamed down her cheek, she tore the letter with trembling hands and vowed not to let her husband know anything about it. As she had done many times before, she begged God to give them a child to silence their tormentors.

Rexy had been a man on his toes most of the time and hardly had enough time to spend with his family at home. He spent most of the day at work and each evening of the week, apart from Tuesdays and Saturdays there was a programme at church in which he participated. Tuesday evenings were reserved for the Women's Movement, so it was not obligatory for the men to attend.

Many nights, by the time he finally settled at home, he would be too tired to do anything or it would be about bed time. Sometimes when he saw David in the morning, he only came to see him sleeping. So one day when he came home a bit earlier than usual, David seized the opportunity to interact with him. He questioned him about the story of David and Jonathan which he had begun but did not finish some time ago.

Rexy gave his son a brief history of the friendship between Jonathan and David, continuing from where he had stopped, after David had killed Goliath. He said the women of Israel were praising David by attributing to him that he had killed tens of thousands and to King Saul they said he had only killed a thousand. This made Saul angry and so he became jealous of David and wanted to kill him. By this time, King Saul's son, Jonathan, had become so attached to David.

"Jonathan loved David so much so that they were almost inseparable. So whenever his father planned to do any harm to David, Jonathan informed him about it and helped him escape. I want you to read it yourself from *1 Samuel chapter 17* onwards, that's the way to learn."

"Thank you, Dad. I will read it and tell Jonathan about it."

"Good boy," said Rexy, tapping his son's shoulder.

That evening, Rexy and his wife prayed at length for Joe and his wife. Beside the letter which Evelyn had torn in his absence, Joe turned a deaf ear to Cornie's requests to go to Diasempa to see her. In fact, both Joe and Evelyn decided not to go to Diasempa for anything. But as the saying goes, 'It's easier said than done,' a time came when Joe had to go home. Someone close to the family died and he could not exempt himself from attending the funeral.

When Auntie Cornie heard that Joe was in town, she sent for Serwaa to come and see her immediately. They planned that Cornie would share a table with Joe at the funeral gathering and Serwaa would then come to them and the game will start from there.

"Will it be a netball or football game? Serwaa asked.

"Time will tell," said Cornie.

Amid smiles, Serwaa gave Cornie some money, like she had been doing many times since Cornie promised to link her to Joe. When Joe arrived at Diasempa, he first went to his parents' house to give them some presents and promised to pick them up to the funeral. His parents encouraged him that one day the good Lord would answer their prayers and bless them with children.

When Serwaa and Cornie were planning how to work on Joe at the funeral, Kwaku was in his room and he overheard a few words. He wasn't happy and so confronted his mother as soon as Serwaa was gone.

"Mum, what's going on between you and Serwaa?" he asked with a serious face.

"Why do you ask that?" asked Cornie.

"Well, it's because each time she comes around, you two seem to be setting a trap to catch someone, whoever that person may be," Kwaku said.

"So you've been listening to our conversation?" asked his mother.

"Of course, I am not deaf, neither do I live outside of this house, so I know bits and pieces of what goes on here," he said.

"What bits and pieces?" Cornie asked again.

"Well, if it's something that could make you regret in future, I will advise that you stop now. That is my opinion. Take it or leave it."

Kwaku slammed the door behind him and left the house. Cornie looked very worried for a moment because she did not know how much her son knew of her plans with Serwaa to make him question her and behave like that.

Kwaku was aware of a letter that his mother had sent Serwaa to deliver to someone and also their conversation confirmed that they were working out plans to trap that person. He had always wanted to ask his mother about her plans with Serwaa but he had no proof to base on. However, today's conversation indicated that whoever they were targeting on was attending this funeral.

Cornie knew that funeral attendance was not Kwaku's cup of tea, so she was sure that he would not be there to see how they would carry out their plot. As Cornie started getting ready to go, Joe also went to pick his parents. Before they left the house, Agya Boakye advised his son to stick to his wife and never think of leaving Evelyn because of their condition.

"I know friends and even some relatives may be giving you series of suggestions, but one thing I want you to recall always is your vows at the wedding - for better for worse," said Agya Boakye.

"I can never think of leaving Evelyn, Paapa. She has been so supportive, honest and encouraging in all things. I'm willing to live with her for the rest of my life, come what may. Thank you for the advice, any way. I know I can brave the storm with you and Maame by my side."

"Thank you, Kwadwo. Don't listen to what others may say to you," said Darkoaa.

Darkoaa was glad about Joe's determination to stick to his wife, irrespective of what others were saying about them. She was aware of all the negative comments some of their own people were making about Joe and Evelyn's condition and so had been praying and encouraging them not to allow anyone to influence them.

During a chat in Serwaa's room before they went to the funeral, Betty commented that a lot of people would be in town and Serwaa, who was dressing up, said that was why she wanted to look extra good.

"I want to make a catch today."

"Have you targeted anyone?" Betty asked.

"Not really. But come rain or shine, I'm going to make a catch today," she said, with Joe in mind.

"What about Kay?" Betty asked.

"Forget about him for once, Betty," said Serwaa.

She had been assured by Auntie Cornie that she would do anything and everything for Joe to marry her. And today being the very first day when she was going to be formerly introduced to him, she was confident that Joe would show some interest in her.

At the funeral, Joe was with his parents when Auntie Cornie came around to greet them. She showed Joe where she was sitting and said she would like to talk to him when he was through with his parents. As Joe conversed on general issues with his parents, two friends who sat a few tables from theirs were also talking about him. One of the friends was a Diasemparian who knew Joe, so he told his friend how rich Joe was but childless. According to him, and rightly so, family members made life unbearable for them because of their condition, so much so that he had to leave the town with his wife.

"He used to own that big shop by the station. It was the best equipped of all the shops in town when he owned it. You can see the state of it now, almost empty," he said.

"Poor lad, where is the wife?" asked the friend.

"I don't know whether she came with him because I haven't seen her here. She is a very beautiful and modest lady," said the Diasemparian. "It is rumoured in town that he might have used his manhood to acquire wealth and others blamed it on his wife as being barren."

"Do you believe in the notion that people exchange their manhood with money?" asked the stranger.

"I've heard of people saying that, but I viewed it as rubbish. Money is not everything, you know. What will I use wealth for if I don't have a family?" the Diasemparian asked.

The friends continued to talk about Joe until he left his parents' table to join Auntie Cornie. Serwaa kept monitoring every movement of Joe's, so as soon as he went to Cornie's table, she popped around to say hello.

"Hi Serwaa, how are you doing?" Cornie asked, acting as if she had not seen her for a very long time.

"Fine, thank you," Serwaa responded.

Just then, someone tapped Auntie Cornie on the shoulder to talk to her, distracting her from the conversation with Serwaa. Joe recognised Serwaa and in order not to leave her standing there like a dummy while Cornie was engaged with the other person, he spoke to her.

"It seems I have seen this face somewhere before," Joe addressed Serwaa.

"Yes. I delivered a letter to you from Auntie Cornie some time ago," Serwaa said, full of smiles.

"Oh, yes, yes, I remember. How are you doing?"

"I am very well, thank you."

"Thank you very much for taking the pain to come back to the shop that day," said Joe.

"Thank you too for, the envelope," Serwaa said.

When Cornie finished with the person she was speaking to, she confirmed what Serwaa said about the letter. She said no one was willing to come to Okaishie that day to deliver the letter and she was lucky to have seen Serwaa who offered to come to his shop.

"Where is your table, Serwaa?" Cornie asked.

"I'm with some friends at the corner near the entrance," she pointed to her table.

"Ok, I will talk to you later then. It's good you are here," said Auntie Cornie.

As Serwaa was going back to her table, Cornie was smiling and kept looking at her in a very admiring way.

"What do you think about her?"

"In terms of what?" Joe asked.

"Her general appearance," she said.

"Well, she is pretty, but appearance can be deceptive, you know," Joe said casually.

When Joe said Serwaa was pretty, Cornie smiled again and nodded. To her, it looked like Joe was getting close to the bait to take a bite or swallow it whole. Serwaa was looking from her table to see Joe's reaction as Auntie Cornie spoke to him about her. She had positioned her seat in such a way that she could see whatever was going on at Cornie's table without having to turn or stand.

Betty was talking with the other lady and, once a while, Serwaa would chip in a word or two to show that she was still with them, but all her attention was on what was going on between Auntie Cornie and Joe. She wished she could hear what Cornie was telling him and his responses.

Since Serwaa was told about Joe, she had spent so much money on Cornie with the hope of becoming Joe's wife, and Cornie had promised her that even if she has to bring heavens down for this to succeed, she was prepared to do so.

'This is the day, a make or break day for me,' Serwaa thought.

Auntie Cornie began her speech in an attempt to convince Joe that Evelyn was no good, and that Serwaa would be a perfect match for him.

"You know I have always wanted the best of everything for you. Since the day I saw Serwaa and sent her to deliver that letter to you, my spirit has been telling me that you should have her as a wife. She is pretty, like you said, and polite, too. Chances are that she would be able to give you a child."

Joe kept silent and looked into his aunt's eyes as she spoke. She had forgotten that Joe was no more the teenager she had controlled in years past. Serwaa could see that Joe's facial expression had changed and was not the smiling Joe any longer. He was not saying a word to Cornie's lectures either. She felt like going closer to ask if all was well, but she restrained her emotions, thinking that after all, what they were talking about at that moment may have nothing to do with her. At a certain point, Betty noticed that Serwaa looked disturbed.

"Are you okay, Serwaa?" Betty asked.

"Oh yes, I'm fine. I was just thinking of an incident that took place at a certain funeral some time ago."

"Stop day-dreaming at this time," said the other friend.

They were interrupted by a service girl who came to ask if they wanted some drinks. The two friends told the girl what they wanted but Serwaa said she didn't want anything at that time. She was busy creating a thought-form to support whatever Auntie Cornie was saying to Joe about her.

"As I have always suggested," continued Cornie, "you must either divorce that unproductive wife of yours or marry Serwaa as a second wife. After all, you've been blessed so much financially that taking care of two women will not be a problem. So that at least you can have your carbon copy on this planet. I hope you understand?"

After taking in a deep breath and exhaling, Joe adjusted himself on his seat and looked around to see if anyone was listening to their conversation.

"Have you finished what you have to say?" he asked.

"Not yet," Cornie replied.

"Okay, go on," Joe said.

He sat back straight on his chair with both hands folded across his tummy and continued to look into Cornie's eyes without saying another word. His posture and expressions should have spoken to Cornie not to say any more, but she continued to talk.

"You see, everyone is talking about you in this town. People even think you are sterile but I know the problem is not with you. That girl is barren. I have inquired from some of her friends. She can never conceive, look at her twin sister, you got married before her and she now has two children. How long do you have to wait, eternally?"

She paused, expecting an answer from Joe.

"Have you finished?" Joe asked again.

"Yes, for now. What do you have to say about that?" Cornie asked.

Joe moved his chair forward a bit, put his elbows to the table and clinging both palms together, he put the thumbs under his chin. He was yet to utter a word, but the look on his face said it all - he was angry.

"I have heard every single word you said, but I am not interested in any one of them. Secondly, I want this to be the last time you will ever talk to me about my wife or marriage."

Cornie took a quick look at Serwaa and their eyes met but she looked away almost immediately. She looked back at Joe who had not raised his voice but meant everything he was saying.

"If it was part of your plot for sending her to me with that letter, go and tell her now that I'm not interested in her and that in spite of our condition, I still love my wife. I am out of this place because of you."

He did not change his posture as he spoke until he had said his last word. He pushed his chair back, stood up and left for his parents' table. To conceal what had just taken place, Joe was all smiles by the time he got to his parents.

"Maame, I hope you will be able to go home by yourselves?"

He was addressing his mother but it was his father who responded.

"Of course, we can."

"Well, I have to see a few people before I go, so I am leaving here now."

Whatever he needed to discuss with his parents or give to them was already done, so he headed straight for the city. Serwaa saw him leaving the hall so she went to Cornie to find out what was going on.

"I saw him leaving and he didn't seem happy," she said to Cornie.

"He is having some misunderstanding with the guy whose plot is next to his house. The guy's brother has been making some provocative comments concerning him, so he is going to sort things out with them," Cornie lied.

Serwaa had hoped to have another short conversation with Joe, at least, but now that he was out of the place she wondered if she would have that chance. She looked confused and worried because she had boasted to Betty about making a catch that day. Auntie Cornie assured her not to worry because she had sown some seeds into Joe's conscience concerning her.

"He will get back to me in a few days," she said.

Funny world! Kay was dying for Serwaa, but she was not interested in him, and Joe, the person she was dying for, was not interested in her. Kay wanted to marry Serwaa, but with Joe in mind, she did not want to introduce him to her people, not even her mother. Kay's mother was also suspicious of Serwaa and so one day she tried to talk to him about her observations.

"I don't think she is really interested in you," she said.

"Why are you saying that, Mum?"

"I am a woman, Kay, and I have been like her before. Besides, I have personally spoken with her on a number of occasions and I don't think she is the type that ..."

"Mum, please can we talk about this later as I am almost late for an appointment?"

285

Kay stopped his mother from further comments about Serwaa. He loved her and wanted her to be his wife at all costs, but his mother had negative opinions about her.

"Okay, but bear what I am saying in mind," said his mother.

What some old people see when sitting down, young people cannot see even if they climb trees, because they have seen life and could somehow tell of the future based on past experiences and current circumstances. This was a woman who did not want her son to walk into danger, because she was seeing far into the future. She did not know Serwaa's background, but since intelligent people learn from observation, she could tell the type of lady Serwaa really was. She knew she could never become a good wife. She wasn't the type she would recommend even to her enemy, let alone her own son.

Kay's mother saw Serwaa as someone who could make life difficult for her son. But Kay had introduced Serwaa to most of his friends and colleagues and would find it difficult going round to explain to them that his mother was not in favour of the relationship. Besides, he loved her and was in no way going to give up on her, if that meant disobeying his mother. Serwaa was also still hopeful of having Joe as a husband because Auntie Cornie said Joe had her in mind.

A few days after the incident at the funeral, Serwaa went to lie to Cornie that she would be going to Accra and was wondering if she had any message for Joe. The fact was that she wanted to go to the mountain herself, if it would not come to her. She had ideas that had made many men fall for her in the past and she could have used the same tactics on Joe if Cornie had not become an intermediary. She did not know what Cornie had said to Joe about her, so she could not go to him without first seeking Cornie's approval.

Auntie Cornie had no message for Joe and told Serwaa that she wanted him to get back to her before taking another step. But Serwaa still decided to go to Accra. Her plan was to walk around the front of Joe's shop several times till he catches a glimpse of her, and if she was lucky, invite her for a chat. If this happens, then she would initiate some of her tactics, irrespective of what Joe had been told about her, and so to Accra she went. Unfortunately, Joe sat behind the till most of the day and could not see much of the outside.

In fact, when Rexy was in the shop, it was he who dealt with customers, so all that Joe did was to collect money from the sales. Serwaa roamed around the shop for more than three hours without seeing the man she had travelled about one-and-a-half hours to entice. At one point, she went so close that she overheard Rexy dealing with a customer. The customer was bargaining for an item and wanted to plead with Joe for further reduction but Rexy would not let him.

"Going to him will mean I don't know what I am up to in the shop. If anything at all, I will have to speak to him to see whether he can help with the price," said Rexy.

"Please tell him I can pay two hundred thousand Cedis," said the customer.

"Two hundred thousand? I don't think he will accept that. Anyway, let me talk to him first."

Rexy went to tell Joe how much the customer was offering, knowing very well that one hundred and twenty thousand cedis would do. But, like any good salesman, he wanted to make more money for his employer. Joe only nodded with a smile and Rexy went back to tell the customer his boss said he should add twenty thousand Cedis to his offer which he agreed. Serwaa was standing close by, listening to Rexy and the customer. Rexy went to tell Joe that he was selling the item for two hundred and twenty thousand cedis while the man was getting his money ready.

"You can go and pay while I parcel it for you," said Rexy.

Rexy was glad for making some profit for his boss, but he wanted a confirmation from him; so soon after the customer had gone, he went to ask Joe if it was a good deal.

"More than good, Rex, I would have sold it for around one hundred and fifty thousand cedis, at most. That is why I want you to deal with them when you are here."

"Don't worry, Boss. If possible, when you see any customer coming to the shop, just pretend to be busy and I will deal with them."

"Good."

Joe dealt with Rexy as his own brother and not an employee. Observing the way they communicated and did other things, anybody seeing them for the first time would take them for brothers or cousins. They respected each other and there was transparency in their dealing at all times.

For as long as Serwaa was lingering in the area, Joe was glued to his seat. It is so amazing how God works to protect His faithful servants from temptation. No sooner had Serwaa left the place to go back to Diasempa disappointed than Joe came out to have a chat with his friend D.D. in front of the shop. She could not achieve her aim of going to the city but, to impress Auntie Cornie more in order for her to press her course for her, Serwaa bought a bag as a present for her. She decided to pass by Cornie's house to deliver the present before going home.

"I am just returning from Accra and I thought I should pass by," she said on arrival at Cornie's place.

"When did you go?" asked Cornie.

"I went this morning. Have you forgotten that I told you I had to go to Accra?"

"Oh yes, I remember," responded Cornie.

"Actually, what brought me here is a present for you. I bought two of these bags and Would like you to choose one for yourself," Serwaa said and put the bags on the table.

Kwaku was reading a magazine when Serwaa arrived and he kept looking at them in anger but said nothing during their conversation.

He hated Serwaa this time because of what he suspected she was planning with his mother.

"Which of the bags do you like, Kwaku?" asked Cornie.

"You may not like what I like, so make your own choice," he said and got up to leave the room, apparently not happy.

"That's a good judgement," said Serwaa, as Kwaku was leaving.

"Well, I have got a light pink scarf which will match this, so I will take the pink one."

Cornie lied to her that Joe had sent her a message the day before, to come and see him so she was arranging to get some transport fare to go. Since getting into contact with Serwaa, Cornie had on many occasions asked for money from her, so when it had to do with seeing Joe, Serwaa was more than willing to give Cornie the required money to Accra and back.

"I'll bring you some money in the evening to enable you go and see him," she promised.

"Oh thank you very much. I will go tomorrow then; you will definitely be my in-law not very long from now," Cornie said in a very low voice because she did not want Kwaku to hear her saying that.

At the back of her mind, Serwaa felt she has wasted the transport fare to Accra. If she knew that Cornie had plans to go and see Joe on her behalf, she would have given that money to her to make this important trip. All the same, she was glad to have brought her the bag as a memorial, and the comment she had just heard from Cornie raised her hopes. She will do anything to become Mrs Boakye. She had already confided in Auntie Cornie that she did not mind being a second wife and, based on that, Cornie had also said to Joe that even if he was not willing to divorce Evelyn, he could take Serwaa as wife number two.

Around that time, the consequences of Brago's action towards Evelyn which led to Jude being sent back to her was manifesting.

Brago had gone bankrupt again and because she could not pay Jude's school fees, he was sent home. After staying at home for a few days, Brago wanted the boy to go back to school while she tried to raise some money.

"Go back to school and tell your teacher that I will get the money for you next week," said Brago.

"You go and tell him that. Until the money is ready, I am not going to school," said Jude. "If it had not been your behaviour towards Auntie Evelyn I would have been with Uncle Joe in the city by now and money would not have been a problem."

"Go to him then."

The boy's entire appearance had changed since he went back to his mother. His academic achievement since then had also fallen far below average and his moral behaviour had a lot of question marks. He had become more wayward and truant than ever before. Some traits of his mother as a Company C comrade were showing in the boy. He was rude to everyone, including his own mother, to put it straight.

"When I was with Uncle Joe there was never a time that I was sent home because of my fees," he said to his mother.

"Shut your mouth!" Brago shouted at him.

The boy left her presence in anger and for some time did not want to talk with her. People who knew about what Brago had done to Evelyn interpreted the boy's behaviour as a curse. Now Brago was bringing up the boy single-handedly, and what would one expect a Company C comrade to impart on a boy in his formative years? Arrogance. The boy had become so arrogant that no one could control him. Even his own class mates dreaded talking to him sometimes.

Although other members of Joe's family had been talking negatively about their marriage because of their condition, Brago and Cornie were real thorns in the flesh. These two were the main reason for their migration to the city, and even there, Cornie would not leave them alone. She had promised Serwaa of doing all within her means to kick Evelyn out of Joe's life to make way for her, but the couple were so much in love that, so far Cornie's plans had not succeeded.

CHAPTER TEN

ORMOAA'S CONCOCTION

When Cornie's effort to push Serwaa to Joe was proving difficult, she decided to deal with him from another angle. She did not go to see Joe but lied to Serwaa that when she went to him, Joe said she should give him a little time to think over it. It had been a while since then and there seemed to be no positive response from him. Serwaa's plans were being thwarted. She had planned to show Kay the red card as soon as she receives the green light, or a sign of it from Joe.

One morning when Serwaa went to inquire if there was any progress, Cornie thought of coming up with her incubating idea and directing Serwaa to follow suit. She had received so much from Serwaa and lied so much to her that she thought the only way to get herself out of it, or so it seemed to her, was to bind Joe spiritually to take his mind off Evelyn and focus on Serwaa.

"It's been some time now and there seems to be no sign at all," Serwaa complained.

"Yes. But there are many ways of killing a cat, you know. You can trap it, shoot it or suffocate it. So far, the traping technique seems not to be working as planned," said Cornie.

"So what do we do now?" Serwaa asked.

There was silence for a while. Cornie knew Serwaa was eager to be Joe's wife, but she was not sure whether Serwaa would agree to what she had in mind so she hesitated for a few more moments while she looked into Serwaa's face.

"What are we going to do next?" Serwaa asked again.

"I know a powerful man at Aboabo who can be of help," Cornie said. "When you are ready, let me know and I will give you the direction to go and see him."

"I am ever ready, I can go there tomorrow," said Serwaa.

"If you get to Aboabo, ask anyone to give you the direction to Kordorbeda. At Kordorbeda, even a kid can take you to the man. He is called Ormoaa, a very powerful spiritualist."

"Okay, I will go and look for him," Serwaa said. "What should I tell him if I go?"

"Just tell him you are in love with someone who is not opening up and you want him to help you."

"I don't know how much he will charge you, but ..."

"I will pay whatever he charges," said Serwaa.

On her way home, Serwaa was wondering how Cornie got to know someone like this spiritualist. She also wondered how many men Cornie might have sent there to be worked on by this man. Exposing her hairy abdomen alone had won the admiration of many men who had fallen for Serwaa in the past. Pretending to be very sick suddenly in the presence of a man she wanted had also worked for her a number of times. But with regards to Joe, Cornie had initiated the whole show, so, like a user of a new gadget, she had to follow the manufacturer's instruction.

Serwaa went to Koforidua that evening for some money from Kay to enable her go and see this man at Kordorbeda the next day. She told Kay her mother had taken ill the previous night and so she needed some money to take her to hospital. Kay gave her what he could afford at the time and when she left, Kay's mother questioned him again about Serwaa and this really bothered him. At work the next day, one of his colleagues noticed that Kay looked worried.

"Kay, you don't look like the Kay I know. What is the matter with you?"

"No problem. I'm fine," said Kay.

"I don't think so. You look a bit gloomy."

Kay didn't know what to say to his friend. He looked at him for a moment and shook his head.

"You should have trained as a psychologist and not a stenographer," he said.

"From the look on your face even a child can tell that there is something wrong with you. And that something is what I want to know, may be I could be of help."

"It's about my mother and Serwaa," Kay said.

He was about to narrate his mother's recent complaints about Serwaa when his colleague had a call from his boss to proceed to his office. *'Don't be stupid. Why share such an issue with a colleague?'* Kay heard a voice telling him after his colleague left his desk, so he decided not to tell him any more than what he had already said. Although his colleague later asked for more information, Kay only told him he had some argument with his mother about Serwaa and that was what was bothering him.

Serwaa was at Kordorbeda at that time of the day in search of Ormoaa and just like Auntie Cornie had said, his place was not difficult to locate. On arrival, Ormoaa asked her the one who directed her to him and she mentioned Auntie Cornie from Diasempa.

"Oh Cornie! How is she?"

"She is fine," said Serwaa.

The way Ormoaa responded upon hearing Cornie's name made Serwaa to believe that he knew her very well. As to how and when he came to know her, she could not ask Ormoaa.

"Now tell me, what brought you here?" Ormoaa asked.

Serwaa did not know how or where to start. She had never tried juju before, but now, because of Auntie Cornie, she sat before Ormoaa, thinking of how to tell him why she was there. After hesitating a little longer, Ormoaa told her to feel free to tell him of her mission.

"I'm in love with a certain rich man in the city. I have tried all my best to make him love me too without success so I discussed it with Auntie Cornie and she said you could be of help."

Ormoaa started to laugh. He broke a piece of the cola he was holding, put it in his mouth and asked if that was all her problem and Serwaa replied in the affirmative.

"It is one of the simplest issues I have been dealing with over the years. In fact, it is my speciality. Cornie can tell you more about me in that area. There are three stages to it. Yours is the first stage, the second is to make the partner love you more and the third stage is to bind the two of you forever."

"I want the first stage for now," Serwaa said.

"It is the easiest and the cheapest."

"How much will it cost me and how does it work?"

"Can you get him to eat or drink something?

"Yes," Serwaa said without thinking of how she could get Joe to eat or drink something.

"Which do you prefer, to eat or to drink?"

"I want the one to be eaten."

"Ok, that will cost you two million Cedis and it could be ready in a week, if your money is ready."

"I can give you half of the money now and bring the rest when I come for it."

"That's fine. I will need a few things from you, by the way."

"What kind of things?" Serwaa asked, wondering if they were things she could provide.

Ormoaa belched and coughed about eight times continuously. He got a piece of cloth from his pocket which served as a handkerchief to wipe his mouth.

"I'm sorry about that, this cola is choking me."

"Don't worry, we all get choked at some point," said Serwaa.

She was gaining some confidence talking to Ormoaa now. Her initial fear was diminishing as she considered the possibility of becoming Joe's wife.

"I will need a few of your pubic hair, hair from you armpit and cuttings from your finger nails. As soon as I have these, the work will start. And very soon he will be in your arms as your lover, doing and giving you whatever you ask of him."

Serwaa said she could bring them the next day but Ormoaa said there was no point coming back the next day because of the items. He pointed to a room across the small compound and told Serwaa to go inside and lock the door behind her.

"You will find a pair of scissors and a razor blade on the table so you can provide all of them now."

Serwaa went in there reluctantly, feeling a bit embarrassed that she was being ordered to shave her pubic hair in broad daylight. The fact that Ormoaa would be looking at her with his mind's eye, stripping and shaving made her feel very uncomfortable, but she had to do it for Joe's sake. If nothing good comes easy, some bad things don't come easy either.

The room had a bed, a table and a chair, all very old and made noises when touched. On the table were two packets of brand new Tatra razor blades, a pair of scissors and a mirror. One of the packets of blade was opened and half of it had been used already. Serwaa could see the used blades in an old bucket which served as a bin.

She raised her skirt and underwear, held the hem tight with her chin against her breast, and then pulled her pants half way down her thighs. Reaching for the scissors, she was about to cut her pubic hair when she realised that it will fall on the floor so she needed something to catch it. She dropped the instrument, pull up her pants to its original position and let go of her underwear and skirt. She looked round the room to see if she could find something onto which to cut the hair but could not find anything suitable. She opened her handbag and was lucky to find some pieces of used tissues.

At first she thought the tissue was contaminated and so could have some effect on what the hair was going to be used for, but she had no choice, so she spread it on the floor between her legs and repeated the process of cutting. She did not ask the man the quantity required so she thought of cutting as much as she could while standing. When she began to cut she realised that some where falling into her hanging panties so she dropped the scissors again and pulled the panties completely from her legs and put it on her bag which she had placed on the bed. She resumed the cutting and when she had cut enough she picked up the tissue and wrapped it. She quickly used her left hand knuckles to brush off the pieces from her tighs and legs and wore her panties.

She did not have problem with shaving her armpit because the blouse she wore had single straps over her shoulders. She just had to raise one arm and used the other hand to shave, also onto a piece of contaminated tissue. She used the same blade to cut her finger nails onto yet another piece of contaminated tissue. When all was ready, she went to give them to Ormoaa with the cash. A day was agreed for her to come for the medicine, with the balance.

Joe was living his life in the city, but for some people in Diasempa, the likes of Auntie Cornie and Serwaa, out of sight was not out of mind, as they sought for him day and night. He had built a nice two-room apartment for his parents not long after relocating to Accra, so they had moved from the family home. His nephew Jude was one of those who sought for him. His uniform was worn out, his PE kit wasn't complete, his fees were always in arrears, etc. Ever since he was sent home for non payment of school fees recently, he had always picked on his mother as being the cause of his woes. So like Jabez in the book of Judges, he decided to do something about his situation. He went to ask Darkoaa if she had heard from Joe.

"Yes, he sent us some parcels two days ago," Darkoaa said.

"What about Auntie Evelyn, is she okay?"

"Yes, they said they are all doing very well. Did you go to school today?"

"No, Grandma. I haven't been to school since last week Monday."

"Why?"

"I need to pay my school fees in full and my mother can't afford it."

"How much is left?"

"Fifty thousand Cedis."

"Fifty thousand Cedis! And what is your mother doing about it?"

"She said she would pay it next week but she..."

"Go and call her for me," said Darkoaa.

Before he left his grandmother's, Jude pleaded with her that if she got in touch with Joe again, she should tell him that he was sorry for what his mother had done to Evelyn. He said he would like to go and stay with them in the city.

"So you know what your mother did was wrong?"

"Yes, Grandma. I have told her that if it was not for her actions, I would have been in the city with Uncle Joe."

Repentance is the gateway to forgiveness and acceptance, so Darkoaa was glad to know that the boy had come to realise that his mother was wrong and wanted her to apologise to his uncle on his behalf. As Jude went back to invite his mother, Serwaa was also reporting the outcome of her trip to Ormoaa's shrine to Auntie Cornie.

"The man says it is not a big deal," said Serwaa. "My only problem is how to get him to eat the concoction that he is going to prepare for me."

"That is not a problem at all. As you know, my fiftieth birthday is due in a month's time. I have invited him and I know he will come to the party, so I can sort that out if only the concoction would be ready by then," said Auntie Cornie.

"I'm going for it next week."

"Good," said Auntie Cornie.

Joe had given his aunt the assurance of attending the party, so she was confident of sorting him out on that day. How true it is that if an outsider could do any evil to you, it is always an insider who leads the way - your own people. Someone who knows your secret and weak point is the one who would sell you to those who are seeking your downfall. Auntie Cornie was leading the way to Joe's downfall and destruction, just the way Judas Iscariot did to Jesus. He knew where Jesus could be found at that time of the night when He was being sought for, so he led the soldiers there and gave them a sign. With a kiss, he betrayed the Master.

Cornie had vowed to bring heavens down to make Joe marry Serwaa to the detriment of Evelyn. Ormoaa had also said to make Joe love her was his speciality so Serwaa had to keep her fingers crossed till the party day.

Evelyn had decided to stay away from Diasempa for some time but after a very long absence, she visited home one Saturday and went to her in-laws' place before going to see her mother. Darkoaa, as usual, gave her words of encouragement to continue trusting the Lord. Evelyn was so grateful to her and said such words always gave her the hope that one day things would be fine.

A boy from Evelyn's mother's area who had come to play in the locality with his mates spotted Evelyn when she parked the car to go to her in-laws. Later on he went to Evelyn's mother to find out about her. Evelyn was always being nice to everyone, even the little children - she gave them presents. So the boy was sure of getting something from her if he went to say hello to her. He hoped that even if Evelyn didn't give him any money he would get some bread or sweet from the city.

"Grandma, is Auntie Evelyn in?" the boy asked Maame Konadu.

"No, she is in the city."

"I saw her going to Maame Darkoaa's house and I thought she had come home so I was coming to say hello to her," he said.

"When did you see her?" asked Konadu.

"Not long ago."

"Are you sure?"

"Yes, Grandma, she was wearing a red top and a black skirt."

"Go back and find out if she indeed was the one you saw and let me know."

She ordered the boy like King Herod said to the wise men from the East, to bring him word after they have found the new born King.

The boy left her presence, promising to give her feedback but he went to play instead. When the wise men did not report back to Herod, the Bible says he got angry and ordered that all the new born boys under the age of two years be killed, but he could not lay hands on the Messiah.

In anger, Konadu went to a woman across the road who owned a small shop to ask her if she had seen Evelyn around. She asked this because she had been out of the house about one hour earlier and was thinking that maybe Evelyn had come and gone during her absence.

"It could be someone who looked like her," said the woman.

"Apart from her twin sister, who else looks like her in this town?" Konadu asked.

"If she is the one, she will come home," the woman said. "It might be Bevelyn."

While Konadu was complaining to the woman about what the boy had said, Evelyn came to the house and was asking a little girl about her mother when Konadu appeared.

"Look, that is Grandma coming," said the girl as Konadu approached, apparently not happy.

"How are you, Maame?" asked Evelyn.

"I'm fine. I hear you went to your in-law's house. Why did you go there before coming here?"

"I had to give them some presents from my husband. Besides, I had to pass their place before I get here."

"You should have come to see me first," insisted Konadu.

"But how did you get to know that I was there?" asked Evelyn.

"Don't you know that you are always being watched? What brought you here today, anyway?" her mother asked as she led the way to the living room.

"Joe sent me to bring some things to you and his parents."

At the mention of *some things to you*, Konadu brightened up and began to smile. Evelyn opened the suitcase and started removing the presents onto the centre table.

"All for me?" Konadu asked.

"Yes," said Evelyn."

Konadu kept smiling and examining the clothes, shoes and other things in the bag. Evelyn opened her handbag and presented her with a fat envelope, full of cash from Joe. Konadu did not even say thank you or ask how Joe was doing as she hammered in her usual question of pregnancy. When Evelyn told her there was still no sign, her face changed again.

"That's why I want you to leave that man; there are many ways through which that shop and house could become yours afterwards, but if you still want to live this life of shame, that is entirely up to you. I'm fed up with all these comments going on around town."

"I did not come here to be bombarded by you, Maame. I came to deliver presents to you from the man that you think is of no use. If you do not desist from such comments and actions, I'll stop coming to Diasempa for good."

"Do you know what people are saying about you?" asked Konadu.

"I no longer care about what anybody is saying. I think I will be better off with my husband in the city than to come here only to be abused and ridiculed by you," Evelyn said, sobbing.

"Don't ever think that your threats would stop me from pursuing the course which I feel is for your own good," Konadu insisted. "I have always suspected that..."

A knock at the door stopped Konadu from completing her statement. She told Evelyn to put the items back into the suitcase quickly before she opened the door. She made sure everything was back in the suitcase and zipped up while Evelyn cleaned her face before she ushered in Bevelyn and her two kids. The way Konadu welcomed them, cuddled the children and the comments she made about them and their father made Evelyn feel like an unwanted material, discarded and good-for-nothing.

The look on Evelyn's face spoke volumes to her sister so she asked her what the problem was. Evelyn told her all that their mother had said since she arrived and she started sobbing again. Bevelyn beckoned for Evelyn to go to the corridor with her because she did not want the kids to see her crying.

"Maame is making life unbearable for me," Evelyn said as she sat on the floor, with her back to the wall.

The way she sat with her arms by her sides like lifeless limbs and her neck tilted to her left shoulder said it all, unwanted and rejected by her own mother. Bevelyn tried to comfort her sister but she could not stop the tears. Konadu called Bevelyn but she did not respond because she was angry from what her sister had told her. She kept calling but Bevelyn still did not respond. After a while when Bevelyn came to the living room, leaving her sister still sitting on the floor and crying, she confronted her mother.

"Maame, why are you still insisting on this issue of divorce? I thought we sorted it out the other day that you should let them live their lives the way they want. I will suggest, like I have always said, that you stay out of it."

"You are just like your twin in your mind. The only good thing about you is that you have a productive man," said Konadu.

"What do you think you are doing and where do you think it will lead to, Maame?"

"It's simple. I want the best for your sister."

"The way you are going about it is wrong. You can't do that."

They argued until the kids stopped playing and stared at them. Sometimes it is bearable when outsiders treat you with contempt and scorn, but when it comes to your own people treating you like that, it's really sad. When a mother who is expected to comfort and support her daughter in times like this turns to nagging, where else could one look for encouragement?

Bevelyn did not want the children to see the state in which Evelyn was, so telling her mother that they were going to see a friend some two houses away, they went for a walk in the neighbourhood to make Evelyn recompose herself. Bevelyn spoke tenderly to her sister, assuring her as always, that it is just a matter of time, that God will visit them one day and change their circumstance.

"If my own mother is treating me this way, what do you expect some of my in-laws to do to me?" asked Evelyn, fighting back the tears.

If Evelyn had the slightest idea about Cornie's plot, she would have asked, *'How do you expect Auntie Cornie to treat me?'*

Meanwhile, Darkoaa had given Brago some money to help pay Jude's fees so the boy went back to school the following Monday. When Evelyn came to the house earlier, Darkoaa had wanted to tell her about Jude's plea but when she discussed it with Agya Boakye he told her not to, because the couple were better off without the boy. Two days after Evelyn's visit to Diasempa, Serwaa went for the medicine from Ormoaa and came to tell Auntie Cornie about it.

"According to the man, as soon as he eats it, even if I am in a hole, he will trace me. In fact, he will not rest until he finds me," she said.

"I told you the man is powerful. Very powerful, I mean," said Cornie.

After showing the medicine to her, Serwaa was going to keep until the party day but Auntie Cornie suggested that since she has brought it to her place and she would be the one to use it, it would be better for her to keep it. Serwaa agreed that it was a good idea.

"The man said just a drop would do," Serwaa said.

She gave the concoction which was in a small bottle, about the size of a child's thumb, to Auntie Cornie. She raised it up, shook it to examine it very well and laughed.

"I will make sure he consumes all of it," said Cornie. "My only worry was that I thought he was going to come with his wife but I learnt three days ago that he would come with a friend instead."

Serwaa was very happy to hear that Joe would not come with Evelyn, because that would give them more room to operate. She had been nervous at Ormoaa's place on the first day, but this time she felt so confident that soon, she was going to become the wife of Joe.

"When you get there don't forget me, Serwaa, because you are going to be rich, I mean very rich," said Auntie Cornie.

"How can I forget you?"

Kwaku was not at home this time so they talked and laughed much as they could about the brighter future that Serwaa was looking forward to. For the first time since they became friends, Serwaa told Cornie about Kay. She says as soon as Joe begins to show interest in her she will tell Kay that her people do not want her to marry anyone from outside Diasempa and so they should go their separate ways.

"In that way you can still be friends with him so he would not think it had been your plan to ditch him," said Cornie.

"I've got plans, you know," said Serwaa.

"Clever plans, I suppose."

"Sure," Serwaa confirmed.

While Serwaa and Cornie were planning to trap Joe, he and his wife were also discussing the power of prayer on their way back from church. A Minister had preached on the topic - *Praying without ceasing.* The Minister cited a lot of examples including those who will come to you as wolves in sheep clothing. For this reason and for God's grace and protection to be abundant, he said we need to pray continually.

"The message was very good," said Evelyn.

"Yes. Deacon C.C. recorded it so I have asked him to get us a copy next Sunday. We really need to intensify our prayers because, like the Minister rightly said, the devil never gives up," said Joe.

"So why should we?" Evelyn asked.

As the discussion progressed, they came to the point that, Evelyn should also start fasting on Saturdays instead of doing it randomly. Joe had been fasting on Mondays for a very long time, and he still fasted on other days with his wife. They seemed satisfied with the arrangement but just before they got home, a new idea dropped into Evelyn's subconscious.

"Joe, I think we can do it twice a week", she said

"How?"

"Both of us can do it on your day and when it's my day, we do the same," she explained

"That's a good idea, we shall start next Saturday, on your day, because it's always ladies first," said Joe.

The couple understood each other so much so that they hardly argued over any issue. Even though they sometimes had different opinions, it never led to any serious argument. They always found ways of sorting things out amicably between them. Most of the time, they thought alike. An example of this was when Joe had the idea that Hagar be taught how to drive, Evelyn had also jotted down the same thing to discuss with him later.

Coming from a humble background and being moulded by Joe and Evelyn's humility and love had made Hagar also a very polite and affable young lady. Whenever she had to go for her driving lessons, she prayed for God to give her the knowledge to grasp whatever she was being taught. She had taken her driving test and went to inquire of the results from her instructor as in those days it took two days for results to be released.

"Congratulations! You did very well, as stated in this letter," the instructor said and gave a letter to Hagar.

It was from the Licence Office. She glanced through it and thanked the instructor.

"So where do we go from here?" he asked.

"We need to apply for the licence, now that you are a qualified driver."

The instructor promised to break the news to Evelyn on phone before Hagar gets home but she begged him not to do that because she wanted to do it herself, in a special way. He gave her an application form for the licence and said he's got friends at the Licence Office so there would be no need to post it; they could take it to them to fast track the process.

"I can't wait to drive in town all alone one day," Hagar said.

"You will soon be doing that," said the instructor.

The form required four passport size photos and a stated fee for processing. Hagar could not stop praising God and her foster parents for what they were doing in her life. She never expected to attain this height. As soon as she left, the instructor called his contact man at the Licence Office that he would need his assistance in a few days with regards to a new licence. Hagar also passed by a photography shop to get the photos ready before going to break the news to Evelyn.

"I bless the day you found me, Mum, and that's why I want to continue to stay around you," Hagar said to Evelyn as soon as she got home.

"Why are you saying that?" asked Evelyn.

"Because since that day I have never regretted nor felt the way I used to feel when I had to stop going to school," she said and handed the letter and the application form to Evelyn. "I've passed my driving test, Mum."

"Congratulations!" Evelyn said and embraced her, dropping the documents on the settee.

Evelyn called to tell Joe about it after reading the letter and glancing through the application form. Joe congratulated Hagar on the phone and said she should go for the photos as soon as possible. Hagar said she was not taking any chances so she got the photos before coming home. She showed the photos to Evelyn who was all smiles. From that time, they started talking about the things that Hagar could help to do to help, now that she was going to drive, like shopping and various errands which Joe and Evelyn had to do most of the time.

Auntie Cornie's birthday party was approaching and Joe had planned to go with his friend, Andy. It was scheduled for a Saturday and as Joe and Evelyn fasted on every Saturday, he confided in Andy that he would not eat or drink anything at the party.

When the day finally came and they arrived at the venue, Joe and Andy chose a table at the corner of the hall. Joe happened to be a very popular man in Diasempa because of his shop. His popularity increased when Akonoba and Akwankwaa tried in vain to use voodoo on him. Some people approached Joe to have a chat one after the other. Andy was surprised to see how popular his humble friend was in his home town. Those who came to him mentioned how deplorable the shop was, compared to when he used to operate it and Andy was impressed to hear these nice comments about Joe.

While food and drinks were being served, Auntie Cornie instructed the service girls not to take anything to Joe's table because she wanted him to be served separately. She explained that Joe did not like too much salt so she had prepared a special stew for him. The girls accepted her explanation because they knew how close she was to Joe and believed that she knew what he liked best. She then went to Joe for a brief interaction.

"I know you don't like too much salt so I prepared your stew separately, the way you like it," she said.

"Thank you and, this is Andy, my friend whom I told you about," said Joe.

"You are welcome to Diasempa, Andy," said Cornie.

"Thanks. Happy birthday to you," Andy said and shook Cornie's hand.

Soon after Cornie left their table, Kwaku approached Joe and after greeting them, he pulled Joe aside to have a word with him. From what he had observed between his mother and Serwaa, he knew for sure that something was going on, although he could not pinpoint what it was.

"If my mother tries to introduce any lady to you or your friend as her friend, ignore her. We will talk later as the party goes on," Kwaku said and left to join Dan.

"That's the birthday lady's son," Joe said to Andy when Kwaku left.

During the afternoon when Serwaa went to check if Joe was in town, Kwaku was at home and overheard them talking about *his friend*. He did not know who the subject-matter was or his friend, but it was obvious that his mother knew this person or his friend more than Serwaa. He had heard his mother talk with Brago before about helping Joe to get rid of Evelyn or take a second wife, so in a way he felt he should tell Joe to be careful with his mother. Joe kept thinking about the meaning of what Kwaku had just said to him. He wondered who this lady friend could be and why he should ignore Auntie Cornie, as warned by her own son.

"If *Opopokyikyie* comes from under the water to say that the crocodile is dead, you don't argue with it," so goes an Akan proverb.

Opopokyikyie, the synodontis, is the largest genus of the cat fishes, of the family Mochokidae. Apart from living in the water together, it has the ability to kill the crocodile, if swallowed, by striking its fins in the liver, hence you don't have to doubt someone who is in the position to know. Kwaku was the one living with his mother so he knew her more than anyone else. For that reason, if he told you something about her, you would be compelled to believe him.

Since the day Cornie spoke to Joe about Serwaa at the funeral and he told her not to talk negatively about his marriage or Evelyn again, Cornie had not mentioned any lady to him again and it seemed to him that his warning did sink in well.

'*We will talk later as the party goes on,*' Joe reflected on these words from Kwaku and wanted to call him outside for details of his warning, but then, he decided to wait and see what would happen first as he kept praying silently.

"Like I said, I will not eat, so I will put the food in this bag if it comes," Joe said to Andy.

Joe pulled a carrier bag from his trousers pocket, showed it to Andy and asked for his assistance.

"I will hold the bag and pretend it's a take-away for my children," Andy said.

Outside the hall, Yaappiah, the mentally disturbed man wanted to get in but he was stopped by the gate-keepers.

"Why won't you let me in? Where there is music and merry there must be food and drink. I want something to eat. I am hungry," pleaded Yaappiah.

"You wait here, when they begin to serve the food I will go and get some for you," said one of the gate-keepers.

"Will you get me drink too?"

"Yes."

"Good! Good! You are a good man," he said and started dancing.

Although he was classified by the locals as being sick in the head, his dancing IQ was above that of most normal human beings. He had entertained many people with his dancing in the past and when he was promised food and drink, he started dancing to the admiration of those at the gate. As people were cheering his dancing, Betty and Serwaa arrived, smartly dressed. After watching him for a while they said what they felt about Yaappiah being there.

"Why do they allow this man here at this time? If he is allowed at funerals and other functions, he should not be allowed at people's private parties," Serwaa said.

"Exactly," Betty agreed.

"You see, so many important personalities will be here today and it's not nice to have someone like this around," Serwaa said again.

"Something should be done about this situation," suggested Betty.

"You wait, if he is still here after we've settled, I will see to it that he is driven away," Serwaa said angrily, gritting her teeth when they were entering the near-fully packed hall.

The disc jockey was playing an old tune from Yamoah's Guitar Band titled *Serwaa Akoto* which talked about a beautiful, humble and respectful lady called *Serwaa Akoto*. Agyaaku, the lead singer, admonished all ladies to behave like her.

"Oh! I like this song," Serwaa said as soon as they entered and started dancing, shaking her buttocks in front of Betty.

"The song is talking about a different Serwaa, not you, so let's find a place to sit," said Betty.

In a moment, Serwaa glanced around the hall to see if Joe was there. She had checked from Auntie Cornie a few hours earlier and she confirmed that Joe was in town. He was sitting at a corner close to the entrance with Andy, but she looked far beyond so she did not see him.

As was her usual practice, whenever Joe was away, either on a business trip or any other trip that kept him away from her, Evelyn would pray for him till he returned. This time around, having in mind the kind of hostility they had faced before moving from Diasempa, and most especially the person whose party Joe was attending, Evelyn intensified her prayers. She committed Joe's life into the hands of the Most High God, that nothing evil befall him while there. Being a Saturday, she was also fasting and the more she thought of how Auntie Cornie had always interfered with their marriage, the more she prayed.

If Evelyn had her way, she would have stopped Joe from going to the party in the first place, but she knew that it would have escalated Cornie's hatred for her if she got to know about it later, so all she could do was to pray, pray and pray till his return in one piece.

When at last Serwaa spotted Joe, she became nervous. She had not spoken to Cornie since arriving at the fuction because they had planned not to talk to each other until the concoction had gone into Joe's system. However, they kept making eye contacts once a while.

When Cornie thought it was about the right time, she went to the service area and managed to distract the girls who were serving. She instructed the girls to take food and drinks to certain guests, leaving only one of them with her. Then she told the girl to get her a tray from behind her, some three steps away. She had the small bottle wrapped in her handkerchief, ready to be used in a twinkle of an eye. As soon as the girl turned around, she sprinkled the entire content onto Joe's plate of rice. By the time the girl brought the tray, she was putting the stew from a different bowl onto the rice.

"This plate is for my son," she said. "Like I said to you earlier, he does not like too much salt so I prepared his stew separately."

"Should I take it to him or you will?" asked the girl.

"Take it to them, but make sure you give this plate to my son and the other one to his friend."

Cornie made sure the girl knew which of the plates belonged to Joe so when she got to their table, she did as instructed.

"Thank you very much, beautiful lady," said Andy.

Joe just smiled and kept praying and thinking of what Kwaku had said to him. When Andy began to eat, Joe also picked his fork and knife and pretended to be eating. He put a chewing gum into his mouth and kept chewing it as food. He kept tossing the food on the plate and, occasionally, he swallowed the saliva as if it was the real food and licked his lips.

Auntie Cornie signalled to Serwaa that everything was under control. When Andy was about half-way through with his plate, Joe opened the bag and emptied most of the content of his plate into it, with Andy's assistance. He continued to toss the remaining food on his plate from side to side with the fork until Andy was done and then they cleaned their mouths and hands with the tissues that were provided.

Upon seeing Joe wipe his mouth, Serwaa got up and started dancing. She pretended not to have seen Joe, but inside, she was rejoicing. All of a sudden, she was extremely happy and Betty asked her the reason why she was so excited. She could not give any other reason than saying party time is meant to be a happy time. Not long after that, Joe went to the gents and another girl came to clean the table while Andy held on to the bag.

As soon as the girl went to clean the table, Cornie called her to the service area and gave her another assignment. When she dropped the bag that contained the extras from Joe's table, Cornie put it straight into the bin to make sure none got to anyone else, knowing the content therein.

Outside the hall, based on the promise from the gate-keeper, Yaappiah was still entertaining the people with his dancing. In fact, this was his happiest moment, when there was a gathering, with food and drink. Such occasions were rare in Diasempa, apart from funerals, so he decided to make the most of the day, doing what he was good at, dancing.

"The music is good, but I want more than that. I want some food and drink," he said.

When Joe retuned from the gents, he suggested to Andy that they go outside for some fresh air because the hall was too hot.

"What about the bag?" Andy asked.

"I will put it in the car," Joe replied.

Andy picked the bag and they sneaked outside where Yaappiah was still displaying his dancing techniques. They stopped to watch him for a while.

"He is a good dancer," said Andy. "Unfortunately, life can be cruel to some people. Is he from this town?"

"Yes," Joe replied.

When Yaappiah realised that they were talking about him sympathetically, he took a good look at them and recognised Joe as the man who used to give him food and money from the shop sometime ago. He asked Joe if he could go and get him some food. Some people had come out of the hall just to watch Yaappiah dance and others passing by also stopped to admire his steps and movement to the rhythm of the music. There were a lot of people out there, some were about to go into the hall and others, like Joe and Andy, had come out for fresh air.

When Yaappiah stopped dancing and asked Joe to go get him some food, all attention was turned to the two friends. Joe was known to most of the the people, if not all. One of his attributes known in Diasempa was being generous, so they waited to see if Joe would ignore Yaappiah or do something about his humble request. Without a second thought, Joe grabbed the bag from Andy and gave it to Yaappiah as the people watched. Andy also opened his wallet and gave him some money.

"Thank you very much, God bless you," Yaappiah said. "You are good people. You will see good and good will follow you. Good. Good. Good people. God bless you."

As Yaappiah was pronouncing those blessings upon Joe and Andy who were walking away from the crowd, he opened the bag and started eating. After a few bites, he turned to the gate-keeper and told him he was still expecting what he promised him and everyone laughed. Joe said hello to a few people before they went to his car. Some were however disappointed that Yaappiah had stopped dancing.

Serwaa had seen Joe going outside so after a few minutes when he did not return, she told Betty she wanted to see if Yaappiah was still out there. She just wanted to be sure that her dream man was not leaving for good, like he did previously at the funeral. She wished to have a chat with Joe so she could entice him with her charming eyes and smooth words as a top-up to Ormoaa's concoction.

There was a young man nicely dressed at the party who had been eyeing Betty from where he sat and as soon as Serwaa left her table, he came to introduce himself to Betty as George and had a short chat with her. He gave Betty his complimentary card and asked her to get in touch. Once outside, instead of Joe, Serwaa found Yaappiah eating happily, nodding his head and still tapping his feet to the rhythm of the music.

"So this man is still here," Serwaa said angrily to one of the gate-keepers. "Why don't you drive him out of this place?"

Yaappiah heard what she said but his mouth was full so he could not speak. He looked at her and continued to munch the spiked food.

"He has been asking for food and one of the guests has just given him some, so I am sure he will go by himself. We cannot force him to leave," said one of the the gate-keepers.

By this time, Yaappiah had swallowed what was in his mouth so he said what was on his mind to Serwaa.

"You are only being jealous. I've got some of the food. You thought you were going to enjoy it all alone."

Everyone's eye was shifting from Yaappiah to Serwaa. Yaappiah did not care about what people were thinking as he continued to eat neither could Serwaa stand there to be addressed like that by this madman. She went back to the hall immediately. She went to complain to Auntie Cornie that Joe was out of the hall and nowhere around the gate.

"Don't worry about him any longer. It's gone into his system and that's the most important thing. If I were you, I would leave this place as soon as possible to go and organise my room, if you haven't done so already, and wait for him to come," said Cornie.

Serwaa adhered to Cornie's advice, as always, and convinced Betty that she had to leave as soon as possible because she had just remembered that Kay was coming to see her around that time. Betty was suspicious of Serwaa's actions. Going outside, talking with Cornie and the sudden change of plan that she was expecting Kay was strange. If indeed Kay was coming to town, she knew Serwaa would have told her earlier. But then, there was nothing she could do to stop her from leaving the venue. Serwaa went home and changed her room to look as if an angel was coming to visit.

Joe and Andy came back to the hall and stayed for about half-an-hour more before telling Auntie Cornie they had to go because Andy also had an appointment in the city. Joe gave her an envelope containing some money and a present which he had gone to collect from the car at the time when Serwaa was looking for him at the entrance. Andy also gave her a card to wish her a happy birthday.

"I thought you were going to spend the night here and go back in the morning," said Cornie.

"No. Like I said earlier, Andy also has a function to attend so we need to go. In fact, we should have been half way through the journey by now."

"Brako said he would be leaving for Accra this evening so he would be able to take Andy with him, if that's okay."

"No, no, no. I brought him here, so I have to take him back to his wfe and children," said Joe.

"Evelyn is also expecting you back this evening, don't forget," Andy chipped in with a smile.

Cornie was trying to convince Joe to stay for the night and see how the concoction would work on him. She trusted Ormoaa so much so that she was sure of Joe going to look for Serwaa within the next few moments. She thought it would not be safe for him to drive under the influence of the concoction, when it begins to work. But Joe had made up his mind to go back to Accra, so they left.

Once at home, Serwaa tried to relax but she could not. The thought that Joe would be coming to ask of her any moment made her restless. Under normal circumstances, whenever she returned from an outing, the first thing she did was to change her clothes, but today she did not. After making sure everything was in place in her room, she still remained in her party dress. Her mother asked why she had not changed and she lied to her that she was expecting a friend and would soon be going out again. So she kept waiting for Joe. She could not go back to the hall, in case Joe showed up in her absence, but the reality was that Joe was on his way to Accra.

Back in the city, Joe and Evelyn held each other's hands and prayed. Evelyn thanked God for bringing him back home safely. She was to go for the results of another lab test on the following Monday, so they prayed about that too, for God to intervene in their situation. Serwaa, however, kept waiting, Sunday morning, afternoon and evening, but Joe never turned up. Cornie had told Serwaa on the Saturday evening that maybe Joe was taking Andy back to the city because of his appointment before coming to look for her, but it had taken more than twenty-four hours.

Ormoaa had said that the moment the concoction got into Joe's system, even if Serwaa was in a hole, he would come and look for her. Monday morning, Serwaa continued to set up her room to make it look more attractive. Every cob-web and dust was dealt with. Items that were not needed immediately were kept out of sight. By lunch time on Monday, there was still no sign of Joe. Whenever someone entered the house, Serwaa would peep to see if it was Joe or if he had sent someone to come and call her for him.

When Evelyn went to see the Doctor whom she preferred to call Elder, she was told everything was normal, according to the test results. Several other doctors had said the same thing to her in the past so she wondered why she could not get pregnant. In her mind, she was beginning to think if what her mother had said about Joe not being able to make her pregnant was true. Her thoughts were disrupted by a statement from the doctor.

"I therefore don't see why you cannot conceive. I will suggest that your husband also comes for a test," said Dr Ankrah-Badu.

"He will be more than willing to come over. When do you want him to come?" she asked.

"Either Wednesday or Friday. Do not panic yet, because the problem could be solved in a very simple way."

"In a very simple way, Elder, did I hear you well?"

"Yes, you heard me right. I have handled several more serious cases than this in the past. Some don't even need any medication and others could be due to the method used during love-making."

Evelyn listened attentively as Dr Ankrah-Badu explained a few points to her. She had heard so much from various doctors already about her condition and was beginning to think that Dr Ankrah-Badu was no different from the others.

"Another area is that some of the couples are not co-orporative, they hide certain facts from their partners, and that too can be very disastrous. You come on Wednesday and we shall continue from there."

Evelyn thanked him and left, promising to come with Joe. By that Monday evening, Serwaa was becoming more worried. The few moments Ormoaa promised her had turned not only into hours but days, and although she was not hiding in a hole, Joe had not come looking for her. Any strange voice in the house, to her, should have been Joe enquiring of her. When it was around 8:00 o'clock in the evening and nothing was happening, Serwaa went to Auntie Cornie. Cornie panicked when she saw Serwaa. She looked pretty as always, and well dressed, but the look on her face told a different story.

"Have you heard anything from him?" Serwaa asked.

"No."

"It's been three days now. But the man said it would be a few hours, if not right after it's gone through his system."

"Why then has it taken three days and no sign at all?" asked Cornie.

"I just don't know, and I am beginning to worry," said Serwaa.

"Well, let's wait a few more days and see," Cornie said.

As they sat facing each other in silence, Serwaa was not convinced of Cornie's suggestion of waiting for a few more days. Kwaku was not at home else, he would have read between the lines and concluded that something had gone amiss.

It does no good to spread the net when the bird you want to catch is watching, so says the good book in *Proverbs 1:17*. In this case, Joe had not been watching, he had not even seen the net being spread to catch him, yet because his Redeemer lives, Cornie and Serwaa's evil plans had been turned upside down. God had thrown them into confusion. His word is true when He says He will watch over your going out and coming in so that no evil befalls you. He will order your steps so that you will not step into the devil's trap. He did just that for Joe. That night, Joe and Evelyn shared a word from *Jeremiah 33:3.*

"Sister Charlotte calls this scripture God's direct number - 333," Evelyn said.

"She is right, because you don't have to go through any operator," said Joe.

Evelyn read the scripture and afterwards Joe held her left hand with his right while they knelt in front of the bed and Joe prayed as follows:

"God, we are standing on your word and promise and call on you tonight, answer us and give us our hearts' desire to the glory of your Mighty Name. Reveal to us whatever is hidden from us that is not making our happiness complete, in the name of Jesus we have prayed. Amen."

When he finished praying, he turned off the main lights and switched on the bedside light instead as Evelyn covered herself with the sheet. Each of them kept praying silently till they fell asleep. The devil's power can harm other people, but not those covered with the blood of Jesus. That blood, powerful as it is, serves as a bullet-proof for the sons and daughters of God. His Name is a strong tower, the righteous run to it and they are safe - *Proverbs 18:10.*

Ormoaa's concoction had gone into the system of Yaappiah and had begun working so he went about in search of Serwaa. Standing in front of the hall where the party took place, Yaappiah scratched his hair and talked to himself.

"I saw her here but I don't know where to find her now. I will comb through this town till I find her, wherever she may be."

He was talking to himself, but he spoke so loud that people heard him and wondered who he was referring to. Some, however, took him to be doing what people like him do and so ignored him while others thought he was now suffering from schizophrenia.

But Yaappiah was seriously looking for the one whose love was attracting him like magnet.

He left the place, still talking to himself and looking for Serwaa. People started talking about him that his situation was getting bad. His people had never thought of making him seek any psychiatric help, but as he kept talking about this beautiful lady, some people suggested that it was about time his family took some steps.

From that time on Yaappiah became restless, moving from place to place in search of this beautiful lady he claimed to have seen at the party. People were beginning to wonder whether the lady was one of the people Auntie Cornie had invited to the party from outside the town or a Diasemparian. Could it be another stage of Yaappiah's condition? And if it was so what other stage would it get to. Would he become normal if he got into contact with this beautiful lady he was looking for? Would he ever find her? If he did or did not find her, what will he do? These were some of the questions that people were asking.

In a dream one night, Joe saw Auntie Cornie trying to pull him away from his wife while Serwaa was standing at a distance and laughing. The dream ended suddenly as Joe woke up in a struggle to free himself from Cornie's grip. Sitting on the bed, he wiped his face with his right palm and looked around the room only to realise that he was dreaming. Evelyn was soundly sleeping. Joe looked at her beautiful face and thought of waking her up to tell her about the dream but he did not. As he prayed and thought about what the meaning of the dream could be, he slept again. In the morning, he woke up before Evelyn and when she did, he told her he had had a dream.

"What was it about?" asked Evelyn.

"Do you remember the scripture we read the other night about calling on God?"

"You mean God's direct number, *Jeremiah 33:3?*"

321

"Yes. Let's read it again before I tell you about the dream."

Joe picked his Bible from the bedside table and gave his wife's to her. He then flicked through the pages till he got to the underlined scripture and began to read.

"It says, 'Call on me...'"

"No, God says," Evelyn corrected him.

"Yes, God says, *'Call on me and I will answer you and tell you great and unsearchable things you do not know'.* You know I've been telling you that Auntie Cornie used to have great influence in my affairs."

"Yes. You've said that many times. What is she up to again this time?" asked Evelyn.

"Before we married, she wanted me to marry her friend's daughter but I refused for some personal reasons."

"What were those personal reasons?" asked Evelyn.

"Well, I just wanted to break away from her and have my independence, because I know if I had married that lady, she would have been controlling the marriage."

Joe paused for a while to see Evelyn's reaction to this revelation, but she was quiet and waited for him to continue.

"There is something that I have kept from you for some time now, but due to the dream I had this night I am going to tell you about it."

Evelyn was still quiet as Joe was speaking. She just kept looking into his eyes, expecting to hear the dream. Joe was now sitting on the bed.

"I did not want to put any negative feelings into you about her, apart from what you have observed yourself, and that's why I have kept it to myself."

"What is it?" Evelyn asked.

She was more interested in the dream and what it had to do with the scripture than the tales about his aunt. She had heard and had enough of Auntie Cornie already. Joe told his wife that his aunt had been suggesting to him that he got a second wife so as to have his own children. Evelyn sat up and looked at Joe more sternly at the mention of a second wife.

"Now, God has revealed her wicked plans to me," Joe said.

Joe told her about the letter Cornie had sent to him through Serwaa, inviting him to come and see her for only God knows reason, but he refused to go. Then he also told her of Cornie introducing Serwaa to him when he attended a funeral at Diasempa as a beautiful lady who could be a better wife.

"In my dream, you and I were walking hand-in-hand when suddenly my aunt appeared and tried to pull me away from you."

Evelyn listened with her eyes wide open. Her heart skipped and beat faster than normal as she wondered what the conclusion of the dream would be.

"In a distance," Joe continued, "I saw this same lady standing akimbo and laughing. I woke up suddenly as I was struggling to free myself from her grip."

"Did you know this lady before she was formerly introduced to you?"

"No. The first time I saw her was when she came to deliver the letter to me."

"Did she come to this house?"

"No, it was in the shop, on the day David had the accident," explained Joe. "The last time I saw her was at Auntie Cornie's birthday party, but I did not even speak with her."

Joe said he had been very suspicious of his aunt since the day she introduced the lady to him and it was for that reason that he had been trying to avoid her lately. Whether it was for a reason or he just forgot, Joe did not tell Evelyn about what Kwaku told him to ignore his mother if she should introduce any lady to him as a friend.

"I know God reveals to redeem so He will take care of us," Evelyn said.

Joe was silent for a while after this assurance from Evelyn and she too was scared of the dream. She had always been confident that no woman would be able to take Joe from her, but she knew how cunning Cornie could be. Later, they held hands to pray to commit their lives to God. It was not one of their days of fasting but they decided to fast throughout the week to seek the face of God in this matter. Evelyn was very worried, because it reminded her of the letter from Cornie which she had destroyed some time back without Joe's knowledge.

When Hagar came to live with them, they advised her to fast once a month, preferably on Sunday, the day she was born. They explained to her that it would bring her closer to God and also be beneficial to her health. Hagar chose the first Sunday of every month as the day of her fasting, and she had been doing it consistently. Coincidentally, it happened to be the communion day at church so those days were very solemn to her.

In the morning Hagar overheard Joe and Evelyn talking about fasting so she later told Evelyn that she wanted to join them in the week-long fasting and prayer. Evelyn was glad to hear this and simply told Hagar that their focus for the week was committing their lives into God's care and protection. Amazingly, from that day, as soon as Joe and Evelyn left home for the shop, Hagar would do all that she had to do quickly and go to her room to pray. She would kneel in front of her bed and commit the entire house - the people and properties in it into God's hand. Sometimes she raised her hands up and thanked God for bringing them that far. She also prayed that God would give her a sister or brother through her foster parents.

Meanwhile, Serwaa was still waiting for the arrival of Joe and because she did not want the search to be difficult for him, she chose to stay at home, where it would be easier for him to locate through Auntie Cornie. And because she stayed at home always, Yaappiah, who was eagerly looking for her could not find her.

Betty had to go to her house to see her after a few days. She noticed the changes in Serwaa's room and recommended that it stay that way always. Serwaa herself was happy with what she had done to the room, but it was yet to achieve its purpose, so, somehow, her happiness was not complete. During their conversation, Betty brought up an issue that made Serwaa feel very uncomfortable.

"Did you see that young man who was wearing white suit with black tie at the party two tables away from ours?"

"Yes. What about him?" Serwaa asked.

"As soon as you went outside, he came over to ask if he could use your chair and when I told him you were coming back, he said he just wanted to have a short chat with me."

"And what happened?" Serwaa asked.

Betty was all smiles as she spoke and this made Serwaa jealous because she could read between the lines to 'smell' the good news that she was yet to hear.

"So we talked till he saw you coming and went back to his table. He gave me his card and we've been in contact almost every day since then."

"Lucky you," Serwaa said from the corner of her mouth and not looking at Betty's face.

"Did you make any catch as you were hoping to?" Betty asked.

"Hmm, no. You know I had to leave early to come and meet Kay," Serwaa said.

"Oh yeah, how is he?"

"He's fine. So who is this guy?" asked Serwaa.

"He is a year older than me and has never been married. He works as Secretary to the Director of SIC (State Insurance Corporation) and above all, we seem to have the same hobbies, that is, music, reading, etc."

Betty's description of the guy was like adding insult to Serwaa's injury. This time she was looking at Betty and forming pictures in her mind.

"So what's going on?" asked Serwaa.

"Actually, I'm seeing him on Friday and the meeting will determine the next step," said Betty.

"If he drags his feet let me know and I will introduce you to someone to work on him, spiritually," said Serwaa

"What do you mean?" asked Betty.

"You may have to bind him to win him, you know," Serwaa said, shamelessly.

"Sorry, I am not into that kind of thing. If he is for me, I will have him. If not, so be it, period."

Serwaa tried to convince Betty to give in to her spiritual assistance but God-fearing Betty would not do that. It was Serwaa's frustration that made her voice out this spiritual assistance to her friend, otherwise this spiritual step she had taken herself should have been a secret. When you are desperate, sometimes you do and say things you shouldn't. Besides, she trusted Betty to keep it between them. By this time, Yaappiah was asking everyone he met if they had seen his lover.

"Oh God, I love this lady. Where can I find her?" he asked a young man.

"Who is your lover?" asked the young man.

"That beautiful girl I saw at the party. She is sweet, sweet like toffee. I love her so much but I can't find her," he said and left the young man.

"This guy's condition is getting worse. He used to bath once in a while but now he is looking dirtier like a real mad man," said another man who was standing by.

Yaappiah was beginning to become the talk of the town. Some people who had been avoiding Yaappiah in the past, this time tried to engage him in conversation in the hope of getting a clue to who this lover was.

CHAPTER ELEVEN

EVERY ACTION HAS A REACTION

One thing leads to another, otherwise how could a young boy's accident and burnt fridge lead to a Bible lesson? David and Jonathan had met at school in the same class and become the best of friends without knowing the history about their names in the Bible. Jonathan's parents were not much of church people like David's, but that did not make them unbelievers, any way. They were very good and kind people, better than some who claim to be Christians.

They chose the name Jonathan for their son because according to his father, a very jovial man, one could get three names from it. He always explained to his friends with smiles that he could call his son Joe, Nat or Nathan and he always added Prophet to the Nathan. He said his son would become a prophet in future and Joe was very simple, just like Nat. The first time Jonathan heard him explaining this to somebody, he was about eight years old and he laughed his head off. David sometimes called him Joe, like most of their mates.

One Monday when they were returning from school, David told Jonathan to go and read *1 Samuel chapters 17 to 20* for them to talk about it at school the next day.

"Why? What is there? Did you go to church yesterday?" asked Jonathan.

"Yes, I did, but it's got nothing to do with what I want you to read."

"I will, but just tell me a little about what is there," demanded Jonathan.

"It's about you and me. You go and read it; my Dad said that's the way to learn," David said.

It was then that Jonathan remembered what David's father had started telling them about their friendship and assumed that Rexy might have told his son the entire story. Jonathan was so excited and promised to read it as soon as he got home. The two friends were so knit together and had nurtured their friendship with sharing whatever each had. They visited each other frequently and so knew what was going on in the other's life at every point in time.

Betty has also come to know that visitation is one of the ingredients of the mortar that binds people together, so she frequently visited George, her new found friend. She had seen Yaappiah going about town asking of his lover, so when she visited George one day, Yaappiah's issue was one of the things they talked about. Betty asked George if he was aware of it and he replied in the negative.

"He was dancing at the entrance of the hall where the party took place," said Betty.

"You mean where we met?"

"Yes," Betty replied with a smile.

"Oh yes. I saw him dancing at the gate when I was entering the hall," said George.

"Yes, he's the one. The man is going around town looking for a beautiful lady that he is claiming to be his lover."

"Was he married before becoming insane?" George asked.

"I don't know," said Betty. "He seems to be madly in love with this person and I don't know what would happen on the day he finds her."

"A mad man madly in love, that's serious! You never know, maybe this lover ditched him and that was what turned him into what he is now," said George.

"It's possible, and now he wants her back. Any way, can you come to town next weekend?" requested Betty.

"Is there anything special going on?"

"Yes, one of the richest men from the town lost has his son in a motor accident and the funeral is taking place next weekend."

"Okay," said George, "but I will have to return the same day."

"You can pass the night at my place, if you wish," suggested Betty.

"I wish I could, but I have other things to do early Sunday morning."

George wasn't taking any chances. He had nothing doing on Sunday morning but he wanted to know Betty more before passing a night at her place. He had told his Diasemparian friend who invited him to Auntie Cornie's party about Betty and the friend had promised to investigate Betty's past and present and get back to him. So until that investigation was done, he viewed the relationship as mere friendship and nothing serious but Betty looked at it differently. She was of age and ready for marriage, George was in good employment, had everything she looked for in a man, so nothing would make her say no to him, if he really wanted her for a wife.

George considered that passing the night at Betty's place won't be an easy temptation to resist since he had decided not to have canal knowledge of her in the meantime. This was one of the reasons which made Betty respect him so much. Most men would like to sleep with you on the first date or soon afterwards, but George had never made any advances on Betty in this wise. To her, it showed maturity, a perfect gentle man of her taste.

She told George that if he did have a change of mind and decide to stay for the night he should call to let her know in advance, but he had already made up his mind. That was will-power at work. There are times when you must stick to your decisions, no matter what others may say or do to influence you. Some people shift their focus as soon as they face a challenge.

George knew that if he went to pass the night at Betty's place and something happens he would have to bear the consequences. He envisaged that she might not be someone that he would like to move with after his friend's investigation. He always maintains that every action we take in life has a reaction, like in Rexy's house where Mr Aki's story was about to become a reality.

Dede's son, Alex, had broken the double glazed window of the house opposite theirs. The landlord, Asomasi, was in the living room when he heard the noise of broken glasses falling on the floor behind him. When he turned around and saw the damage, he rushed outside to where a group of boys were playing football. It was the only open space in the immediate surroundings where kids could actually play ball games, but Asomasi's glass window was their problem. Whenever he was around the boys dared not play there. But when the cat is away the mice do play.

Normally when Asomasi was at home, he kept the windows open. But this day, as fate would have it, even though he was in the living room, the windows were shut, so the boys thought he was absent. When Alex kicked the ball which broke the glass, he left the place immediately while the other boys waited to see what would happen. Asomasi started shouting as soon as he saw the boys with long faces.

"I have been warning you not to play football here. See what you have done now? Who did it? Who kicked the ball?"

"It was Alex," one of the boys said.

"Where is he?" Asomasi asked furiously.

"He has run away," said another boy.

In a rage, the man went to their house to look for Alex. He met Mr. Aki at the entrance and asked him if he had seen Alex and when he said no, Asomasi asked for his parents. Dede came out of her room when she heard the man enquiring of them.

"What is the matter, Asomasi?" asked Dede.

"Come over here and see for yourself what the matter is. I fixed this window not long ago, as you know."

Asomasi was fuming as he led the way, followed by Dede, Aki and other tenants. He pointed to the broken window and said:

"It cost me a fortune to get this done and so I want it fixed as soon as possible."

"How did you know that it was Alex who broke it?" Dede asked in her usual arrogance.

"Ask the boys he was playing with and, if he wasn't the culprit why did he run away while the others were still here? Where is he?" he asked.

"I don't know," she shrugged her shoulders in a careless manner. "You just have to be patient till he comes home. He may not be the one who did it."

All the boys confirmed that they saw him kick the ball and even showed the direction in which he fled. Asomasi got angrier when Dede talked about patience.

"Don't make me get mad at you. Do you know what patience is?" he asked. "We were all here when you asked Rexy to replace your fridge at a time he needed your sympathy. I can't have this window stay like this through the night. I want it back as it was, now. I mean now, otherwise there will be trouble."

By this time other neighbours had gathered at the scene. Everyone in the vicinity knew Asomasi to be jovial but harsh and Dede very arrogant and disrespectful. Mr Aki approached Akyaa and used his palm to shield a part of his mouth and whispered to her.

"Do you remember the story I told?"

"Yes, about Mr Salt and his neighbour, Mr Shea Butter," Akyaa said in a low voice.

Akyaa started putting the pieces together to see where salt and shea butter fitted in this scenario. After reconstructing her mind of the past events and the current happenings she understood Mr. Aki's story very well. Asomasi emphatically told Dede that if she had pardoned Rexy and his wife regarding the fridge, he would have done the same.

"Take it easy, Asomasi," pleaded Dede.

"Why didn't you take it easy when the couple's son was in agony? You were determined to milk them dry because of an old fridge and now you are telling me to take it easy. I will rather take it hard, very hard," he threatened.

Dede, now looking sheepish, continued to plead with Asomasi to wait till her husband's return from a trip. Mr Aki, pretending to sympathise with her, went between them to plead on her behalf.

"Asomasi, please have mercy on her, and wait till her husband ..." Mr Aki was saying.

"I would have had mercy, Mr Aki, if she had shown any to Rexy and his wife. I hear it was you who presented the fridge to her on their behalf. Mercy is shown to those who are merciful and you do to others as you want them to do to you. I want the window fixed as soon as possible."

Those who knew what she did to Rexy and his wife sided with Asomasi, but others who did not know of the past assumed that he was over-reacting. Alex had absconded and when it was almost dark and he had not shown up, his mother was getting worried more about him than Asomasi's threats. She went out of the house in search of him but could not see him anywhere.

Yaa Basoa was also so much concerned about her daughter,

Serwaa, for being single when most of her mates had got married. She questioned Serwaa about Kay, saying she was not getting any younger.

"You have to settle down with him before another lady comes his way."

"Don't compare me to my mates because everyone is different, Maame. Kay doesn't have money; besides I'm not really interested in him."

"I did not expect this statement from you, Serwaa. When I met your father, he was a mason's apprentice, without money, but I loved him for who he was. I don't want a situation where you would be blaming other people in future, when you have lost your beauty, well advanced in years and no one coming forward to ask your hand in marriage."

"Your days were different from the present age, Maame," Serwaa said and started walking away from her mother.

"Why don't you stop seeing him then if you are not interested in him and look for someone else to settle down with?" asked her mother.

There was no response. Although Serwaa had not formally introduced Kay to her mother, the woman knew about their relationship, so she was taken aback by her daughter's comments. Basoa saw Kay as a gentleman but Serwaa had made it clear to her that he wasn't her kind of man.

It had been many days since the party and Serwaa was wondering if the medicine would eventually start working and force Joe to come knocking at her door. But Joe was rather pursuing the course that could possibly give them a child. Together with Evelyn, they visited their District Pastor to ask for his support in prayers. They had embarked on twenty-one days of prayers and fasting, asking God to visit them and it was in the remaining last week that they went to speak to the Pastor. Pastor Odei told them that being their spiritual father, it was his responsibility to help them in this direction. The

Pastor had planned a seven-day prayer and fasting session for the entire district in the coming week and this visit made him change the focus of the coming programme, apparently to support the couple.

"I am going to send information to all the Presiding Elders to announce on Sunday that everyone should endeavour to attend the programme."

Joe and Evelyn looked at each other in shock. They thought all attention at the meeting was going to be on them. Immediately, through discernment, Pastor Odei explained his idea to them.

"Don't be alarmed because I won't mention you," the Pastor said. "God would give us the wisdom to deal with it in a way that would please Him."

"Thank you, Pastor," said Joe. "You know we have been ridiculed for a very long time and we don't want a situation where everyone would be staring at us at the church services."

"Brother Joe, nobody would know that the programme is being organised with you in mind."

Joe and his wife felt very uneasy, so Pastor Odei kept assuring them that there would not be a slightest hint for anyone to link them to the programme. After he had prayed with them, they left the mission house.

In Diasempa, Adamfopa's son's funeral day for which Betty had invited George finally arrived. Some people had planned for weeks towards this funeral, and so, right from the morning the atmosphere in the entire town was different from what it had always been. The funeral was to be held at the town's largest open grounds where festivals and other big events took place. Any programme held there was given a special recognition, and so was this funeral.

Serwaa was at this time beginning to doubt the efficacy of Ormoaa's concoction and the frequency at which she visited Auntie Cornie's house had also reduced. She decided that staying indoors might not be a better option after all so she would attend the funeral. Secondly, because the funeral was for the son of a rich man and Joe was one of the rich by Diasemparian standard, she thought he might be in attendance. She was of the view that Joe may catch a glimpse of her to activate the concoction in his system.

As she always did on such big occasions, Serwaa was dressed to kill and headed for the funeral grounds. She was a very beautiful lady; her height, curves, eyes and everything about her would make many a man fall for her, as some had in the past. Whenever she wore tight jeans or a skirt that showed her shape, any man who walked pass her turned around to take a second look at her. When Serwaa arrived at the funeral grounds to join some of her friends, the programme was at its climax.

Adamfopa's son was buried a week after the accident and this was the fortieth day anniversary. It was more of a party then a funeral. So much had been spent to provide food and drinks and everyone ate and drank to their fill. This was the happiest moment for Yaappiah, when drinks and food were in abundance. He was around and feeling a bit tipsy because a few people had offered him alcohol.

He moved from one group of people to another, asking if they had seen his lover. Sadly, no one seemed to know who this lover was and so could not tell him where to find her. Serwaa, always seeking to be admired by dignitaries at such occasions, asked one of her friends for a dance but the friend declined. Live band was playing and Serwaa kept pulling her friend to accompany her to the dance floor.

"You don't know who is watching you," said her friend.

"Come on, let's do justice to our shoes," Serwaa said.

"There are so many strangers here so I would rather tap my feet and enjoy the music right here."

"What about those dancing, are they not being watched too?"

"Serwaa, I just don't want to dance, so leave me alone."

Serwaa's pressure on her friend to the dance floor could be likened to an incident concerning Deer and Tortoise. In the days of old, the two were very good friends who lived and did everything together. Once they were invited to a party by the Tiger where there was a lot of drumming and dancing. Deer liked dancing and so, no sooner had they arrived than she took to the floor. After dancing for a while, she asked Tortoise to join her but Tortoise refused.

She told Deer that she did not want to dance because dancing with her could be to her detriment. Deer did not grasp the wisdom in Tortoise's words and kept pulling her to join her and the others who were merrily showing their dancing skills. Deer knew her friend to be a good dancer, but considering the circumstances and whose party they were attending, Tortoise decided to observe what was going on rather than taking part in it. But her friend would not let her, so she finally gave in and started dancing.

You needed to see Tortoise and her movements to the sound of drumming. She danced *kete, fontonfrom, konkonma, osode*, etc, but *adowa* was her best. At a point, everyone stopped dancing and was admiring Tortoise. The way she wriggled her feet behind her and moved her hands was such an amazing sight.

Even when the drummers were tired and wanted to have a break she told them to continue playing harder because she was yet to show them her best styles. They continued to play until the leading drum split beyond repairs. At that time, Tiger was having a discussion with some VIAs (Very Important Animals) in chambers and when he was informed of the damage he asked if Deer was still around.

"Yes, she is around," said the informant.

"Good," said Tiger. "You know that from the time of our forefathers, we have not used any other skin than that of the Deer in making drums, so if she is still around, do what you have to do," Tiger ordered the stewards.

337

Immediately, the Deer was bundled up and taken to the backyard, apparently to be killed for her skin to be used for another drum. As she was being led away, she cried to the Tortoise to come to her aid but there was nothing her good friend could do or say to change the orders of Tiger.

Such was Serwaa's doom. She should have listened to her friend to stay away from prying eyes. But whatever has to be must be, for no sooner had she taken to the floor with her friend in the hope that Joe might see her, if he was around, than she was spotted by Yaappiah.

"Yes! Yes! There she is at last. I have seen my lover," Yaappiah kept saying.

He made his way through the crowd to embrace Serwaa from behind. Serwaa pushed him away but Yaappiah insisted on kissing her, causing a lot of confusion. Some people laughed and others wondered about what was going on. The guy got frantic and bit someone who tried to restrain him. There was complete higgledy-piggledy! Everyone in Diasempa by that time knew about Yaappiah and his search for a lover, but no one expected this lover to be the high society city girl like Serwaa.

"Leave us alone. She is my lover. She is the only one I love. Nothing will stop me from marrying her," said Yaappiah as people tried to barricade him from Serwaa.

There was pandemonium as Yaappiah intensified his efforts, pushing her to the floor to lie on her. Some people, however, managed to get Serwaa from beneath him and from the crowd. Others obstructed Yaappiah as Serwaa was taken to a near-by car. When the car drove away, Yaappiah followed its direction until it was out of his sight. The disturbance almost brought the funeral to a halt as everyone talked about the scene.

"What are we seeing, man? Something like this has never happened in this town. In fact, I have not heard anything like this before," someone said to his friend.

"There is always a first time, you know. There must be something serious to this, I bet," the other man said.

Auntie Cornie was at the funeral and witnessed the incident. She was shocked to the bone and wished she had been told about it instead of her having to tell others. A woman who knew her to be friends with Serwaa asked her if it wasn't Serwaa that was being attacked.

"Yes, it's Serwaa. There must be something wrong," said Cornie, almost trembling.

"She needs some serious protection," said the woman.

"Yes, because if Yaappiah gets to know where she lives, he could attack her at home," Auntie Cornie said, as she tried to move away from the crowd.

The band stopped playing. Some of the bandsmen left the stage and were now in the crowd trying to find out what was going on because not all of them saw the attack. Adamfopa went to the platform to grab one of the microphones to address the gathering.

"Ladies and gentlemen," he started, "and most especially guests who have come from outside Diasempa to witness and support this occasion, I am very sorry for what has just happened. In fact, we are all surprised about this incident and I really apologise to you all."

Some people were listening to him while others discussed the incident. There were two schools of thought. One school said someone was trying to use voodoo on Serwaa and another school said it was a curse. Both, however, agreed that it must be something spiritual. But the big question was why Yaappiah picked only on Serwaa among the numerous ladies at the gathering.

"Please bear with us and take the man as he is, insane, and he is only doing what such people do. I am very sorry," said Adamfopa.

Yaappiah's search for his lover had taken him to the length and breadth of the town of Diasempa prior to this day. Even some people from neighbouring towns and villages were aware of a mad man going around looking for his lover. So when he pounced on Serwaa and wanted to do whatever he had in mind with her, many were those who felt they should have allowed him to have his way. One young man said, though Yaappiah may be sick in the head, he could still see the beauty in the opposite sex and be attracted, and that was why he picked on Serwaa.

When Yaappiah got to the lorry station without seeing the car, he returned to the funeral grounds, almost wailing. What a sight it was! Yaappiah, the vagrant crying because of a run-away lover!

"Where is she?" he asked no one in particular. "They have taken my lover away in a car. They don't want me to have her but they can't hide her from me forever."

He changed his wailing into a threat in a moment when he noticed that every eye at the gathering was on him.

"I will find her. I will make sure no one takes her as a wife but me."

Betty and George were very close to the scene and had vividly witnessed everything that happened. Some ladies started leaving the place one after the other. Those who left said they did not know what Yaappiah would do next and they talked about the attack as they went. None of the ladies wanted to be the next victim, especially those who had come without a man to protect them. Cornie was worried and scared as people kept inquiring about Serwaa from her, so she left the place and met Kwaku on the way.

"Mum, have you heard what I am hearing?" he asked.

"About what?" Cornie asked in return.

"Were you not at the funeral grounds?" Kwaku asked again.

"I was there earlier," she said.

"Did you see Serwaa? I hear Yaappiah is chasing her as his lover."

"Yes, I was there and saw it all. Everyone, including myself, is shocked about it. It almost brought the funeral to an end."

"Why do you think this is happening?" Kwaku asked.

"How will I know, Kwaku?"

Kwaku gave his mother a questionable smile and walked on towards the funeral grounds. As he went, he thought of his mother's plans with Serwaa and wondered if it could have any link to what was going. Cornie was determined to help Serwaa catch Joe like a fish with a hook. Unfortunately, the hook had snapped to hook the thrower.

Although Joe had been suspicious of his aunt, he did not have the slightest idea that she could go that far. For the rest of the evening, the incident dominated every conversation in the town and the visitors also took it to their various towns.

Onlookers have managed to get Serwaa from Yaappiah's fierce, vice-like grip but, would they be able to continue to protect her from him forever? Would Yaappiah give up his search for her? How is this incident going to affect Serwaa and, together with Auntie Cornie, what are they going to do about their evil plot which has backfired? What about Kwaku, would he press for more facts from his mother? What is Serwaa's family and that of Yaappiah going to do about this issue? Indeed, there are more questions than answers, but somehow, someday we must find the answers to this mystery.

END OF PART ONE

Lightning Source UK Ltd.
Milton Keynes UK
UKOW04f2326290615

254329UK00002B/120/P